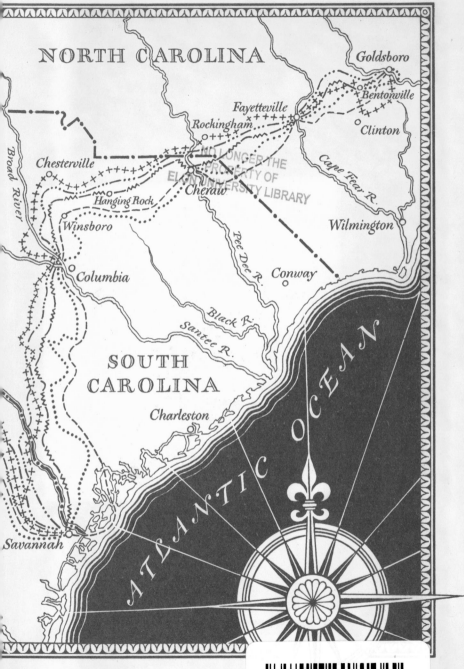

NORTH CAROLINA

Goldsboro

Bentonville

Fayetteville

Rockingham

Clinton

Chesterville

Cape Fear R.

NO LONGER THE
PROPERTY OF
ELON UNIVERSITY LIBRARY

Cheraw

Hanging Rock

Wilmington

Winsboro

Broad River

Pee Dee R.

Columbia

Conway

Black R.

Santee R.

SOUTH
CAROLINA

ATLANTIC OCEAN

Charleston

Savannah

Jubilee

Jubilee

BY JOHN BRICK

Doubleday & Company, Inc.

GARDEN CITY, NEW YORK

WITH THE EXCEPTION OF ACTUAL HISTORICAL PERSONAGES,
THE CHARACTERS ARE ENTIRELY THE PRODUCT OF THE AUTHOR'S
IMAGINATION AND HAVE NO RELATION TO ANY PERSON IN REAL LIFE.

for Dorothy

Bring the good old bugle, boys, we'll sing another song;
Sing it with the spirit that starts the world along;
Sing it as we used to sing it, fifty thousand strong,
While we were marching through Georgia!

Hurrah! Hurrah! We bring the jubilee.
Hurrah! Hurrah! The flag that sets you free.
So we sang the chorus from Atlanta to the sea,
While we were marching through Georgia.

Part One

"It is about time the North understood . . . that the entire South, man, woman and child is against us, armed and determined. It will call for a million men for several years to put them down. . . ."

(W. T. Sherman to John Sherman, 1862.)

1

In eighteen hundred and sixty-one,
Hurrah, hurrah!
That was when the war begun,
Hurrah, hurrah!

In eighteen hundred and sixty-two
Both sides were a-falling to,
And we'll all drink stone wine when
Johnny comes marching home.

THE SLANTED RAYS of the afternoon sun bounced brazenly on the choppy surface of the river, paining the eyes and blurring the vision of anyone who looked long at the water. Far downstream, the bulk of the Highlands cut off the sun and the river was dark with the shadow of the mountains. The wake of the steamboat was still visible there, a thread of light color on the dark blue water, stretching into the distance and vanishing as the Hudson itself narrowed and vanished in the forested Highlands.

One passenger stood alone near the stern, as far from the rhythmic thumping of the steam engine as he could get. There were no passengers nearer him than five yards in either direction, although a pair of frolicking boys tumbled on the deck near enough to his feet to force him to move a step or two.

His name was Jefferson Barnes. He was a second lieutenant in the United States Army, holding the temporary rank of captain.

For the fourth or fifth time that day he took a folded telegraph message from an inner pocket of his blouse. He had already read it so many times that the flimsy yellow paper was tearing at the seams. The message wasn't long:

COME HOME IMMEDIATELY. HIGHLAND COUNTY REGIMENT FORMING. YOU WILL COMMAND.

The message was addressed to him in care of the War Department in Washington, where he had spent the past year serving on the staff of General Winfield Scott. It was signed by his father, Stephen Barnes. An official letter from Governor Morgan of New York had followed the message, asking if he was available for field grade commission with a volunteer regiment.

Barnes repressed a grin as he read the message. This was his chance to get into the war. It seemed to him that the year he had spent in Washington had been the longest of his life. Here it was July of 1862, the war was more than a year old, and he had not yet seen a rebel soldier or heard a shot fired. At last, however, he was being given a command.

He was so eager to get home to Highland Landing that he had been fretting for the past three hours about the steamer's seemingly slow progress up the Hudson. Actually, the *Oregon's* side wheels were pushing the big white steamer at a speed approaching twenty miles per hour, good time for a river boat.

Barnes put the telegraph message back in his pocket, then stared fixedly at the steep wooded height of Storm King Mountain, as if he could see through to its other side. In a manner of speaking, he could. The United States Military Academy was hidden from view by the flank of the mountain. He had spent four years at West Point. Now he was getting his chance to use the training he had received; he would serve his country with all his mind and body and heart.

A cheerful voice broke his thoughts. "Jeff Barnes! How are you?"

Jeff turned from the rail to face a handsome young man with a pleasant smile. He knew the fellow's face but he couldn't find a name in his memory to go with it.

The young man laughed. "You don't remember me, do you? No reason you should, I suppose. It's been a long time. I'm Edward Boudrye."

"Of course," Barnes said, nodding. "How are you? And the sheriff?" He remembered now that Boudrye had been a skinny youngster in a lower class at Montgomery Street Academy, and that his father was, or had been, sheriff of Highland County.

"He's fine. He's looking forward to your arrival. As a matter of fact, the whole town is."

Barnes was surprised, and showed it. His father was not given to discussing personal affairs with outsiders, and certainly the Governor hadn't made a public proclamation of the appointment of one field officer.

"What do you mean, the whole town?" he asked.

Boudrye laughed, showing even white teeth below his thin black mustache. "Folks are pleased as punch to have you come home to command the regiment. The committee let the news out because they're planning to make you the guest of honor at a ball in the Huguenot Hotel."

"What the devil are they doing that for?"

"It's all for the regiment, really," Boudrye told him cheerfully. "To whip up public spirit and bring the men in to enlist. You'll probably have to make a tour of the county to let the boys see their dashing commander."

Boudrye might have found a word more calculated to rile Barnes if he had searched his vocabulary thoroughly and if he had known what he was seeking, but "dashing" would do well enough. To Jefferson Barnes that word was synonomous with "reckless" and "flamboyant." Moreover, he had heard young and pretty ladies in Washington apply it affectionately to George Armstrong Custer. Barnes would be damned if he'd let himself be compared, however unintentionally, with the D'Artagnan of the Class of 1861, U.S.M.A.

"There will be no dashing," Barnes said swiftly, concealing his momentary irritation. The young man had meant no harm, after all.

There was another interruption, by a girl in a blue dress who came walking quickly along the deck. "Ned, is the baggage all right?" she asked. She looked at Barnes and smiled. "Hello, Captain Barnes. How are you?"

"You remember my sister, don't you, Barnes?" Boudrye asked.

"How do you do, Miss Boudrye?" Barnes said easily.

He brought his head up from the stiff nod that passed for a bow these days in Washington society. He looked into dark eyes. Her small, even-featured face was framed by swirls of black hair that whipped and twisted in the breeze. Her mouth was crinkled by a pleasant smile.

"I'm very well," she said. "We're glad to have you home again."

Barnes held his black slouch hat in his hand searching his mind for a memory of Edward Boudrye's sister. He could find none. He told himself that he should remember, even if she had been only a little girl when he was going to school with her brother, because he instantly decided that she was the loveliest woman he had ever seen.

Perhaps his appraisal was wrong, because lovely women were everywhere in wartime Washington, but, in credit to his judgment, she was beautiful. Her eyes were very dark and set wide apart under long, full brows that added strength and angularity to her thin face. She was taller than most women—he didn't have to look down to meet her eyes. Her body was slim and graceful. He was sure of this because she was less flounced and skirted than was the fashion, or perhaps her dress was cut in simple lines. He didn't know much about women's apparel, but he thought she was dressed in the best of taste as he was able to determine it. He imagined that she was twenty or perhaps twenty-one.

"Life has been so exciting since the county started raising the regiment," she said. "I think it's wonderful. Did Ned tell you about the ball, Captain Barnes?"

"Yes, he did," Jeff said.

"We're all working for the regiment," she told him. "My father and yours are on the committee, and Ned is raising a company. He'll be a captain as soon as he gets enough men."

"Bill Colden and I are racing to get the first company complete. You remember Bill, don't you, Barnes?"

Jeff nodded. Colden had been in his class at Montgomery Street Academy.

Boudrye laughed. "My sister said she'd give him his ring back if he didn't beat me."

Barnes looked quickly at the girl. "You're engaged to Bill Colden?"

"Yes, I am."

Boudrye picked up the conversation again and carried it for a few minutes more, telling Barnes that he and his sister had been to New York on a shopping trip—she to buy a new gown for the ball, and he to be fitted for his uniforms as an officer in the new regiment.

"We'll be there soon, Ned," the girl said finally. "We'd better see to our baggage."

When they'd left him, Captain Barnes leaned against the railing and reached for a cigar. He bit off its tip, spat the tobacco flakes into the river, and struck a match on the railing.

Cigar smoking was a habit he'd picked up during his year in the War Department. A man couldn't very well avoid it, unless he had prejudices against smoking. Fine cigars were thrust upon him by congressmen seeking commissions for constituents, by state governors who visited the War Department to expedite the mustering of militia into federal service, by manufacturers and merchants who wanted to sell equipment and supplies to the army, by civilians in brand-new uniforms, wearing eagles or stars on their shoulders, who sought favorable assignments for their regiments or brigades.

At first Jeff Barnes had refused the cigars, knowing how often he would have to bar the donor's way to General Scott or Secretary Cameron. He soon learned, however, that the proffering of a cigar was as much a part of a Washington introduction as a handshake.

Many of the cigars he had smoked during the past year had come from the hands of men whose names had since become well known to the nation: Hooker, Burnside, Pope, Butler, McClellan, Halleck. Others hadn't yet pushed their way into the newspapers. Barnes remembered with a faint smile one officer who had not offered him a cigar. That had been his classmate George Custer, resplendent in his own conception of what a cavalryman should wear, who had breezed into Secretary Cameron's office with the assurance given him as aide to General McClellan. He'd had only a slap on the back for his old friend Jeff Barnes—a fatherly slap, for George Custer took himself most seriously. Barnes remembered thinking that Custer's uniform had probably cost so much that there hadn't been any money left for complimentary cigars.

As the steamer entered the wide bay in the Hudson at Highland Landing, Barnes left the rail and moved slowly forward among the passengers who were also leaving the boat at Highland Landing. He smiled, thinking of the Boudrye girl. He'd certainly dance with her at that ball they'd talked about even if she was engaged to Bill Colden.

He noticed his fellow passengers only casually; he was conscious that they were staring at him, but he was used to that. Army officers were still objects of curiosity everywhere in the Union except in Washington. The war was little more than a year old; it had not yet become a long and terrible nightmare to civilians. People were beginning to realize that it was somewhat less of a circus than it had seemed when the first volunteers had marched away, but it was still novel and exciting.

The *Oregon's* passengers were cast in the placid civilian mold—men, women, and children were for the most part comfortably dressed, looked well nourished, and evidently were middling-prosperous. They were the type of people one would expect to find on a steamboat offering luxury accommodations for the trip from New York City to any one of a dozen landings on the Hudson.

There were soldiers aboard, a dozen or so. Barnes saw five of them squatting in a circle beside a lifeboat, concentrating on playing poker for small stakes. They were all bearded, and their uniforms were worn and faded. They were that rare breed among the hundreds of thousands who now comprised the Union army—veterans of the first year of fighting. They glanced casually up at Barnes as he passed, then back at their cards. A year ago, in their first exciting days as soldiers, they would have leaped to attention. Now they pretended they didn't see him.

Barnes met the Boudrye girl again as he passed the huge wooden housing of the side wheel.

"There you are!" she said brightly. "Will you share a hack with us when we land? Ned's going to rush off and hire one before they're all gone."

"Thank you very much," he said quickly. "I'd be pleased."

There was considerable comment among the crowd when Captain Barnes came down the gangplank of the steamer with the sheriff's daughter on his arm. People knew who he was; his arrival had been announced in the Highland Landing *Statesman*. Barnes didn't no-

tice the buzz of interest. She was touching his arm lightly with her
hand, smiling at him. His spirit was singing with rare pleasure for a
young man who considered himself wholly dedicated to the task before him.

2

In the army there's sobriety,
Promotion's very slow,
So we'll sing our reminiscences of
Benny Havens, oh!

HIGHLAND LANDING was a city of perhaps sixteen thousand
people in 1862. It was on the west shore of the Hudson, somewhat
closer to New York than it was to Albany. It was a logical market
center for the thousands of farmers who cultivated the fertile rolling
country that stretched between the river and the Catskill and
Shawangunk mountains to the west. Before the war the city's merchants and manufacturers had depended largely on the farmers of
Highland County and neighboring counties for their income. River
traffic had always been brisk, but in addition to its commercial
piers the bay at Highland Landing held several small shipyards.

With the war, Highland Landing changed from a quiet river town
to a hustling center of industrialization. The Bellnap Harness Works
had been converted to making army shoes and boots; Hasbrouck's
Farm Implement Company was working two shifts a day to pro-
duce artillery carriages and caissons; the Storck Woolen Mills turned
out hundreds of blue uniforms every week; Chapman's Bleachery
had abandoned the manufacture of washing chemicals to make gun-
powder; the shipyards were employing hundreds of men in the con-
struction of gunboats for the Union navy.

Walking the streets of the city on the night of his return, Jefferson
Barnes was quickly made conscious of the changes. Saloons were
crowded with men in work clothes; the Academy of Music on

Broadway, advertising a dramatic company on tour, was fronted by a column of people, four abreast, waiting patiently to get to the box office; the streets were busy with carriages and buggies of every type. The many pedestrians all seemed to be hurrying, as if they were already late for appointments. Barnes could remember well the quiet, lazy city he had known as a youth, when it was customary for young folks to complain that the city fathers took in the sidewalks at nine o'clock. Now the city reminded him unfavorably of Washington, with its noise, its smells, its appearance of being far too busy to clean itself up.

Barnes was content, however, that all the passers-by seemed too preoccupied to pay much attention to a soldier strolling along the street. There'd been too much fuss already in the three hours he'd been home.

Dinner had been an uncomfortable meal for him, although the food was good: roast lamb done with his mother's usual skill. The trouble was that he had been unprepared for his family's varying attitudes toward him.

His father, who had always been a forthright, unassuming man, treated Jeff with deference, as if his son were a major general.

His mother fluttered about him, forcing food upon him, refilling his water glass, tinkering with the table setting, and frequently murmuring such comments as, "My, my, Jefferson, you do look handsome in your uniform," or, "The mustache becomes you, Jefferson, but I must say it makes you look thirty instead of twenty-three," or, "Just think of it, Stephen! Only yesterday he was a boy, and now he's a colonel in the army."

Her words were difficult to bear in silence because, for one thing, he had grown the sandy mustache for the specific purpose of looking thirty instead of twenty-three and, for another, his parents had always opposed his dreams of an army career. He remembered how his mother had cried the day he came home from his visit to Congressman Cathcart's office to tell them that he had an appointment to West Point. His father had said no good would come of it. In those days the word "soldier" in Highland Landing meant one of two things: either one of the disreputable hangers-on in the waterfront taverns of the city who were often found on the streets with their hands out to sober citizens asking folks to help an "old solger," or one of the wild youths from unsavory families who ran away to the West to join the army and fight Indians.

His brother Walter was the source of even further discomfort. Walter was twenty, a tall young man with a full, open face and a heavy body, who moved slowly and talked slowly. To Jeff, seeing him after several years' separation, Walter seemed well fitted for his occupation as clerk in the Barnes hardware store. The two brothers had never been comrades in spite of the fact that there was a difference of only three years in their ages. Walter had always preferred to hang around the hardware store helping his father. He'd never had much interest in sports, or in hunting and fishing, and not once in his boyhood had he read a single one of Jeff's books about wars and soldiers.

They'd seen very little of each other since 1857, and Jeff now viewed Walter with curiosity, as if he had never considered that Walter would one day grow to manhood.

It was Walter's conversation about the new regiment that made Jeff uncomfortable. It was quickly evident that Walter expected to be an officer, and as far as Jeff could see, he had no qualifications whatsoever.

"I wouldn't expect to start off any more than second lieutenant," Walter told Jeff placidly. "I'll be in Ned Boudrye's company. I've been helping him get recruits, and he says I can have the job. I guess there's a million questions I've got to ask you, Jeff, about uniforms and a sword and such that I'll need."

"It's not as easy as you all seem to think," Jeff said sharply.

Walter laughed. "We know it's not, Jeff. That's your job, to teach us. I've been keeping a list of questions for you to answer. Every time I think of one I write it down."

"We'll have classes for that," Jeff said. "You'll drill all day and go to school at night. Listen, Walter, why don't you enlist in the ranks? There'll be promotions when you prove your ability."

"Why, Jeff, I never heard of such a thing!" his mother exclaimed. "Billy Hasbrouck will be an officer, and Ned Boudrye, and Bill Colden, and a bunch of others. Walter is as good as any of them. Why should he take a back seat?"

"That's right, Jeff," Walter said. "We're all starting from scratch. They don't know any more about it than I do. It ain't as if I want to be captain right off, you know."

"You'll have to let Jeff decide what you're going to be," Stephen Barnes said. "He's going to be the boss, you know." He smiled proudly at his elder son.

"You'll get along just fine with all the boys who are slated to be officers, Jeff," his mother said. "You went to school with most of them."

"We'll have a prime regiment, Jeff," Walter said. "You think we'll get into the fighting by September?"

"Listen to me!" Jeff said abruptly. "This is no schoolboys' game, nor a church social, either. It's a hard, mean business, and I intend to be the hardest, meanest commanding officer in the army until the men under me are all first-class soldiers. Now they're farmers and clerks. I have to teach them how to kill rebels, kill as many rebels as they can as fast as they can, or they'll all get killed themselves. I'll have to start right at the beginning. Put hay in the left shoe and straw in the right. Hay-foot, straw-foot! So you want to be an officer, Walter? All right, you can start right now."

Jeff got up from the table and crossed to his baggage, piled at the foot of the stairs in the hall. He rummaged in a valise and brought out a slim book. He went back to the table and slapped the book down before Walter.

"There you are. Start studying. That's 'Hardee's Tactics.' That's your Bible from now on. Learn it backwards and forwards and inside out. And I want to tell you right now that the officers in this regiment will hold their commissions by ability. Friendship with me, or family connections, or political influence will cut no ice."

His mother spoke in a disturbed voice. "Why are you yelling at Walter, Jeff? What's he done wrong?"

"He's getting the first sample. One thing more. Some regiments while they're training work from sunup to sunset. This one is going to work from can to can't. That includes everybody, Walter."

His brother blinked and looked at the book in his hand. "Sure, Jeff," he said slowly. "I'll work as hard as you want me to. Hard as anybody else does."

"Maybe harder," Jeff said harshly. "Maybe you've got a longer way to go. You've never even fired a rifle, Walter."

"Don't get off on the wrong foot, Son," his father said soberly. "Everybody is willing to do his part. I know that. I'm on the committee, and I know how hard everybody has worked so far."

"I'm not getting off on the wrong foot, Pa. I know what this job is like. I'm going to have to drive 'em. I know it. They may all hate me when I'm finished, but by God, they'll be soldiers."

His mother clucked her tongue. "Now, Jeff, you remember what I always used to tell you when you were little. You'll draw more flies with sugar than you will with vinegar."

"We're talking about soldiers, not flies, Ma."

"Another thing, Jeff," his father added. "The way things are, the officers are pretty well lined up, you know. There's not much can be done about changes now."

"I know that, Pa. I helped work out this system down in Washington. I also know just how fast I can get rid of them if they don't pull their weight."

"Maybe you'd like to tell the committee how you plan to work. There's a meeting tonight at the sheriff's house. Congressman Cathcart called it. He's got something on his mind, but there's probably going to be time for you to say your piece if you want to."

"Not tonight, Pa," Jeff said. "I thought I'd take a walk around town." He looked at his mother. "Boudrye was with his sister on the boat. I didn't remember her. What's her name?"

"Kathleen," said Mrs. Barnes in surprise. "You must remember her, Jefferson. Kate Boudrye. They lived near us on Liberty Street when you were only a youngster."

"The white house near the library?"

"That's right. They still live there."

He shook his head. "It was a long time ago, Ma. I don't remember her."

He thought about the name. Kathleen. Kate. It sounded just right for her dark beauty. He repeated it in his mind. Kathleen Boudrye.

When his father left for the committee meeting, Jeff took his baggage upstairs to unpack. His mother went with him. She pointed out happily that his room was kept exactly as it had been before he went away to West Point.

"Even your guns, Jeff," she said, indicating the glass-fronted gun case which held his shotguns and rifles. "Walter cleans and oils them for you." She paused. "He's a good boy, Jeff. Be patient with him, and with the rest of them."

"I'll be as patient as the time allows, Ma. Eight weeks is all we have. They've got a lot to learn."

"I don't know a thing about soldiering, Jeff, but it seems to me that they'd do better for you if you forget your West Point discipline."

"You let me handle it, Ma," he said with a smile, thinking at the same time of the regiments he had seen marching through Washington, headed by officers who didn't know the first thing about West Point discipline. Out of uniform, out of step, out of hand, with non-commissioned officers who whistled at girls just as loudly as did the men in the ranks, while the officers dropped out of the column and headed for the nearest saloons. Such regiments had scattered at Bull Run, and had been worthless in other early battles of the war.

Jeff recalled the story that had been told in the War Department about Mr. Lincoln's visit to the bivouac of General Sherman's brigade after Bull Run. He told his mother how it had been: a captain who had wanted to go home to New York had complained to Lincoln that Sherman had threatened to shoot him if he left his company.

"Threatened to shoot you, did he?" Lincoln asked, looking from the irate captain to the stony-faced Sherman. Then he bent close to the captain and whispered loudly, "Well, if I were you, and he threatened to shoot, I wouldn't trust him. I believe he would do it."

Jeff's mother didn't laugh at the story.

"Sherman was a colonel then," Jeff explained. "A few days later Lincoln made him a brigadier general."

"Sherman?" she said. "Isn't he the general out West that the newspapers said was crazy?"

Jeff started to protest, but then shrugged and laughed. "All right, Ma. I guess the story isn't as funny as I thought it was."

When he was leaving the house to take his walk around town, Jeff saw Walter at the dining-room table, his head bowed over "Hardee's Tactics." "Don't try to learn it all in one night," he called.

Walter looked up woefully. "I guess I'll never learn any of it."

With Kathleen Boudrye on his mind, it came as no surprise to Jeff that he found himself walking on the broad blue flagstones of the sidewalk on upper Liberty Street, above Broadway. Neither was it surprising that, while he was still a block away from the library, he was trying to remember whether the white house with the green shutters, the clipped privet hedge, the long, low veranda shadowed by honeysuckle vines was the second or third house beyond the red brick hulk of the Highland Landing Free Library.

It was the third house. He slowed his pace as he approached it, noticing that the hedge had grown much thicker but was still clipped to waist height, that the honeysuckle now almost covered the veranda, that the house gleamed brightly as the moonlight fell on its white façade.

"Captain Barnes. Good evening."

It was her voice, cool and quiet, but carrying in the still night air. There was no inflection of surprise in it; for a moment he thought curiously that she might have been expecting him. She was standing on the veranda near the steps, dressed in white that made her clearly visible against the shadows trapped by the vines.

He turned back, went through the gate and along the walk until he had reached the foot of the steps, where he stood looking up at her. "Good evening," he said. "I was taking a walk."

"I'm glad you came this way," she said quietly, as if it had been most reasonable, most natural circumstance to have him come walking out of the darkness of Liberty Street to find her waiting to greet him. "Come sit down, Captain Barnes."

There were wicker chairs in the cavern formed by the honeysuckle and the roof. He pulled one forward, holding it until she was seated. He took another for himself. There was a table to one side. He heard the clink of a glass, the sound of liquid being poured.

"Iced tea," she said. "Unless you'd prefer my father's brandy."

"This will be fine," he answered. "Thank you."

He held the cool glass without drinking. "You're alone," he said. The statement was really a question; if she didn't want him to stay, she could tell him she was about to go inside when he came, or she was waiting for Colden, or some other excuse.

"Yes," she said. "The meeting inside is in full blast. I made the iced tea for them, but they prefer brandy. I came out here to get away from the talk and the cigar smoke."

She paused. He looked at her in silence, sensing that she was about to speak again. There had been an undertone of concern in her words, as if she were trying to tell him something about the committee meeting.

"Mr. Cathcart is in there," she said evenly. "With your father and Judge Crist and Mayor Hasbrouck."

"My father told me," he said. "What are they doing, having a Republican caucus?"

She didn't laugh. "You might say so. They're trying to convince Cathcart that he should run for Congress again. He says he doesn't intend to be a candidate."

"He'd win in a walk, wouldn't he?"

"He would, but he doesn't want it this time."

"Why not?"

"He's been to Albany to see Governor Morgan," she said. "He brought the commissions for the regiment back with him today."

"The field officers' commissions?" he asked wonderingly. There was something wrong, and she was trying to tell him. He put his glass down, waiting.

"He brought back three commissions. One is for Billy Hasbrouck as major. The other two are for colonel and lieutenant colonel."

"I think I know what you're going to say."

"Yes," she said. "He's an old friend of Governor Morgan. He helped get Morgan the nomination in 1858. He went to Albany and asked for the command of the regiment. The Governor gave it to him. You're to be lieutenant colonel."

This was bitter news to take, but somehow it neither shocked nor surprised him. He felt almost as if he had been expecting it, or some similar political trick. He had seen it happen time and again in Washington during the early days of recruiting volunteer regiments. Many a capable regular or militia officer, under orders to assume command of a volunteer unit, had suddenly found himself superseded by a local politician. The aggrieved officers had brought their problems to the War Department, but there was nothing that the Federal government could do about them. The organization of volunteer regiments was an affair for the states to handle, and the War Department could not interfere until the regiment was mustered into Federal service. Any attempt then to remove incompetent political officers was usually followed by a storm of Congressional protest; therefore the politicians kept their commissions unless they were so inept that they could be forced to resign under threat of court-martial.

"They've been arguing with him for an hour," she said, "but Mr. Cathcart just smiles and says that you and he will get along fine. There's nothing that Father and the rest can do, without destroying the unity of the Republican County Committee. Judge Crist and my father can't buck Cathcart."

"I see," he said. "The Republican Party is more important than winning the war. Cathcart is no soldier."

"What will you do?" she asked.

He got up from the chair and walked to the edge of the porch, looking out into the quiet street. He clasped his hands tightly behind his back, fighting the anger that rose inside him. Giving way to emotion would serve no purpose.

"What will you do?" she asked again.

He turned his head and looked at her, smiling briefly. "I don't know," he said slowly, managing to keep the bitterness out of his voice. "Only one of two things, I guess. Refuse the commission and go back to the War Department, or take it and serve under Cathcart. I'll have to think about it."

"If I were a man, I know what I'd do," she said fiercely. "I'd go in there and punch that fat schemer right in the nose!"

Barnes laughed. "If the Governor swore him in, he's already a colonel. I'd be court-martialed."

"It would be worth it!"

They were silent for a little while, until she said unhappily, "I suppose you'll decide to return to Washington."

He shrugged. "I don't know what I'll do. It's not the rank that bothers me. It's the command. I've been trained for it since I was eighteen years old. The army needs me. I'll have to decide how I can serve the army best."

"I'll tell you what I think. You ought to stay here. Cathcart can't train the regiment. You can."

"Did you ever hear of General Sherman?"

"General William Sherman? The one in the West that the newspapers say is crazy?"

"That's how my mother identified him tonight. Newspapers! Sure they say he's crazy. He speaks his mind. He says the war will last for years. He says that we could take a dozen Richmonds and still lose the war, unless we take and hold the Mississippi. Those aren't popular ideas, so they say he's crazy."

"Why are you talking about Sherman?"

"I met him in Washington several times last year. He and his brother, Senator Sherman from Ohio. The Senator told me to see him when the new levies were ordered this year. I think I could have an Ohio regiment if I wanted it."

"Will you go to see him?"

"I'm tempted," he said simply.

"We want you to stay here, Jeff."

He looked quickly at her when she used his first name.

"It will take time to decide. That ball you told me about—it's next Saturday night?"

"Yes. Will you come?"

"If you'll dance with me."

"Of course I will."

He picked up his hat from the table. "I'd better go now," he told her, "before Cathcart comes out. I'm afraid I might take your advice and punch him in the nose."

She held out her hand. "How shameful that he did it. I'm sorry, Jeff."

"Don't let it worry you," he said, taking her hand in his. "I'm looking forward to Saturday night." Tenderness and longing swept into his voice with the touch of her hand. She looked up swiftly, meeting his eyes in wonder.

Her voice was very low. "So am I, Jeff."

Her hand trembled. She stepped back. He could scarcely hear her whispered, "Good night." Before he could answer she had reached the door and vanished into the house.

He walked home through the dark streets with a spirit that was soaring in spite of his sudden loss of rank. He gave little thought to Cathcart; his mind and heart were caught up by the promise he had seen in her eyes and had heard in her voice.

His common sense told him to stop indulging in foolish dreams. She was engaged to Bill Colden, wasn't she?

Why is it, he thought, that I am attracted by women who have already promised to marry someone else?

His mind returned to his Academy days, to the winter of 1860–61. There had been a new instructor in military drawing that winter, a middle-aged lieutenant named Meyer. Jeff had been invited to Sunday-afternoon tea at Lieutenant Meyer's quarters with a group of first classmen. The lieutenant had a daughter named Ruth, a girl with gay blue eyes and straw-colored hair. Jeff's best friend, Paddy O'Rorke, had taken all her time that first afternoon, but such a flirtation was a routine matter to Paddy. Jeff Barnes had stood aside, in sober conversation with her father, yet watching Ruth

Meyer all the time. For the first time in three and a half years at the Academy, Jeff paid more than passing attention to a girl.

Another cadet at the Meyer house that afternoon, a southerner named George Corwin, had fought the battle of states' rights in the Meyer parlor, arguing vehemently with other cadets that secession was the God-given right of any state in the Union, and that there were millions of men ready to fight for it.

Jeff gladly accepted the invitation of Ruth's mother to call again. He visited the Meyer quarters at every opportunity, and before the snow was off the ground he knew that he was in love with Ruth. He had competition, however. Cadet Corwin was there as often as he was.

In the early days of 1861, George Corwin resigned from the Academy to go South to fight for secession. Ruth Meyer married him in the Episcopal church in Highland Falls. She went South with her husband. Jeff never heard from her or about her since that day.

Now he tried to remember her more clearly, but all he could bring to mind was the straw-colored hair blowing in the wind that swept up from the river and across the parade ground.

He brought his mind back to the present as he passed a recruiting poster for the Highland County regiment pasted to a billboard on the side wall of the Academy of Music. He paused and studied it briefly, but his thoughts wandered almost immediately back to Kate Boudrye. The professional soldier would worry about the regiment in the cold light of day; tonight, with the moon and thousands of stars shining overhead, the discipline and dedication of his youth gave way to love.

3

The sun's low down the sky, Lorena. . . .

THE BALLROOM of the Huguenot Hotel had never been intended for such a crowd; before the evening was fairly started, there was little room for dancers, and none at all for spectators. The overflow spilled into the high-ceilinged lobby and into the main dining room. More guests arrived by the minute, until it seemed that every woman in Highland County who owned a dancing gown, every man with evening clothes, was trying to get into the hotel.

Many of the late-comers, particularly those whose years made dancing more a chore than a pleasure, made no attempt to reach the ballroom. The gentlemen lit their cigars and joined discussions in the lobby or the lounge; the ladies filled the tables in the main dining room, where harassed waiters were trying to fill orders of tea and cookies, ices, or punch supplied by the dance committee.

Many of the men had no interest whatsoever in the dance. They had attended for one or both of two reasons—either to support the regiment or at the command of their wives, who had declared that "everyone will be there." They tended to deposit their wives in the dining room and then retire to the wide stone porch of the hotel, where they could smoke and talk in comfort, able to make themselves heard when they had something to say instead of fighting a losing battle against the music and the chattering of women. There, too, a squad of waiters was kept busy filling glasses with cracked ice, whiskey, and water.

While they watched amusedly the efforts of the hotel's stableboys to reduce the congestion among the carriages that deposited guests in an unending procession, the men on the porch were gossiping just as much as were their ladies inside. The topic was Jefferson Barnes.

The entire county knew by this time that Cathcart had snared the command of the Highland County regiment. The Highland Landing *Statesman* had announced the Governor's appointment on the day after the committee meeting. The question at hand was what did young Barnes intend to do? Would he go back to Washington, or would he serve under Cathcart?

The group on the porch was evenly divided as far as guesses went. No one knew for certain; Stephen Barnes had told people he didn't know what his son would do. There were several Democrats on the porch who suggested that Cathcart's trick was no more than one might expect from such a worthless fellow. They quoted the editorial which had appeared in the *Statesman*. Young Adam Colden, the editor, who had fought Cathcart for the Republican nomination for

Congress in 1860, had scored the policy of political appointment of
army officers.

"The liberal dispensation of brandy and cigars," the editorial had
said, without naming Cathcart, "does not qualify a man for high rank
in the army. It seems to us that our fighting men are ill served when
a politician has the power to substitute himself for a qualified field
officer, a graduate of West Point. Regimental committees should not
be forced to submit to such injustice."

In saying that, of course, young Colden was just spitting into the
wind. Cathcart was colonel, and colonel he would stay. The interesting issue was what young Barnes would do. There were friends of
Cathcart who asked what all the shooting was about; a young fellow
of twenty-three, West Pointer or not, was doing right well to be commissioned a lieutenant colonel.

When Jeff Barnes walked quietly up the smooth sandstone steps
of the Huguenot Hotel, accompanied by his brother Walter, the men
on the porch almost missed him. They were busy greeting Judge
Homer Crist and Mrs. Crist, with their beautiful daughter Martha,
who had walked up the steps just ahead of the Barnes brothers. It
was good business sense these days to come forward to shake the
hand of one of the county's most powerful Republican leaders and
to bow to his prim-looking wife and his handsome daughter.

Jeff and Walter Barnes almost slipped through the crowd before
they were seen. Logically enough, it was Judge Crist, who had
trained himself to notice what went on around him, who greeted
Jeff Barnes.

"Good evening, Jefferson," the judge said amiably.

"How are you, sir?" Jeff answered, touching his hand to his hat in
the direction of the judge and his ladies. He didn't interrupt his step,
but continued into the hotel with Walter at his side.

The men on the porch, after making way for Judge Crist's party to
enter, crowded through the doorway to watch developments. They
were disappointed. Young Barnes didn't head immediately for the
group in the corner of the lobby that was dominated by Colonel
Cathcart's florid face and spanking-new uniform. Instead, Barnes
paused before the group of middle-aged ladies who were selling
tickets under this sign:

THE BOYS OF THE 195TH NEW YORK VOLUNTEER INFANTRY
THANK YOU FOR YOUR GENEROUS CONTRIBUTION TO THEIR
WELFARE WHILE THEY SERVE OUR COUNTRY.

The ladies refused to take his money. He was an honored guest, they said. The committee insisted.

He bowed politely, handed his slouch hat to the cloakroom attendant, and walked immediately to the ballroom. Whispers seemed to ripple like waves across the lobby, the lounge, and the dining room. Barnes apparently did not notice the stir he was causing. His brother Walter did. With a face that grew redder by the second, he whispered an excuse to Jeff and retired to the sanctuary of a group of young men and girls near the stairway.

People moved aside to allow Jeff to enter the crowded ballroom. He stood quietly in the entrance, his eyes on the dancers.

The only person who had been sure he would come to the ball was Kate Boudrye. She had been dancing for a half hour now, in the arms of one young man or another, always managing to look at the doorway every few seconds as she whirled around the polished floor.

She saw him as he entered even though she was on the far side of the crowded room. She watched him standing there with his eyes sweeping the dancers. For a few seconds he failed to find her. She could feel her heart beating more rapidly; she was smiling so happily that anyone who happened to be looking at her would wonder what might be the fascination her dancing partner held for her. In truth, she didn't hear a word that rather ungainly young man was telling her. He was Bill Colden's cousin, and he was relating, detail after dull detail, how he had recruited sixteen farm boys into his cousin's company. He told her that he certainly deserved a second lieutenancy.

His eyes were on the floor as he talked, watching his clumsy feet pick out the intricacies of the waltz. He was not in time with the music and he knew it. He'd never been in time with the music in his life, and he was worried about it. How could he lead his men in parades and such if he couldn't keep time?

He didn't notice that the girl who had obviously resigned herself to his clumsiness had suddenly been transformed into the most radiant woman in the room. It was unfortunate for him that he was watching his feet instead of her face; otherwise he would have imagined that his words had the ability to charm, and he would have been much more sanguine about approaching Cathcart and his cousin for his commission.

As it was, he was startled to hear her voice say happily, "If you don't mind, Tom, I'd like to stop dancing now."

The joyous tone was the surprising thing. Usually girls who asked him to stop dancing had sore feet and ankles. He looked up to find her looking not at him, but at the doorway of the ballroom. He stared that way also, wondering what had caught her eye.

"There's Barnes!" he exclaimed. "They said he wasn't coming."

"Yes," she answered softly. "Will you get me a glass of punch, Tom?"

"All right," he answered. "I wonder whether he's met the colonel yet." He held out his arm to lead her off the floor.

"Leave me here," she said. "Thank you, Tom."

Barnes had already started to thread his way through the dancing couples toward her. She went to meet him. She knew that everyone in the room was watching them, but for all she cared, they might have been alone with each other. She knew also that her quickened breathing had brought unladylike color and motion to the low neckline of her gown; her mother had warned her that the exertion of dancing in this dress would bring too much of her bosom into view. Probably her mother was watching now, clicking her tongue. Kate didn't care about that, either.

She had her eyes fixed on Jeff's shoulders as he came forward, and she saw with warm pleasure that he had made his decision. He no longer wore the twin golden bars of a captain, but had replaced them with the oak leaves that signified a lieutenant colonel's rank. He had decided to stay.

They met in the center of the floor. Without taking his eyes from hers, he bowed. "Will you dance with me, Kate?" he said.

She nodded in answer because she didn't think she could speak; her throat had constricted and she was unsure of what she might try to say. She closed her eyes when she moved into his arms; she was afraid she might cry if she kept them open.

He danced gracefully, with the polished ease of four years' instruction at the Academy and one year's practice in Washington ballrooms. He kept his eyes on her face, waiting for her to look at him.

She spoke before she opened her eyes. Her voice was low but clear. "You're wearing the oak leaves. You're staying."

"Didn't you know I would, Kate?"

Now she looked at him. "Yes, I knew."

"Kate," he said softly, smiling.

"Yes?"

"Nothing. Just Kate."

She held his hand tightly when the waltz ended. She hadn't realized that the other dancers had been leaving the floor since Jeff had taken her into his arms; now they were alone in the center of the ballroom, with everyone in the place staring at them. She was startled by the sudden burst of applause that rose vigorously and continued under the smiling leadership of Judge Crist, who was slamming his hands together at a great rate. The applause began to die away, then volleyed again as the judge renewed his clapping.

"Why the devil are they doing that?" Jeff demanded.

She looked up to see his brow creased and his lips drawn into a tight line. "It might be for our dancing," she said, laughing, "but I doubt it. I think it's for you. I'm not the only one to notice the change in the insignia on your shoulders. They know you've decided to stay and they're happy about it."

"Oh, I see," he said.

"Bow to them, Jeff. Go ahead."

He frowned again, but bobbed his head slightly toward the crowd. He offered Kate his arm. "Let's get off the floor," he muttered. "I'm not used to being a popinjay."

She smiled. "You're something more now, Jeff. You're a politician, whether you want to be or not. I suspect that Judge Crist was leading that applause just to make Cathcart uncomfortable."

He couldn't reply, because now that the ice had been broken by the applause, people crowded around him to shake his hand, to welcome him home, to overwhelm him with chatter. He saw Kate slipping away from his side as people pressed to speak to him.

The members of the committee got busy and formed a receiving line, with Jeff at the end of it, pumping hands and returning greetings with scant courtesy for a few seconds, until he realized that he could not escape. Then he fixed a smile on his face and braced up to the ordeal.

Suddenly there was an arm around his shoulders; somebody was standing beside him. He turned to find Colonel Cathcart, whose florid face was beaming above his trim mustache and carefully shaped beard.

"I've come to share the burden of handshaking, Jeff," Cathcart said jovially. "I'm an old hand at it, you know. How are you, my boy?"

"Fine, sir. And you?"

"Ready to go to work, Jeff. We ought to start getting our plans in good shape. I see you're sporting your new rank. You deserve it. I've kept track of you since the day I gave you your appointment to the Academy. I'm proud of you, my boy."

"Thank you, sir."

A woman was talking into Jeff's ear, telling him about her boy, who was sixteen and wanted to enlist. "—and I said, 'Nothing doing, young man. You'll wait two years.' The war will be over then, won't it, Colonel Barnes?"

"I hope so, ma'am."

Jeff had an inspiration. He bowed to the woman and said politely, lifting his voice somewhat to be heard above the chatter of people pressing along the line, "Ma'am, I'd like to present Colonel Cathcart, my commanding officer."

"Oh, I know Bert Cathcart!" she said. "My husband got his job through Bert Cathcart, didn't he, Bert? You know, Colonel Barnes, that my husband is superintendent of the county poor farm—— Why, Bert, he's gone!"

Jeff had backed away when Cathcart moved forward, ducked out of the line, and walked swiftly away.

"So he has, Mabel," Cathcart said. "So he has."

"Such a nice young fellow," the woman said, looking at Jeff's broad back.

"He'll be a big help to me, Mabel," Cathcart said genially.

"You'll need help, Bert. Whatever gave you the idea you were cut out for a soldier?"

"Never mind that, Mabel." Cathcart leaned close. "Don't go telling people I gave Fred his job. It doesn't sound right."

Jeff saw Kate Boudrye standing near the orchestra, talking to his parents and to her own. He started toward them, but brought himself up short as a tall, broad-shouldered man with darkly handsome features took Kate into his arms and swung her onto the dance floor. Jeff watched them for a few seconds, then went to join his mother and father. He knew the young man. He was Bill Colden. He realized that until now he had forgotten all about Colden.

A few minutes before, he'd had no doubts. He'd found the only woman who stirred him so completely as to force into the background of his consciousness all that had been of paramount importance in his life. The army, his career, the war, the duty and discipline that had shaped him: they had all vanished from view. He had fondly imagined that all he had to do was speak to her of love and she would answer swiftly. Now he saw that Colden held her with possessive tenderness, that she smiled up into his eyes, that she laughed lightly when he spoke to her.

He was drawn immediately into conversation with Sheriff Boudrye and his father. They wanted to talk about the regiment. Stephen Barnes was still storming about the injustice of Cathcart's commission. He voiced his anger loudly, careless of Cathcart's presence in the ballroom. His wife tried to calm him, but he would not be silenced.

Boudrye was far more reasonable. He told Jeff that the committee was powerless; they had to accept the Governor's decision. The sheriff was concerned with the future of the regiment. How could it function under a man with no military training at all?

Jeff was impressed with Boudrye. The sheriff was a husky man, tall and broad, with a weathered, lined face and keen blue eyes set deep and wide in his pouched face. His voice was slow, deliberative, and controlled. Jeff considered that since he had to deal with politicians, here was one he could trust.

"Kate told us that you would decide to stay," Boudrye said, smiling quietly. "I admit we didn't believe her. In fact, until I saw those doodads on your shoulders, I was sure you'd already bought a ticket back to Washington."

"I still think he should," Stephen Barnes cried. "He can have his choice of commands."

"He's made up his mind," Boudrye said with a quick grin. "Quit trying to discourage him, Steve." He looked at Jeff. "Do you think you can get along with Cathcart?"

"I don't see why not," Jeff said, "as long as he gives me the opportunity to train the men."

Boudrye laughed. "It's all yours. He's the first one to admit he doesn't know a thing about the army. All he wants is to be colonel. You can do the work."

"All right," Jeff said. "We won't have any trouble."

He turned to the others to excuse himself, and found Kate's eyes meeting his. Colden was talking to the sheriff. The band was beginning the gentle, slow-moving strains of "Lorena."

"It's not proper for me to ask you. I know that. Will you dance with me, Jeff?"

Slowly and gracefully they moved to the haunting sweetness of the ballad. Neither of them spoke. She was not smiling now. Her face was calm, her eyes were closed.

The music changed, grew softer until the violins and the woodwinds were only breathing the melody across the crowded floor. One of the violinists, scarcely more than a boy, put down his instrument and stepped before the orchestra. People stopped dancing and stood attentively. Jeff did the same. Kate opened her eyes as a hush came over the room.

"Tim Tuggle," she whispered. "He sings like an angel."

The young man smiled at the crowd, lifted his head, and began to sing. His boyish baritone, clear and gentle, gave a rare beauty to the sentimental words of the ballad:

> The years creep slowly by, Lorena,
> The snow is on the grass again;
> The sun's low down the sky, Lorena,
> The frost gleams where the flowers have been;
> But the heart throbs on as warmly now
> As when the summer days were nigh;
> Oh, the sun can never dip so low,
> Adown affection's cloudless sky.

Young Tuggle smiled and bowed. The audience gave him a storm of applause. When the band put aside its instruments, signifying intermission, people began to leave the ballroom.

Jeff and Kate stood where they had been, both caught in a moment of understanding wonder.

"Kate," he said, as he had before.

She gripped his hand. Her lips trembled. "Jeff. Oh, Jeff, do we have to stay here?"

"No, Kate."

"Then let's go. Now. Anywhere but here, with the lights and all these people."

"Right now," he said softly. "Do you have a wrap?"

"Yes."

Swiftly they moved through the milling crowd. People spoke to them; they nodded and smiled but didn't stop. At the door she whispered, "My mother is watching us. She'll think I'm out of my head."

She knows, he thought. Somehow her mother knows. She must have seen it in my eyes.

His happiness with the moment ebbed as they approached the cloakroom. "What about Colden?" he asked quietly. "Are you sure you want to leave with me?"

"Yes, Jeff. I'm sure."

While the attendant was bringing his hat and her wrap, they were standing silently together. Both of them knew that heads were turning in their direction.

Kate took his arm and they walked the few steps across the lobby to the door. A curious silence fell across the room, a silence that lasted until they were through the door.

Then Highland County started to talk. The word passed quickly into the other rooms. Within thirty seconds everyone in the place knew that Colonel Barnes had left the dance with Kate Boudrye on his arm, and everyone was trying to find someone who might know what it meant. Only Bill Colden was left alone at the foot of the stairs, his troubled eyes fixed on the door.

4

Yes, these were words of thine, Lorena,
They are within my memory yet. . . .

THE PASSING of a folded greenback from Jeff's hand to one of the hotel's stableboys brought a horse and buggy in less than five minutes; the Bellnap livery stable was just around the corner on Second Street. While they waited, Jeff and Kate stood silently on the hotel steps, aware that the men in the shadows of the stone porch were watching them.

As they walked to the buggy, Kate said quietly, "We'll be the talk of the town by morning."

"Yes," he said. "Do you want to go back?"

"No. Let's go."

When they were in the buggy and away from the hotel, she moved close to him, touching his arm with her shoulder. Slowly he lifted his arm and put it around her. He felt her trembling. She drew her cloak closer about her body.

"Are you cold? Is that why you're shivering?"

"No, Jeff. That's not the reason."

The horse was now walking slowly through the dark streets of the "Old Town," that part of Highland Landing where the stone houses built by the Dutch in the second decade of the eighteenth century were still standing. Hundred-year-old maples towered above the bluestone sidewalks, closing out now the moonlight that had lighted the buggy.

He was silent; she wondered if he could hear her heart beating. She reached up and touched his hand against her shoulder. She held it tightly and she trembled again.

He faced her. The moonlight was shining on his face. He isn't handsome, she thought wildly, not like Bill. His face is hard, stern— she thought of a word: disciplined. And he's so young! She imagined that his hard mouth would crush hers if he kissed her.

Suddenly she was afraid. She didn't want him to kiss her. A week ago her life had been flowing in a course that would be marked by happiness, contentment, richness. There were no unknowns. Her life as Mrs. William Colden of Highland Landing would be secure and rewarding.

She had seen her danger in the eyes of Jefferson Barnes the day she met him on the *Oregon;* she had heard it in his voice. With rare perception for her years, she had known that no woman would ever bind him to her with the simple ties of love and devotion. He was bound by three mighty chains; she had little knowledge of the Military Academy and less of the army, but she had heard of those three chains. Before she met him she would have considered them abstract words, having no meaning of themselves, but only suggesting a vague code of principles. DUTY. HONOR. COUNTRY. Now she was afraid of them, afraid that they were so mighty that the feeble chain of love could never hold against them.

She had only to say, "Let's go back, Jeff," before he kissed her. Then there would be no reason to be afraid. She didn't say it. She closed her eyes as his lips came to hers.

His kiss did not bruise, but it was demanding, insistent, on her trembling lips. When he released her, she leaned against him and buried her head against his shoulder.

"Kate, I love you."

"I love you," she whispered.

In the darkness he kissed her again. Then his lips moved against her hair, his voice said softly, "Will you marry me, Kate? Soon?"

"Yes, Jeff. Tomorrow if you want me."

5

Dearest love, do you remember . . . ?

SUMMIT HOUSE was located near the top of one of the highest mountains in the Shawangunk range. It had been built on the southern slope, at the crest of a ridge. Below the steep face of the ridge was a beautiful little lake in the center of a wooded plateau. The oval shape of the lake was so nearly perfect that it looked man-made, as if some person of great wealth had hired thousands of workmen to construct it for a child's pleasure. Its glacial origin, however, was clear on close inspection of the great cuts of rock that formed its perimeter.

The hotel itself, a popular resort among people of wealth in New York City and the Hudson Valley, was a great sprawling building, white with green trim, that could be seen for twenty miles on a clear day. Eastward it overlooked the trim orchards and fields of High-

land County, all the way to the river; to the south were the wooded
Shawangunks; west and north, shaded blue by distance, were the
higher and wilder peaks of the Catskills.

The only way to reach Summit House was by way of a private
road which wound for several miles along the mountainside, a broad
avenue of red-hued shale bordered by massive hemlocks. Only guests
and hotel personnel could use the road; the only vehicles allowed
were rubber-tired carriages supplied at the entrance to the road by
the gatekeeper. No ruts or bumps marred the perfection of the
packed red road.

On the Tuesday afternoon following the ball Jeff and Kate rode in
one of the resort's carriages along the Summit House road. They were
driven by a towheaded boy in green-and-white livery, whose mountain speech and raw-boned features were in strange contrast to his
neat uniform, the splendid carriage, and the team of coal-black
horses that drew it.

Even the horses, Jeff noticed, were equipped to protect the road.
They were shod with broad thick shoes without flanges. These are
summer shoes, he thought. They'd slide all the way down the mountain on those things in the winter.

The driver rode stiff and straight on his seat, never speaking after
he'd picked up the reins. Once he broke into a kind of tuneless
whistle, then cut himself short abruptly, as if he'd remembered that
a Summit House employee must never disturb the guests.

"Isn't it lovely?" Kate asked softly, her eyes on the road ahead—a
winding red path, edged by the green hemlocks, and vanishing as
it turned upward into the brilliant clear blue of the mountain sky.

"It should be," Jeff said, thinking somewhat ruefully of the hole it
was going to make in his pocketbook. He regretted the words immediately; these days must not be marred in any way. "For us, I
mean," he added quickly.

She smiled and held his hand. He would have kissed her if he had
not the curious idea that the mountain boy on the driver's seat had
eyes in the back of his head.

This was their honeymoon. They had six days, until Sunday. On
Monday morning Jeff had to be at the new camp of the 195th New
York Volunteers at Chapman's Lake outside Highland Landing. The
regiment was to be activated although the rolls were not yet completed.

They had been married an hour before in the village of Cedar Bush, a few miles away at the foot of the mountain. The minister, all his life a back-country pastor, had been reluctant to perform the ceremony. To him this couple who knocked at the door of the parsonage at lunch time were simply a soldier and his girl who had suddenly decided that they'd better get married before he went back to the war. The minister advised them to go home and think it over, to consult with their parents first. After all, he reasoned, they were eloping, otherwise they would have had both families with them.

The minister knew nothing of uniforms or insignia.

"What is your name, soldier?" he asked the young fellow in his best fatherly tone.

"Jefferson Barnes," the soldier answered impatiently.

The minister knew he should recognize the name. It had a familiar ring. Where had he heard it?

"And the young lady's name?"

"Kathleen Boudrye," Kate said. "If you won't marry us, Mr. Comfort, we'll find someone who will."

"Boudrye!" the minister exclaimed. "Your father is the sheriff?"

"Yes."

"Oh, my goodness! And does he know you came here to marry this young soldier? I think you'd better go back to Highland Landing and think about this. I really do."

"This young soldier," said Kate, "is Lieutenant Colonel Jefferson Barnes, of the 195th New York Volunteer Infantry, and my father and mother know him well, Mr. Comfort."

A lieutenant colonel! The minister was amazed. He had seen the story in the *Statesman* about this young fellow, but he had pictured a middle-aged man. Mr. Comfort wasn't sure just how high in the army hierarchy a lieutenant colonel might be, but he knew it was well above captain. And this man, this young fellow, would be in charge of Samuel. He'd have to marry them! He'd be happy to, in fact.

"Of course," he said, "that's different, Miss Boudrye. Come right in. Come right in—uh—Lieutenant Colonel. Do you have any witnesses with you?"

"We hope you can supply them, sir," Barnes told him.

"Of course I can. My wife and my son Samuel. He will be—uh—in your charge, Lieutenant Colonel. He has enlisted."

The minister shook his head again as he led them into his study. Such a young man! Just a few years older than Samuel. He looks competent, however.

Mr. Comfort considered himself, by the very nature of his calling, a thoroughly qualified judge of character. He decided that his son Sam, whose mind was a bit slow when you came right down to it, and whose body was even slower, would be quite safe under the guidance of this lieutenant colonel. He'd teach Sam how to dodge rebel bullets.

They were married a few minutes later. Jeff kissed Kate tenderly, with Mr. and Mrs. Comfort smiling benignly upon them. Sam stood by in bug-eyed wonder. This man in the handsome blue uniform was a real colonel in the real army, and the pretty girl was the sister of the fellow who had enlisted him. Sam was almost beside himself when the officer shook hands with him. All he could say was, "Looks like I'm goin' to work for you. I joined up."

"So your father said. You look as if you'll make a good soldier." Privately Jeff was telling himself that this lad would have to lose forty pounds in two months. He had the shape of a pickle barrel.

"I can work hard," Sam said. "I ain't afraid of work, nor guns either."

They sat down, on the Comforts' insistence, to a lunch table filled with so much good food that Jeff could understand Sam's girth. Mrs. Comfort kept talking about her son, listing his accomplishments, most of which seemed to be in the housekeeping line. He'd worked at Summit House before he enlisted, she said, and he'd learned a lot there in addition to what she'd already taught him. Mr. Comfort smiled somewhat shamefacedly. This was no way to talk to an officer about a future soldier. He tried to make a joke of his wife's carrying-on.

"Sam will make some girl a good husband," he said. "He can cook and sew and do a dozen other things better'n most girls. He's all man, though, Sam is."

The subject of the conversation was sitting quietly. He hadn't said a word since Jeff had shaken hands with him.

When Kate and Jeff were leaving for Summit House, Mrs. Comfort drew Jeff aside for a few seconds.

"You'll look after my boy when he comes to the army, won't you, Colonel?"

"I'll look after him personally, Mrs. Comfort," Jeff said with a winning smile. "You say he can cook?"

"He cooked the lunch we ate," she said proudly. "Most as good as I could myself. They had him in the kitchen at Summit House."

"Fine, Mrs. Comfort. That's fine," Jeff said. He turned to the young man. "When you get to camp next week, you ask for Colonel Barnes. Tell them I want to see you. Don't take no for an answer."

"Yessir," Sam said.

As soon as he and Kate were away from the parsonage, Jeff began to laugh.

"I'm glad you're happy to have a wife," Kate said wonderingly, "but why laugh about it?"

"I got more than a wife back there in the parsonage," he told her. "I got a housekeeper, too."

Her face clouded. "I should have warned you about that. I don't know a dust mop from a broom."

"I'm not talking about you," he said, hugging her to him with his free arm. "I'm talking about Samuel Comfort. I'll have an orderly who can cook, and mend clothes, and iron shirts! I'll look after her boy all right. I won't let him out of my sight—Cathcart might grab him!"

During the long ride up the mountain Kate sat quietly in the fold of his arm. He thought he knew why. Any girl had a right to a gala wedding, with her friends and family about her to laugh and cry and rejoice with her. Kate would have had such a wedding, probably followed by a magnificent reception in the Huguenot Hotel, if he had never come home. Instead, he'd taken her alone to a country parsonage, to an abrupt and simple ceremony which, although employing the same words that were used before a church full of people, seemed even to him to be somehow ineffectual.

All four parents had begged them to wait. Mrs. Barnes and Mrs. Boudrye had cried together; Stephen Barnes and the sheriff had spent a perturbed hour trying to change Jeff's mind. In the end, they all gave their reluctant blessings.

So Kate had lost her wedding day, Jeff thought, but he'd make up for it. This week, for instance. They would always remember it. He was glad he had thought of Summit House. He'd always heard that it was expensive, luxurious, and peaceful. On Monday morning, when he'd decided to take her there, he'd been worried about accommodations. There was no time for a letter to go from Highland

Landing to Cedar Bush. Sheriff Boudrye furnished the answer: Jeff went to Judge Crist, who wrote a letter to the resort owners, whose legal affairs he handled. Jeff had the letter; Judge Crist had assured him it would take care of everything.

"There it is," Jeff said to Kate as the carriage pulled around a curve and the hotel on the ridge came into view. He studied the building, which reflected the sunlight from hundreds of windows. "I hope they don't put us in a cubbyhole under the roof."

The driver brought the carriage into the semicircular drive before the wide shaded veranda that stretched the length of the hotel. There were at least twenty people, perhaps thirty, seated in wicker chairs taking the cool breeze that swept across the mountain. The veranda furnished a twenty-mile view of the mountains and the valley in three directions, but the guests—all of them except a few who were napping—watched with pleasant curiosity the young couple who came up the bluestone walk to the wooden steps.

The man at the registration desk watched Jeff hold the door for Kate to enter. He allowed himself the brief luxury of a frown, but it lasted only an instant. He was used to problems, and this was one of the common kind. Whoever the officer was, Summit House expected no guests today. This couple—they had the look of newlyweds—would have to be turned away.

He watched them start across the lobby, his face impassive. It's a shame, he thought. And there's nowhere within twenty miles they can go. How am I going to make it easy for them?

He straightened to greet them. He was tall and lithe, with straight brown hair that was swept back from a high forehead above keen gray eyes. His face was strangely weathered for his occupation; darkened by wind and sun, it added several years to his apparent youth. While Jeff Barnes tried to look thirty with some success, this young man achieved it without trying. He was actually no more than twenty-five. He was clean-shaven and dressed in a light gray suit.

"How do you do?" he said pleasantly as Jeff and Kate reached the desk. "I'm Michael Stewart. What can I do for you, sir?"

"Good afternoon," Jeff said. "We'd like to register, please. Jefferson Barnes is my name. This is Mrs. Barnes."

"I'm sorry, sir," Stewart said evenly, knowing that his resolve to turn them away was already crumbling under the direct gaze of the girl's dark eyes. "You aren't expected, Colonel Barnes. We must have advance registrations."

As Stewart had expected, the girl's bright eyes lost their glow. She looked at her husband with concern.

"I have a letter here," Jeff said quickly. "Judge Crist thought that you might be able to arrange something for us." He took the letter from the inner pocket of his blouse. "It's addressed to Mr. John Stewart."

"My father," Stewart said. "He's not here today. He and my uncle are in New York. Do you mind if I read the letter?"

"Go ahead," Jeff told him.

Stewart opened the letter and glanced rapidly through it. He'd already made up his mind. All the letters Judge Crist might write would never change a Summit House policy, but the judge's words confirmed Stewart's idea that they were just married. His father would have been reluctant to accept them; his uncle would have been adamant against it. Michael Stewart, however, sometimes paid little attention to the established rules of the resort.

Furthermore, Judge Crist said that this officer was with the Highland County regiment. That in itself would probably have been enough for Michael Stewart, without considering Mrs. Barnes's beauty at all.

"Yes," Stewart said easily. "How long will you be staying with us, Colonel Barnes?"

"Sunday," Jeff said quickly, smiling at Kate. "We'll have to leave Sunday afternoon."

"All right," Stewart said, offering pen and ink. "If you'll register, please."

With amused pleasure, Jeff wrote "Lt. Colonel and Mrs. Jefferson Barnes," using his firm masculine script. Kate, looking over his shoulder, was surprised to find herself thinking that those strange words from this day forward meant that Kathleen Boudrye no longer existed.

"You left a carriage at the gatehouse?" Stewart asked.

"They said they'd take care of the horse until we left."

"If you'll follow me," Stewart said. He called an elderly man from an inner office to take over the desk. To Jeff's surprise, Stewart started for the door that led to the veranda.

"The big house is crowded," Stewart explained as he held the door for them. They preceded him to the veranda. "We have several cottages down by the lake. Many of our guests come back year after year to stay in the cottages. They like the privacy, without the hustle and bustle of the hotel."

As Stewart led the way to the cottage, the guests on the veranda exchanged smiles. Their speculations were justified; newly married couples almost always picked a cottage if any were available.

One of the men, an elderly gentleman dressed in riding clothes, puffed happily on a cigar as he watched Jeff and Kate vanish down the face of the ridge. He reached to the next wicker chair and tapped his wife on the hand very gently.

"You were as pretty as she is, my dear."

"Was I, George? Thank you. That was a long time ago."

"You still are, my dear."

6

How swift the hours did pass away,
With the girl I left behind me.

THE COTTAGE was wonderful, or at least it seemed to be wonderful while Stewart was showing it to them. It was built of fieldstones and situated in the heart of a grove of the hemlocks that grew everywhere on the mountain. The trees had been cut away toward the lake, with a path leading to the water. There were no other cottages within two hundred yards, Stewart said. They would have all the privacy they wanted.

There were two rooms in the cottage, equal in size, with a massive fireplace in each room. The summer nights were cold in the mountains, Stewart said. They'd need fires. He showed them the cordwood stacked between a pair of hemlocks, and also a pile of chunkwood for the stove in the bedroom. He'd send a man to make the fires each evening, if they wished. Jeff said he could do it perfectly well. A maid would be assigned to the cottage, Stewart said. She'd arrive at ten o'clock each morning, if that wasn't too early.

That would be fine, Jeff said.

The carriage driver arrived with their luggage, and Stewart went back to the hotel with him, telling them to ask for anything they needed at any time.

Then they were alone, and it was not so wonderful. They stood in the center of the living room, pretending that they were interested in the furniture—which was artfully constructed to offer both rustic appearance and comfort. Jeff admired the soft rug that covered the floor; Kate remarked about the size of the fireplace. He reached for her hand, but she did not draw closer. He sensed the constraint that held her tightly, and he didn't know what to do about it.

She withdrew her hand and said in a small voice, "I'll unpack our things."

"Good idea," he said. "I'll bring in some of that wood. It'll be dark before we know it."

That was the wrong thing to have said, and he knew it instantly, but it was beyond him to add anything to it or to try to change it. She left him with rapid steps, disappearing into the bedroom, and he went outside, cursing himself for a blundering fool.

When he had finished with the wood, he went to the doorway of the bedroom. She was hanging his extra uniform in the closet; he was wearing his light one.

Jeff couldn't help staring at the tremendous bed, which looked big enough to sleep four in comfort. She turned suddenly, sensing that he was in the room. She followed his gaze to the bed, and then looked at him again. Her face was flushed but she met his eyes easily enough.

"Kate," he said too loudly, as if his normal voice wouldn't carry the length of the room, "I'm sorry about the wedding. Maybe we should have waited."

"You didn't want to wait, did you, Jeff?"

"No, dear. But it's been only a few days. We don't even know each other."

She crossed quickly to him and he took her in his arms. She kissed him fiercely, then whispered, "We have all afternoon, then dinner, then the evening. There's time."

"What can I tell you about me?" he asked. "Where do I start? Do you want to hear about the Point? Or about my wasted year in Washington?"

"Just talk, Jeff. I'll listen."

"T. J. Barnes—the T. stands for Thomas—always wanted to be a soldier. When he was ten years old, he found out there was a place called West Point. The army became his entire life."

And now it's my life, too, she thought as she listened to his account of how he had planned and schemed and studied to enter the Academy.

I'm part of it now, she told herself, and I'll have to learn all about it in the little time we have before he goes away. Most of all, I'll have to learn what those three words mean to him. He's so far ahead of me with those three. The fourth one we are learning about together. Duty, Honor, Country, and Love. They will determine the rest of my life.

7

Oh, Johnny has gone for a soldier. . . .

MICHAEL STEWART dipped his oars quietly into the water, pulled gently, lifted the oars, and waited. He didn't have to count while the rowboat glided over the surface; he had been fishing in this manner for so many years that the oars dipped and pulled again automatically when five seconds had gone by.

The tips of his twin trolling rods, set in braces at the stern of the boat, bobbed and dipped unevenly against the pull of the heavy lures deep in the lake. At the age of ten, when he spent most of his days on or near the lake, he had started experimenting on a sure-fire method of catching trout in the warm summer months. It had taken him several years to develop the technique, but now it was second nature to him.

Trolling for trout was one of the prime pleasures of Michael's life on the mountain. He had always been wary of inviting guests to share his solitary mornings on the lake; in all his years of fishing he had found only a few whom he felt could properly appreciate the quiet beauty of the rising sun, the swirling night mist that lay in drifting layers over the water, the querulous peeping of wood ducks in the reeds, the cautious gliding of a deer coming down to drink at dawn. Most people, he had found, wanted to go fishing to catch fish.

Michael had been pleased to discover that Jefferson Barnes could be ranked with the company to whom the taking of trout was supplemental to the enjoyment of a fishing trip. Michael had asked Jeff to fish on Thursday morning and again on Friday morning.

Stewart had become much interested in Jefferson Barnes, because as soon as he had heard the name, he knew that his future would be linked with this man. On the coming Saturday, Stewart intended to enlist in the Highland County regiment.

There had been little conversation between Stewart and Barnes during the few hours they had spent together on the lake, and what there was had been concerned almost entirely with fishing. The rest of the time they had engaged in that mystic series of grunts, groans, grimaces, and profanities which pass for communication among fishermen. Jeff had proved himself without words, however. He had admired the boat, quickly mastered the tackle, listened attentively to Michael's instructions, adeptly put them into practice, and had done no bragging about other fishing he had done.

They talked considerably at breakfast after fishing on Friday morning. Mike had asked a few questions about the war, none of which drew Barnes out, until Mike suggested that there must be a clear reason why so many Union regiments broke and fled under fire. At Bull Run they had panicked, and at Shiloh thousands of men had huddled in terror under the bluff below the battlefield.

"Of course." Barnes nodded soberly. "The answer is clear enough. We have a vast army of men who were civilians a few months ago. They need time to learn how to fight."

Stewart understood that Barnes was willing to talk about this subject because the exclusive society of professional soldiers to which he belonged was not at fault—the material it was given to work with was not suitable to the job—and secondly, training was his immediate concern.

"They'll learn," Barnes said. "They are young men thrust into peril for the first time in their lives whether they come from the farms or the cities. Many of them have never fired a rifle until the day they are marched up to face the rebels. Their officers are for the most part unequal to their commands. If all the fresh regiments received proper training, they'd stand and fight. There are two ways of molding a good regiment. The first is to expose them to battle until they learn that they are soldiers. That way is expensive and dangerous, but we've had to use it so far. The second way is to make soldiers of them beforehand."

"And your regiment?" Stewart asked. "How long will it take you to make soldiers of them?"

Barnes frowned. "It's not my regiment. Colonel Cathcart commands. To answer your question: They will be soldiers when they are as hard as the ground they're going to sleep on, when they can march as far and as fast as I can lead them and have enough energy left to curse me for making them do it, when they can fire a rifle with the knowledge that they can hit what they aim at, when they respond to a command without pausing to consider it, when they know themselves to be better men than the rebels they're going to face. How long will that take? I can't tell you that."

After two days of fishing with Barnes at dawn, Michael wanted to be alone on Saturday morning. This was the day when the recruiting party was scheduled to be in Cedar Bush. After breakfast he would be leaving Summit House to enlist, and he did not intend to return. Barnes had said the regiment would be activated on Monday morning, and Michael meant to go directly to Highland Landing from Cedar Bush. This was therefore the last morning he had for fishing.

As he rowed quietly through the mist, watching the rod tips for the sudden bend that would indicate a strike, Michael wondered how he would tell his father about his decision. No Stewart had ever carried arms, in the United States or earlier in England. How could he explain to that man of peace that he intended to go to war? The old man simply would not understand. He had reared Michael as a Quaker, and in spite of his son's somewhat worldly ways, John Stewart firmly believed that Michael would turn, with the passage of his youth, to the reverence of God and the worship of Him in the manner ordained by the Society of Friends.

There was in Michael's mind no yearning for adventure or glory; he had read extensively of wars and the men who fought them, and he knew something of their brutal and bitter pattern. Nor was he stirred by rallies and slogans; this war was no crusade, although politicians referred to it in crusading terms. Rather, Michael considered the war a cruel and bloody test of the endurance of the Federal Union. Every man who owed his freedom to the basic principles of the Republic must be prepared to sacrifice himself in order that others might continue to enjoy that freedom.

He remembered one of his professors at Yale, more than five years before, speaking wise words that he had never forgotten:

"Gentlemen, I am an abolitionist. Most of you know that, and some of you do not approve. However, the issue that faces this country in these times is not one of slavery; the question of which states shall be free and which shall continue to hold men in bondage—or even whether the entire nation shall be either free or slave—is but a tributary to the main stream of argument. The question that we must answer, and I rather think we will answer it before we are much older, is this: Will the Federal Union be preserved, or will it perish?

"I believe that the issue can be faced and the decision made to preserve the Union by the continued insistence upon the abolition of slavery in these United States. However, if reason could convince me that the Union will perish if abolition sentiment prevails, I would cease, then and there, to insist upon abolition. That is the heart of my political philosophy: that the Federal Union must be saved."

And that, thought Michael Stewart, is the reason I'm going to war. Father will never acknowledge that it's valid. He has a very short list of things in this world which are to be rendered unto Caesar, and none of them involve his heart and mind.

Michael's musing was broken abruptly by the sharp dip of one of the trolling rods. The wooden reel clicked wildly. He dropped the oars, grabbed the rod, set the hook firmly, and felt the fighting surge of a good trout. The struggle lasted almost five minutes before a three-pound trout lay flopping in the bottom of the boat. Michael killed it quickly and stowed it in a basket of wet ferns under the seat.

He reeled in the second lure, which had fouled the bottom when the boat stopped moving. He looked at the sun. It was time to quit.

The mist was rapidly lifting from the water as the sun's early warmth began to tell.

Michael tied up his boat, stowed his rods in the boathouse, then took the basket of fish up to the hotel. Now he'd have to face his father.

He left the fish in the kitchen, went to his room and changed his rough clothing for a gray suit, then sought his father in the hotel office. His uncle Ephraim was there with John Stewart, complaining bitterly that four more employees were leaving to join the army.

Ephraim was accusing the four employees of ingratitude and dishonesty as well as complete senselessness for leaving the hotel at the beginning of the season. He vowed that at this point he was in favor of helping them down the road with the toe of his shoe.

"What can we do?" John Stewart said mildly. "We cannot keep them here against their will. Thy temper, Brother, is running wild again."

"Temper, is it?" Ephraim cried. "I can't understand how thee can sit there quietly when we lose four men in one day. They're leaving this morning, the four of them."

"Five," Michael said quietly.

His uncle stared at him. "Another one! Who is it this time? Not the pot-washer, I hope? Three pot-washers this month!"

Michael shook his head. "No, Uncle Ephraim, not the pot-washer. I am the fifth one."

John Stewart looked up quickly. Ephraim ruffled his thinning hair with his fingers, trying to control himself.

"No jokes, Michael," John said. "Thy uncle is already angry."

"I'm not joking, Father. I'm going down to Cedar Bush this morning to join the army."

Ephraim stared in disbelief, then cried to his brother, "He is mad, John! He has lost his senses."

John Stewart shook his head. "No, he has not. I have seen it coming. I know my son. I've heard him talking of the war and I have seen in his eyes the look of a man who has lost his faith in our ways. He is not mad, Ephraim, unless the whole world be mad."

"A Friend cannot bear arms!" Ephraim cried.

Michael spoke gently. "It has been many years since I've considered myself a Friend, Uncle Eph."

"Go to the war, my son," John said quietly. "And may it spare thee until thy faith returns. The Lord in His wisdom will give thee the chance to become one of us again."

"Forbid it, John!" Ephraim said. "Forbid him to go."

"He is a man. I can forbid him nothing. I can only counsel him. Remember, Michael, the Lord's word: *Thou shalt not kill.*"

Michael hesitated. "I will do my duty, Father."

His father nodded sadly. "As thy soul reveals it to thee."

"I'm leaving now, Father, and I won't be coming back. Can I have your blessing?"

His father looked into his eyes for a long moment, then shook his head. "Not for such an undertaking, Michael. Not for war and killing. My heart goes with thee, and my love. Not my blessing."

They shook hands, then Michael put his arms around his father and hugged him briefly. He shook hands with his uncle, whose mouth was working in an effort to control either his anger or his sentiment; Michael knew that Ephraim Stewart loved him.

"Take a carriage and driver," Ephraim said. "No need to walk before the army orders it."

"I'll walk," Michael said. "It may be a long time before I see this mountain again. I want to enjoy it this last morning."

He went into the lobby, picked up the carpetbag he had left at the registration desk, and started for the door. He looked back once at the office. Through the open door he saw his father sitting at his desk with his head in his hands while Ephraim Stewart talked earnestly to him.

8

Oh, there was an old soldier. . . .

JEFF and Kate were halfway down the mountain in one of Summit House's rubber-tired carriages when they saw the man walking the road ahead of them. He stepped aside to let the carriage pass as the sound of hoofs and wheels reached him.

"It's Stewart," Jeff said. "Wonder where he's going."

"Give him a ride," Kate said lightly, "and then we'll find out."

Jeff pulled up the trotting team. "Can we give you a lift?" he called.

Stewart appeared to hesitate, then smiled. "Don't see why not, Colonel, even if I did have it in mind to walk to town."

"It's a long walk," Jeff said. "And that sun is getting hotter."

Stewart climbed into the carriage, sitting beside Kate on the front seat. He put his bag on the floor boards at his feet.

"We're going to Cedar Bush ourselves," Barnes said. "There's a regimental recruiting party there this morning. They're making a last swing around the county to pick up a few more men."

"I know," Stewart said. "That's why I'm going down."

Kate looked up quickly from her study of her husband's strong brown hands on the reins. "You're going to enlist, Mr. Stewart?"

"I am," he said.

"But I thought——" She hesitated. "You're a Quaker, Mr. Stewart. You don't have to serve in the army, not even when the conscription laws take effect."

"No, Mrs. Barnes, I don't have to. I could stay there on the mountain until the war is over. My father's religion would shield me."

Barnes had been studying him soberly. Now he spoke in a level voice. "There is good reason, Stewart, for exempting pacifists from the draft law. I don't mean to offend you by saying this, but the man who shoots his rifle into the air instead of at a rebel is dead weight. Worse than that, he's a danger to his comrades. Such a man is apt to be a convincing talker. It's possible that he could persuade other men to fire their rifles into the air."

"I'll hit what I aim at, Colonel Barnes."

"Again, I mean no offense," Jeff said quietly, "but what will you aim at?"

"No offense taken, Colonel. I'll aim at Confederate soldiers."

"All right," Barnes said, smiling. "I'll take your word that you will. Tell me this—why did you decide to join the army?"

Stewart grinned. "Colonel, you sound as if you doubt that I'll make a good soldier."

"Not at all," Jeff said. "You'll probably be an excellent soldier. All I want to know is why you're going to enlist."

"It's hard to put an answer to that question in so many words. I'll try it this way: I think it's the duty of every able man to shoulder a musket now. A lot of us will have to die to save the Union. To use a word you are quite familiar with, I think it's my duty."

Kate spoke up. "It's my brother's company that's recruiting in Cedar Bush today. I'm sure he'll be glad to have you, Mr. Stewart."

The recruiting stand was set up on Main Street in Cedar Bush in a vacant lot between a feed store and Mr. Comfort's church. There was a carnival spirit to the crowd that listened to a five-man band playing martial airs. Children and dogs raced around the lot making more noise than the band. Occasionally Ned Boudrye, neat and handsome in a smart new uniform, mounted the steps of the stand and motioned the band to stop playing. His exhortations to enlist in Company A of the 195th New York Volunteer Infantry didn't bring many young men to the booth. Recruiting parties had already picked Cedar Bush and the other rural towns of Highland County almost clean of adventurous young fellows. Jeff Barnes, standing behind the recruiting booth where his brother Walter was handling enlistments, was pleased to see that the men who stepped up to the booth from time to time were in their twenties, sober and more mature than the boys who had rushed to enlist during the first calls for volunteers in 1861.

If new regiments all over the North were drawing this kind of man —recruits who left wives and families and jobs to march off to war, then it was certain that the people were settling down to the terrible job ahead of them. For himself, Barnes would prefer to have every man in the regiment at least twenty-one but not more than twenty-five. Extremes, either in youth or in age, were unstable and susceptible to sickness and disease.

When Michael Stewart came out of the church basement, where Dr. Renwick from Highland Landing was examining applicants for enlistment, Jeff Barnes took his brother's place in the booth in order to fill out Stewart's papers himself. When all the blank spaces were filled with information, Barnes swung the papers around and held out the pen for Stewart to sign.

Barnes smiled at Stewart and said, "All right, soldier. You're in the army. Next man!"

Stewart turned to the man behind him in line, saying, "Go ahead, Jack. You're next."

"Name?" asked Barnes.

"John Hanford, sir."

"Place of birth?"

"Cedar Bush, New York."

"Date of birth?"

"June 14, 1820."

Barnes looked up quickly, studying the man for the first time. He saw a broad, powerful body dressed in farmer's denims. The man's face was tanned and lined by the weather. His hair was black, streaked with dull gray. He stood easily at attention, his eyes straight forward, looking over Barnes's head.

"That makes you forty-two years old, Mr. Hanford."

"That's right, sir."

"And you want to join the army?"

"Yes, sir."

Barnes scanned the man for a few seconds in silence, seemed about to speak, then looked back at the paper. "I think I know the answer to the next question, Mr. Hanford. Previous military service?"

"Yes, sir. Twenty-two years, sir."

"The army?"

"Yes, sir. Twelve years in the 1st Infantry, ten years in the 3rd Infantry, sir. Service in various posts in the United States, in Mexico during the war, in the Indian territories, and in Texas."

"I think I can answer the next question too, Mr. Hanford, but I'll ask it anyway. What grade did you hold when you were discharged?"

"First sergeant, sir. For twelve years."

"Do you have your enlistment records with you, Sergeant?"

"Yes, sir." Hanford handed a brown envelope to Barnes.

Barnes looked at its contents briefly and then looked back at Hanford. "Sergeant, have you considered applying for a commission?"

"Yes, sir. I decided I'd do a better job without bars. Chevrons would be better, sir, if you see fit."

"All right, Sergeant. I'll see to it. Sign here and you're back in the army."

Hanford relaxed and bent over the writing surface of the booth. He grinned broadly, showing strong yellowed teeth.

"I been behind the plow for three years now, sir. And every damn night of them three years I woke up thinkin' I heard the bugle blowin'. I couldn't hold out no longer."

"I'm glad you didn't, Sergeant. We need you."

Hanford swung a smart salute, which Barnes returned with a smile. He watched the big man join a lithe, tanned woman in a sunbonnet.

Forty-two years old, Barnes thought. And he'll march the rest of them into the ground and still keep going.

Jeff felt absurdly happy. Between Hanford and me, he told himself, we'll make soldiers out of them. If I could only get a dozen more like that, I'd have the best regiment in the world.

9

They took away my brogues
And they robbed me of my spade;
They put me in the army
And a soldier of me made.

VIEWED from the ridge on its eastern border, the swamp stretched four miles long and a half mile across. It had been a beaver pond many years before, although the beaver were gone and the dam had long since given way to the force of annual spring torrents.

The swamp was bordered on the north by Chapman's Lake, on the east by the ridge, on the south by the Gardinerville road, and on the west by the rolling heights of forested land that were topographically known as the Deerkill Mountains, although local hunters called them the "Gardinerville Hills."

Among the gaunt sticks and broken stumps of trees killed long ago by the water of the beaver pond, there were six long files of men strung out in broken erratic formation. They were making clumsy progress through the water and the marsh grass toward the ridge.

Twenty yards in front the tall, lithe figure of Jeff Barnes was splashing through the bog. His blue denim field breeches were plastered with mud and slime, his shirt was sweat-soaked, and his face was streaked where perspiration had trickled through the coating of dust that covered it. Behind him lurched the fat figure of Private Samuel Comfort, exhausted to the point of nausea but too proud of his place as the lieutenant colonel's orderly to fall back among the stragglers.

The six companies of the 195th New York Volunteer Infantry pushed doggedly through the swamp, their faces drawn and twisted with fatigue, their bodies coated with muck, their rifles held high by weary arms, their eyes fixed on the man in the slouch hat out in front, whose blue back never bowed, whose legs kept driving inexorably forward. There were eight hundred pairs of eyes fixed on Jefferson Barnes, some of them with pure glittering hatred, others with fear, more with desperation, and a few—a very few—with grudging admiration. Here and there in the files of men there were eyes that shone with worship; they belonged to boys like Sam Comfort, who were young enough still to believe that there were men like gods in this world, and that they had found one of them in the iron man who led them.

Jeff Barnes didn't have to turn around during the passage of the swamp to see that the regiment was still coming. After eight weeks of training he knew that the chain of command that he had forged was dragging them after him. From company commander down to corporal, every man with authority was applying the whiplash to those weary men, knowing that if he did not it would be applied with blistering effectiveness to him.

The exhausted soldiers who stumbled and fell in the muck were dragged to their feet by the men behind them. Here and there a man carried an extra rifle while two of his comrades supported the rifle's owner on dragging legs. They cursed and cajoled to keep a straggler going; they abandoned him only when he became a dead weight on their own bowed shoulders. Then they passed him back along the files, keeping him out of the water, until the doctor and his orderlies could handle him.

The doctor, Captain Wilson Renwick, who had been one of Highland Landing's most popular family doctors a few weeks before, managed to deal with the men who came back to him only because there were so few of them. Even though his voice with the stragglers was quiet and gentle, his eyes were bitter when he looked ahead at Barnes. The doctor was convinced that Barnes was a madman who would never stop driving the men until he had killed them all. Flesh and blood, mind and heart could stand just so much brutal treatment. Then they would collapse. Dr. Renwick had been expecting catastrophe as a result of Barnes's training methods; it would surely come, although the doctor had to admit to himself that on this, the most strenuous of the forced marches that had started eight weeks before, there were fewer exhaustion cases than ever before. There came a breaking point, however, and he was positive the men had reached it.

Jeff Barnes waded out of the water onto the rising ground. The face of the ridge stretched upward, covered with brush, brambles, and the precise stone walls of an abandoned farm. He turned to face the regiment, lifting high his right hand, which held a gleaming new Colt's .44 cap-and-ball revolver. His eye sought the head of the first file on his left, Captain Boudrye's Company A. At Boudrye's side the exhausted bugler was struggling through a mass of cattails, his bugle fastened high on his shoulder by a shortened lanyard that kept it out of the water.

"Bugler, sound the charge!" Barnes shouted.

Captain Boudrye poked the bugler in the ribs. The man struggled with the lanyard for a couple of seconds, then raised the bugle to his lips. The call was weak and halting, but it carried across the swamp. Barnes lowered his arm, turned, and ran for the ridge. Behind him he heard the growl that swept through the ranks, then the thrashing of marsh grass as it was trampled into the muck by feet that somehow had reserved the final strength for running.

Barnes climbed the first stone wall on the face of the ridge, turning briefly to look back. They were coming at a run, weary faces straining with the effort. They stumbled and fell, pushed themselves up and forced their legs to pump again. Even the stragglers tried to run, staggering along with flailing arms. Private Comfort sprawled on the stone wall beside Barnes, grunted, and crawled over the stones before he got to his feet to run again.

"Yell, you devils!" Barnes screamed hoarsely. "Yell! Yell!"

A low roar swept from the dry throats, halting at first and then swelling in rage and hatred to become a wave of savage sound.

Barnes turned and ran up the hill, yelling madly. He passed Sam Comfort, lifted his revolver, and fired one shot. He heard the panted commands of officers that followed the shot, and then the first volley of rifle fire slammed into the still air. Rifles cracked steadily, feet pounded the hard ground, and with a wild mixture of screams and shouts, the regiment rolled up the hillside.

Barnes reached the crest of the ridge, turned again, and stood there panting, watching them come. A dozen or so were only a step or two behind him. They'd put out their final strength to beat him to the crest, but they had failed.

Now as they passed him, he shouted with straining throat and lungs, "Steel! Give 'em the steel! Drive 'em! Drive 'em!"

Company commanders screamed the same wild words, mixing them with curses and inarticulate cries. They led their men over the crest, a raging horde with bayonets flashing in the late-afternoon sun.

Barnes stood where he was until the six companies had poured by him. His face was fixed in a distorted, humorless grin as he stood motionless in the middle of the wave of troops. When the last stumbling figures had gone by him, the noise subsided. The regiment was sprawled on the ridge, hundreds of men covering the ground, some of them in the last stages of exhaustion, others lying with heaving chests and open mouths, sucking in air. There were a few score men still on their feet, most of them officers or non-commissioned officers too proud to be caught on their backsides if Barnes issued another order.

He did not, however. He stood there watching them, still wearing the grin on his lean face, his breath whistling through his nostrils with rhythmic harshness.

They did it, he thought jubilantly. Twenty miles out, bivouac in the rain, and twenty miles back. Then they charged this hill the way they'll have to do it when we go after the Johnnies.

Eight weeks ago they'd have fallen by the hundreds in that swamp. Just eight short weeks and now they're ready. They're soldiers and they know it. They're proud of it. They may hate me, but they know what I've done to them. Probably there's a lot of 'em who've already promised themselves that they'll put a bullet in my back first chance they get. Maybe there's one among 'em who is foolish enough, or brave enough, or mad enough, to do it. That's the chance I'll have to take. But the rest of 'em, hate me or not, will follow me all the way to hell and back again just to prove that they can do it.

Good men, he thought. Good men. Even the ones who couldn't make it tried their best. They're all good men.

He turned to face a pair of officers who were approaching along the crest of the ridge. Both were colonels. One of them was Albert Cathcart, looking stout and uncomfortable in his rumpled uniform. There was perspiration on his florid face and his spade beard needed trimming, but he was smiling jovially as he came forward. The other colonel was an inspector general of the New York State adjutant general's department. He had been, before his commissioning, a judge in Dutchess County and a power in the Republican Party. His name was Dunham. He was middle-aged and stout, like Cathcart, and he also wore a spade beard. His face was puffed and veined from too much whiskey too often. He had sharp, alert eyes, however, and he had a reputation for efficiency in his job so long as such efficiency did not interfere with the awarding of highly profitable contracts to loyal Republicans.

Jeff Barnes, watching them come toward him, was reading Cathcart's mind. The jovial smile, Jeff knew, had no relation to Cathcart's thoughts.

Colonel Cathcart, Jeff was certain, was deeply concerned that Colonel Dunham, the Governor's military representative, should be pleased by the appearance of the 195th N.Y.V.I.

And how could he be impressed by eight hundred wet and muddy scarecrows who came staggering out of a swamp dog-tired and filthy?

Dammit all to hell, Jeff imagined that Cathcart was telling himself, that young fool Barnes knew that Dunham would be here today. Why'd he have to do this to me? Forty miles in two days, and he didn't even take 'em along the road in military fashion. He had to bring 'em across that goddamn swamp!

Jeff also knew that Cathcart's red-veined eyes had already surveyed his subordinate's uniform—boots coated with muck and slime, breeches sodden, faded blue shirt dark with sweat and the sleeves rolled above the elbows.

That's the worst thing of all, Jeff thought with wry humor. He's boiling because I led the men every step of the way. He probably thinks it's conduct unbecoming an officer.

Jeff saluted casually as the two colonels reached him.

"Tell me, Colonel Barnes," Dunham began curtly, "why you forced the men to plow through that wilderness when they could have reached camp an hour ago by way of the road."

Barnes's face didn't change expression, but his gray eyes flashed as he looked straight at Dunham. Cathcart, sensing a caustic reply, interrupted hastily.

"Jeff thinks the men should get used to battle conditions," he said soothingly. "You know, Dunham, that we have a very rigorous training program. This young man is responsible for it."

That's either blame or absolution, Jeff thought, depending on which way Dunham's mind is running.

Dunham grunted. "There's no need to ruin trousers and shoes by crossing swamps when there are perfectly good roads to march on. You must realize, Colonel Barnes, that the taxpayers have to pay for the men's equipment. That little jaunt across the swamp has probably cost several hundred dollars."

Barnes's face stiffened and his lips drew to a thin line, but he didn't answer. His gaze went to the swamp, then to the western sky, where the sun was just starting to slide down to meet the Gardinerville Hills. High against the orange-colored sky a pair of black ducks were swinging to come into the swamp for the night. As he watched, the ducks suddenly swerved and fled, startled by the mass of soldiers who were sprawled on the ridge.

When he spoke, Barnes's voice was controlled; his anger was concealed. "I agree that training is hard on uniforms and equipment, sir. As for the swamps, the men have to get used to the kind of country they're going to be fighting in. The map of Virginia is dotted with swamps, sir."

"I'm sure that General McClellan prefers to use the roads," Dunham said harshly. "You're driving your men too hard, Barnes. How many desertions have you had?"

Cathcart winced. He answered hastily. "Just a few, Dunham. All bad actors at that."

"How many?" Dunham asked.

"Twenty-nine," Barnes said.

"Good God, man! Twenty-nine desertions before you're under fire! Your harsh measures are driving them away, Barnes."

"The provost's guard brought back twenty-six," Barnes answered evenly. "They were punished and returned to duty, most of them. Two of the other three are in civilian jails for armed robbery, and the last man is still missing. We've only lost three men, sir."

Dunham had no answer to that, but he had another question. "Where did you ever get the tomfool idea to charge that ridge? No general would order such a stupid action."

Barnes flushed. "Many generals have! I want these men to know how to make a frontal assault. The regiment has crossed that swamp and charged the ridge six times. They're learning."

"They're learning how to waste powder," Dunham said crustily. "One shot apiece when they went up the hill would have been enough. They were firing as fast as they could load. They were running. The shots would have been wild."

Jeff hid a grin. Lucky thing that Dunham hadn't been around when the men were on the rifle range. Marksmanship training was frowned upon by the adjutant general's department. It was a rare Union regiment so far in this war which went into battle knowing how to use its rifles. Well, what Dunham didn't know wouldn't hurt him.

"You may be right, sir," Jeff said equably.

"I know I'm right. Powder is expensive and scarce. Watch the waste in the future, Colonel Barnes."

Barnes nodded. "I'll bring the men in to camp, sir," he said to Cathcart.

"Fine, Jeff," Cathcart answered. "Colonel Dunham and I will see you later. Give the men a rest now, Jeff. They deserve it."

"All in all, an interesting exhibition, Barnes," Dunham said. "As soon as you get a few of those West Point ideas out of your head, you'll be a good officer. You've got to learn that these men are citizen soldiers, not dumb brutes in the regular army."

A hot reply came to Jeff's lips, but he flushed and swallowed it. Only a week more of this, and then he'd be able to start proving his training theories.

Cathcart and Dunham left him, walking toward an orderly who waited with their horses. Barnes turned away, toward the regiment. His legs ached, his feet hurt, and he was dog-tired. He'd like nothing better than to lie down and sleep for twelve hours, but there was work to do, and he remembered that Kate wanted him to come home tonight. She'd said to be there for dinner. He'd try to make it when he got the work cleared up.

The men were sprawled everywhere on the sloping plateau beyond the crest of the ridge. He passed among them silently, oblivious to the bitterness in their eyes. He joined a group of regimental officers who were leaning against or sitting on a rock outcropping in the center of the plateau. They came to attention as he approached. He put them at ease.

"A good job, gentlemen," he said, smiling. "Form your companies. I want to talk to the men."

When the regiment had assembled, Barnes climbed to the top of the rocks. "Colonel Cathcart wants me to tell you that you did splendidly."

There was scornful laughter from the rear ranks. Barnes smiled. "A few weeks ago you couldn't have made this march. A few weeks more and maybe you'll begin to look like soldiers."

There was more laughter and some catcalling. Company officers spoke sharply, but Barnes was still smiling.

"I suppose you're tired," Barnes said.

Groans, howls, and jeering negatives rose in chorus. A boyish voice shrilled, "I ain't tired. Let's do her again, Kernel!"

Barnes laughed with them. He could afford to laugh now that the job was done. "My eyes and nose tell me," he continued, "that you all need soap and water. Let's get back to camp and clean up. One thing more. You men know we're leaving next week. Colonel Cathcart has asked me to tell you that half the men from each company will receive a furlough starting with the sunset gun tonight. You'll be back at reveille on Thursday morning. The other half of the regiment will leave for home with the sunset gun on Thursday. They'll be back for reveille Sunday morning."

His last words were lost in an excited murmur that swept through the ranks. A happy voice cried suddenly, "Three cheers for the Ramrod!" The cheers rolled out, "Hurrah! Hurrah! Hurrah! Ramrod Barnes!"

Company officers looked startled and some were embarrassed, both by the breach of discipline and the use of Jeff's newly acquired nickname. They thought he didn't know that virtually every man in the regiment, as well as most of the officers, already called him "Ramrod" when they weren't calling him worse.

He knew it, just as he knew many other things that they thought he could never know, and the name pleased him mightily. It meant that they understood what he was trying to do, that they were equal to his harsh treatment of them in the past few weeks, that they had labeled him for exactly what he was. He also knew that Cathcart had not been honored with a nickname, not even the usual one given to commanding officers, the "Old Man," and he was human enough to be vain about his own distinction. When the regiment moved into the Army of the Potomac next week, the men would brag to soldiers of other regiments that a man didn't know what soldiering was until he'd served under Ramrod Barnes. Not many of them liked him, and some of them hated him, but they'd all brag about him.

He held up his hands for silence. The regiment quieted again. "The only men who will be denied furloughs," he said harshly, "are those whose pieces were fouled in crossing the swamp. Six times you've crossed that swamp, and six times you've been told that your rifle must be ready to fire on command. Company commanders will inspect all weapons. Any man whose rifle has not been fired by reason of fouling will draw three days of company punishment."

Groans and curses rippled through the ranks like a gust of wind across a placid lake. Barnes climbed down from the rocks. The commander of Company B, Captain Colden, came toward Barnes determinedly. He was making no effort to control the anger that darkened his sun-tanned face. His eyes were flashing and when he spoke his voice was harsh.

"That order is unfair, sir!"

Barnes looked at him coldly. "How so, Captain?"

"Men who fell in the swamp shouldn't be punished for falling. You know damn well that most of 'em were out on their feet! They all did their best to keep their cartridges and their rifles dry. I won't obey your order, sir. Every man in my company will have his furlough!"

"You'll obey any order I give, Captain, or you'll be out of this regiment so fast it'll make your head swim. Remember that."

"I've got a lot to remember, Colonel Barnes."

Barnes nodded. "Do you acknowledge the order, Captain?"

"Yes, sir," Colden snapped. He turned on his heel.

"Captain Colden," Barnes said quietly.

Colden looked back. "Yes, sir?"

"I supposed you would use your judgment about the execution of
the order. You will report to me in camp the names of the men who
will receive company punishment. I'll expect that report within an
hour. In the meantime, I suppose I'll hear a few rifle shots."

"Yes, sir!" Colden said, flushing. "I understand, sir."

Barnes walked well ahead of the column on a wood road that led
directly to the training camp of the 195th, a mile or two to the north-
east on the shores of Chapman's Lake. Every few seconds during the
march some fortunate swamp stumbler would manage to clear his
rifle and fire it into the air. With every shot a rousing cheer lifted
from the ranks.

Barnes grinned to himself. Colden was the best officer in the regiment in spite of his dislike of Jeff Barnes, or, perhaps, because of it.
There were others almost as good. He was pleased and in good
spirits, although he was bone-tired.

The men were, too, but the prospect of going home for a few days
exhilarated them. They began to sing their favorite song. Barnes
listened through a line or two, then lifted his own baritone in the
words that some versifier among them had grafted to an old tune:

> *"We're from Highland County,*
> *And we'd like to have you know*
> *That Highland is the county*
> *Where the luscious apples grow.*
>
> *They call us apple-knockers,*
> *And they needn't take it back,*
> *'Cause the apple-knockers are the boys*
> *Who drink the applejack!"*

A ready-made name, Barnes thought. They'll sing it and other
outfits will hear them. "You see them York Staters over there? Apple-
knockers, that's what they are. The 195th New York, the apple-
knocker regiment." They may laugh when they say it, but they won't
laugh long. These are soldiers, these Highland County boys.

10

> *But I couldn't beat a drum,*
> *And I couldn't play a flute,*
> *So they handed me a musket*
> *And taught me how to shoot.*

SUNSET was throwing a golden light across the smooth surface of Chapman's Lake when Barnes reached camp. Private Comfort managed to have a steaming kettle of good hot water on the washstand before Barnes finished stripping his body of its mud-caked and sweat-stained clothes. Sam Comfort stood beside the stand in what might possibly be termed a position of attention while Barnes started to lather his face with his shaving brush. No uniform had been found to fit Sam Comfort. Army life, which usually turned flabby flesh into hard muscle and erased rolls of fat, had had the opposite effect on Sam. He cooked Barnes's meals, and he had not yet learned that Jeff could not stow away an entire beef pie or two fried chickens at one sitting. As a result, Sam had to eat twice as much as he ever had just to prevent the spoiling of good food. His belly and his backside rolled in most unsoldierly fashion when he walked, his face was round and puffed with flesh, and his thick neck was ringed with rolls of fat.

Jeff was amused and somewhat alarmed at Private Comfort's propensity to add padding to his body, but he reasoned that field rations would trim him down. Certainly the boy's mother wouldn't be able to complain that Jeff Barnes hadn't taken care of him.

"Will the colonel want anything else, sir?" Comfort asked. His voice, as always, had a somewhat dolorous quality, as if he were sure that Barnes was about to give him a measure of the same harsh discipline to which the rest of the regiment was subjected. "A hard man, the Ramrod," Comfort often said to other soldiers. "Real hard. You ought to be glad you don't have to work for him." The truth was that Jeff had never yet had occasion to speak a sharp word to Private Comfort. The boy was a perfect housekeeper, devoted to his job. He complained constantly about Barnes's stern nature only because he thought it was expected of him. He really couldn't understand why so many of the men grumbled. They were soldiers, weren't they?

"Thanks, Comfort," Jeff answered. "That's all, if you've put out a uniform for me."

Comfort stayed where he was, his face twisting with indecision. Barnes glanced at him, saw that the orderly was trying to say something, then looked back into the mirror above the washstand. He knew he'd throw Comfort into confusion if he tried to read his mind. Whatever it was the boy wanted, he'd get to it eventually.

"If the colonel please, sir——" Comfort began.

"Yes, Comfort?" Barnes said mildly, forcing his irritation away. Why couldn't the man speak up? Barnes's temper was on edge after two hard days, but he always tried to control it with Comfort. Barnes supposed that the boy would go off and cry if he were reprimanded.

"I wondered, sir, if the furlough for the men, sir, that you said——"

"Yes?"

"Well, sir, I wondered if that went for me, too."

"Good God, yes, Comfort! Go home and see your family. Stay until Sunday. Tell the adjutant I said it was all right."

"Just till Thursday is enough, sir. Thank you, sir."

"Until Sunday, Comfort. That's an order."

"Yes, sir. Till Sunday, sir." Comfort sounded upset, and Barnes almost laughed. He was sure that the orderly would spend his furlough worrying about what he'd done to make the colonel want to get rid of him.

"You can go now, Comfort. When you get home, give my regards to your mother and father."

Sam Comfort went down to the lake to do his washing before he left for home. He found two men from Company A, which carried Comfort on its rolls, at the same task. They were debating the wisdom of staying home for six days instead of three. They were sure to get company punishment for it, but they didn't care about that. They were troubled by the rumor that Barnes had a new punishment for absence without leave; they'd heard that anyone who overstayed his furlough would be trussed up by the thumbs for the length of his delay.

Sam Comfort felt the compulsion to show himself as a devil-may-care veteran. "I'm stayin' home till Sunday," he said to the others with a show of grimness. "I don't care what he does to me."

"Are you, Comfort?"

"That's right, even if he hangs me by the thumbs."

"If you do, I will, too," one of the men said.

"Sure," the other said. "You'll get worse than we will 'cause you work right for him."

"That's right," Sam said. "He'll give me bad trouble if I stay over, but I'm goin' to."

He bent over his washing guiltily. Now why had he told such a dang lie? And his father a minister, too. Why hadn't he told the plain truth, like he always used to before he joined the army? When he wasn't punished at all, these fellows would know he'd been lying. So he'd have to invent some kind of story about Barnes's horrible treatment of him, and that would be another lie.

Back in the tent, Barnes was carefully shaving two days' stubble from his jaw. As he relaxed under the touch of the razor, his tension fell away.

Barnes finished shaving, then lathered himself from head to toe with soap. His nose wrinkled a bit when he smelled the soap. It was faintly perfumed; Kate had given it to him from her own supply. He used it because it lathered well, and good soap was hard to come by. He hoped the smell didn't linger; the men shouldn't be given reason to snicker at him.

Barnes took the kettle of water, cooling now, outside the big Sibley tent. He doused his naked body to wash off most of the lather, then took the towel that Comfort had put out for him and jogged for the edge of the lake, about fifty yards away.

Barnes was unconcerned by the fact that a hundred men were watching him run naked through the camp. He'd been doing it at least once every day since camp had been established on the shores of Chapman's Lake. His dignity, which he usually guarded carefully, was not in the least endangered. He knew that his body had not an ounce of extra flesh on its hard frame.

Sometimes, when he was making the run to the lake, he imagined what a spectacle Cathcart would make if he followed the same practice. There was no chance of that, however. Cathcart took his baths in comfort at his home in Gardinerville, where he spent most of his time, or in the room at the Huguenot Hotel in Highland Landing where he had what he called his "headquarters."

There were twenty or thirty soldiers swimming in the lake when Barnes came running to the shore and launched himself in a long, shallow dive into the clear blue water. With their respect for rank, they left plenty of room for the colonel to swim. He was an expert swimmer, far better than most of the men, who floundered and splashed near the shore. With long, hard strokes of his perfectly conditioned body, Barnes was soon far out in the lake. All his cares and irritations abated; he stopped worrying about the things he might have forgotten to do—some order neglected, some training enterprise that had slipped his mind, some detail overlooked—things that would one day tell against the regiment when it moved into combat.

He swam for ten or fifteen minutes in the cool water, until his tired body was completely relaxed, almost enervated. Then he slowly made his way to shore, picked up his towel—an outsized affair that Kate had provided, wrapped it around his hips, and walked back to his tent.

Two officers were awaiting him. One of them was Colden; the other was Ned Boudrye, who was sitting on Barnes's cot smoking a cigar while Colden stood stiffly beside the field desk. Boudrye greeted Barnes's smile with a wave of the cigar and a languid comment: "How was the water, Jeff?"

Jeff's smile faded when Boudrye failed to get up from the cot. "It was cold, Ned," he answered shortly, proceeding to towel himself. He withheld his intended rebuke, although he told himself that the status of brother-in-law went just so far in the army, and it did not extend to lounging on a superior officer's cot unless you were invited to do so.

"My company report is on your desk, sir," Colden said abruptly.

"Thanks, Bill. I'll look at it later." Barnes grinned suddenly. "How many men can't go home because of fouled rifles?"

"None, sir."

Barnes nodded. "Good. They worked hard."

"Thank you, sir. If you'll excuse me now——"

"Go ahead, Bill. Good night."

"Good night, sir."

Barnes watched Colden leave. The captain's stiff back scarcely bent as he went through the open fly of the tent. Without thinking, he remarked, "You think he'll ever consider himself a friend of mine?" He regretted the words instantly; he disliked letting Ned Boudrye see his mind so openly.

"Never," Ned answered with a swift laugh. "Why should he? He courted Kate for three years. You came home and married her in a week. You blame him?"

"I guess not," Barnes answered shortly.

"You don't make it easy for anybody to be your friend, Jeff," Ned said slowly. "You've been driving us like mules, you know."

"You needed it."

"Sure we did. And now we're ready to go prove you did a good job. You got a drink around here, Jeff? I need it after that expedition you took us on. My tail was bumping the ground with every step."

"In the washstand," Barnes said. "Bourbon and apple."

Ned poured bourbon whiskey into two tumblers and handed one to Jeff. "Drink a toast with me," he said. He held up his glass. "To the 195th New York Volunteers, the best damn regiment in the Union army."

Jeff nodded, smiling. "To the Highland County apple-knockers."

He tossed off his drink and continued to dress. He heard the bottle gurgling again and turned to see Ned returning to his place on the cot with another drink in his hand. Barnes swallowed his intended rebuke once more. Instead, he said sharply, "You turn in your report, Ned?"

"On your desk," Boudrye said. "I brought along the rest of them, too. Billy Hasbrouck invited most of the fellows to his house tonight for supper and a poker game. They were glad to get out of camp. Jeff, can I ask you a personal question?"

"Ask away."

"When are you going to stop doing Cathcart's work as well as your own?"

Barnes looked swiftly at Boudrye, about to tell him to tend to company matters and leave the regiment to him, but he tightened his lips and didn't answer. He stepped around the desk and sat down, picking up the reports, assuming that Boudrye would take that action as a signal of dismissal.

"All right, then," Boudrye said, "put it this way. How do we tie a kite to Cathcart? There must be a way to get rid of him."

"I've never paid much attention to politics," Jeff said, rustling the reports impatiently.

"It's important, Jeff! You know that he isn't worth a damn as regimental commander. And he'll stay in command until we do something about it. It's a nice soft job for him. You do all the work. You ought to wear the eagles."

"What are you suggesting, Ned?" Barnes asked sharply.

"Maybe an election. If we primed the men beforehand, they'd throw him out and put you in his place."

"You'd better shut up, Ned. You're close to the line. If this conversation were overheard, you could be brought before a court."

"Oh hell, Jeff! Who's going to hear me? Besides, all I'm saying is that the men could elect you colonel if they wanted to. You know yourself it's been done a dozen times."

"And what would they elect you, Ned?"

"Maybe major. Billy Hasbrouck could take your rank."

"That's enough, Ned. I don't want to hear any more. And don't carry on with it outside this tent."

Ned flushed. "That an order, sir?"

"That's right." Jeff's anger flared although his voice was level. "So you want to be a field officer? You have the best company in the regiment. Do you know that?"

"Sure I know it."

"You had nothing to do with it, Ned. Sergeant Hanford did it in spite of you and in spite of my brother Walter. I'm telling you this for your own good, Ned. I've watched you these past few weeks. You leave everything to Hanford. You take advantage of his abilities. The result is an excellent company, with a commander who shirks his duties. And my brother follows your example. Poker parties, dances, church socials, drinking bouts! Brace up, Ned. You'll never be a field officer on my recommendation until you show that you can command your company."

Boudrye's eyes flashed and his face was red. He stood stiffly beside the cot. "Thank you, sir! Do you have anything else to say?"

"Don't get your back up, Ned. You had to be told sometime, and I'm the only one to tell you."

"Is that all, sir?"

"That's all for now."

"Thank you, sir, for the lecture. Perhaps you'll be able to expand on it at dinner tonight. You'll have a captive audience. Walter and I promised Kate we'd be there."

"Dinner?" Jeff asked.

"At your house," Ned answered angrily. "Perhaps you'd prefer that I didn't come? It's probably not quite fair to surround you with in-efficiency when you're not on duty."

"Don't be childish, Ned. There was nothing personal in what I said."

"I think there was, sir."

Ned left the tent. Jeff looked after him, wondering about the din-ner. Had Kate told him about it? He'd last seen her three days ago. He couldn't remember her saying anything about a dinner party.

All right, it had slipped his mind. Anyway, there was time to work another half hour. Then, if he pushed his horse, he could get to High-land Landing in fifteen minutes. It was six o'clock now. Kate liked to start dinner at seven.

He was tired. The reports refused to transform at a glance from inked figures on paper to a comprehensive picture of the regiment. Sick lists, disciplinary measures, supply reports, training details—all contributed daily to his evaluation of the training regimen he had instituted and conducted. But they meant nothing now; his mind was a blank.

He picked up the whiskey bottle that Ned had left on the field desk, poured himself another drink, put the bottle back in the wash-stand, then dashed down the whiskey. It warmed his stomach agree-ably. He yawned and stretched, and told himself that the reports could go to the devil tonight.

He'd known for a long time that he'd have to dress Ned down. Walter was next. One was as slipshod in his duties as the other. He hadn't expected that Ned would take the rebuke as a personal af-front. Jeff decided to be a shade easier with Walter, who, after all, was only following Ned's example.

His feet hurt, and he decided to change his boots. He had a pair of dress boots that were softer and lighter. As he took off the heavy field boots, he toyed with the idea of taking a few days' leave. He and Kate could leave in the morning for Summit House. Maybe they'd get the same cottage again. It was September; the mountain would already be subtly changing to autumn colors. She would love it, and he needed a rest.

He lay back on the cot, swinging his stockinged feet up and wriggling his toes. He put his hands behind his head and looked up at the tent wall, thinking about the cottage, the glowing fires that gave it warmth and light, the wind sighing through the hemlocks. He thought of Kate tenderly, knowing that the best farewell gift he could give her would be a few days for them to spend together.

He sighed. It was impossible. The regiment was leaving next week. There was too much to do between now and then, and he couldn't leave important details to Cathcart, on the one hand, or to the rest of the staff, on the other. He was the only one who could handle the job.

Even though the men of the 195th would have said that Barnes was an iron man, there was a limit to his endurance. He had almost reached it. His fatigue and the two drinks of bourbon dulled his mind. His tired muscles relaxed. His eyes closed. He fell asleep.

Sam Comfort was ready to leave on his furlough. Some of the Cedar Bush boys were waiting for him impatiently, but Sam was sure that the colonel had some last-minute task for him.

"He'll skin me alive if I don't see him before I go," Sam said. There were four others leaving for Cedar Bush, including Mike Stewart and Hanford.

Sam entered the Sibley and found Barnes sleeping on the cot. Sam was distressed; the colonel was wrinkling his best uniform.

Sam wrestled with a decision for almost a minute. Should I wake him up, or should I let him sleep? If I wake him up, I may have to fix him some supper. If I let him sleep, he'll get some rest and I can get home quicker. I'll let him sleep.

Sam tiptoed to the tent fly, released it to close the tent in darkness, then hurried off to join his comrades.

11

Come fill your glasses, fellows,
And stand up in a row. . . .

SHE could hear the clock ticking even though the others were talking. They talked loudly, unnaturally, as if words could cover their regret, but still she could hear the clock. She wanted to cross the room, open the glass face, and stop the pendulum with her hand. She sat quietly, however, listening to her brother's story of the training exercise. She watched his mobile face instead of the clock.

Ned finished his story, stood up, and walked to the dining room, where Jeff's whiskey was kept in the sideboard. That was Ned's fourth trip. He was drinking too much, she thought. She looked at her mother, who was watching with troubled eyes Ned's swaying progress toward the dining room.

Walter Barnes got up also and stepped toward the dining room. His youthful face was flushed to a deeper red than his sunburn accounted for. His eyes were bloodshot. He'd made three trips to the sideboard.

"Walter," said Stephen Barnes quietly, "we'll be having dinner soon."

Walter looked slowly around, smiling foolishly. He shook his head. "Not if we wait for him," he said. "Don't you know he's got to put the regiment to bed first?"

"You'd better sit down, Walter," Stephen Barnes said sternly. "You're not used to that stuff."

"Got to get used to it," Walter said solemnly. "Officer and a gentleman, Father. Got to hold my liquor."

"Sit down!"

Kate interrupted. "I'll tell Mrs. Fulton to serve dinner."

Walter shook his head again. "Got to wait for the Ramrod," he said. "Court-martial ev'body if we don't wait for him."

Ned returned to the room and guided Walter to his chair. Both Mrs. Barnes and Mrs. Boudrye looked pleadingly at Kate. She nodded with sudden decision. "Mrs. Fulton!" she called.

At that moment they heard a horse trotting down the hard-packed street. Kate listened attentively. The horse and rider went by without stopping.

"Yes, Mrs. Barnes?" Mrs. Fulton asked. "You want me to serve?"

"Yes," Kate said abruptly. "We won't wait."

Walter managed to push himself from his chair, offering his arm to Kate. "Take you to dinner, Mrs. Barnes. Your husband detained by duty." He frowned. "Always detained by duty, ain't he?"

"Walter Barnes, behave yourself!" his mother said angrily.

"Am behavin' myself," he grinned. "Get court-martialed if I didn't. Good ol' Ramrod court-martial his own brother."

He looked around him unsteadily. "You think he wouldn't? He hates me and Ned. Me and Ned, his own family."

"Stop that nonsense!" Stephen Barnes said.

"Ain't nonsense, Pa. Ned tole me all about it. Jeff says we're only two no-good officers in the whole regiment. That's what he said. Says we don't attend to duties. To hell with him and duties! Ain't said a friendly word to me since I put on the uniform!" Walter sat down in his chair again and began to cry. "Ramrod! Ramrod! Goddamn him!"

"Stop it now, Walter!" his father cried. "You're drunk!"

"Sure, I'm drunk," Walter sobbed. "Rides me all the time 'cause I'm his brother. Got to be perfect, just like West Point!"

He jumped from the chair and walked clumsily to the door. Ned Boudrye followed, saying to the others that he'd take Walter home.

The meal went quickly and unhappily. Mr. and Mrs. Barnes, with Mrs. Boudrye, prepared to leave right after dinner. They refused coffee. Mrs. Barnes managed to say a few words privately to Kate.

"I'm terribly sorry, my dear, that one of my sons made a fool of himself and the other one didn't even come. They ruined your party. I'll vow that Jeff forgot it was his birthday."

"It's all right," Kate said quickly. She didn't want to talk about it.

"No, it's not all right," Mrs. Barnes said firmly. "I intend to speak to him about it."

Kate shook her head quickly. "I'll speak to him myself."

Mrs. Barnes looked steadily at her. "Yes, Kathleen. Maybe it's best you do. He's given you very little of his time."

Kate smiled. "It will be all right."

"I hope so. Good night, Kate."

Kate stood at the window after they had gone, hoping to see him ride out of the darkness.

He could have come, she thought. Whatever it was that delayed him wasn't so important that it couldn't have waited until tomorrow. He should have been here. I have never complained when he stayed at camp night after night, but this was his own party. He should have been here.

She left the window, turning her mind away from her disappointment. She thought instead about the news she had to tell him.

I won't tell him tonight, though, not when I'm angry. Next week, before he goes away, I'll tell him.

She smiled to herself. He wanted children, but she was sure that he had never considered having any girls. All boys, one after another —as many as half a dozen, and each of them slated to enter the Academy at the age of seventeen.

They'd talked about children at Summit House.

"If the first boy is born next year," Jeff had said, figuring rapidly on his fingers, "he'll enter the Academy with the class of 1884."

"Suppose he wants to go to Yale or Harvard or Princeton?" she'd asked teasingly.

He nodded. "Couple of years at a good college would help him. He'd learn enough to keep him in the first quarter of his class all the way through the Point. That would be important to his career."

She laughed. "Suppose he can't get an appointment?"

"Appointments can be managed," Jeff answered. He grinned at her. "Your brother will be a politician. He might be Highland County's Congressman by that time. Maybe even Senator."

It has to be a boy, Kate told herself fiercely. The first one has to be a boy. Thomas Jefferson Barnes, Jr., class of 1884, United States Military Academy. That's what he wants and that's what I will give him. If I can. Dear Lord, let nothing go wrong to prevent it.

"Mrs. Barnes," Mrs. Fulton said from the doorway of the dining room, "I've cleared the table. Shall I hold a warm plate for the colonel?"

"No, I'll take care of it when he comes. You go home, Mrs. Fulton.
You've had a long day."

"And so have you." Mrs. Fulton's voice was kind. "Give him a
piece of your mind when he comes in. Forgetting his birthday
party!"

Kate nodded. "He's very busy, you know."

"Give him a bawling out, anyway. It'll do him good. Anything
more I can do before I go?"

"Yes, there is," Kate decided suddenly. "Will you please stop at the
Bellnap livery stable and have them send a buggy I can drive myself?"

"You goin' out to that camp?"

Kate nodded.

"You better not do that, ma'am. Not at night, with them soldiers
on the roads. They got no respect for a lady."

"It's all right, Mrs. Fulton."

"Just you be careful, hear?"

"I will. Good night, Mrs. Fulton."

"Good night, ma'am."

When Mrs. Fulton had left, Kate put out the gaslights and went
outside to wait for the buggy.

The night was clear and somewhat cool, as if the weather were
hesitating on the boundary between summer and autumn. There
were lights in the houses along Grand Street, and somewhere, faintly
heard, girlish voices were singing.

The Barnes house was a three-story square brick affair in the Old
Town. It had once been the rectory of St. Paul's Church, but the
church had been burned in 1860, and the rectory had been unoc-
cupied since. Sheriff Boudrye had convinced the church board to
rent it to Colonel Barnes, at least until the church was rebuilt. The
house was far too large, with its twelve rooms, but it was comfortable,
well furnished, and cool in the summer heat.

Kate would have traded it in a moment for a one-room cottage
near Camp Chapman, but there were no such cottages available.
If there had been, she would be able to see Jeff every night. As it
was, most evenings of the week, she and Mrs. Fulton rattled around
in the big house until dusk, when Mrs. Fulton went home. Then
she was alone. She could read or sew or play the untuned piano in
the living room. Then, whenever she finally admitted to herself that

he wasn't coming home, she could go to bed. Some evenings she entertained her mother and her mother-in-law, and on other evenings Ned dropped by with a brother officer or two, but mostly she was alone.

Until tonight she hadn't blamed him for leaving her alone. Three nights a week, from seven o'clock until nine, he conducted an officers' training course, and on three other nights he had a similar class for non-commissioned officers. She knew that he had to be the instructor; there wasn't anyone else who could do it. When the courses were ended each night, he had to return to his tent to do the paper work that he didn't have time for during the day. Then he had to plan training exercises for the next day.

She told herself repeatedly, I'll never see him at all when they go off to the army. At least now I see him sometimes.

There were nights when Jeff finished his day's work by ten or ten-thirty. Then he came home, to share a late supper with her, to talk for an hour or so before they came to that quiet moment when, as if by some unconscious signal to each other, they decided it was time for love. He would see to the doors, she to the lights, then, arm in arm, they would climb the carpeted stairs. Before dawn he would be gone again. She might not see him for three or four days.

He's too tired to come home every night, she had always told herself. It's too much to expect of him. It's so much easier for him to sleep on his cot instead of riding into town. And he doesn't need me to look after his clothes or food. He has Comfort for that. He just doesn't need me.

But he could have remembered tonight, she thought. He didn't know that it was to be a party, but he knew I wanted him to come for dinner. Mrs. Fulton is right. I'll give him a piece of my mind. He's never seen me angry.

She saw the buggy coming down Grand Street. She walked to the sidewalk to meet it.

Whatever he's doing, she told herself vehemently, he can put aside. He'll come home with me and we'll have the rest of the night together, anyway.

She passed soldiers all the way along the county road that led to Camp Chapman. Some were alone, others in groups. This was the night, she remembered, that half the regiment went on furlough. One soldier in a group of five raised his forage cap as she guided the buggy past on the narrow road. She threw a quick glance at him, seeing his face clearly in the moonlight. She was startled to see that it was Michael Stewart. She had thought of him often in the past eight weeks, remembering with pleasure his courtesy at Summit House.

She felt a trace of guilt that she hadn't stopped to speak to him, or even lifted her hand in greeting as she went by; the horse was spirited, and she needed both hands on the reins. She hoped he didn't think he'd been snubbed; that was far from her intention. As a matter of fact, she would have long since suggested that Jeff bring Michael Stewart home to dinner some night if she had not already learned that she would have to be snobbish to be a good army wife; privates were not the social equals of officers of field grade, whether or not the private or the officer liked it.

She passed a freight wagon full of soldiers, which pulled to the side of the road to let her by. One of the men shone a bull's-eye lantern upon her face, whistling ribaldly in appreciation of her beauty. She heard a startled voice say harshly, "Shut up, ya durn fool! That's the Ramrod's wife."

She was not any more displeased by Jeff's nickname than he was; she knew it had been given to him in respect, almost as a mark of appreciation for his work.

The camp was quiet when she reached it. The men due for furlough had already left or had turned in before taps to get an early start in the morning. The rest of the regiment, worn out from hiking, also sought sleep, except for sentries and the men of the provost's guard.

Kate went directly to Jeff's Sibley tent, accompanied in spite of herself by one of the provost's men who was going to follow his orders about women in camp at night even if this one was the colonel's wife. At first, because the tent wasn't lighted, Kate thought Jeff wasn't there. When she opened the fly of the tent, however, she heard his harsh breathing in the darkness.

"All right," she said to the soldier. "Colonel Barnes is here. You can go now."

"Yes, ma'am," the soldier said.

She went into the tent, moving cautiously in the darkness until she found the oil lamp with the box of matches beside it. She lit the lamp and turned to look at her husband.

Instantly her resolve to show her anger vanished. She guessed that he had fallen asleep while he was dressing to come home. He hadn't forgotten, then. Should she wake him or should she let him sleep?

She stood beside the cot looking down at him. His face, even though sleep had relaxed it, was etched with care. There were puckering lines at the corners of his eyes. The skin was drawn tightly across the angles of his face. His brow, burned by sun and wind to a deep tan, had lines of worry traced across it. He twisted in his sleep, and she saw the muscles working in his jaw.

She smiled softly, thinking that it was his birthday, and no matter how tired he was, how soundly he was sleeping, he would have to share with her the few hours remaining in the day. She put the oil lamp on his field desk, turned back to the cot, and knelt beside it.

She kissed his eyes, his face, then his mouth. Her lips touched his easily, then drew away. "Wake up, Jeff," she whispered. "Wake up. Happy birthday, darling."

He opened his eyes, closed them again, then smiled.

"What are you doing here?" he asked.

"I came to take you home. It's your birthday." She bent down and kissed him again. "I love you, Jeff."

"And I love you, Kate."

He held her tightly to him in a kiss that took her breath away. She pulled out of his arms, laughing.

"Come on, Colonel Barnes. Time to go home!"

12

Sitting by the road side on a summer day,
Chatting with my mess mates, passing time away . . .

MICHAEL STEWART turned his head to watch the buggy roll down the road toward Camp Chapman. He knew that she'd seen him tip his forage cap; even by moonlight he had seen the trace of a recognizing smile on her face. He also knew that she had been too busy with the frisky horse to reply to his greeting.

I had forgotten, he thought, how lovely she is. Or at least put it out of my mind. And I'd better keep it out, he told himself in sad humor. Somewhere among the Articles of War must be one that prohibits the private soldier from looking upon the colonel's lady with admiring eyes.

"Looks like you know her," Jack Hanford said quietly. "Colonel's wife, wasn't it?"

Stewart nodded. "They stayed at the hotel when they were married."

"Pretty girl," Hanford said. "She good enough for him?"

Stewart smiled and nodded again. "She seems to be, Jack. I liked her."

Hanford pursed his lips and spit tobacco juice to the side of the road. "Regular officer needs a good wife. Helps him a lot. I seen some bad ones in my time."

"I know her, too," Sam Comfort said proudly. "I stood up for 'em at the wedding. My father married 'em. Colonel says to me, he says, 'Comfort, you come see me when you get to camp,' he says. 'I'll give you a good job,' he says."

"Good job!" sneered Jacob Wagner. "Dog-robbin' for 'im. If I was you, Comfort, I wouldn't brag I worked for that bastard."

Adam Youngblood, fifth man of the group, glanced over his shoulder at Wagner, a look of distaste on his face. He didn't say anything, though. Youngblood wasn't much of a talker.

"Tell you what, Wagner," Hanford said laconically, "you keep that line of talk up from here to Cedar Bush, sooner or later I'll bust your jaw for you."

"Don't git yer back up, Sarge," Wagner said uneasily. "Just tell this dog robber here to shut up about High-and-Mighty Barnes. When I git a few days away from him, I don't want to hear about him. If you was to tell the truth, Sarge, you'd say you didn't like him no better than I do."

"I always tell the truth, Wagner," Hanford said softly. "Don't you forget it. And I'll tell you some of it now. I don't know whether I like Barnes or not. I ain't known him long enough to say. But I do know this. He's a good man, one of the best I ever seen. And I seen a lot of 'em. The day is comin' when every man in the 195th will be glad we got him."

"There's some that's got other ideas," Wagner said darkly. "He better watch hisself when we git to fightin', else he'll end up with a Minié ball in his back."

"That's happened before," Hanford agreed, "by accident or otherwise. It ain't goin' to happen to him, though. I'll tell you why. There's only five or six men in the regiment that's fool enough and got nerve enough to lay an Enfield on him and pull trigger. You're one of 'em, Wagner, and I could name you the others. By the time we get fightin', as you say, them others will likely be too busy lookin' out for their own health to worry much about shootin' Barnes. Not you, Wagner. You're a bad actor. I'll keep my eye on you. Happen the colonel gets a Minié ball in the back, I'll empty a .44 into your head. Get me?"

"Hell, Sarge," Wagner said roughly, "you know I was just talkin'. Trouble with you is you've got the damn army on the brain. Lots of ways you're just as much of a dressed-up soldier boy as Barnes is."

"I wish I was," Hanford said. "I just wish I was. Like I told you, he's one of the best I ever seen. He's young, and he don't do everything just right, but he's learnin'. I got more days in this blue suit than you got rocks on that mountain patch of yours, Wagner, and I seen officers come and go. Good ones and bad ones, in Mexico and California and on the Plains. That boy is awful good, Wagner, so you remember what I say. Watch what you do with that Enfield. I'll take it personal if you ain't careful where you point it."

"Aw, fergit it, Sarge. I was only havin' a joke."

Hanford laughed mirthlessly. "I ain't jokin', Wagner."

Yes, Wagner, be careful, Stewart thought. Because he isn't joking. He's another good one. One of the few really good ones we have. They take a long time to develop.

Stewart looked up at the moon and the stars, turned his eyes toward Hanford, then looked ahead, surveying Wagner's hunched shoulders, Comfort's rolling walk, and Adam Youngblood's straight young farmer's body.

"What made you go back into the army, Jack?" he asked.

"They needed me," Hanford said simply. "I knew they needed me after I read the papers some. A whole army of lunkheads."

"Lunkheads," Stewart said, grinning. "You think I'm a lunkhead, too?"

"Sure. All of you. Even Barnes. You know why?"

"No, I don't."

"Because you ain't seen the elephant yet, not you nor them three, nor the officers, nor Barnes himself. Cathcart don't count, of course. He'll never see it."

"What do you mean, we haven't seen the elephant?"

"What happens when the circus comes to town? All the kids, and the old folks too, holler that they want to see the elephant. After they've seen him, then they're different. They're changed, 'cause they've seen something they never seen before, a strange thing that they'll remember for the rest of their days."

Hanford paused. When he continued, his voice was quiet, sober. "Well, that's the way it is with young soldiers. Green ones. They holler like hell to see that elephant, the first battle. They talk about it all the time, what they're goin' to do and how they ain't goin' to be afraid, how they're all goin' to be heroes. Then some mornin' they march out, all brave and ready, and there's the elephant! Right smack square in front of 'em. When they march back or forward, however way the fightin' goes, they ain't green no more. They ain't lunkheads. They seen the elephant at last, and there ain't a one of 'em won't tell you, happen you should ask, that he sure to God is a big one, and they don't give a goddamn if they never see him again."

"I see," Michael said quietly. "And next week we're off to the circus to see the elephant. How do you think we'll come out of it, Jack?"

"Pretty good, I'd say, if Barnes is half the officer I think he is. Like I said before, Cathcart don't count. Most of us will make it all right. It's a good regiment, Mike, or it will be, when you all stop bein' lunkheads."

13

I have seen Him in the watch-fires of a
hundred circling camps. . . .

THE HOUSE, of course, was dark and silent when Adam Youngblood came down the lane. His father went to bed regularly at nine
o'clock.

There were apple trees on both sides of the lane between the
county road and the house. He was deep in their shadows when he
saw his foxhound Joe come loping out of the woodshed and stand
in the moonlight beside the house, nose high in the air.

Adam smiled. Before the dog rolled a deep-throated challenge,
Adam whistled once, softly. The dog hesitated for an instant, then
came running. He was all over Adam, whimpering with frantic joy,
licking Adam's face, pawing and jumping, crying out his loneliness.

"Hush up, Joe," Adam whispered. "You'll wake Pa up."

Gradually the dog quieted, and Adam walked the rest of the way
down the lane. It wouldn't do to get his father out of bed at this
hour. Adam, with his hand on Joe's neck, went into the woodshed.
He found a pile of gunny sacks where he'd left them in July, picked
up a half dozen, and went out to the barn. He lifted Joe into the
hayloft, them clambered up beside him. He arranged the gunny
sacks across the hay, let himself down with a weary sigh, and went
to sleep, with Joe curled tightly against him.

He was awake at dawn's first light. One of the bantam cocks that
were his father's pets was crowing a shrill greeting to the sun. Adam
went into the pasture beyond the barn and, with Joe's eager aid,
rounded up the dozen cows that were milking. He brought them
into the barn, found his three-legged milking stool right where he'd
left it, sat himself down on the right side of the first cow, tucked
the tuft of the cow's whipping tail into the crook of his bent knee so
she wouldn't slap him in the face with it, and began to milk.

The milk rang rhythmically into the pail as he squeezed the teats. Zing-*zing*, zing-*zing*, zing-*zing*—first the right hand, then the left. Joe stood by, his head cocked, watching Adam's hands and waiting. Adam grinned at the dog, turned his right hand, and directed a jet of milk at Joe. The dog licked his chops enthusiastically, grumbling with happiness.

As the bottom of the pail filled with milk, the sound changed. It became swish-*swish*, swish-*swish*, softening all the time as the milk foamed.

There was a shadow in the open barn door. Adam looked around into his father's weathered face. "Mornin', Pa," he said softly. "You sleepin' late these days?"

William Youngblood clenched his hands tightly, clamped his jaw, and swallowed heavily, making his Adam's apple bob up and down again. He put out his hand to pat Joe's head gently, not taking his sad eyes from Adam's face. A faint smile touched his lips.

"Mornin', Son. I see you ain't forgot how to milk."

"Feels good, Pa," Adam said softly. "Feels awful good."

"I mind the time you thought it was a chore, Son."

"Not now, Pa. Just like to sit here a-milkin' all day long."

"That army is short on cows, I s'pose?"

"Not a cow, Pa."

"You can milk 'em all," William Youngblood said, "but first you better get up from that stool and give me a proper greeting."

Adam nodded solemnly, set the milk pail on the floor, got up from his three-legged stool, and held out his hand to his father. They clasped hands for a few seconds, looking into each other's eyes, and then William Youngblood put his arms on his son's shoulders, hugging him briefly.

"It's good to see you, boy."

Adam's voice was broken. "Ah, Pa, I can't tell you——"

"That's all right. That's all right, boy. How long they give you, Adam?"

"Three days is all."

William Youngblood's eyes clouded, but then he smiled. "That ain't much, but we'll make the best of it."

When the milking was done, they went to the house for breakfast. Adam looked around him with keen pleasure, seeing everything just as it had always been, neat and clean and orderly.

"You're still keepin' it just the way Ma had it."

"It's a pleasure to me," William Youngblood said.

Adam figured rapidly in his hand. His father was only forty-five. That was young. Sergeant Hanford was more than forty.

"Pa, it seems to me you don't have to keep on like that. You got a long time to live. You could marry again. There's lots of women would have you, s'posin' you had it in mind."

William Youngblood shook his head. "I had the best, boy. There ain't another like her."

Adam nodded. "Long as you ain't too lonely here, Pa. I may be gone a long time."

"I can wait," his father said. "You'll be the one to bring another woman here, Son. After the war you'll find you a good one."

"Never thought much on it, Pa."

"You will, boy. You'll meet one sometime."

"Maybe so," Adam said agreeably. "Not in that army, though. Drill and sleep, sleep and drill. Ain't time for much else."

"Your letters make good readin', Adam. You don't send enough of 'em is all."

"They keep us awful busy, Pa. Maybe there won't be so much drill and such when we get to——" Adam paused, looking up into his father's eyes.

"That time has come, has it?"

"Next week, Pa."

William Youngblood nodded. "You'll do your best, Adam. I know you'll be careful as you can, without shirkin' your duty."

"That's right, Pa. They taught us pretty good, it seems to me."

"This head man of yours, this Barnes you wrote about—what kind of man is he, Adam?"

"Young, Pa, but somehow he seems lots older than me. And hard —hard as a hickory block."

"That ain't a fault in a thing like an army. You put trust in him?"

"I do, Pa. I'm ready to go anyplace he says. He's a good man."

"All right, Adam. With him out in front of you and the Lord up above you, I ain't goin' to worry too much."

14

Come all you wild young men
And a warning take by me
Never to lead yourself astray
Into no bad company.

JACOB WAGNER had it all planned. He wasn't as dumb as that big ox Hanford thought he was. He'd get home, put Mag to work packing the stuff, and in the morning he'd hitch up the horse to the wagon. Oh yes, he'd have to burn the damn blue suit. They'd go to New Jersey, maybe, to start off. Pick one of the big towns, rent a little house for Mag to live in, and he'd pick out another regiment to enlist in. He'd be careful in his choice; some regiments paid bigger bounties than others.

He'd stay until the first furlough time, then he and Mag would pack up again and head for, say, Pennsylvania. Another regiment, another bounty, another furlough, and off again. There were lots of places a smart man could work the trick. He could get rich doing it. He'd heard some of the boys say that a man could get two or three hundred dollars in some states just for signing the paper and putting on the blue suit.

Not near as dumb as Hanford thought! That bastard. He'd like to stay in the 195th just to take care of Hanford. In his mind's eye he could see the broad blue back topped by the gray-black hair. He could look along the barrel of his Enfield until his sights lined on the patch of wrinkles in the blue jacket, caused by Hanford's habit of keeping his shoulders racked back.

He'd do it if the bounty money wasn't so attractive. He couldn't pass up money so easy to get.

He thought about Mag, considering leaving her right where she was. No, he couldn't do that. Might be a long time, or maybe never, before he found another one like Mag. It'd be a nuisance dragging her around with him from one state to another but, in the long run, she'd be worth it. He thought of her full, warm body with an animal pleasure. She'd be sleeping when he got home, but by God, she'd wake up fast enough. He grinned, showing big yellow teeth in the moonlight and quickening his steps up the rutted mountain road.

She was all right, Mag was. She liked his kind of life, which involved no fancy fixings of any kind—just living in the old slab-sided shack on the mountain. No work to speak of most of the year. A little hunting, a little fishing, some very cautious burglaries in the valley when he needed cash money, and a garden patch to scratch in.

She was a good old girl, Mag was. A tongue too rough to suit him, sometimes, when he'd been laying around on his butt too long without bringing in the what-for, but she forgot that soon enough when he grabbed her and held her tight. And an eye that wandered whenever she came up against a strange man but, as far as he knew, the back of his hand had always cured her.

He scowled when that thought came into his head. Just let him catch her! Just once!

That was the night he caught her. It was almost two o'clock in the morning when he reached the shack at the end of the rutted road. He opened the door softly and stepped inside. He didn't want to make enough noise to wake her up before he had a chance to light a lamp and stand over her in the bed. That was a pleasure he'd savored ever since Stewart had dropped him at the foot of the road. Just looking down at her for a while before he put his hands on her to wake her up.

He went directly to the table, his hands searching in the darkness for the lamp. He heard her breathing heavily in her sleep, but he also heard another sound that shouldn't have been there at all. It was a low, rasping snore, pitched higher than her breathing. He struck a lucifer and lit the lamp.

He looked at the bed. She was sleeping all right, with one arm thrown around the shoulder of one of the redheaded Watson boys from the far side of the mountain.

He stared at them for a full minute. He saw why the light hadn't awakened them. There was a stone jug lying on its side near the bed. The stopper lay on the floor.

Wagner crossed the room noiselessly, reached to the rifle rack on the wall, and took down his old cap-lock rifle. Carefully he loaded it with powder and ball, set a cap in place, and raised the rifle.

He took a few seconds to decide, then aimed and shot young Watson in the head. Then he stepped swiftly to the bed, before she could get up from her drunken sleep. He used the barrel of the gun in a few swift blows.

Wagner was tired from the two-day hike. He picked up the jug, drained the few ounces of whiskey that were left in it, then decided to get some sleep in the barn.

Lying on the hay, however, his cold rage left him. He began to shake and shiver. Damn fool, he told himself. I could of run him and beat hell out of her, and things would of been the same. Now I'm in sure bad trouble.

He lay there unable to sleep, his brain working wildly. First thing is get rid of 'em and any sign of what I done. Second thing, leg it for someplace else.

No, no! Runnin' won't do. Damn provost's guard might find somethin' when they come after me for desertin'. They don't do much to you fer runnin' off from the army, but they sure as hell hang you for what I done. I got to stay now. I'll go down to town tomorrow and whine around that Mag's left me. They'll all think she run off with Watson. I got to make it look good, so nobody will come snoopin' around.

I'll go back to the army and go off to the fightin' with 'em just like I'm s'posed to. Then nobody'll think anything's wrong. Poor old Jake, they'll say. His wife run off and left him.

15

Where have you been all the day, my boy Willie,
Where have you been all the day,
Willie, won't you tell me now?

SAM COMFORT let himself into the parsonage and headed directly
for the kitchen. He lit a lamp, took off his blouse, dropped his sus-
penders over his hips, and opened the top button on his breeches.
He grinned happily, looking around him at the bountiful evidences
of his mother's skill with food. There was a huge layer cake on the
table. He lifted the cover, broke off a good chunk with thumb and
forefinger, popped it into his mouth. He opened the oven of the
stove, scowling when he saw the crock of beans bubbling with the
slow heat of an all-night fire. Beans were army food. He went into
the pantry and brought back in two trips several covered dishes and
a jug of milk from the cooler.

He heaped a plate with cold beef hash, cold baked potatoes, a
few slabs of fresh white bread, plenty of butter. Swiftly the mound
of food disappeared, and Sam sat back for a minute of relaxation
before he tackled the cake. There was no cook in the world like his
mother! He was pretty good himself, but he couldn't hold a candle
to her.

With a magnificent sigh of pleasure, he cut a huge slab of cake.
Holding it with both hands, he brought it to his mouth.

"Gol!" he said aloud. He took another bite. "Best dang cake I ever
et," he said.

"Who's there?" a frightened, whispering voice called from the
stairs outside the kitchen.

"Me, Ma," Sam called. "It's Sam, Ma."

She came running into the kitchen in her nightdress, her eyes wide
with disbelief.

"Oh, Samuel!" she cried. "Oh, Sam, you're home!"

Sam grinned. "Best durn cake you ever made, Ma."

She tried to kiss him and got her mouth smeared with frosting for her pains.

"Wait, Ma!" he said, laughing. "Lemme finish the cake."

The Reverend Mr. Comfort's head, covered by a tasseled nightcap, poked into the kitchen. "Sam, boy! You're home!"

"Sure am, Pa. Pull up a chair and have a piece of cake."

Mrs. Comfort pursed her mouth. "Sam, do they feed you all right?"

He grinned. "Don't you worry, Ma. I'm the colonel's orderly, and I eat better'n most. He just don't like the kind of food that puts meat on a feller's bones."

"Is he good to you, Sam?" Mr. Comfort asked.

"He's a prince, Pa. But I don't dare say so to the other fellers. Most of 'em don't like him much."

"You stick close by him, then. He'll look after you. How do you like being a soldier, Sam?"

"I think it's fine, Pa. I ain't never had such a good time in my life."

16

> *If ever I should see the day*
> *When Mars shall have resigned me,*
> *Forevermore I'll gladly stay*
> *With the girl I've left behind me.*

THE HANFORD FARMHOUSE was situated on the Hollow Creek about two miles from Cedar Bush. Actually the house was on an island in the creek, if the division of a stream twenty feet wide to pass around a high point of land could be said to have formed an island.

As soon as Jack Hanford set foot on the bridge that spanned the creek, his stepson's dogs began to bark. There were three of them, short-legged hounds with flopping ears that young Pat called beagles. Hanford called them "rabbit dogs" because running rabbits was their only accomplishment. Not that Hanford found any fault with that; he and Pat had spent many a winter's day tramping through the brush following the frantic yapping of the beagles.

Hanford tried to quiet the hounds when they reached him, but they kept up the racket all the way to the house. By that time the kitchen door was open, and by the light of the moon Hanford could see the tall frame of his stepson in the doorway.

Hanford's heart leaped when he heard the note of honest pleasure in Pat's greeting.

"Hey, Sarge! You're home!"

"I am, Pat. For three days."

The boy came out to shake Hanford's hand. "This is great, Sarge. Wait'll I wake Ma!"

"No need to wake me, Pat," said a quiet but deep-throated voice behind him. "Your dogs did that. Hello, Jack."

"Carrie," he said, coming forward. The boy stepped aside. Hanford took his wife in his arms, feeling his blood race suddenly as her warm full lips touched his briefly, as his hands rested on the firm body beneath the old flannel robe she was wearing. "By God, Carrie!" he whispered.

She smiled at him, pulling gently away from his arms. He knew why she did that. They had always been careful in front of Pat. The boy remembered his father; probably he had seen many displays of affection between his parents.

"Come in, Jack," Carrie said. "I'll put on a pot of coffee."

While she put chunk wood in the stove to get the pot boiling, Hanford walked around the kitchen, coal oil lamp in his hand, touching this and that and the other thing. He felt his eyes smarting. He thought it was the oil smoke. He wasn't crying; he'd never cried in his life.

"Nothing's changed, Jack," Carrie said, watching him.

"I know," he said. "I got to take it all in, though. This is the first time, all the years I spent in the army, that I ever came *home* on furlough."

"We got three calves, Sarge," Pat said. "An' a litter of seven shoats. The wheat and rye's been threshed. I'm cuttin' silage this week."

Hanford smiled. The word "Sarge" came easily to the boy's lips. Probably the chevrons on the sleeve of the blue blouse helped. It had been difficult four years before to decide what Pat should call him. "Pa" wouldn't do; Carrie insisted "Jack" was too familiar; "Mr. Hanford" was a symbol of the barrier that had to be broken. "I been 'Sarge' for fifteen years," Hanford had said. "It fits comfortable." So it had been agreed, although Pat had seldom used the name in the first two or three years.

"I'll help with the silage," Hanford said. "That's a dirty job."

"Nothin' doin', Sarge!" the boy exclaimed. "Me and Ma decided that was the army to let you come home, you wouldn't do a darn thing except fish in the creek. I got a stump jumper Ma hired to help me. I'll get on back to bed, Sarge. You and Ma sleep late in the mornin'. I'll take care of everything."

When the boy had gone, Hanford shook his head puzzledly. "Has he growed any in two months, Carrie?"

"He's sixteen, Jack. He's growing all the time."

"Soon be a man."

"Yes," she said quietly. "That's what I'm afraid of. You going to get that war over and done with soon, Jack?"

"I sure to God hope so, honey."

She turned away from the coffeepot to face him. She smoothed her hair away from her brows and smiled happily at him. "You come here now, Jack, and kiss me proper."

17

Mine eyes have seen the glory . . .

THE 195th had come the long way round into Highland Landing instead of going directly from Camp Chapman along the North Plank road. That route, several miles shorter, was considered by the Republican politicians and Colonel Cathcart as undesirable. The streets were narrow. The vast crowd that had come from all over Highland County, as well as from Orange, Ulster, and Rockland counties, just to see their boys march off to war could not be accommodated along the tenement-hedged strip of North Water Street.

The parade had been scheduled for nine o'clock. It got under way at nine-forty. The city and county officials, the police and the volunteer firemen, and two fife and drum corps stepped down Broadway. Company buglers in the regiment lifted their bugles on signal to blare the call to fall in, and as the notes lifted sharp and clear, the men of Company A heard First Sergeant Hanford's rich baritone lift in mockery of the call:

> *"Fall in, ye pore devils,*
> *As fast as ye kin,*
> *And when ye git tired,*
> *I'll rest ye agin."*

One by one the companies stepped out to the cheers of the crowd and the tapping of the drums. Ahead of the regiment the two groups of musicians vainly tried to drown each other's tune.

Buildings were decked in bunting, crowds of small boys tripped along beside the marching column, and the vast crowd cheered its heroes lustily.

Jeff Barnes, riding easily in the comfortable saddle of a horse from the Bellnap livery stable, grimaced at the wailing music that rolled back to the regiment. Billy Hasbrouck, a likable young man, noticed Jeff's disgust. He grinned sympathetically.

"I'll fix that," he called to Jeff. He reined in his horse and waited until the regimental musicians had caught up with him. He spoke a few words to one of the drummers, who nodded eagerly and called to his companions.

Hasbrouck rejoined Jeff. "Bless old Ossawattamie Brown," he said. "Here they go!"

The regimental drummers essayed a few preliminary taps, then shuddered into a steady beat. The fifers, one at a time, picked up the tune. The rhythm rolled back across the regiment; in company after company the sergeants grinned and began to count cadence on the beat of the drums. Then, in the front rank of Company A, young Tim Tuggle, who had sung "Lorena" at the regimental ball, lifted his youthful voice fervently in the first line:

> *"John Brown's body lies a-moulderin' in the grave."*

A ripple of sound went through the regiment. A few voices from Company A joined Tuggle in the second line:

"John Brown's body lies a-moulderin' in the grave."

A hundred men picked up and repeated the line the third time, and fully half the regiment shouted out the final words of the verse:

"His soul is marchin' on!"

The words rolled out like thunder as more than seven hundred men roared the chorus:

> *"Glory, glory, hallelujah!*
> *Glory, glory, hallelujah!*
> *Glory, glory, hallelujah!*
> *His soul is marchin' on!"*

The crowd went wild. Already deeply stirred by the pageantry of the parade and by pride in their boys, each of whom was marching out to be a hero, the people on Broadway abandoned all effort to hold their emotions in control. Women cried, babies screamed in terror, and men removed their hats and joined shaking voices in singing with the soldiers. A mob of boys materialized beside the column, young throats straining to achieve a manly tone in singing "John Brown's Body," while short legs pumped valiantly to keep step with the men.

Before the parade started, Colonel Cathcart had instructed the Gardinerville Fife and Drum Corps that they should play "Hail, Columbia." The rolling thunder from behind him, however, carrying an almost physical impact as it went by, thoroughly blanketed the efforts of the Gardinerville musicians. The drum major, resplendent in red and yellow uniform and a magnificent shako, looked over the heads of his minions toward the colonel on the big black horse. He shrugged his shoulders, gave the band a sign to pick up "John Brown's Body." Even then the squeal of the fifes and the rattling of the drums were drowned in the pounding, rhythmic wave of singing.

Colonel Cathcart's ability to react swiftly to public opinion was phenomenal. Before the regiment had fairly started on the second verse, the colonel had observed the weeping women, the singing men, the general surge of emotion that rippled through the crowd. Furthermore, several pretty young ladies dashed into the street and showered him with cut flowers. His anger vanished; there was more than one way to catch the crowd's fancy with a stirring song. His mouth lost the trim military straightness that had marked it at the beginning of the parade, and he joined in the second verse:

> *"He's gone to be a soldier in the army of the Lord,*
> *He's gone to be a soldier in the army of the Lord,*
> *He's gone to be a soldier in the army of the Lord,*
> *His truth is marching on!*
>
> *"Glory, glory, hallelujah!*
> *Glory . . ."*

The third verse roared down the broad street:

> *"John Brown's knapsack is strapped upon his back . . ."*

Jeff Barnes turned his horse to the side and cantered back along the left side of the column. He noted carefully the effect of the singing as it was reflected in the seven hundred and some perspiring faces. Not a man was out of step, not an eye turned right or left to watch the crowd, not one head was bowed to watch the paving stones underfoot.

> *"His pet lambs will meet him on the way. . . ."*

Fine, Jeff thought. If that's what singing does to them, we'll have 'em singing all the time. It will shorten marches, make 'em forget they're tired, pump courage into 'em when they're shaking in their boots.

> *"Glory, glory, hallelujah . . ."*

Jeff pulled in beside the ambulance that followed Company F, preceding the supply wagons. A corporal handled the reins; beside him sat Dr. Renwick, staring lugubriously across the sea of bayonets that bobbed before him. The corporal was singing lustily, but Renwick's mouth was clamped on an unlit cigar.

"Why aren't you singing, Doctor?" Jeff shouted.

"Got nothing to sing about," Renwick yelled. "This is no picnic we're going on."

Jeff nodded and rode back toward his place at the head of the column.

He's right, Jeff told himself, it's no picnic. And that's why I'll let them sing themselves hoarse if they get pleasure from it, if it takes their minds from what they're going to do.

Passing Company A, he saw that First Sergeant Hanford's broad shoulders were braced as stiffly as the youngest recruit's, and that the sergeant's lined, weathered face was flushed, the cords in his neck were strained, and his mouth was wide open, shouting in time to the step:

"We will hang Jeff Davis to a sour apple tree . . ."

Even the old-timers, who knew better, had caught it. Hanford, who had seen the elephant so many times, was marching off to glory.

18

We are springing to the call of our
brothers gone before. . . .

THE *OREGON'S* whistle tooted twice, impatiently, startling small children and stray dogs. The crowd knew that the time had come. The politicians had all made their speeches, and the regimental colors had been presented by the ladies of the committee auxiliary.

Parents, friends, sweethearts, wives, and children broke from the orderly ranks of spectators to give a final tearful farewell to the boys in blue.

Tim Tuggle's weeping, gray-haired mother clawed her way to her embarrassed son, hugging him, kissing him tearfully, yet managing to rattle off a series of instructions: "Wear your wool drawers all the time, Timmy. Catch a cold in summer just as well as winter. Don't you dare take a drink of whiskey! Hear me, now!"

"Sure, Ma," young Tuggle blurted. "You better get back now. We're goin' aboard."

"Good-by, Timmy darlin'. Good-by."

Men who had no one to see them off watched this scene with misty eyes; they weren't inclined to laugh at young Tuggle's discomfiture. They wished they had someone to kiss them and cry over them.

The weeping and wailing continued for a minute or two until the *Oregon's* whistle blasted again three times, imperatively. Jeff Barnes lifted his hand and shouted an order. Hanford and Captain Boudrye began steering the front rank of Company A toward the gangplank at the end of the pier.

Kate Barnes pushed her way through the crowd that massed before the reviewing stand. She could see Jeff's tall figure ahead of her, where he watched the men start to file aboard the boat.

No tears, she told herself. Not a single tear!

"Jeff!" she called.

He turned and came toward her. "There's not much time, Kate. I'm glad you got through the crowd."

"Let the boat wait," she said swiftly. "And let's get out of this mob so we can say good-by properly."

He laughed. "All right, dear. I guess they can get aboard by themselves."

He took her arm and led her to the far side of the broad landing, where they were alone. She stood on her toes and kissed him lightly, then smiled and looked up with shining eyes.

"I saved you a surprise," she said, "for a going-away present."

"You gave me the field desk with your picture," he said. "You didn't have to get something else."

She laughed. "It isn't that kind of present, darling. It will be a long time before you see it." She took a deep breath and said the words quickly. "We're going to have a baby, Jeff."

"We are! Well, by God, that's fine. That's fine, Kate." He took her hands and held them tightly. "You take good care of yourself, dear. If I can manage it, I'll be home when it's time. Do you know when, Kate?"

"April, I think. Late April. Will he be old enough for the class of '84, Jeff?"

Jeff laughed. "Sure he will. That's a wonderful present, Kate. Thank you."

"You're quite welcome," she smiled. "Now remember, darling, as soon as you're free of duty, wherever it is you go, you find housekeeping rooms so I can come."

He frowned. "You think you ought to? I mean—the baby changes things, doesn't it?"

"Don't try to back out of your promise. If you end up in Washington or Baltimore, I'm coming down."

"All right, I'll find somewhere for us to live."

"I'd be satisfied with a single room, Jeff, just to be with you. Now kiss me before you go."

Their kiss was long and fierce. Then she broke from his arms, gasping for breath. "Go put your precious regiment on the boat, Jeff. Good-by."

"Good-by, Kate," he whispered. He turned away and dashed for the gangplank, where the soldiers were beginning to crowd and shove.

Tempers were fraying in the rear ranks, when Mrs. Tuggle provided the note of humor that was needed. She elbowed her way through the soldiers to the end of the gangplank. Tim was at the steamer's rail, looking down at the confusion.

"Timmy," she shrilled, "you forgot your calomel!"

She held up a brown paper sack tied with string. Tim pretended not to hear, ducking away from the rail, but his comrades began to laugh, then they took up Mrs. Tuggle's cry.

"Timmy, you forgot your calomel!"

Again and again they repeated it while Barnes and the line officers were bringing order to the crush at the gangplank.

"Timmy, you forgot your calomel! Timmy, you forgot your calomel!"

A soldier grabbed the package from Mrs. Tuggle's outstretched hand and passed it forward. Up the gangplank it went, held high by blue-clad arms, with the plaintive chant for Timmy following it every foot of the way.

Company A was already aboard, and the other companies were pressing down Front Street. Before he went up the gangplank, Michael Stewart stopped for a few seconds before Kate Barnes. She was watching her husband. She was the only woman there who was smiling instead of crying.

"Good-by, Mrs. Barnes," he said quietly.

She looked at him quickly, absently for a second before she recognized him. "Oh—good-by, Mr. Stewart. Good luck to you."

"Thank you," he said. The men behind him pushed him on. He

managed to look back once more, to see her watching her husband again.

A moment that I can remember, he thought. If only there were any hope that she will remember it, too.

A half hour later, two hours behind the scheduled time of departure, the *Oregon's* captain eased her away from the pier, put into play the steam in her iron boilers, and wondered if he could coax twenty miles an hour from her with every available foot of deck space occupied by a soldier. She'd been carrying regiments down-river all summer; the captain was sick and tired of such assignments. He wanted to get back to the luxury of passenger traffic, New York to Albany.

Damn brainless idiots, the captain thought irritably. Going off to war shouting, "Timmy, you forgot your calomel!"

His temper eased somewhat, however, as the *Oregon* responded to the cylinder stroke. She began to move in her proud fashion, as sleek and almost as fast as any boat on the river.

The captain looked at the two officers of the 195th whom he had invited to the wheelhouse with him. The fat one, the colonel, smiled happily and offered the captain a cigar. The other one, the lieutenant colonel, was looking down-river.

Wonder what he's staring at down there, the captain thought as he looked again at the lieutenant colonel after a few minutes of pleasant colloquy with the colonel. There ain't a thing down there on that side but West Point.

Part Two

"I would banish all minor questions, assert the broad doctrine that
a nation has the right, and also the physical power to penetrate to
every part of our national domain, and that we will do it—that we
will do it in our own time and in our own way; that it makes no
difference whether it be one year or two, or ten or twenty; that we
will remove and destroy every obstacle, if need be, take every life,
every acre of land . . . that we will not cease till the end is at-
tained. . . . The South has done her worst and now is the time for
us to pile on blows thick and fast."

(W. T. SHERMAN TO ABRAHAM LINCOLN, 1863.)

19

. . . He has loosed the fateful lightning . . .

ALL DAY LONG the artillery had thundered from the left. There were so many guns firing that sometimes their incessant booming drowned out for long minutes the spiteful crackle of musketry. Sometimes, however, the cannonade stopped suddenly, as if gunners on both sides had prearranged a signal to rest and cool themselves and the guns.

During these interludes the men on the far right of the Union line listened soberly to the rattle of thousands of rifles. They could hear faintly the hoarse, never ending yelling of the Union troops, and sometimes, borne on a changing wind, the undulating, high-pitched scream of the rebels. It came down the wind in succeeding waves, striking them with that same dread of the unknown that twists the hearts of children when the north wind howls through the naked trees on a winter's night. Sometimes, too, they could hear the terrible cries of the wounded when ambulances clattered along in the dust of the Baltimore Pike on the way to field hospitals in the rear.

It was, in a way, a comfort to hear the guns begin to boom again. That was an impersonal noise, one that they had always expected to hear in battle, and it threw a curtain of sound between the right wing and those poor devils on the left. It blotted out the screaming and the vicious cracking of the rifles.

The XII Army Corps under Slocum held the right wing of the Union line, southeast of Gettysburg. On the extreme right, near a wooded bend in Rock Creek, flanked by Union artillery on McAllister's Hill, the 195th New York Volunteer Infantry waited for something to happen. This was their second day of waiting, along with the rest of the 1st Division of the XII Corps. It was July 2, 1863. All through July 1, the XII Corps had waited for orders at Two Taverns, a crossroads hamlet near Littlestown, eight miles from Gettysburg. Before dawn of July 2, when Longstreet's guns started to pound the Union left near Little Round Top, the XII Corps moved into its position on the right. Then the waiting started again.

Early on the first day of the battle, when the men waited in pastures, hayfields, and along the roadbed of a spur of the Gettysburg and Hanover Railroad, the entire corps had been jumpy. If a courier came from the direction of the rumbling cannon, companies immediately began to form, regiments fell into their brigade positions, and brigade commanders rushed to division headquarters for orders. False alarms continued all day long; hard-riding couriers became only subjects of speculation. Toward evening of July 1, the men of the XII Corps kept right on playing cards, cooking meals, writing letters, or singing songs, no matter how many dust-covered lieutenants leaped from sweating horses at Slocum's headquarters.

When they moved into the line, on July 2, however, where they could hear the savage sounds of battle, the screams of the wounded in the ambulances, where the acrid powder smoke stung their eyes and set them to hacking and coughing when the wind was right,

they lost the nonchalance so quickly gained a day before. The card
games in the 195th suffered from a dearth of players; even the
inveterate gamblers tucked their grimy packs of cards into their left
shirt pockets, since it was a well-known fact that many a man's life
was saved every day by the provident presence of a Bible next to
the heart. Lacking Bibles, the gamblers used the next best thing.
There was no singing in the lines that day, although scores of men
kept their courage up with tuneless whistling. Many sought absolution in the hurried writing of letters long delayed; the mails were
always jammed when battle was imminent. Some soldiers prayed
silently, others annoyed their neighbors with nervous repentances of
their evil ways; others found things for their hands to do, like
whittling or buffing their rifles with emery paper, because busy hands
keep a man from dwelling on the dreadful future. The non-commissioned officers were helpful; there were dozens of details to be
assigned even though the breastworks were completed. Almost every
man in the 195th, however he was occupied, nevertheless took
frequent occasion to stop what he was doing to look across Rock
Creek at the rolling wooded hills and the trim fields of Gettysburg
farmers. That land held the rebels. They'd be coming across the
fields and through the trees when they came. They'd been seen,
infantry and cavalry, moving in the distance. There were thousands
upon thousands of rebels out there. The 195th waited for them
nervously.

The rebels didn't come. Morning wore on toward noon, and then
the sun began to decline. News trickled through from the left, some
of it true and some of it disturbing rumor. There had been terrible
fighting on one of the hills held by the Union left, a spot on the map
called Little Round Top. Thousands of men lay dead and dying.
Rumor had it that the rebels had broken through, that their artillery
was now enfilading the entire left wing. Word came to the 195th from
the 2nd Massachusetts, who had it from the 3rd Wisconsin, who had
it in turn from the 27th Indiana, and so on, regiment by regiment,
that the battle had been lost and that the III and II Corps were
running for their lives. The alarm was immediately dispelled by another rumor that Lee's army was licked and was in full flight. So the
day wore on. Occasional shells from rebel batteries screamed overhead to burst in the fields along the Baltimore Pike; others plowed
into the banks of Rock Creek or lifted geysers in the stream itself.

For the first time in almost a year with the 195th, Lieutenant Colonel Barnes found himself with nothing to do. He, too, could only wait. He knew that action was coming. It was inevitable. Both Lee and Meade were committed to a crushing engagement. An entire corps would not be left to cool its heels much longer. Regiment after regiment was being smashed on the left. Fresh troops would be called for soon.

Jeff Barnes knew more about the battle being fought so savagely a mile and more away than any other officer in the 3rd Brigade. Three times that day he'd visited corps headquarters, situated between Culp's Hill and the Baltimore Pike. He'd been sent each time by Colonel Cathcart. Jeff hadn't wanted to go; it was ridiculous to imagine that Slocum's staff had time to chat with regimental officers at such a time, but Cathcart had insisted.

"Find out the situation, Jeff," the colonel had said. "They'll tell you over there. You know people on Slocum's staff, don't you? He's from the Academy, he must have West Pointers on his staff. Find out what they want us to do."

"They want us to wait for orders, sir," Jeff had told him.

"What orders? What will they be? You go find out, Jeff."

"Look, sir," Jeff said patiently, "it's no use to ask. They don't know themselves. Unless those rebs out there attack us, we'll stay in line until they need us on the left. That's all there is to it."

"You go on over, Jeff. See what they say. That's an order."

Jeff was doubly reluctant to go: in addition to knowing that no one on Slocum's staff could tell him anything, he was afraid an attack would come while he was crossing the half mile between the 195th's position and corps headquarters. Cathcart would be helpless if the command were left to him.

On his first trip, in midmorning, Jeff talked to a few officers who were having coffee outside Slocum's tent, received from them the details of the fighting that morning on the left wing, and returned to the 195th.

Cathcart sent him again at noon. This time Jeff had more luck. A classmate, a major named Archie Smith, was one of Slocum's aides. He invited Jeff to a hasty lunch—half of a cold fried chicken and bitter coffee—and talked volubly of the battle.

"The III Corps is catching hell over there," Smith said. "So is the II. The rebs are throwing all they've got. I heard Sickles had the III

Corps 'way out in front this morning. There's a peach orchard there
where it's real hot, Jeff. Sickles was out too far and Longstreet hit
him with everything but the mules. The III Corps had to pull 'way
back, and the rebs are still hitting 'em."

"What about us, Archie?"

Smith shrugged, taking a huge bite of chicken. He chewed the
meat awhile before answering. "Slocum thinks that Johnson over
there"—he paused, pointing toward the rebel positions beyond Culp's
Hill—"is going to come at us sometime today. He also thinks Meade
will send some of the XII Corps to the left wing. If that's so, it'll be
Williams's division. That's you, isn't it, Jeff?"

Jeff nodded. "195th New York, 3rd Brigade."

"You been with your boys right along?"

"A year now. No action yet."

Smith grinned humorlessly. "This is the place, boy. And today's the
day. You better go get 'em ready."

"They're ready," Jeff said slowly. "I've spent a year waiting for this."

Smith nodded. "I bet they're good, Jeff. Take care of yourself."

"I will. Thanks, Archie."

On his return Jeff found Cathcart anxiously pacing the wooded
knoll into which the 195th had dug its breastworks. He had a pair
of field glasses around his neck. From time to time he stopped pacing
and studied the terrain across Rock Creek.

"What'd you find out, boy? What is it?"

"Johnson's division over yonder," Jeff said. "If they leave us alone,
we'll be pulled out and sent to the left. Third Corps, probably.
They're in trouble."

"Bad, Jeff? Did they say it's bad over there on the left?"

"Bad enough, I guess."

"My God, Jeff! You suppose we're in for it?"

"Yes, sir. I think we are."

Jeff had suspected Cathcart of hitting the bottle all day. Later in
the afternoon, when the colonel sent him to corps headquarters for
the third time, he was sure that Cathcart was half drunk. He could
smell the whiskey, and the colonel's voice was thick.

"Go over and get some news, Jeff! This damn waitin' is too much.
Go get some news."

Jeff hurried this time. If the rebels were to attack the XII Corps
position, they'd be coming any time now. Jeff knew he had to get

back. The shock of an attack would sober Cathcart, but by that time the damage might be done. He didn't mind how much Cathcart drank when he, Jeff, was around to handle the command, but if he were absent when the attack came, Cathcart could destroy the regiment in a matter of seconds with just one foolish order.

Major Smith had more news. "They're holding over there, Jeff. I don't know how the hell they're doing it, but they are. There on Little Round Top and below in the valley. They've been going hand to hand for hours. Some regiments have been cut to pieces. You'll be going in there, Jeff. Pretty soon now."

"I'd better get right back," Jeff said.

"That's right," Smith said. Suddenly he smiled. "Tell your Nervous Nellie not to send you over here again. The general's orders, Jeff."

Jeff laughed. "Thanks, Archie. I'll tell him."

Suddenly Smith sobered. "One thing more, Jeff. I almost forgot to tell you. Bad news. Somebody in the V Corps sent word on casualties. One of 'em is Paddy O'Rorke."

"Dead?" Jeff asked.

Smith nodded. "On Little Round Top. In the thick of it."

"That's where he'd be," Jeff said quietly.

"He was one of the best. He was slated for stars, you know."

"He should have been."

"I know you two were close," Smith said. "I'm sorry as hell, Jeff."

"Thanks, Archie."

"Take care of yourself," Smith said.

Handsome, gallant O'Rorke was dead. First man in his class, first man to die. He had been sure of a brilliant career. Now he was just another name on a casualty list.

As he rode slowly across the fields toward the regiment, Jeff remembered sadly how much pleasure O'Rorke had contributed to those four grinding years at the Academy. There were three or four men now serving in the Army of the Potomac—Archie Smith was one of them—who had been hauled by the seat of the pants through that academic maze by Paddy O'Rorke.

There would never be a day, until the last man of them had died, when someone, somewhere, would not have reason to remember Paddy O'Rorke. And maybe that's enough, Jeff thought suddenly. Maybe that's all any of us is ever supposed to do. Just leave something behind that's worth all the time and the work and the energy.

Jeff found Cathcart face down on the cot in his tent, reeking of
bourbon and snoring noisily. Jeff shook him vigorously. It took a
minute or two to get Cathcart awake.

"You'd better get hold of yourself, sir," Jeff said coldly. "Our orders
are coming. You can't even get on your horse."

"A few minutes, Jefferson," Cathcart mumbled, blinking his reddened eyes. "Only had a couple of drinks."

"You shouldn't have had any, sir."

Cathcart grinned weakly. "Don't scold me, Jeff. Be all right, you'll
see."

"I hope that's true, sir. Major Smith said we'd be sent to Little
Round Top. They've been fighting there since morning."

"Don't worry 'bout me, Jeff. Just one thing. You and I stay close,
boy. Right?"

"Yes, sir," Jeff said. He turned on his heel and left the tent.

It was five o'clock. There were no couriers from corps headquarters, no orders from General Williams, division commander, or
General Ruger, brigade commander. The battle on the left was thundering fitfully.

Comfort had fixed a meal of cold beef, fried potatoes, and coffee.
He set it out for Jeff in the shade of a maple tree at the edge of the
wood lot behind the position occupied so nervously by the 195th.
Billy Hasbrouck, Ned Boudrye, and the regimental adjutant, a bank
teller from Gardinerville named Jeptha Bookstaver, were all in the
line with the men, so Jeff ate alone.

With his coffee, Jeff lit a cigar and stretched his legs. He got up
from the three-legged stool that Comfort had foraged somewhere.
He sat on the ground, back against the trunk of the maple. He tried
to relax for a few minutes, smoking the cigar slowly and appreci-
atively. He knew that the feeling of weariness that gripped him was
the result of sustained tension.

Finally he flipped away the cigar butt and got to his feet. He
walked to the breastworks. Company A was the first company on
the right. Jeff saw Ned Boudrye leaning indolently against a stone
wall that formed part of the breastworks. Boudrye was talking
casually with Walter Barnes while they both watched the wooded
slopes across Rock Creek.

Jeff looked critically at Company A's position. He spoke abruptly
to Boudrye.

"Get your men ready to move, Captain. They've dumped their gear all over the woods as if they expect to spend the campaign here."

"Hell, Jeff," Ned said easily, "the rebs are sitting tight over there."

"You heard what I said! Get your company ready."

Ned flushed but managed to nod agreeably. "All right, Jeff. They'll be ready when they're needed."

Jeff looked at his brother. "You'd better get your men, Lieutenant! What do you people think this is, a game?"

Walter turned stiffly and walked away.

"What's the matter with you, Jeff?" Ned asked. "You don't have to put on a West Point show for us."

"Don't be flip! Get this company ready to move."

"Yes, sir," Ned answered harshly. "Right away, sir."

Jeff walked away. He tried to dismiss the matter from his mind, but he couldn't. He need not have spoken sharply, even if Ned's careless attitude had angered him.

My nerves are on edge, he thought. It's the waiting.

20

We fought them full nine hours
Before the strife was o'er.
The like of dead and dying
I never saw before.

THE BRIGADE moved out at six o'clock, joining a hurrying column of other XII Corps units. They crossed the fields and wood lots that lay between the flanges of the rough horseshoe pattern of the Union line. They would move into position to the right of Little Round Top, near the Trostle house, scene of bloody fighting earlier in the day.

They relieved shattered regiments of the III Corps, which had turned back blow after savage blow from Longstreet. The III Corps soldiers, powder-blackened and soaked with sweat, stumbled wearily to the rear, moving aside patiently, with dull eyes, to let fresh brigades go in.

These men paid little notice to the new troops, although the 195th New York caused some stir among them. Derisive grins crossed dirty faces as their bloodshot eyes took in the neat uniforms of the Highland County men, the new Enfields, the full field equipment. Greenhorns! The word passed, with mocking laughter, among the veterans of Second Bull Run, Fredericksburg, Chancellorsville, and now, the Peach Orchard and Little Round Top.

The men of the 195th knew why they were being laughed at; they were suddenly ashamed of their spick-and-span appearance and their shining rifles.

Their brigade stumbled to a halt, briefly, in a field being crossed by a ragged column of another New York regiment, coming off the wooded slopes of Little Round Top. The veterans slouched by, grim faces relaxing somewhat as they looked at the greenhorns. This was, in fact, the 140th N.Y.V.I., of the V Corps, which, until a few hours before, had been commanded by Colonel Patrick O'Rorke.

"Who are you, sonny?" one of them called to Tim Tuggle.

"Highland County," Tim answered swiftly.

"Apple-knockers," said the soldier with a grin. "We thought you boys was safe and sound in Baltimore."

"We came in yesterday," Tuggle answered. "What's it like up ahead?"

"It was rough, sonny," the soldier said easily, scanning the anxious faces before him. "It's over for today. You won't get hurt now."

"What about tomorrow?" Tuggle asked.

The soldier nodded. "That's another day. You fellers is liable to see the elephant tomorrow."

He and his comrades moved on, and the 195th went into the line on the slope between Little Round Top and the Trostle house. There had been a lull in cannonading, but the guns began to slam again. Shells whined and screamed overhead, but apparently the 195th wasn't under fire of the Confederate guns. There was no show of motion from the rebel lines, but bodies dressed in butternut or gray lay everywhere beside the Union dead on the contested ground.

Some of them were alive; their crying could be heard faintly through breaks in the gunfire.

This, then, was combat. The Highland County men waited for the shock of battle in spite of the advice of the soldier from the 140th who had said the fighting was over for the day. The men whispered to each other about the sprawled bloody bodies that lay in every direction. Few soldiers had eaten since noon, but none now wished to chew cold beef and bite into hardtack in view of the bodies lying so still.

Toward dusk hospital orderlies on both sides began to move slowly into the open ground, bearing stretchers and paying no attention to the artillery fire. Both armies were using sharpshooters in the heavy cover of the wood lots, but none of them fired upon the hospital men, who moved in pairs, pausing for a few seconds at each sprawled figure.

Michael Stewart, watching a pair of stretcher-bearers moving into the gully to the left, between Little Round Top and the Devil's Den, where rebel sharpshooters were hidden, wanted to warn them to be careful. They were brave men to venture into range of those deadly rifles across the way. Because of training and tradition, he should be out there with them, but instead he lay safely behind a breastwork of log and stone, waiting with quickened heart to add to the carnage they were inspecting.

His hands tightened around his Enfield; he took his eyes away from the orderlies to look at the weapon. He had sighted it in with care. It was a good rifle. He could use it. Would he kill rebs with it? He didn't know yet for sure, but he thought he would. He owed his comrades his best, and his best was deadly because he was an expert rifleman.

The stretcher-bearers started back across the open ground, checking body after body, whether dressed in blue or butternut. Stewart watched them, then lifted his shoulders above the breastworks. He whistled to draw their attention. The men of Company A looked at him curiously.

"Over here," Stewart said, pointing to a pair of bodies that lay twenty yards or so from Company A's breastworks. "I thought I saw one of 'em move."

The orderlies brought their stretcher and bent over each body in turn. One of them, a man whose cadaverous face and long, skinny body fitted perfectly the popular caricature of an undertaker, looked back at Stewart and shook his head. He touched one of the bodies with his toe and called out tonelessly: "Somebody's darlin'. Both of 'em."

The words were grim and calloused, but the man had a dreadful job. He had to harden himself to it. In camp or music hall, his eyes would probably fill with tears and his throat would constrict when he heard the sweetly sentimental words of the song:

> *Somebody's darling, somebody's pride,*
> *Who'll tell his mother where her boy died?*

Stewart watched the stretcher-bearers until the dusk had closed them in farther along the regimental position. Then he turned his back on the ground that stretched beyond the breastworks, settling himself against the log. An attack was unlikely now that darkness was settling.

He saw that Hanford evidently had the same idea. The sergeant was stretched out with his back against a neighboring log, smoking his pipe dreamily, looking as if he might be ready to doze. His heavy-lidded eyes moved here and there, however, watching the men. He looked as if he hadn't a care in the world.

Stewart took his eyes from Hanford, looking at the other men. Tim Tuggle sat behind a portion of stone wall, his eyes fixed on the darkness that hid the rebels, his face tight and pale. Jacob Wagner was paring his nails, his face a mask. Too dumb to be scared, Hanford had said. Somebody in the company had his eye on Wagner all the time. He'd tried to desert three times while the regiment had been stationed in Baltimore.

Adam Youngblood was dreaming again. He was a good soldier when under orders, but give him free time and his eyes picked out a faraway spot and he began to dream. A half-smile would dance on his lips, and sometimes he would whisper to himself. Stewart had heard at times the words that came so softly. "Get the hayin' done this week, Pa, and we can cut brush before the oats are ready." The war that had changed so many lives so drastically, had ended so many others, was to Adam Youngblood a long, troublesome trip away from home on necessary business.

Stewart looked at Captain Colden, standing straight and tall at the far right of the company position, his eyes on the darkening slope of the Devil's Den. Colden was listening to Captain Boudrye, his face impassive as usual. He was a good officer—the best in the regiment, next to Barnes. The men of Company B were fond of him; they admired Barnes and respected him, but they liked Colden.

In the center of the line Lieutenant Colonel Barnes was thinking that tomorrow would be the day. He was listening to heavy artillery fire on the Union right, accompanied by intermittent bursts of musketry.

He realized that Cathcart was talking to him, and had asked him a question. He had been half listening to Cathcart, who was carrying on a rambling conversation with Major Hasbrouck about the news they'd had of the day's fighting.

"Don't you think they'll hit the road back to Virginia, Jeff?" Cathcart was saying. "They took an awful beating today."

Jeff shook his head. "Another try, sir. They'll have to do it. All Pennsylvania lies in front of them, with food and clothing and horses and a hundred other things. Washington and Baltimore are like plums for the picking if they can break us here. They'll make another try tomorrow."

Cathcart looked dubious. "They lost a lot of men today."

"So did we," Jeff said. "Tomorrow is another day."

"Will they come through here, Jeff?" Hasbrouck asked in a quiet voice. "Do you think they will?"

Jeff shrugged. "As likely here as any place. We won't be here, though. Hear those guns, Billy?" He gestured toward Culp's Hill, hidden in the twilight haze and the gunsmoke. "I'll bet a month's pay we get orders to go drive them out of our old position."

Cathcart and Hasbrouck stared toward Culp's Hill. The artillery flashes were orange dots dancing across the haze. As night came down more swiftly, the thunder of the guns died away.

Marching orders came at nine o'clock. The men had already settled for the night; they cursed and grumbled as they formed in the brigade column to go back across the wheat fields and pastures to the right wing. It was very dark now. Walking was difficult in the shell-torn fields, littered with the debris of battle. The head of the column had to pick the way carefully. Bodies of dead and dying men were trod upon in the darkness. The reformed regiments of the V Corps and fresh troops of the VI were going in as the 1st Division of the XII Corps came out.

The moon began to shine brilliantly as the 1st Division reached the Baltimore Pike. The column halted in the fields near the road. The word from Generals Williams and Ruger came back through the regiments: "Fall out and bivouac here. Rebels up ahead. Fall out and bivouac."

Long before dawn the Union artillery that had been brought up during the night began to pound the rebel lines on Culp's Hill. Bugles blared throughout the XII Corps. By daylight the fight was already raging furiously, with the 2nd Massachusetts and 27th Indiana of the 1st Division suffering heavily in attacks upon the entrenched rebels. The 195th New York went into line of battle with orders to fire into the heavily wooded valley that fronted Culp's Hill. The woods were branched low and full of underbrush, and there was seldom a target to be seen.

The regiment was relieved after two hours and returned to the bivouac area near the main road.

Then the time came. Major Archie Smith arrived with orders for General Ruger. Regimental commanders gathered around the general at the side of the dusty road to get their assignments. Cathcart and the colonel of the 107th New York were shown their objectives. They would make the attack on the right.

Archie Smith walked over to Jeff. He nodded at Culp's Hill with a grim smile. "That's your beauty, Jeff. We've got to have it. Good luck."

"Thanks, Archie."

The regiment moved into the line and waited. The Union guns roared incessantly, sending screaming shells into the rebel lines on Culp's Hill. As always with troops waiting for the signal to attack, there were various signs of religion and superstition along the battalion front. Here and there a man went to his knees and prayed aloud unashamedly. None of his comrades laughed; some moved their lips with his: *"Our Father, which art in heaven . . ."*

Colonel Cathcart looked at his watch for the tenth time in five minutes. His florid face had lost some of its color and his jaw muscles twitched.

"Five minutes, Jeff," he said hoarsely. "We go as soon as the guns stop."

Jeff nodded, but didn't take the field glasses from his eyes. He was studying the breastworks that had been occupied the day before by the 195th, which now had been turned around by the rebels. There were shell-torn trees and heavy underbrush all the way. They'd slow the men down, but they'd offer cover at the same time. It would be hand to hand when they got there. Bless the 2nd Massachusetts for their morning's work! They'd torn themselves to pieces attacking those works, but they'd dealt a heavy blow to the rebs. The blue-clad bodies that lay among the trees were matched by as many in butternut behind the breastworks.

"Jeff," Cathcart said, "listen to me, boy."

Jeff took the glasses away from his eyes. "Yes, sir."

"Just a few minutes, Jeff. That's all we've got. I want to say something."

"Yes, sir."

"I'm scared, boy." The colonel smiled nervously. "I think we all are. Right?"

Jeff nodded.

"This is your regiment, Jeff. You taught them and trained them and made soldiers of 'em. I want you to take them in there."

Jeff's eyes narrowed and his lips tightened. He might have expected this. At the last minute, the very last minute, Cathcart was pulling out! The men would start forward and Cathcart would stay behind. They'd see him desert and they'd break at the first volley. Bitter words rushed to Jeff's tongue.

"Wait!" Cathcart said, holding his hand up. "Wait till I finish, boy."

"You can't, sir——"

"I said wait! You're going to take them in. You've prepared all your life for this moment, and now you're going to do it."

"It's your duty, sir! I'll be damned if——"

"Jeff, listen. I'll be right alongside you. I'm no coward, boy. I'm not stupid, either. I got these eagles by pulling political strings. You've earned the right to take these boys up that hill. You give the orders. You make the decisions. Take us in there, Jeff."

Barnes stared amazedly. He had never expected humility from Cathcart. He didn't know what to say.

"All right, Jeff? You and I, side by side, but you lead the men. Let's shake hands before we go."

"Yes, sir." Jeff put out his hand and they shook briefly.

The Union artillery on the right suddenly stopped firing at the rebel position on Culp's Hill. Major Billy Hasbrouck came running. His voice was unnaturally loud now that the guns had stopped. "The 107th is moving out, sir."

"Yes, Billy," Cathcart said hoarsely. "And so are we. God bless us and keep us." He lifted his sword high above his head. "All right, you apple-knockers!" he shouted. "Here we go!"

Bugles shrilled. The men clambered over the breastworks, yelling savagely. Rebel rifles on Culp's Hill began to bark.

The first casualty was Sergeant Jedediah Matthews, the regimental color-bearer. A rebel bullet hit him in the shoulder, but he didn't fall. He jammed the flagstaff into the ground and leaned upon it, gasping. A second bullet struck him in the temple. He was dead before he hit the ground. The colors started to fall. Private Comfort, trying valiantly to cover the rough ground on the heels of Colonel Barnes, grabbed the flagstaff. He lumbered forward, trying for a time to carry both the colors and his rifle. Then he dropped the rifle. He held the colors high. He was suddenly transfigured. No dog robber now! The fear that had twisted his boyish face was gone. The whole regiment was following him! He didn't even hear the bullets whining around him. He didn't feel the sharp tugs on the staff as Minié balls tore through the flag. His mouth was open in a savage yell, although the words were lost in the tumult: "Highland County, follow me!" He'd never known he could run so fast. He was passing Cathcart, Barnes, and Hasbrouck. "Come on, you apple-knockers!" Wild glory transfixed his face as the colors streamed above him.

Company A, on the far right, poured into the shallow valley and headed for the slope. They curved forward on the tip of the scimitar because the underbrush was sparse on the right. Their first burst of yelling died away and they ran silently, but for a few chopped words or shouts.

Jack Hanford, out in front with Boudrye, kept turning to see that they were coming all right. Once he ran backward for a few steps, jolting his big frame along awkwardly. "Go, boys, go!" he yelled. "Yell! Yell yer damn lungs out! Go it, boys!"

Some of them yelled and others took it up. Hanford's long-jawed face was slashed by a savage grin, then he yelled too, a deep-throated roar. Looking back again, he saw one man spin and insanely keep spinning until he fell on his face. Another stood still for a second or two, then grabbed frantically at his stomach, screaming with pain. He went down quickly and lay still.

Men were stopping to fire into the dark waves of smoke that crested the hill. Hanford and Boudrye waved them on. "Hold your fire! Hold your fire!" They yelled it again and again, but the words were lost in the overwhelming roar of the battle. The line held its shape, however. No man wanted to be left behind. The only safety lay in the rebel breastworks.

Jake Wagner ran with the rest, cursing his bad luck. He didn't yell, or stop to fire his Enfield, or flinch when a rebel ball clanged through his canteen. He just ran for the top of that hill because that's where the rest were going. Once or twice he looked at Hanford's broad back with a gleam in his narrow eyes. His hands tightened on the Enfield, but he didn't dare aim it. Too many eyes to see. He'd never thought it would be like this. He shouldn't be here. He should be off getting rich on bounty money. He would, too, soon as Hanford was dead and Barnes was dead. Maybe they'd be killed right now. Maybe he wouldn't have to kill them to be free. His eyes flashed with hope, and he ran on with the rest.

This is it, Michael Stewart told himself. I don't have to wonder what I'll do. I've got to kill as many as I can.

His mouth opened wide and his lungs strained as he yelled as wildly as the rest of them. The shining tip of his bayonet was pointed at the crest of the hill.

Like bees, Adam Youngblood said wonderingly to himself. Sounds like a whole goldurn hive of bees goin' over. They're shootin' too high. That's why it sounds like bees. Or maybe it is bees. I guess they got bees here in this country well as anyplace else. Nice country, but not as nice as it is to home. If we don't get up there faster than this, ain't one of us ever goin' home. We'll all be killed.

At the other end of the scimitar Companies E and F, crossing a clearing, caught the withering fire of rebel rifles just a few yards from the breastworks. Their ranks broke, but a few men dashed over the stones and logs and closed with men in brown and gray. The rest of the two companies, faltering for only a few seconds, followed them as soon as they realized that the terrible rifles were still.

Company A took the desperate final volley as they surged toward the breastworks. The line shuddered and swayed like an old wooden fence in a gust of wind. A few men fell, but the rest followed Hanford and Boudrye into the flashing rebel bayonets.

The rebels in the center, distracted by the struggle on the wings, wasted their fire power. Scattered shots struck the mass of men lunging forward, but there was no smashing rebel volley to break them. They kept coming, a shouting horde of blue demons, led by a crazy fat boy bearing the colors high and screaming his head off. The rebels were battle-worn and weary. They'd spent the night turning Yankee breastworks; they'd taken the shock of an attack by the veterans of the 27th Indiana in another part of the line. They were ready to call it quits for the day; they awaited the order, but it didn't come. So they rose with bayonets and clubbed rifles, tensed for impact.

One rebel fired a final shot at the color-bearer just before the fat boy reached the tumbled logs in front of the breastworks. The shot missed the color-bearer, but the rebel grunted in satisfaction when he saw the lumbering red-faced colonel take it in the chest. The rebel didn't see the colonel go down; the Yanks were coming over the logs with a final hail of bullets and then stabbing bayonets.

Private Comfort jammed the flagstaff into the soft earth of the breastworks, turning to yell, "Come on, boys! Clean 'em out!"

A lean, grim-faced rebel reached forward and jabbed the end of his bayonet into Private Comfort's backside. Comfort went flat on his face with a yell.

Jeff Barnes leaped to the top of the breastworks and balanced himself on a log, firing methodically with his Colt's .44 revolver. Before he could empty it, the trench below was filled with too many men in blue to risk any more shooting.

Jeff looked along the line swiftly. On the wings the rebels were falling back. They were already out of the trenches, still resisting stubbornly, but being forced toward the other slope. The scimitar had curved back upon itself.

Then the Confederates in the center, bone-weary and outnumbered, broke off the fight and ran for the trees. In a matter of seconds the knots of struggling men in the shallow trench fell apart. The rebels scrambled away.

Swift orders held the men of the 195th where they were. They'd done their job. There were other rebel troops in the trees below Culp's Hill. There would be no pursuit of the rebels who had fled.

The men slumped in the trench for protection against the Minié balls that were already humming out of the rebel woods. They looked at each other wonderingly. They'd done it! By God, they'd been told to take their breastworks back and they'd done it.

On the slope below, Dr. Renwick and his orderlies were already working on the wounded. There were half a hundred men lying there, more than twenty of them dead.

Jeff Barnes demanded of his mind that it begin to work again. It had been trained for this moment, trained to be clear and quick. It wasn't that way now. His head throbbed dully, and he couldn't follow a thought to its conclusion.

His hands shook and his legs trembled. There was a burning sensation along his ribs on the right side. He touched the place and found that he had been scraped a glancing blow by a Minié ball. He looked at the dead and dying on the slope and he felt sick. He fought the nausea, shuddering at the image of himself yielding to such a weakness before the men.

The entire regiment was looking to him for orders. Captain Bailey of Company E was pulling at his arm, saying, "Sir, listen . . ." saying it over and over again.

"Just a minute, Sam," he said. "Let it wait a minute."

Wearily, slowly, he climbed the breastworks, with no mind for the rebel bullets thunking into the logs and whining off the rocks. He walked five paces and stood looking down at the body of Colonel Cathcart. The body lay face up, with a wide wet stain across the chest. Cathcart's face had slackened in death to a tired, peaceful expression.

He turned away from the body slowly, blinking his eyes. When the haze lifted from them, he straightened his shoulders, holstered the revolver that he was still carrying in his right hand, and ducked back across the breastworks. His eyes were hard and clear when he faced Sam Bailey, the first of a dozen officers who wanted to speak to him.

"What is it, Sam?" he said quietly, thinking of all the things there were to be done and of the decisions he alone had to make. "Make it brief, Sam," he added. "We've got a lot to do."

The heavy fighting on Culp's Hill continued through most of the morning as the XII Corps fought to secure the works it had regained.

The 195th New York waited and listened and crouched low when the rebel shells screamed overhead. Then the musketry died away as Ewell's rebels gave up the attempt to seize the barb of the fish-hook with bare hands. The artillery continued, however, past noon. Then, at one o'clock, the sporadic booming of the guns increased to a steady, ear-pounding roar. Every Confederate gun on the Union left was thundering, and the Yankee guns replied.

For almost two hours the tremendous cannonading tore the green hills of Gettysburg to shreds, and then suddenly the thunder died away. Smoke drifted over the hills.

The 195th had already been relieved and marched across the fields with other XII Corps regiments to back up the Union left.

They waited, unable to see anything of the mile or so of shell-torn ground that stretched between the lines. They wondered what was happening out there. The men in the line, however, battle-worn veterans of the II Corps, knew what was happening. They tensed and stared at the wall of smoke that shrouded the rebel positions.

The smoke lifted briefly. Under its cover a wave of gray and brown was rolling forward. Fifteen thousand of them were in the wave.

That was Pickett, and that was the end of the three days at Gettysburg.

21

We'll give the hero three times three;
Hurrah, hurrah!

THE TRAIN puffed slowly to a stop at the depot in Dunning's Point, New York, directly across the Hudson from Highland Landing. Several passengers descended the high steps of the coaches, among them an officer and a sergeant. The sergeant came down the steps first. Shouldering aside the waiting conductor who tried to help him, the sergeant reached up and took the officer's arm.

"All right, Comfort. I can make it."

"Yes, sir. Watch your step, sir."

The officer nodded to the conductor, smiling. He could see that the man was somewhat put out by the sergeant's brusque treatment. "Thanks for a good trip," he said.

"Glad you enjoyed it, Colonel."

Sergeant Comfort picked up the colonel's bag. "Ready, sir? The ferry's in the slip."

"Lead off, Comfort."

Jeff Barnes smiled as he watched Comfort stride for the ferry slip opposite the depot. Shoulders racked, back stiff, head high, and right leg pulled unbending in an exaggerated limp. Ever since they'd left camp at Kelly's Ford in Virginia, Comfort had been stumping proudly on that right leg. His limp was his badge of honor. He intended that everyone should know he was a wounded veteran.

Comfort stopped at the passengers' entrance to the ferry.

"I'll get the tickets, sir. You go aboard."

Jeff nodded. He walked onto the ferry, went through the passengers' cabin on the right, and out to the bow of the boat. A brisk breeze was sweeping down-river from the north. Jeff pulled his slouch hat down over his forehead. He adjusted it awkwardly with his right hand. His left was bound in a sling under his blouse. Only the fingers showed. They were pale and puffed. He flexed them, making a fist of his hand, but they couldn't draw together in a tight grip. He felt a flutter of pain in his shoulder as his arm muscles contracted. He relaxed his hand, frowning. It would be weeks before he could use the arm again.

He heard Comfort stumping through the passengers' cabin. He looked up to see the sergeant shouldering his way through the swinging door.

"You all right out here, sir?" Comfort asked. "Maybe we'd better go in and sit down."

"You're the invalid, Sergeant. You go inside if you want to."

"Right here is fine, sir."

"Your leg giving you trouble, Sergeant?"

"Stiff from the railroad ride, sir. It doesn't hurt."

Jeff hid another smile. He knew damned well it didn't hurt, but he'd bite his tongue before he'd say so. Comfort had earned the right to show off his second wound.

Jeff remembered Comfort's agony in the first three weeks after Gettysburg. He'd been plagued by every man in the regiment about the first wound. Not even his promotion to sergeant, as permanent color-bearer, had tempered the good-humored ridicule of the men. Many times a day someone would say slyly to Comfort, "How's your wound, Sam? Can you sit down yet?"

Or the question might be, posed in mock seriousness, "How can a color-bearer get wounded in the butt, Sam? I'd hate to think our color-bearer was runnin' the other way."

Or, "How'd that rebel sneak up behind you, Sam?"

Comfort had reacted, of course, by blushing and stammering out a confused explanation, and that only made it worse. The men kept telling him he'd turned tail, until finally he was almost convinced that he had. He couldn't quite remember just what he'd done in that mad dash into the breastworks on Culp's Hill. His spirit languished under the banter in spite of the assurances of Barnes and Hasbrouck, who had seen him plant the flag in the earth of the breastworks.

For three weeks after Gettysburg, Sam Comfort avoided his comrades on every possible occasion. From dawn until dark he tried to stick close to Colonel Barnes, where the gibes and banter couldn't reach him. Then the 195th New York reached Kelly's Ford on the Rappahannock. Cavalry clashes had marked the slow-moving pursuit of Lee and the Army of Northern Virginia, but the rebel infantry had managed to escape the ponderous grasp of the Army of the Potomac.

At Kelly's Ford there were two troops of Confederate cavalry waiting, concealed in a wood lot that bordered the river. Barnes had led a party of skirmishers toward the hamlet at the ford. The bulk of the regiment was several hundred yards away, followed at some distance by the rest of the brigade, and farther back the division. The rebel cavalry opened fire on the skirmishers, who immediately ducked for cover. The only casualty was Jeff Barnes. A rebel ball broke his shoulder and knocked him from his horse. He lay unconscious in the open road, in full view of rebels and Yankees.

Sam Comfort dashed from the cover of the rail fence to which the skirmishers had retreated, ran to Barnes and bent over him. A rebel bullet hit him in the thigh, in the soft, thick flesh just below the wound he'd received at Gettysburg. Sam fell down, but pushed himself to his knees immediately. Somehow, in spite of pain and shock, he managed to haul Barnes's limp body onto his back. Under heavy fire from the rebels he struggled to his feet and half carried, half hauled Barnes to the safety of the rail fence.

So Sergeant Comfort was wounded for the second time in less than a month and became a hero for the second time. No one joshed him about the new wound, although it was only a few inches below the first. There was some speculation about the likelihood that Sam Comfort was the only soldier in the Union army who'd been wounded in the backside twice, but none of it reached Sam's ears.

The regiment camped at Kelly's Ford and stayed there while the armies maneuvered for future action. Dr. Renwick kept Sam Comfort in bed for two weeks, but then Sam was up and stumping around proudly on his stiff leg. He was a bona fide, dyed-in-the-wool, first-class, A No. 1 hero, the only one the regiment had. He didn't brag, but he did exhibit his game leg every time he had the chance. There was no denying his courage; the entire regiment had seen it. No man dared call him dog robber now; he was still the colonel's orderly, but he was also a sergeant and the regimental color-bearer. During his time in bed the fat had melted away from him like butter exposed to heat. He was still heavy, but he'd found a uniform to fit him neatly, and his big frame carried his weight easily. He bore himself with confidence and pride befitting a twice-wounded hero.

I guess he's grown-up, Jeff Barnes thought, watching Comfort standing tall and broad on the ferry's deck. How old is he? Twenty? He's turned from boy to man. His mother will cry when she sees him.

"Your folks will be glad to see you, Sergeant," Jeff said. "You'll have two weeks of your mother's cooking."

"Two weeks, sir?" Comfort exclaimed. "No, sir. I figured to get there for a couple, three days later on, sir. When you're able to manage for yourself."

Jeff frowned. "You planned to stay in Highland Landing with me?"

"Yes, sir. Cap'n Renwick said to take care of you, and that's what I'm goin' to do."

"I have a wife, Sergeant. And a mother, and a mother-in-law. They are perfectly capable of attending to my needs. This is a convalescent leave, Sergeant. You go to Cedar Bush and convalesce."

"Sir——"

"That's an order, Sergeant."

Comfort squared his shoulders. "Yes, sir."

"I'll expect you to join me on the first of October, not before."

"Yes, sir. I understand, sir."

Jeff smiled and turned his head to look across the river at Highland Landing. He searched for the red brick height of the library, then moved his gaze north to the white frame house where Kate was waiting for him. Kate and his son! He wished now that he hadn't advised her to give up the renting of the parsonage at St. Paul's in favor of living with her father and mother. It would be difficult to make this a second honeymoon with the sheriff and Mrs. Boudrye in the house.

Sergeant Comfort shifted his weight, favoring his game leg. "Shall I rent a hack when we get ashore, sir?" he asked.

Jeff shook his head. "It's only five blocks, Sergeant. I'd like to walk it if your leg can stand it."

"Sure can, Colonel." Comfort beamed. The idea of walking through Highland Landing's business and shopping district pleased him enormously. His tall, handsome colonel with his arm in a sling, and he with his game leg—folks would know for sure that two real heroes were walking the streets.

Kate had been trying assiduously to read how Grant had captured Vicksburg, but the sense of it kept dancing away from her. The words of one sentence, the sentence she'd been reading for ten minutes now, said, *To prepare for Sherman's attack across the swamps of the Yazoo . . .* , but her mind repeatedly transformed them into other words, *Maybe he'll come today. God, let it be today. Please let him come today.*

The prayer stopped instantly when she saw him coming down Liberty Street. Like most supplicants whose prayers are suddenly answered, she forgot all about giving thanks.

She jumped to her feet, whispering, "Jeff! Oh, Jeff!" *Harper's Weekly* fell to the porch floor. Little Jeff began to wail when his cradle stopped rocking. Mrs. Boudrye came to the door, followed by Mrs. Barnes.

"What is it, Kate, for heaven's sake?" her mother asked.

"Take care of the baby," she whispered. She gathered her skirts and ran down the steps.

He stopped to wait for her to reach him. Her heart hammered and her voice caught in her throat when she saw how his blouse was buttoned over his left arm. He took her in the fold of his right arm and held her against him.

"Jeff! Oh, Jeff," she cried.

"All right, Kate," he said softly.

She saw in an instant how pale he was, how the skin stretched tightly across his cheeks and jaw. There were lines in the corners of his eyes, etched deeply into the flesh. The muscles of his neck were ridged against the stiffness of his collar, which was grimy with soot and dust from the train.

"I'm not as neat as I might be," he said quietly. "A man can't fix himself up with one arm."

"Oh, Jeff, you're home. That's all I care about."

"Come along, Sergeant," he said to Comfort, who had been standing by, eyes fixed on the maples overhead while his colonel kissed his wife.

Jeff kept his arm around Kate's shoulders until they reached the porch under the curious eyes of the neighbors. He went forward with a smile to kiss his mother, who stared fearfully through her tears at his misshapen shoulder.

"Your wound, Son——" she said tremulously. "Be careful, Jeff."

"It's in good shape, Mother," he said easily. He turned to Mrs. Boudrye. "How are you, ma'am?"

"Welcome home, Jefferson," she said quietly. Instead of kissing him, she took his hand. "You must be hungry. I'll fix something." She turned and went into the house.

Mrs. Barnes took her son's arm. "You've changed, Jeff. A great deal." Her voice was troubled and her mouth trembled.

"I'll be all right, Mother, soon as I can use this arm again."

"I'm not talking about that," she said quickly. "You've changed inside. You're hard and cold. I can see it. You're not the same boy. What's the war doing to you, Son?"

He stopped at the screen door and looked into her eyes. "What is it, Mother? What's the matter?"

"Nothing," she said hastily. "You go in to Kate and little Jeff now. It's nothing."

After lunch, when Kate had nursed the baby, he watched silently while she tucked the child into the crib. She turned brightly and came to kiss him. She took care not to press against his bad shoulder.

"Come on," she said, "I'll give you your bath."

"I can make out," he said.

"Somebody has to scrub your back. Come on."

The tub of steaming water drew a happy sigh from him when he relaxed in it. "It's been four days since I had a bath," he said. "And that was with a sponge and a bucket. You're a much prettier back-scrubber than that Sanitary Commission nurse."

"Nurse!" she said. "You let a woman give you a bath, Jeff?"

"They're all men," he said, grinning. "In field hospitals, anyway." He lathered himself with some of Kate's perfumed soap, wrinkling his nose. Then he looked up soberly. "All right, Kate. Now tell me what's bothering your mother. We'll start with her."

"It's nothing. Really it's not. Forget about it, Jeff. She's very happy to see you."

He shook his head. "You know what it is. Tell me."

"Well, I think I do. You see, Jeff, everybody thought that Ned should have been promoted. After Gettysburg, I mean. He expected it, too. At least he hinted at it in his letters."

"I see. And you all think that I should have recommended him as a field officer."

She spoke spiritedly. "Don't say it like that, Jeff, as if we were try-ing to interfere. Let's not discuss it now. Hold still while I cut away that bandage."

"I want to discuss it now, Kate."

"No," she said firmly. "Let's not argue about it."

"All right. So that's one thing. Now the other. What's bothering my mother?"

"She's the best one to tell you that, Jeff."

"Suppose I tell you, then," he said. "Walter has been writing home that his hardhearted brother treats him like a dog. He gets all the dirty details, he gets a tongue-lashing every time I see him, he's still a second lieutenant after fourteen months. He thinks I'm a son of a bitch on wheels, doesn't he?"

"Now look here, Jeff! Let's not spoil our day with these things. I'll just say this. Nobody here understands what you're trying to do be-cause they don't understand the army."

"Do you think I should have seen to it that your brother and Walter were promoted?"

"Not if they didn't deserve promotion. Now that's all I'm going to say about it."

"Let me tell you about the promotions," he said quietly, "and then we'll forget the whole thing."

"If you want to tell me," she said, "go ahead, but it isn't necessary."

"Billy Hasbrouck was a good-natured boy when we went away. He wanted to be a schoolteacher, and his father wanted him to be a lawyer. Politics being what they are, Billy was commissioned a major." Jeff looked up soberly. "He was worthless in the beginning, Kate, but he wanted to learn. Now he's a good officer. Maybe he's capable of handling a regiment himself; there are plenty of colonels not half as good. I use the iron fist, Billy uses the velvet glove. When I was lying out in that road with the Johnnies shooting at me, Comfort was the only one who came out to get me. There were a dozen men who could have but didn't. If it had been Billy lying there, the entire regiment would have fought the whole rebel army to get to him. I'm not complaining about that. They love Billy, but I'm the one who made soldiers of 'em. He can handle them now, but it's a good thing he didn't have to in the beginning. That explains, I think, why he's now a lieutenant colonel."

He stopped talking while she finished cutting away the grimy bandage that covered his shoulder. He winced when she pulled the cloth away from the wound. She cried out when she saw the raw flesh puckered around the black hole in his shoulder.

"It's not as bad as it looks," he said gently. "Let me finish my bath and you can tie it up again."

Carefully he lathered the shoulder. He began talking again. "Sam Bailey was one of my two best company commanders. The other was Bill Colden. I offered Bill the promotion, and he refused. No comment, no explanation, just plain no. Your brother Ned is a nice fellow, Kate. Personable, handsome, and intelligent. He's not a soldier, though. The men of his company would walk all over him if they got the chance. I see that they don't get it. He's not a good officer, Kate, and he'll never be promoted while I have any say about it. If he'd knuckle down, he could change. I don't think he will. He evidently thinks that this is a game we're playing. He's damn lucky he's got Jack Hanford for his first sergeant."

"I can't argue with you, Jeff," she said sharply. Her face was flushed. "It just seems to me that you forget too often that these aren't regulars you're dealing with."

"They should be the equal of any regulars who ever lived!" he exclaimed. "They've had more than a year of training. They've fought in the biggest battle this country has ever seen. They've skirmished with Stuart's cavalry. They're not recruits any longer, Kate. They deserve the best leadership I can give them. Now about Walter," he said slowly. "He's only a boy who got started on the wrong foot. He copied Ned's tactics of taking the whole thing as a joke. Walter can lead his platoon and that's about all he can do. He's never tried to learn any more. Last July I growled at him a few times, the way I growled at every man of 'em. Walter was hurt. He thought I should treat him like a brother. He crawled into his shell and he's stayed there ever since. If he'd used his head then, he'd have realized he was getting the same treatment all the rest were getting. I won't recommend Walter for promotion until he grows up. That's it. Now what do I say to your family and mine?"

"You had best say nothing, Jeff. Let it pass."

"If you say so," he said. "I don't care either way. Their opinions wouldn't influence me in any case. I hope you didn't mind, Kate, that I spoke so frankly about your brother."

"No," she said. "Come out of the tub, Jeff, and I'll dress that shoulder. Will you have to see a doctor while you're home?"

"No. Renwick said there wouldn't be any more trouble with it."

Dinner that evening was marked by constraint. Only Kate managed to display the normal merriment that should have marked such a reunion.

Mrs. Boudrye was reserved during the meal; the sheriff was uncomfortable; Stephen Barnes was silent; his wife was nervous, and Jeff was irritated by their various attitudes.

Kate ran out of topics during coffee. The silence was broken by the sheriff, who summoned his usual affability to ask Jeff why Meade hadn't come up to Lee and whipped him again after Gettysburg.

"We didn't catch him," Jeff said abruptly.

"I know that," Boudrye said pleasantly enough, "but there must have been a reason, Jeff."

"They marched faster," Jeff said.

The sheriff flushed and set his mouth.

Jeff immediately regretted his rudeness, but he thought he had reason. This silent disapproval was getting on his nerves. He'd better have stayed with the regiment.

Kate suddenly spoke up. "All right, let's talk about it. Jeff, tell them why you didn't promote Ned and Walter."

He looked at her in surprise. He hadn't expected her to bring up the subject. He was glad she had. It could clear the air even if what he had to say didn't salve anyone's feelings.

He deliberately chose softer words than he'd used to Kate. "Kate told me you were all wondering about the promotions. All I can tell you is that I picked the officers most qualified. Bailey is an older man, more mature in his judgments, less easy in his discipline. Ned's got a lot to learn yet, and he'll learn it more quickly as a company commander. His chance will come. This is going to be a long war. As for Walter, Pa, you and Mother know that he's just a boy. He's not ready yet for heavier responsibility. He's still learning how to handle his men. It wouldn't be fair to him or to his company to promote him now."

Mrs. Boudrye spoke evenly. "From all I hear, Jefferson, you are inclined to be—what is the word? A martinet. You expect too much. I suppose it's understandable. You went to West Point."

"I'll tell you, ma'am," Jeff said as politely as he could, "this war is a serious, deadly business. I was trained for it. The men I command were not. I've done everything I humanly could in the last year to make them the best soldiers in the Union army. I haven't succeeded fully. I know that. There must be other regiments, particularly veterans of two years, who are head and shoulders above the 195th. But our boys will get there if I have to drive 'em into the ground."

"It seems to me that you've been doing exactly that, Jefferson," said his mother unhappily. "Walter writes to us that you're needlessly harsh, almost cruel."

"That's right, Jeff," his father said quickly. "Walter says your methods are too rough. He says the men need more consideration."

"I'll tell you what Walter needs, Pa," Jeff said. "He needs the flat of your hand on the seat of his breeches, just the way he got it fifteen years ago." He smiled suddenly, warmly. "You people stop worrying. Ned and Walter both are fine officers. They'll be moved up in time. A couple more battles like Gettysburg and we'll run out of field officers."

22

Where are you going, soldier,
With banner, gun and sword?
We're marching south to Canaan
To battle for the Lord.

KATE had been awake for the past hour, aroused not by the noise
rising from the shipyards on the waterfront, but rather by the insistent buzzing of a mosquito that had slipped through the screening.
The baby's crib was protected by netting, but still she worried lest he
be bitten.

It was a warm night, and in the moonlight that streamed through
the windows she saw that Jeff had kicked away the linen sheet that
had covered them. She looked at the long whiteness of his body with
the stirrings of remembered desire.

How strange it had been, fourteen months ago, to find herself
married to a man whom she had known only a few days. The strange-
ness of it had been manifested suddenly on their wedding night,
when she discovered that she was married to a man who never wore
night clothes. She remembered the thought that had repeated itself in her mind: He should have told me that he sleeps that way!

Perhaps there were many things we should have told each other,
she thought. I have known him now for more than a year. I have
given birth to his child, and sometimes I wonder if I know him at all.

We were so close to a quarrel today. I should have defended Ned,
perhaps. I know him better than Jeff does. He's my brother; surely
he's a better man than Jeff believes him to be. He is, by any standards
other than Jeff's, which are too stern even for himself.

Look at him: worn, tired, tense even in his sleep. I used to smile
secretly at the mustache that made him look older than his twenty-
four. Now he's twenty-five, and if the mustache does anything for

him, it keeps him from looking ten years older. It hides the tightness of his jaw and the lines around his mouth.

Are they all wearing themselves out the way he is? All his friends from the Academy, those hard-eyed young men I met in Baltimore and in the two weekends we spent in Washington? Some of them must already be dead like Paddy O'Rorke, or wounded and broken. They're not all the same, though, just because they went through that machine inside the gray walls. O'Rorke had a sense of humor that Jeff can never have. And Jeff has written about Major Smith, who drinks too much. Jeff will never take to drinking heavily. And Custer. He must be different, from all Jeff has said. He's never liked Custer —I suppose it's because Custer is dedicated to Custer above Duty, Honor, Country . . .

Finally she fell asleep, although it was uneasy slumber, disturbed by a dream. She could see him clearly in the dream.

He'd bought himself a horse in Baltimore, a bony, hammer-headed gray beast that wasn't much good for anything but matching all day long the thirty-inch stride of the infantry. He was mounted on the horse, riding along at the head of the regiment in the sunlight of a summer's day. His shoulders were back, his face was tanned, he was looking into the distance with keen, speculative eyes. Behind him rode other officers, their faces indistinguishable, and then came the marching men. Curiously enough, some of their features were quite clear. Sam Comfort, limping with the colors; handsome, sober Michael Stewart; young Tim Tuggle, his face aglow. The men were singing:

> "He has gone to be a soldier in the army of the Lord,
>   His soul is marching on!
>   Glory, glory, hallelujah. . . ."

Almost imperceptibly the scene began to change as the road pitched higher, growing rougher and darker. It was no longer summer. Fallen leaves swirled in the ditches, tossed by a strong wind. The sun was gone, the sky was gray and darkening.

There were vacant places in the ranks. The men were bearded, most of them, and their uniforms were hard-used. They looked weary but their marching belied their looks. They had stretched their stride until they seemed to be traveling at a swinging lope.

The officers came into view, marching with the column or riding at its head. Then the colonel, out in front as always. Who was this man? Gaunted, slumped in the saddle, seamed face that showed gray against the gray sky, eyes like burning coals set deep in bony sockets. He was still staring into the limitless distance. The only sound was a keening wail that could not be the wind.

Kate woke up shivering. Jeff slept peacefully at her side. The baby was crying. His wail had pierced her dream. He always cried when he was wet and uncomfortable. She got up to change him.

23

'Tis nothing, a private or two now and then
Will not count in the news of the battle. . . .

JEFF walked down to the *Statesman* before breakfast the next morning to get the paper. A sleepy-eyed office boy brought him a copy on which the ink was not yet dry. Jeff glanced briefly at the telegraphic news on the second page (the first page was devoted to advertisements and the daily installment of a serialized novel), noting the reports of cavalry skirmishing in Virginia.

When he returned, he sat at the breakfast table with the sheriff, who seemed to have forgotten the constraint of the day before. The sheriff talked about politics most agreeably; Jeff listened attentively.

The ringing of the front door bell interrupted their conversation.

"I'll get it," Kate said.

She was back in a few seconds looking puzzled. "For you, Jeff. Mrs. Johnson. I don't know her. She insists on waiting outside."

"Johnson?" he said. "I don't think I know any Johnsons. Not here, anyway." He got up and walked to the front door. Kate followed him to the kitchen doorway.

"Yes, ma'am?" he said to the woman who waited on the front porch. She had a slight figure, gray hair, and was shabbily dressed. She peered up at him from narrow eyes.

"Are you Barnes?" she said in a trembling voice.

"That's right, ma'am."

"I'm Mrs. Amy Johnson."

"Won't you come in, Mrs. Johnson?"

"I wouldn't come in your filthy house!"

He stared at her in amazement. His face colored. He heard Kate breathing at his shoulder.

"What's the matter?" he asked. "What do you want?"

"You brute! You put my boy in prison! He'll die there!"

Then he remembered. Private Zach Johnson, Company A. Sleeping on picket duty the day after Gettysburg. Tried by general court-martial of the XII Corps and sentenced to five years at hard labor. The boy had been sent to Forest Hall Military Prison at Georgetown.

"Yes, now I know," he said quietly. "Come inside and I'll tell you about it, Mrs. Johnson."

"I don't want to hear your lies!"

The woman was sobbing convulsively. Suddenly she moved before Kate could stop her. She slapped Jeff's face with one hand, then punched him with the other. She hit him several times. He stood stiffly, his face white and his eyes closed, taking the blows without any effort to defend himself.

Kate grabbed the woman's arms. Mrs. Boudrye and the sheriff, who had come running from the kitchen at the sound of the scuffle, pulled Jeff into the house. The sheriff went outside to help Kate.

Jeff stood in the hallway with his hand on the bannister of the stairs. His head was bowed, his eyes were still closed. The woman had punched him in his wounded shoulder. He fought off the nausea that gripped him. Kate came in and ran to him.

"My father will take her home, poor thing. Did she hurt you, Jeff?"

He shook his head.

"Come have another cup of coffee, darling. Come on with me."

He felt better as soon as he had some hot coffee. He told Kate the bare facts about Private Johnson.

Her face was sober when he finished. "Five years is a long time," she said, "just for taking a nap. He's so young, Jeff."

"He should have been shot."

"Oh no, darling!"

"The court was too lenient. Johnson should have been shot as an example to the rest of the division. Rebel cavalry were on the roads that night. I found him snoring under a tree when I made the grand rounds with the O.D."

"You found him, Jeff? Then you were responsible. Didn't he have any excuse?"

"There's no excuse, Kate."

"Jeff! He must have had some story."

"Yes. It was a beauty! He told the court that the captain of Company A had always covered up for men who fell asleep on guard. He said it had happened many times before. He'd have been all right, he said, if the colonel hadn't made the grand rounds that night."

She stared at him angrily. "Now you're accusing Ned! It's Ned's fault that the boy is in prison?"

"My God, Kate, let's drop it!"

Mrs. Boudrye spoke nervously from the other side of the room, where she had been listening. "You can't drop it, Jefferson. You've brought Ned into it. What did you mean by that?"

"All right," he said, pacing up and down beside the kitchen table, "I'll explain it to you." He paused as the sheriff came back into the house.

"She's gone," Boudrye said. "I guess I talked some sense into her." He looked quickly from his daughter to his wife. "What's the matter here?"

"Jeff is about to tell us," his wife answered, "why it's Ned's fault that young Johnson is in prison."

"What the hell does that mean?" Boudrye exclaimed, his face flushing with anger.

"That is not what I said!" Jeff told them. "Let's get this straight. The Johnson boy told his story to the court. His captain had never turned him in for catching forty winks before. That's what he said. It was his bad luck that I was the one to catch him this time."

"He was in Company A?" Boudrye asked.

"He was. What he said was true. I asked Sergeant Hanford, who admitted that Ned had never taken such things seriously. The boy should have known better; Hanford, the only old army man in the company, should not have kept quiet about it, and Ned should have taken a more responsible attitude toward discipline. Most of the fault lies with me, however. I should have known what was going on. I had a rough half hour with General Williams because of it. It won't happen again."

"I can't see where it's my son's fault that the boy is in prison," Mrs. Boudrye said coldly. "Certainly Ned appears to have made a mistake, but you and he could have corrected it together, Jefferson."

"Why didn't you, Jeff?" Boudrye asked. "You and Ned could have given the boy the scare of his life, and then made sure that it didn't happen again. It's a terrible thing to send a boy to prison for a crime that nobody else was ever punished for."

"It was out of my hands," Jeff said slowly, emphasizing each word. "Can't you understand? I had no choice. I found the boy sleeping. I turned him over to the division provost marshal. The court took it from there."

"How was it out of your hands?" Kate asked. "You could have questioned him, found out the trouble, and reprimanded Ned. You knew the boy might be shot, didn't you, Jeff?"

"I expected that he would be."

"Then why, Jeff, in God's name, did you turn him over to the provost marshal? That's what I can't understand."

"Neither can I," Boudrye said harshly. "You and Ned could have worked it out."

"I've told you," Jeff said with bare control of his patience. "It was my duty."

Kate nodded slowly, staring at his tense face. "Yes, Jeff, I can see that you'd think so."

That ended the discussion. The sheriff went to the courthouse, Kate and her mother had the house and the baby to care for, and Jeff, feeling the strain of a hectic half hour, took a book to the shelter of the front porch, where he sat in a comfortable wicker chair, hidden from passers-by by the curtain of honeysuckle vines. He couldn't read. The book was Irving's *Sketch Book*. He didn't get beyond the first page.

He closed his eyes and tried to relax in the chair. He found himself wishing that he had not come home. He threw that thought aside, reflecting that neither Kate nor her parents—his own also, for that matter—could understand the rigid, uncompromising rules upon which his command of the regiment must be based.

He wished he could tell them in his own terms what he had accomplished. In that attack on Culp's Hill his methods had been proved. Some regiments in the XII Corps, commanded by former civilians, had wavered and broken with heavy casualties. In others soldiers had panicked, throwing the assault into confusion. In the 195th, however, although the men had been just as frightened under fire, the long, harsh training to which he had subjected them had told its story. Not a man had turned tail in that long run to the rebel works. None had stopped to help the wounded; as far as Jeff knew, not a man had fired his ramrod out of his rifle. They'd been green troops, and they'd looked like veterans.

It's impossible for civilians to understand the army, he thought wryly. And I guess it's impossible for us to understand them.

Kate came out on the porch, hesitating at the door when she saw his eyes closed. He looked up when he heard her step. She smiled at him.

"Do you think the neighbors could see me kiss you, Jeff?"

"Do we care if they do?"

She knelt beside the chair and kissed him longingly.

"We shouldn't argue, Jeff. It hasn't been pleasant, has it?"

He smiled and kissed her again. "Let's not worry about it, Kate. There are other things to think about. What are we going to do during this two weeks I'm home?"

"That's the secret," she laughed mischievously. "I have it all arranged. It's time to tell you. We're going to catch the afternoon stage to Cedar Bush, then go up to Summit House. Mr. Stewart has promised us the same cottage."

"Wonderful, Kate! But what about the baby?"

"He goes with us, and so does Mrs. Fulton to help me take care of him and still have some time to spend with you."

"Kate, I'm very glad you thought of this. It wouldn't be very pleasant here under the circumstances."

She shook her head. "There won't be any more trouble, Jeff. They love you. They don't know anything about the army or about the difficulties of command." She hesitated. "I shouldn't bring it up again, but will you promise me something, Jeff?"

"Whatever you ask."

"Will you try to do something for Private Johnson?"

He frowned. "For God's sake, Kate! He's been tried and convicted. I can't change that."

"You can try. Don't get angry again, Jeff. That boy shouldn't have to spend five years in prison because my brother didn't do his job properly. Promise me, darling."

"What do you think I can do?"

"You were in the War Department for a year. You have some influence in Washington. You know Mr. Stanton, don't you?"

He acknowledged defeat with a smile. "All right, Kate. I'll stop in Washington on my way back. One of General Halleck's aides was at the Academy with me. He'll work out something. A pardon will have to come from Mr. Lincoln, of course. It can be done. Now, is that the end of it? I want to enjoy the rest of this leave."

24

Give him a kiss but for somebody's sake,
Murmur a prayer for him soft and low. . . .

JEFF sat on a bench outside the cottage by the lake. Kate was taking an overdue nap while Mrs. Fulton watched the baby. Little Jeff had been sick since they'd arrived at Summit House four days ago.

Fortunately, there'd been a doctor among the guests at the hotel. They'd called him the first night when the baby ran a fever. An infant's sore throat, the doctor had said. He'd been reassuring, but the baby was no better. He was worse, Jeff thought.

Jeff was weary from lack of sleep himself. He dozed in the bright September sunshine.

He was roused by the approach of a young man in work clothes who came down from the hotel. Jeff placed him as the driver of the express stage from Highland Landing.

"Got a telegraph message for you, Colonel," the young man said. "Brought it from Highland Landing."

Jeff took the soiled yellow envelope and handed the young man a greenback. "Thanks," Jeff said absently, tearing at the flap.

"Thank you!" the young man said, touching a finger to his cap. He turned and went back to the hotel.

The message was from Archie Smith, addressed to Jeff at his father-in-law's house in Highland Landing. It was dated September 22.

COME BACK IMMEDIATELY ACCORDING TO OUR AGREEMENT.

It was signed: A. SMITH.

When he'd left Virginia, Jeff had arranged with Archie Smith to wire him if any major operation was planned for the XII Corps. Obviously something was up, but the telegraphic reports in the newspapers in the past few days had given no indication that the Army of the Potomac was priming for a battle.

Jeff remembered rumors that one or two corps from the Army of the Potomac would be sent West. Could that be it? Maybe so. Bragg had soundly whipped Rosecrans at Chickamauga just a few days before. The meager newspaper accounts said that Rosecrans' army was bottled up in Chattanooga. Maybe the XII Corps was being sent to relieve Rosecrans.

He went into the cottage. Kate was still dozing in the chair beside the crib. Mrs. Fulton was lying on the sofa beside the baby's crib. The baby was quiet.

Without waking Kate, he went into the bedroom. He took one of the bags from the closet and started to pack his clothing. A minute or so later Kate came into the room rubbing her eyes sleepily. She saw what he was doing.

"Why are you packing?" she asked quickly.

"Orders, Kate," he said, handing her the telegraph message.

She read it swiftly, then looked up puzzledly. "What does this mean, Jeff?"

"I think we're going West," he said. "It seems likely after Chickamauga."

"You're not going to leave now," she said quickly.

"I have to, Kate. There will be a million details that Billy Hasbrouck can't handle. Moving a regiment by rail is a big job. I don't want anything to go wrong."

"The baby, Jeff! You can't go while he's so sick."

He crossed quickly to her and put his arms around her. "Kate, don't worry so about the baby. Didn't Dr. Townsend say it always looks worse than it really is? He'll be fine. Tomorrow or the next day. You and Mrs. Fulton can stay here until the doctor says the baby can travel."

"I don't think he's going to be fine, Jeff," she said soberly. "There was blood in his diaper the last time I changed him. You know what that means, don't you?"

He nodded. "Yes, Kate. Dysentery," he said slowly. "I'll go get the doctor."

The baby was wailing weakly when Jeff returned with Dr. Townsend. Kate stood by the crib looking down at him. Mrs. Fulton showed the doctor the diaper she had just removed from the child.

"Looks like dysentery," the doctor said, nodding. "There's no immediate danger. And we're not helpless, you know. Let's get to work and make the little tyke as comfortable as we can. The more we do for him, the better off he'll be."

The doctor's presence was reassuring, although it was obvious to Jeff that there was very little the man could do except wait and see how the disease developed. When he had the chance, Jeff took the doctor aside.

"I have notice to return to my regiment," Jeff said. "What do you advise?"

The doctor shrugged. "You can't do anything here except make things easier for your wife. It's up to you, sir."

"I'd like to be here if he got worse."

"All we can do is wait, Colonel Barnes. I can't predict anything."

"I see. Thanks, Doctor."

Jeff figured that he had just about time enough to get back to Virginia before the trains started to roll West, if that was the move in the wind. If he missed the regiment now, it might be weeks before he could manage to rejoin it in Tennessee. A great battle might have been fought with Bragg's rebels. Suppose he hadn't been at Gettysburg? Could Billy Hasbrouck have led the attack on Culp's Hill?

He had to go back, he decided. He couldn't risk leaving the command to Hasbrouck. Not yet.

When the doctor left, Kate sank wearily into a chair. She stared at the little row of bottles ranged on the table beside the baby's crib. Her voice seemed angry when she spoke to Jeff. "What good is the medicine? He throws it right up! I wish we could do something except wait."

"The doctor says he's not in immediate danger. You've got to believe what the doctor says." Jeff looked at her with deep concern. "Don't make yourself sick with worry, Kate."

She nodded and smiled. "At least you're here, Jeff. I'm glad you're going to stay."

"I'm not staying, Kate. I'll have to go back."

She got up from the chair and crossed quickly to him.

"You don't mean it, Jeff! The baby may be dying."

"If I don't catch the regiment now, it may take me weeks to get to wherever they're going."

Her eyes flashed, and color mounted to her face. "You think it's your duty to go back now?"

"Yes, Kate."

"Go, then!" She turned her back and stood again looking down at the baby. He watched her for a few seconds without speaking, then went to the bedroom to finish packing. It took only three or four minutes. He went into the other room with his bag. Kate didn't turn around.

"I know you'll look after things, Mrs. Fulton," he said. "We'll never be able to thank you for what you've done already."

"Yes," she said firmly, her lips tight. "You're picking a mighty poor time to leave us."

"I must," he said, flushing. He turned to Kate. "I'm going now," he said.

"You can go," she said coldly, without moving.

He stood there for a few seconds, then went to the door. Mrs. Fulton followed him. She helped him with the door.

"You ain't doing the right thing, mister," she said in a quiet voice.

He heard the baby cry out suddenly as he left the cottage.

25

All quiet along the Potomac tonight—
No sound but the rush of the river.

THE JOURNEY had begun at Bealton Station, Virginia. The rail-road was the Baltimore and Ohio. The route was to Alexandria from Bealton, over the Long Bridge into Washington, on to Baltimore, and then the sharp turn westward.

There were twenty thousand men to be transferred to eastern Tennessee, the XI and XII Corps of the Army of the Potomac. Before the operation was completed, six hundred trains would rattle over the long route, carrying men, artillery, baggage, ammunition, supplies, horses, mules. The men went first, carrying cooked rations for five days, two hundred rounds of ammunition per man, and their personal equipment. Everything else would follow. There were no coaches; they were packed fifty to a boxcar, each boxcar fitted with transverse seating of wooden planks, upon which fifty men in each car could find seats if they were all thin and if they all stopped breathing. Before the first train reached Alexandria, adventurous spirits had climbed to the roof of each car, where they lashed themselves with canteen straps or gun slings to the raised plank that topped each boxcar. They enjoyed the fresh air and the unobstructed view of the countryside. There were only a few tunnels to shower them with sparks from the locomotive and to envelop them in sooty, choking smoke.

The train carrying the 195th New York Infantry clattered over the Long Bridge into Washington. It stopped and waited its turn at the water towers in the freight yards. As soon as the train stopped rolling, guard details from each company jumped to the doors to keep the men in the cars. Lieutenant Colonel Hasbrouck had planned well. No potential bounty jumper could leave the train. The freight yards were patrolled by men of the provost marshal's command, but full

precautions were necessary. There were many men in the boxcars
who wanted nothing to do with eastern Tennessee.

Jeff Barnes, with Billy Hasbrouck and Adjutant Bookstaver,
walked the length of the train. The men were boisterous; the trip
was a great adventure, if an uncomfortable one. Soldiers out of sight
in the boxcars shouted ribald remarks at their commanding officer as
he passed.

"Hey, Ramrod! You think we're sardines?"

"Colonel, we snuck a girl in here! Come on in. She ain't particular
about officers."

"Hey, Colonel, the last thing they carried in this car was sheep.
Your soldier boys are beginning to stink."

Jeff walked to the head of the train and then back, paying no attention to the catcalls and obscenities, which he knew were signs of
the men's high good humor. Occasionally he stopped to look over
the interior of a boxcar, or to check a soldier's rations and equipment.

Hasbrouck had done a good job. There was no question of that.
Jeff knew now that he could have stayed at Summit House without
fear that anything would go wrong. Furthermore, he might have
missed the shipment of the regiment and still been delayed only a
few hours. Other officers who arrived at Bealton after their regiment
had left were simply put on the next train to leave. It was a well-
planned operation.

He was glad he had returned in time, however. Anything might
go wrong, and if there was trouble ahead, he wanted the responsibility.

He returned to the crowded caboose, which carried the train crew,
Jeff, Hasbrouck and Bookstaver, Majors Bailey and Hornbeck, and
Sergeant Comfort.

"You've done a good job, Billy," he said to Hasbrouck, pausing
at the high iron steps to light a cigar. "I can see that I needn't have
rushed back."

"Thank you, sir," Hasbrouck said, smiling, "but it was all done on
the company level. I just gave the orders."

"That's all you were supposed to do," Jeff said evenly.

They were interrupted by the approach of a tall officer who was
walking swiftly alongside the train toward them. It was Archie Smith,
with brand-new silver eagles gleaming on his shoulders.

"Hello, Arch," Jeff said. He pointed with his cigar. "When did you get 'em?"

"Yesterday." Smith beamed. "General Hooker moves fast. He took me away from Slocum because he found out I'm an artilleryman. That's what I am, my lad. A first-class gunner. I'll be directing the batteries the next time this division fights."

"Uh-huh." Jeff nodded. "I'll tell my boys to keep their heads down."

"Don't you worry. Fighting Joe Hooker and I will take care of you."

"How is he, Arch?"

"He seems fine, Jeff. He's delighted with this command. Of course, he's only been here a few days. It's too early to tell much about him. He's all right with me, though. Slocum didn't like it, but I wasn't kicking—not when Hooker jumped me two grades."

"Well, congratulations, Archie."

Smith touched one of the eagles with affection. "Pretty little things, ain't they?" He laughed, then reached into the inner pocket of his blouse. "Got a telegraph message for you, Jeff. It came to the head-quarters train in Alexandria, and the adjutant gave it to me to deliver. I checked the transport schedule, found your train running three behind ours, and came back here when they started to pile up at the water towers. Here you are."

He handed the envelope to Jeff.

"I've got to get back," he said. "We're ready to pull out. See you in Tennessee, Jeff."

Jeff turned the envelope over, inserted his finger under the loose flap, hesitated, then mounted the steps to the iron railing of the caboose. Hasbrouck and Bookstaver followed. Comfort was already inside.

Hasbrouck hesitated at the door. "News from home, sir?" he said quietly.

"I think so. Go on inside, Billy. Hornbeck and Bailey want to take your money in that poker game."

"Yes, sir. Call me if you want me."

Jeff pulled the flap of the envelope open, withdrew the yellow message paper and unfolded it. The address was longer than the message itself. He read all of the address carefully, keeping his eyes from the words below. "COLONEL T. J. BARNES, 195TH N.Y.V.I., 2ND BRIGADE, 1ST DIVISION, XII ARMY CORPS, ARMY OF THE POTOMAC."

Then he read the message:

THE BABY DIED TODAY STOP CAN YOU COME HOME.

It was signed: KATHLEEN BARNES.

He gripped the wrought-iron railing tightly. He closed his eyes, shutting from view the skyline of Washington in the afternoon sunlight, the long lines of gleaming tracks, the puffing locomotives, the splashes of blue where soldiers moved through the yards.

For a few seconds he felt nothing, then slowly the sorrow overwhelmed him. Curiously, he could not see the baby as it had been during the few days he'd been home—an infant wrapped in blankets and lying in its crib or feeding at Kate's breast, but instead he saw a succession of scenes in which the boy grew as years went by, tall and slender and smiling. It seemed to him that the child that was dead was not a baby, but a grown son in whom all his hopes were blossoming. He heard his own voice saying, "He'll enter the Academy with the class of 1884. . . ." He heard Kate saying, "Thomas Jefferson Barnes, Jr. That's his name, darling."

He wanted to weep, but his eyes were dry. He wanted to cry out, but his throat was constricted. He wanted to mourn, but he didn't know how.

Kate, he thought. I should have stayed with her. She faced it all alone. She will never forgive me for leaving her, and I will never forgive myself. He would not have lived had I stayed there, but at least I could have comforted her. All alone. Poor Kate.

It was then that he felt the tears in his eyes. He brushed them away with the back of his hand. He put the envelope and the message in his pocket. His lips moved slightly. "I'm sorry, Kate darling," he whispered.

He turned around, composed, when he heard voices beside the caboose. Ned Boudrye was at the foot of the steps looking up at him. Ned's face was slightly flushed; it was obvious that he'd been drinking again.

Jeff's jaw muscles set, but before he could speak, two more men came into view. One was Adam Colden, the other was his cousin, Captain Bill Colden. Adam Colden had come down to Virginia a few days before to visit the 195th New York in the field. He planned to write a series of articles about the regiment for the Highland Landing *Statesman*.

"We brought you company for the ride," Ned Boudrye said thickly.

"Adam can't ride in with the men. Better he rides with you, Jeff. That all right?"

Adam Colden smiled at Jeff. "Only as far as Baltimore, Jeff. Then I'll leave you."

"You've been on this train?" Jeff asked evenly.

Adam Colden nodded, laughing. "Packed in with the rest of the sardines in Company B."

"By whose orders did you ride in that car?"

"Why, Bill here said it was all right, Jeff. I spent my time with the boys and now I'm going back to Highland Landing. I'll write some good stories about the regiment."

"Captain Colden," Jeff said coldly, "you heard the reading of General Hooker's special orders on transport arrangements. What did they say about civilians?"

Bill Colden flushed, his eyes meeting Jeff's. "There were to be none in the troop cars, sir. It mentioned sutlers and other civilians accompanying or on duty with the army."

"And you deliberately violated those orders?"

"Sir, I thought Adam——" Colden stopped. His face stiffened. "Yes, sir, if you want to put it that way."

"I'm not putting it any way, Captain! The orders were explicit."

"I just hooked a ride, Jeff!" Adam said quickly. "What's all the fuss about? I'm only going to Baltimore."

"Not with us, Adam!"

"Why not, for God's sake?"

"I've explained. General Hooker's orders. Now you'd better leave these yards before the provost marshal's people arrest you."

"Goddammit, Jeff, what's the matter with you?" Ned Boudrye cried. "This is a friend of ours. He wants to write some articles about the regiment. You know as well as I do that every train on the line has correspondents and sutlers and railroad officials and God knows who else on it. Why can't Adam ride to Baltimore?"

"For the last time, General Hooker's orders. I'm sorry, Adam. You'll have to leave the yards."

Colden nodded slowly. "All right, Colonel Barnes. Just as you say. You've got to follow orders." He turned his back and walked away. His cousin turned to follow.

"For Christ's sake, Jeff, what'd you do that for?" Boudrye asked.

"You'd be under arrest, Ned, if I could prove you're drunk."

"Hell, a couple of drinks with Adam! Jeff, when are you going to understand that this isn't the regular army? No wonder everybody hates West Pointers. You make it awful tough to like you."

"And you don't like me, do you, Ned?"

"Not at all," Boudrye said bluntly. "But I can get along."

Jeff pulled the envelope from his pocket and handed it to Ned. "I just got this," he said. "It's from Kate."

Ned read it quickly. "Jesus, that's too bad, Jeff. I'm sorry. I'm really sorry. Kate thought the world of the baby."

"I thought you'd want to write to her."

"First chance I get. Meantime, you tell her how badly I feel when you see her. I suppose you'll be leaving the train at Baltimore?"

Jeff shook his head. "I can't go home. You forget where we're going."

"My God, man! You're not going home? Don't you know how she must feel? Haven't you got any heart at all?"

"That's enough, Ned."

"The hell it's enough! I'm going to tell you something that's needed telling for a long time. Put me under arrest for it if you want. You know what you are, Jeff? You're a cold-blooded son of a bitch. That's what you are. You're not a man, you're a goddamn machine!"

"Get back to your company, Captain."

"I'll be damn well glad to. Aren't you going to arrest me first?"

"Not now. Don't let me catch you drinking on duty again, Ned."

"A cold-blooded son of a bitch!" Ned Boudrye turned on his heel and walked away.

Jeff stood at the railing with his face set and his jaw clamped tightly. His hands clenched the railing. He had held himself in when Ned had called him the name. A punch in the mouth wouldn't solve anything, especially when Ned was half drunk.

I'm wrong about Colden, he thought suddenly. The news about the baby upset me. If it hadn't been for that, I'd have let Adam ride to Baltimore. What's the matter with me? Maybe I am too hard. Maybe I should roll along and have a good time like the political colonels. I didn't have to get hard and mean.

I know how Kate will feel when I don't come home, and maybe that's why I got up on my horse. Why should I care whether Ned takes a few drinks? Why should I care whether Bill Colden gives his cousin a ride?

Kate, I can't come home. Can you understand that? I've got to go
with the regiment. There'll be fighting. I've got to go.

"Sergeant!" he shouted through the doorway of the caboose.

Comfort came on the run. "Sir?" he said.

"Pencil and paper," Jeff said.

Comfort was back with them in ten seconds. "Take this message
and have the telegrapher send it to Mrs. Barnes," Jeff said. "Just see
that he accepts it. He's probably too busy with army messages to
send it now, but make sure he has it on his sending spike." Jeff put
the paper up against the wooden siding of the caboose and poised
the pencil.

He thought of the words. MY HEART IS WITH YOU. I AM SORRY I
CANNOT COME HOME NOW. That wouldn't do. He tried again. WE
MOURN TOGETHER ALTHOUGH I CANNOT BE WITH YOU. Neither would
that. Once more he tried. ALL MY LOVE IN THIS SAD HOUR. REGRET I
CANNOT COME HOME.

Finally he wrote: REGRET CANNOT COME HOME BUT WE MOURN HIM
TOGETHER.

He handed the paper to Comfort. "That's it, Sergeant. Hurry back.
We shouldn't be here much longer. And on your way tell Captain
Colden that—— Never mind, I'll tell him myself."

Comfort hurried off, and Jeff climbed wearily down the steps again
to go forward to Company B's cars. He knew he'd been wrong. Torn
with grief, he'd taken it out on Bill Colden. Now he'd apologize.
And if he could find Adam he'd offer him a ride to Baltimore.

Captain Colden nodded coldly at the stiff apology. Adam Colden
had already left the yards. Jeff walked back to the caboose alone.

26

There's only the sound of the lone sentry's tread,
As he tramps from the rock to the fountain,
And thinks of the two on the low trundle-bed,
Far away in the cot on the mountain. . . .

THE TRAIN shuddered to a stop at the foot of a long uphill grade in the mountains of Tennessee. Seven hundred soldiers howled their protests. They knew what was coming; it had happened twice before on the way down from Cincinnati. Almost any other locomotive in Union service could have pulled that grade; the one that had hauled the 195th's cars ever since Louisville was an old-timer, long overdue for the scrap heap. The men would have to walk to the top of the incline.

Private Adam Youngblood was one of the last men off the train. Most of the regiment had already started trudging alongside the roadbed toward the top of the hill. Adam had been standing in the doorway of Company A's boxcar looking at the countryside. Ever since Gettysburg, when he had discovered that combat was far more terrible than he had imagined, that during it and after it he felt brutalized, numb with horror and disgust, Adam had allowed his mind to retreat from the war. Although his body performed capably the everyday motions of soldiering, he kept his spirit at a distance. Farmer born and bred, he sought with his mind the refuge of the safe, eternal land as well as he could amid the exigencies of war. His chief interest now, other than the determination to stay alive until it was time to go home, was the study of farmland that passed his view. He had long since decided that there was no country anywhere he had been—Virginia, Maryland, Pennsylvania, Ohio, Kentucky, Tennessee—that could match Highland County, New York.

He would have been unable to explain his intense interest in each of the thousands of farms he had passed, and if pressed, he would have said simply that farms were the main things that concerned him. Actually, although the condition had become intensified since Gettysburg, it had been with him ever since he'd left the Catskill foothills in July of '62. He was the victim of one of the severest cases of homesickness ever to strike a Union soldier.

Adam was not an imaginative man, therefore he had never been plagued by changes in the only dream that had filled his sleeping hours since he'd left home. He still dreamed often that he was walking up the lane to the farm on a bright warm day. It was September, he thought, because the trees were heavy with apples. In the dream he could see his father in the barnyard, shading his eyes with his hand as he watched the blue-clad soldier come up the lane. That was the end of the dream. He never reached the house. The nightly disappointment and awakening did not disturb Youngblood greatly. He was satisfied with his dream. Other men dreamed of Culp's Hill at Gettysburg. Adam was certain that someday, when the war was over, he would go home; he would walk up the lane past the orchard, he would shake his father's calloused hand.

Homesickness was the cause of many thousands of desertions from the army; most other soldiers caught by it as badly as Adam Youngblood would have long since taken French leave. But Sergeant Hanford, who had his eye on Jake Wagner during all the time that Wagner spent out of the guardhouse, never once imagined that Youngblood would pull foot. Adam Youngblood was a man of his word. He'd signed for three years; he'd stay his time.

Furthermore, as anyone who knew him would have pointed out, Adam Youngblood was an obedient son. His father's last words to him when Adam was leaving for Highland Landing and the regiment had been, "You got to go, Adam. Do the job as best you can, stay till they're whipped, and then come home."

Since he was a good, reliable soldier, none of the officers on company or staff level, nor any of the sergeants, noticed that Youngblood, the last man to get off the train, was straggling as the blue columns walked up the hill beside the laboring train. None of the men noticed, either; Youngblood was a quiet fellow with no close friends to look around to see where he was. Mike Stewart might have noted that Adam was falling behind, but Mike was caught up in his own dream; unlike Youngblood's, it had myriad variations, but in all of them Kate Barnes's eyes were shining on him and her low voice whispered words he knew he'd never hear. That dream had been with Stewart too in all his days in the army, but it also had been intensified at Gettysburg and since, when he saw death come close and pass him by and knew that it was entirely possible that he'd never see her again.

So no one noticed Youngblood, who was walking very slowly on the rock ballast of the roadbed. His eyes were fixed on the gradual rise of land to the right of the tracks. A slow smile worked across his lean, weathered face. His messmates would scarcely have recognized him at that moment. He looked younger; his face had lost its usual solemn placidity, seeming to be flushed with pleasure; his shoulders lifted from the marching slouch habitual to Union infantry. His messmates might have wondered where Adam had found the whiskey. On the other hand, a woman might have said he was thinking of a girl. Both guesses would have been wrong; Youngblood didn't drink, and he had never courted any girl in his twenty-three years.

The reason for the transformation was simple. There on the hillside was the first place he had seen in all his travels that reminded him of home. There was a lane—it was grass-grown, to be sure, but a lane, nonetheless, of the proper length and turning. Beside it was an orchard enclosed by a rail fence. Some of the fence rails were missing and the trees needed pruning, but it was an orchard just like the one at home. He saw the red spots of ripe apples among the green leaves. Baldwins, from the look of them.

Beyond the orchard were a house and outbuildings. They were weather-beaten and dilapidated, but once they might have been painted—the house would have been white like the Youngblood house, and the barns red like the Youngblood barns. As his eyes returned to the orchard, Youngblood wondered absently what kind of man it could be that would allow his place to go to seed like that.

He imagined that he could taste the apples. They were tart and juicy as his teeth crunched through their skins. He'd like to have a shirtful of them.

He would, by thunder! A shirtful! Youngblood, without a thought for the regiment climbing steadily up the grade, stepped away from the tracks, pushed through the brush that bordered the parallel wagon road, and headed with a quick step for the lane that led to the orchard. No one saw him go; no one missed him. Had any sol-

dier in the regiment been intent upon deserting while the grade was
being climbed, he would have been caught before he'd covered fifty
yards. Private Youngblood, who wanted only a few apples, walked
away as if he were invisible.

The trees were old. Their heavy-fruited branches hung over the
rail fence. Youngblood stopped at the first tree. He leaned his Enfield rifle against the fence and climbed to the top rail. He picked
one red apple and stood balancing precariously on the rail while
he gnawed the apple to the core. Then he opened the first two
buttons of his shirt and began dropping apples into the gap. He
stopped to eat another after picking a dozen or so. The juice ran
down his chin and bits of apple clung to his dark brown mustache.
Private Youngblood was happy for the first time since he'd left home.
He forgot duty and discipline in the joy of eating ripe apples.

He didn't give a thought to the special orders that Colonel Barnes
had issued when the train had entered Tennessee. No straggling,
no coffee-boiling, no berry-picking. The people in these hills hated
Yankees. Anyone who straggled during stops might be shot by bushwhackers, as the army called the guerrillas who roamed the wild
country along the railroad. These men weren't rebel soldiers subject
to discipline, but bandits who robbed and killed when and where
they pleased. They didn't confine their crimes to Yankees or Yankee
sympathizers. Anyone with food, clothing, or money might be attacked.

Youngblood remembered quickly enough, however, when a woman's voice cried, "Git off that fence!" He dropped the apples and
grabbed for the Enfield. The move threw him off balance. He
tumbled back, trying to save himself from falling by propping himself with the rifle. It slipped and fell from his hand. His head hit a
big flat rock in the ditch. The world seemed to explode in a blinding
flash. Youngblood had knocked himself senseless.

When he came to, his head was aching with pain severe enough
to make him groan. His eyes watered when he blinked them, and
he couldn't see through the haze. There was a cold wet cloth across
his forehead. He put his hand up, rubbed his eyes, winced with pain;
then he could see. He was lying in the ditch. His rifle was beside
him. Looking down at him were a woman and a boy. They looked
so much alike he decided they were mother and son. The boy was
six or seven years old.

Youngblood's hand went to his rifle. He started to get up. The pain bounced around inside his skull. He gritted his teeth.

"Easy," the woman said. "You had a bad knock."

The boy spoke in quiet wonder. "Looks like an aig on the back o' yore haid."

Youngblood had always had trouble interpreting southern speech. "Looks like a what on my what?"

"An aig," the boy repeated agreeably. "You know. What a chicken lays."

"Oh." Youngblood nodded slightly, feeling the spot. It wasn't as big as an egg, but it was big enough and sore enough. Suddenly he remembered duty, discipline, and the fact that he was a Yankee in rebel country. He brought his Enfield up to his waist. "How long have I been laying there?" he asked the woman.

"Hour and a half, I reckon. Maybe more."

He looked up the lane toward the house, then toward the railroad; the tracks were shining brightly in the afternoon sun at the top of the grade. There wasn't a spot of blue on the landscape. The train was perhaps twenty miles away now unless it had hit another grade.

He realized the danger he faced. His eyes narrowed and his lips tightened as he appraised the situation. "Anybody in the house?" he asked the woman.

She shook her head.

"Any neighbors?"

She hesitated, studying his face. Most people had little trouble in determining that Private Youngblood was an honest, kindly young man in spite of his veteran's grim look, as much a part of him as his uniform. Apparently she was reassured.

She answered quietly. "None nearer than a mile."

"How far to Chattanooga?"

She shrugged. "I don't rightly know. I ain't never been there. Train makes hit in two hours, I reckon."

"Any Yankees around here?"

"Ten mile that way," she said, pointing to the grade. "They keep the railroad up."

So he was ten miles from safety. He looked at the tracks and then back at the woman. He'd best not risk walking the roadbed in daylight; he'd be in plain sight of bushwhackers.

He had a choice. There were many more regiments coming through on the railroad—probably several of them today. He could wait until a train hit the long grade. It would be easy to hop aboard. On the other hand, bushwhacking country was no place for a Yankee to wait out trains that might have been delayed in Kentucky or northern Tennessee for any number of reasons.

His alternative was to hide out here until night came and then hoof the tracks to the army post she'd mentioned, ten miles away. That would be best, he thought. If no train came through by nightfall—he'd be able to hear one long before it hit the grade—then he'd risk walking the tracks.

"Let's go to the house," he said. "You and the boy walk ahead."

Her face reddened and anger flashed in her eyes. "We got nothin' fer you to rob, mister. No money or silver."

"I wouldn't rob you, lady. All I want is something to eat before I start walking. I'll pay you."

"Ain't much to eat. Pork and beans with sorghum. Some bread."

"Sounds good to me. Let's go."

"Want me to carry hit fer you?" the boy asked, pointing to the Enfield. His eyes were shining with anticipation, but his narrow little face was impassive.

Youngblood laughed shortly. "I'll keep it, sonny. You walk ahead with your mother."

She took the boy's hand and started up the lane. Youngblood pulled up his shirt and let the apples fall into the ditch. He took a long look at the tracks and the wood-covered hills beyond them, then followed the boy and the woman toward the house. He remembered a question he should have asked.

"Lady!" he called.

She turned from the steps and looked back.

"Where's your man?"

"Pittsburg Landin'," she said quietly.

He was puzzled. Pittsburgh was in Pennsylvania. What was a rebel doing in Pennsylvania? Suddenly the name caught his memory. "Shiloh," he said aloud. "You mean Shiloh."

"He was killed the first day."

The death of a soldier, Union or secesh, meant little any more to a man who had seen many men die, yet Youngblood felt the need to say something. "I'm sorry, ma'am."

She nodded, turned, and went into the house. The boy held the door for Youngblood.

"What's your name, sonny?" the soldier asked.

"Tom. What's yourn?"

Youngblood told him.

"I'm goin' to the army when I'm bigger," Tom said. "You reckon I can git me a gun like that 'un?"

Youngblood smiled. "There won't be a war by that time, Tom. We'll finish it soon now."

The boy nodded unhappily. "I reckon," he agreed.

While the woman worked at the stove, preparing his meal, Youngblood looked around the house. It was a small, poorly furnished place. There were three rooms and a lean-to woodshed. It would qualify as a shack back home in Highland County, the kind of place that stump jumpers like Jake Wagner lived in. It was neat enough, but Youngblood noted the absence of an indoor pump, the windows patched with oiled paper, cracks everywhere in the plastered walls, sagging floor boards. It wasn't her fault, he supposed. Maybe her husband had been shiftless.

He opened the two doors leading from the kitchen. Each entered into a bedroom. Both were sparely furnished, but he saw women's fixings in one and a few makeshift wooden toys in the other. He turned from her room to find her eyes on him.

One of his rare smiles showed his strong white teeth. "They might have been filled with rebs, ma'am."

"They might," she said flatly, "but they ain't."

"No," he said, seating himself at the table. "I'm satisfied."

He studied her carefully for the first time. She was his own age or no more than a year older. He had appraised very few women in his lifetime, so he was no expert, but he thought she was pretty. Her hair was honey-colored and fastened in a bun at the back of her head. Her eyes were light blue, curiously light. He couldn't remember ever having seen that color in anyone's eyes. Her cheeks were high-boned, and her mouth was wide. She was tall, maybe five feet eight or nine. Tall women were more graceful than short ones, Youngblood reflected. A little banty of a woman was always scurrying. It'd make a man nervous to have one around.

This woman was different from all the rebel females he had seen in Maryland and Virginia. They'd had bitter tongues and made no attempt to hide their hatred of everything labeled "Yankee." This one, although she didn't talk much, seemed almost friendly. Maybe there was a different breed of rebel in Tennessee.

She opened the oven door and bent to take out a crock of beans. Her dress tightened against her thigh and hip. Youngblood's face reddened and he looked away. He had suddenly imagined that the rest of her was bound to be as attractive as her face.

She brought the food to the table. He managed to lift his eyes to hers. "Would a greenback cover this meal and maybe a snack for the road?"

"More than enough," she said, nodding quickly.

He knew that a dollar was too much. He was surprised at himself. He'd always been very careful with money; he'd been raised to respect it. Somehow it didn't matter. Come to think of it, he'd give her two dollars. She could buy the boy something.

"What's your name, ma'am?"

"Connor," she said. "Susan Connor."

"Mine is Adam Youngblood. I come from Highland County, New York. It's a fine place." That seemed to exhaust the conversation for the time; Youngblood began to eat the plate of pork and beans. It was delicious, even to a man who'd been eating beans almost every day since he'd joined the army.

She fixed plates of food for herself and the boy, and the three ate together without talking. From time to time Youngblood found himself looking into her light blue eyes. A glow of contentment went through him; he ascribed it to the satisfaction of a good meal.

"That's fine cooking, ma'am," he said, putting down his fork.

"Hit ain't much," she said.

"How come you run this place all by yourself?" he asked. "You farm it?"

"We can't do much. We had to stay here when—after Pittsburg Landin', I mean. None of our kin would take us in."

"I can see the land hasn't been worked."

"I couldn't," she said. "It ain't mine. My husbin rented. I ain't had crops to keep up the shares. Now we got word to git."

"What will you do?" Youngblood asked, trying to grasp the meaning of it. Back where he came from everyone had his own place. A man belonged to the land, and the land belonged to him.

"I dunno," she said, her voice betraying hopelessness for the first

time. "I reckon we'll try Chattanooga. I could do washin' and house-
work for the officers."

"That's no proper life for you," he said sharply. "Nor for the boy
either. The army is no place for a woman. How come your folks
won't take you in?"

"You don't want to hear my troubles," she said abruptly. "I'll fix
some grub for you to take along."

"I'm beholden to you," he said. "You could have run for your neighbors or took my rifle and run me off. I'd like to help you."

"What can you do?" she said matter-of-factly. Then she answered
her own question. "Nothin'. It's gittin' dark. You'd best move along."

"Not yet," he said. "I want to stay off the tracks until full night
has come, if you don't mind my company. You wouldn't have any
coffee, Mrs. Connor?"

"Ain't seen a coffee bean since last year. We made some from
acorns, but it don't taste like coffee."

He laughed boyishly and reached for the cartridge box at his belt.
He drew out a cloth sack. "Keep forty rounds in my pockets," he
grinned, "and a pound of coffee in here."

She clapped her hands in sudden delight and ran to the stove to
put water to boil. Youngblood, with a piece of stove wood, tapped
the cloth sack until the beans were crushed. Tom watched the operation solemnly.

"I ain't never had no coffee," the boy said eagerly. "Reckon I could
have a taste?"

"A whole cup, by thunder!" Youngblood said. "That is, if your ma
doesn't mind. Coffee's not for young lads."

"He kin have some," she smiled.

A few minutes later, over a steaming cup of black coffee, Youngblood began to talk. His messmates would have been amazed. He
had been known to go through an entire day without saying a dozen
words. Now he carried on like a revival preacher at a tent meeting.
He was talking about home.

"My pa," he said, "tries to keep things the way they were when
my mother was alive. Our kitchen shines like a new penny, there's
flowers all around the house, and always kittens underfoot. You go
to the springhouse, you'll find a bucket of buttermilk cooling in the
spring, and maybe some ginger beer to wet your throat when you
come in from the hayfields. We've got banty chickens scratching

around; they're no earthly use to anybody, but Ma liked 'em. When the preacher comes to visit—him and his wife—they get served tea in the parlor. Some folks say that Pa ought to forget about Ma and the way she did things, but we think it's a nice way of doing. We like it that way."

"It sounds real fine," she said softly. There were tears in her eyes, but Youngblood couldn't see them. His own eyes were fixed on the ceiling, as if he could see there the green fields of home.

"We keep twenty cows or so, and sell the butter and cheese. We raise wheat and oats and corn. There's a good market for 'em in Highland Landing—that's the county seat. And apples! Lord love you, we've got wonderful trees. A hundred bushel every year goes to market. I hear tell they sell 'em in New York City. Highland County is the world's best place for apples, far as I know."

"We got apples," Tom said. "Them you was stealin'. They got worms in 'em. Ain't ary apple I had without a worm in hit."

"No worms in our apples back home," Youngblood said. "Why, we've got a song the regiment sings—the boys are mostly from Highland County—and it's all about our apples. I'm not much on singing, but I'll try it:

> "We're from Highland County,
> And we'd like to have you know
> That Highland is the county
> Where the luscious apples grow.
>
> Oh, they call us apple-knockers,
> And they needn't take it back,
> 'Cause the apple-knockers are the boys
> Who drink the applejack!"

Youngblood smiled. "Applejack is whiskey. I don't hold with drinking, but it's a nice song. Makes a fellow think of home."

Tom was trying to repeat the song, his thin child's voice stumbling over the words. The soldier laughed and tried to help him along, but he looked at Mrs. Connor and stopped in the middle of the first verse. He saw the tears on her cheeks.

By thunder, I'm a fool, Youngblood told himself. Here she's getting put out of her home, and I go raving along about what a fine life we all have back in Highland County. I'm a pure fool.

"I'm sorry, ma'am," he said softly. "I didn't think."

She managed a smile. "It's all right, Mr. Youngblood. You didn't mean bad. I was thinkin' about little Tom here, and a place like that. Banty chickens and dogs and kittens——"

"Them banty chickens," Tom interrupted, "air they purty?"

Youngblood nodded. "Pretty as can be, Tom."

Susan Connor had regained her composure. "It's real dark now," she said. "You'd best git along."

He knew it was time. He had enjoyed his couple of hours of happiness, and now he had to go back to the harshness, the bitterness, the monotony of a soldier's life. He was indebted to her. He wanted to tell her, but the words didn't come easily. She was a good woman even if she was a rebel.

"When I get to Chattanooga," he said haltingly, "I'll speak to Colonel Barnes. Likely he'll know of work you can do and a place for you to live. You come on when you can. Find the 195th New York Infantry. I'll be watching for you."

"I dunno," she said. "You don't have to put yourself out——" She was interrupted by the sound of horses in the lane.

"Ma! Bushwhackers!" Tom yelled.

Youngblood grabbed his Enfield and started for the door. He was instantly the veteran soldier again. His mind called back the lay of the land. There was a wood lot beyond the orchard. If he could reach the trees he'd be able to head into the hills.

The door had a tight latch. He fumbled at it. She was at the window peering into darkness. She called to him, "No! They're too close! Go in my bedroom!"

He took Tom by the hand and ran for the bedroom. In the darkness he did his best to calm the boy. Finally he held the small figure pressed gently to him. The boy was shaking. Youngblood could see most of the kitchen through wide cracks in the door.

He debated his wisdom in hiding. After all, she was a rebel. Her husband had been killed by Yankees at Shiloh. Why would she protect him from her own people even if they were lawless bushwhackers?

He looked behind him. There was a window on the far wall. He knew he should go through the window and make a run for it. Common sense told him he was a fool for staying.

He heard her opening the kitchen door. She had no trouble with the latch. He saw a figure in the darkness on the veranda, and he heard her say something in a soft voice.

The stranger answered roughly, "My boys are takin' the rest of yer hens. You don't need 'em no more. Got any flour?"

He pushed her aside and entered the kitchen. He was a burly man with a ragged black beard. He wore a tattered Confederate jacket and Union breeches tucked into a scuffed pair of boots. A revolver was holstered at his hip.

Youngblood waited tensely for her to speak. He imagined her voice saying, "There's a Yankee in that room."

She didn't say anything while the bushwhacker was roaming the kitchen, examining the cabinets, the stove and the pans and kettles on it. He picked the half-eaten loaf of bread from the table and began to wolf it.

He spoke to her with his mouth full. "Where's the flour?"

"I used it all for that bread."

He looked at the remains of the meal on the table. His hand swooped out and picked up the cloth sack of coffee. He grinned crookedly. "Damn! Real coffee! You had Yankees here, didn't you?"

She shook her head fearfully.

"I tole you last time we was here what would happen if you took up with Yankees. I said we wouldn't have Yankee-lovers round here. Them railroad bluecoats been here, ain't they?"

"No," she said, backing to the wall.

"Don't lie to me! You're too purty fer 'em to leave alone." He moved toward her. "And too purty fer me to leave alone. What's good fer Yankees is better fer me." He put out his hands; then stopped suddenly and crossed to the open door. The squawking of chickens sounded in the night.

The bushwhacker called to his companions. "You boys camp in the orchard. Save me some chicken. I'll be down later."

A chorus of laughter answered him. He slammed the door and turned to the woman.

Youngblood had eased the latch on the bedroom door. He'd have to be very careful. A shot would bring the rest of the guerrillas. He hoped that Susan Connor wouldn't give him away by screaming for him. She looked frightened, but she stood quietly. She was nearer the bedroom door now.

The bushwhacker came swiftly across the room, grabbing her

shoulders as she tried to twist away. His face bent to hers. "Don't yell, Yankee-lover," he whispered harshly. "Nobody but my boys will hear you."

Youngblood swung the door open and took two swift steps. The barrel of his Enfield cracked against the man's skull. Susan Connor leaped back and the bushwhacker fell to the floor.

Youngblood didn't give the man a second glance. He took Susan Connor's arm and pulled her into the bedroom. She was sobbing. He held her roughly by the shoulders. "Hush, now! Listen to me. We've got to run. He's not dead. If the rest don't come up to the house for a couple of hours, we can get away."

"What we goin' to do, Ma?" Tom cried in terror.

"We're going to run," Youngblood said gently, "and you'll have to keep quiet, Tom lad. Now through the window with you, and no noise."

They made their way silently through the fields, going slowly along shadowy fences until the noise of the bushwhackers in the orchard faded with distance.

When they reached the tracks near the top of the grade beyond the Connor house, Youngblood hoisted the boy to his shoulders. He gave Susan Connor the Enfield to carry.

"Ten miles at night is a good march," he said. "Can you make it?"

"Don't worry about me," she said, "I'll stay with you."

Neither of them spoke again until they reached the downgrade, where the light of the moon on the roadbed made walking easier.

"I'm sorry," he said suddenly, "you had to leave because of me."

"His brother owns the place. Likely he would of put us out anyways."

"There's something I don't understand. He kept talking as if you were a Yankee, not a rebel."

"I didn't tell you," she said. "My husbin was killed at Pittsburg Landin', all right, but he was in your army. He was a Union man. There's lots of 'em in Tennessee."

"That's why your folks won't take you and the boy?"

"His kin too. They're all rebels."

He nodded but didn't answer. He had a lot to think about. There was a strange idea jumping around in his mind—an idea that would have shocked him a few hours ago. He was wondering if that blow on the head had addled his brains. His head still hurt.

By thunder, he was going to say it. What matter if he made himself out a fool?

"Ma'am," he said, then corrected himself. "Mrs. Connor—I mean— Susan. When we get to Chattanooga——"

Tom's sleepy voice interrupted him. "Tell me about them banty chickens. I never seen one."

Youngblood laughed. He could feel his blood pumping wildly. He felt like singing and shouting, but he tried to keep his voice calm. Nonetheless, it trembled when he spoke.

"I was going to tell your mother about banty chickens and other things, Tom."

"Tell about the banty chickens," Tom murmured. Youngblood knew that the boy was almost asleep. He slipped the little body from his shoulders and made a cradle of his strong arms.

He looked at Susan Connor. Her eyes met his, and he marveled at the way the moonlight bathed her face.

"They paid us before we came West," Youngblood said. "I've got three months' pay pinned in my pocket. It will buy passage on the train to Highland County."

She smiled sadly. "You're mighty good to say it. But we can't. What would your pa think of me? I can't talk fine. I don't have nice ways. It's crazy to think it. Don't say no more."

"Pa's lonely. He likes children. Take Tom up there. Say you'll do it, Susan."

"No! It's crazy, I tell you."

"No more crazy than this whole war. You don't have to stay there after I get home. When the war's over, I mean. You can come back to Tennessee."

"No. Don't say nothing more about it."

There was a note of pleading in her voice, as if she were afraid that he would keep talking, keep trying to persuade her. He laughed in triumph. "You don't want me to say more because you know you'll say yes. Well, I won't stop talking, Susan—and that's a wonder for me—so you might as well say yes now and get it over with."

"Let me think, Adam. It's wild to say we could do it."

"Think all you want," he said. "There's only one answer I'll take."

She didn't reply. They walked for another five minutes before she touched his arm. She was very close to him.

"Is it hill country in Highland County, Adam?"

"Hills all over," he laughed. "Mountains in the west."

"Hill country is the best," she said. She slipped her arm into his. They walked the tracks toward Chattanooga.

From this night on Adam Youngblood's dream would be changed.

He would march along, wherever the war took him, a good soldier to the end, unmindful of the names of places that were to become household words across the nation. He would dream his dream of a lane and an orchard and three people waiting for the blue-clad soldier.

27

When a horseman passes, the soldiers have a rule,
To cry out at their loudest,
"Mister, here's your mule!"
But another pleasure, enchantinger than these,
Is wearin' out your grinders,
Eatin' goober peas!

THE MEN of the 195th New York Volunteer Infantry claimed that somebody in corps headquarters had handed them the dirty end of the stick. Upon reaching Tennessee, most of the XI Corps went into camp near Bridgeport, on the Alabama border. The XII Corps, with headquarters at Tullahoma, north and west of Chattanooga, was scattered, regiment by regiment, to guard the Nashville and Chattanooga Railroad from rebel cavalry attacks.

The 195th New York shuttled back and forth between Tullahoma and Bridgeport, as if General Slocum were playing musical chairs with the regiment. Then, with the arrival of Grant to take command at Chattanooga, the Highland County regiment became a road gang.

With Bragg's pickets and skirmishers holding the Tennessee River and the last few miles of railroad into Chattanooga, supplies for the Army of the Cumberland in the city could not be brought in from

Bridgeport. Instead, they were freighted along roundabout mountain roads running north of the river. These roads, rutted and humpbacked in good weather, were practically impassable in the autumn rains. The Highland County men rolled up their sleeves and went to work with pick, shovel, and ax. They were spread out over the mountainsides, filling in potholes, hauling stone and gravel, and felling trees to corduroy the bogs. A hundred times a day work parties dropped their tools and stepped into the mud to put their shoulders to the wheels of wagons that mules couldn't haul. The men were sure they were being discriminated against because they were from the Army of the Potomac. They didn't stop to consider that the regiments that labored alongside them were westerners, while most all the other XII Corps regiments were doing lazy guard duty on the railroad.

Then Grant's engineers built a steamboat that could make the run from Bridgeport to Kelly's Ferry on the Tennessee. The XI Corps under Hooker was assigned the job of securing the twelve-mile "Cracker Line" from Kelly's Ferry into Chattanooga. On the night of October 29, Hooker took part of the XI and XII Corps against the rebels in Lookout Valley and in brief but severe skirmishing drove the rebels across Lookout Creek. The "Cracker Line" was open into the city, and hardtack began to roll by wagon train to the hungry men of the Army of the Cumberland. The 195th New York was shifted from the mountain road to the river road beyond Kelly's Ferry. The picks, shovels, and axes were brought into play once more. The men groused at their labors.

In point of fact, the western soldiers kept them steamed up. Although not a man in the 195th New York owned a paper collar for his uniform, the westerners never failed to call them "paper collar soldiers." Everywhere the New Yorkers went, marching in formation according to Colonel Barnes's orders, the undisciplined westerners would jeer in time to the step:

"PAPE-R   COL-LAR!   PAPE-R   COL-LAR!"

Although the non-existent paper collars were the prime expression of western contempt, there were hundreds of varied gibes hurled at the Highland County men. "Fancy Dans," they were called. "Mama's Boys." "New York Dudes." "Runners from Bull Run." The names couldn't be reconciled with their appearance while they worked on the roads; if anything, they were even dirtier and more ragged than the westerners. Nor did they know that the other eastern regiments were getting the same treatment; the 195th thought it was singled out for western contempt.

The contrast between Hooker's regiments and those in the Army of the Cumberland, and in Sherman's Army of the Tennessee, now on its way from the Mississippi, was striking. The easterners, when they weren't working on the roads, wore complete uniforms, reasonably clean and neat. They had forage caps and full equipment, including haversack, knapsack, cartridge box and bayonet. They marched with the thirty-inch stride common to the Army of the Potomac, and their endless drilling in the early days of the war showed results now. Their orders were to keep themselves as neat as possible, with hair cropped and beards trimmed.

The westerners, on the other hand, wore anything that suited them, so long as it was government issue. They favored slouch hats over forage caps, scuffed boots instead of brogans; they seldom put on blouses, but sported wool shirts crisscrossed with wide galluses, and few of them even owned greatcoats. The veterans among them had discarded haversacks and knapsacks on a hundred southern roads even before Shiloh; recruits were quick to copy the old-timers. Each soldier rolled his possessions in his blanket, rolled the blanket into half of the shelter tent he shared with a messmate, and slung the bundle across his back with strap or rope. The western men were bearded and long-haired; the discipline imposed by their officers was chiefly remarkable by its absence; they seldom marched in formal military style, but when they did, their stride was a long, loose-limbed stretch of thirty-three inches, developed in more than two years of one forced march after another in the fluid warfare along the Mississippi. They made a raucous, wild-spirited, frontier army, and they were as cocky as jaybirds. The newly arrived easterners were natural targets.

Brawls were the inevitable result. Several times a day provost guards' whistles shrilled along the road. The men of the 195th were greatly outnumbered by the western soldiers, and they suffered for it—not because the westerners piled on in superior numbers, but because every man in the 195th faced a fight at any time a westerner had the inclination.

After one such scuffle on the road in the rugged hills near Whiteside, Tennessee, First Sergeant Hanford sent Mike Stewart to regimental headquarters with a request for more men to fill out his working party. Barnes's office was in an abandoned boxcar, without wheels or trucks, perched on a sidehill in the Whiteside Valley. Sam Comfort was outside the boxcar when Mike approached, leaning indolently on an ax he was supposed to be using to split wood for the potbelly stove in the boxcar.

Comfort grinned at Mike. "What was the hoorah we heard down the road? Did they call you 'Paper Collar' or 'Dude'?"

Mike shook his head. "This time it was Hooker. One of 'em said Hooker wasn't fit to be Thomas's orderly, and Tim Tuggle yelled back that he was so. They started to laugh their heads off at that, and Tim got sore at himself for falling for such a moss-grown trick. He took a swing at one of 'em. He got knocked flat on his back. Then I had to handle the fellow that started on him, and first thing you knew, everybody was in it."

"You fighting, Mike? I thought you didn't believe in it."

"I don't. The fellow in front of me didn't give me a chance to tell him about it, so I had to pacify him."

Stewart looked ruefully at the skinned knuckles of his right hand.

"Wisconsin or Illinois?" Comfort asked.

"Neither. That Michigan bunch we had the tussle with last week."

"Who beat?"

"They did. They always do, don't they? Can I see the colonel?"

"Why not?" Sam said laconically, picking up a chunk of pine and setting it carefully on the block. He eyed it speculatively and hefted the ax. "Hot work," he said, putting the ax down again and pulling out his pipe. "Wish I was with you fellers workin' on the road. Nice easy job you got, a shovelful of dirt every time the sergeant looks at you."

"Any time you want my job, I'll split that wood, Sam."

"Colonel needs me here," Comfort said quickly. "Go on in and see him if you want."

Mike went up the pair of steps to the open door of the car. Colonel Barnes was reading a letter at his table beside the stove. Adjutant Bookstaver was shuffling company reports at another table. Barnes looked up.

"At ease, Stewart," he said. "What is it?"

"Sergeant Hanford sent me to ask for more men, sir."

"He's got twenty," Barnes said sharply. "Just to fill four potholes before dark. What's he need more men for?"

"We had a little trouble with a work party from that Michigan regiment, sir. Three of our men were hauled off by their provost, sir, and three have gone back to camp to get their cuts and bruises fixed up by Dr. Renwick."

Barnes's face tightened, then suddenly he laughed. "This is a hazardous duty. All right, Stewart. I'll send a half dozen men from the other side of the hill. Anybody badly hurt?"

"Corporal Tuggle has a three-inch slash on his neck, sir. One of the Michigan men had a knife. I had to take it away from him."

Barnes frowned. "I'll speak to their colonel next time I see him. By the way, Stewart, is Private Wagner in your work party?"

"Yes, sir."

"Tell him I want to see him. You bring him back here with you and tell Hanford I'll send eight men instead of six."

"Yes, sir."

"Has Wagner ever talked about his wife since he claimed she ran off?"

"Not that I heard, sir."

"He probably hasn't said a word to anybody. Well, I have news for him." Barnes looked at the letter in his hand, then frowned impatiently as if he regretted the necessity for being garrulous. "This letter is from my father-in-law, Stewart. It says that Wagner's wife was supposed to have run off with a young fellow named Watson about a year ago. The Watsons didn't believe it. Now they've found two bodies in one of those old quarry holes on the mountain above Cedar Bush. So the sheriff wants Wagner put in the guardhouse and held until he sends for him."

"Yes, sir," Mike said.

"You'd better take this," Barnes said, reaching to the end of the table and picking up his holstered Colt's .44 revolver. He unbuckled the flap of the holster and tucked it in behind the gun.

"Put it on your belt," Barnes said, "and watch Wagner. He may guess why I've sent for him."

Wagner noticed the .44 immediately. He knew that Stewart had no ordinary reason for wearing a sidearm. "He give you that to bring me up with? What's he want me for?"

"I don't know, Jake," Stewart answered carefully.

"The hell you don't! What for?"

"All I know is that he had a letter in his hand and said he wanted to see you."

"A letter? Who from? There ain't never been a letter about me before."

"Look, Jake, I don't know anything about it. He told me to get you, that's all."

"All right, he must of tole you why he was givin' you the gun. Why?"

Mike didn't answer. He nodded in the direction of headquarters.

They walked together along the road, leaving the working party behind them. Faintly they heard the leisurely pounding of Sam Comfort's ax.

Suddenly Wagner stopped walking. He turned swiftly and grabbed for the revolver. "Gimme that gun!"

Mike leaped aside and drew the .44 from the holster. "Stay back, Jake!"

Wagner grinned. "You won't shoot. You wouldn't kill a man, Stewart."

"I'll shoot, Jake. Put your hands on your head and walk ahead of me to the boxcar."

"Gimme the gun!" Wagner took a step forward. "I know all about you. I heard you and Hanford talkin'. You wouldn't kill a man, even a reb. It's against your church. Gimme the gun."

"Don't take another step, Jake."

Grinning coldly, Wagner stepped forward. Mike aimed high over Wagner's head, pulled the trigger, the gun jumped, and the shot whined off through the air. Wagner leaped for the gun, got both hands on it, and wrested it away. He laughed wildly and swung the weapon. The barrel slashed against the side of Stewart's head. Stewart fell.

Wagner turned and ran. He went up the steep-cut bank of the road like a deer bounding up a ridge. He disappeared into the heavy stand of pines that bordered the road.

Stewart got to his hands and knees. His head was bleeding and he was dizzy, but otherwise he was all right.

A squad of provost guards came around the bend in the road,

rifles ready. Barnes, Comfort, and Bookstaver were running from the other direction.

Stewart explained what had happened.

Barnes sent half the provost's men along the road to flank the mountain above them from the west, the other half to guard the road into Chattanooga. A mile or so beyond the mountain was the Tennessee River. Barnes sent Bookstaver to post guards on the other side of the mountain, on the trails that led to the river.

"All right," the colonel said. "How'd he get the gun, Stewart?"

"He took it from me, sir."

Barnes nodded. "You could have shot him, but you didn't. Is that right?"

"That's about it, sir."

Barnes looked at him grimly. "Have you ever fired a gun at a man, Stewart? Gettysburg? Kelly's Ford?"

"Yes, sir. I have."

"Did you hit the men you aimed at?"

"I can't say."

"All right. You and I will climb that mountain to get him. Comfort, give me your sidearm and give Private Stewart your Enfield."

"Ain't I comin', sir?"

"You stay here in the road. Bookstaver will send some more men. When they come, have them spread out and move up the mountain. He'll have to stay ahead of them."

"Yes, sir. You be careful, Colonel. That Wagner is crazy as a bed-bug."

Barnes nodded. "Have you climbed this mountain, Stewart?"

"No, sir."

"I have." He pointed. "See that notch up there? It's the only way he can go through to the other side. On both sides of it there's a fifty- or sixty-foot drop from the hogback. It'll take him some time to work his way across to the notch when he finds he can't get down any other way. We'll go right to it now and wait for him."

It took them about ten minutes, moving silently along the pine-needled floor of the mountainside, to reach the notch through which Wagner must pass. They took positions on either side of the cleft in the rocks. Stewart lay flat behind a gnarled, storm-twisted pine. Barnes crouched in a jumble of rocks above the narrowest stretch of the notch.

They waited for another ten minutes. There wasn't a sound in the dark pine forest except once the far-carrying thumping of a startled deer far down the mountainside. Barnes looked across at Stewart and pointed down, indicating that Wagner had spooked the deer. Stewart nodded. It would be perhaps five minutes, from the sound of the deer, before Wagner reached the pass.

They were wrong. Something or someone other than Wagner had startled the deer, because a minute had not gone by when he appeared, standing against the skyline on the hogback. He looked down at the notch and saw Colonel Barnes crouched among the rocks. Mike Stewart saw Wagner as soon as Wagner saw the colonel.

Mike saw the .44 in Wagner's hand lift and steady on the colonel's back. The man wouldn't miss, taking deliberate aim at twenty yards.

Mike leveled the Enfield quickly, aimed at Wagner's chest, and squeezed the trigger.

The force of the Minié ball slammed Wagner back and twisted him around before he fell. He managed to fire the revolver, but the ball screamed away into the distance when it hit the rocks. Wagner twisted once on the smooth face of the hogback, rolled over, and then slid down the high-pitched ridge, crashing into the stunted pines below and disappearing from sight.

Barnes stood up and brushed the dirt from his uniform. Mike crossed the notch and joined the colonel.

"Thanks, Mike," Barnes said. "I had a glimpse of him just as you fired. He was about to shoot me, wasn't he?"

"Yes, sir," Stewart said quietly.

"Do we have to go down there and look for him?"

"No, sir. He's dead. I hit him in the chest."

I killed him, he thought. I had to do it.

"Let's get off this damn mountain," Barnes said abruptly. "I'd like to talk to you when we get down."

"Yes, sir," Stewart said.

Back in the boxcar, Barnes chunked the stove with wood, filled two mugs with steaming black coffee, and offered one to Stewart. They sipped the coffee in silence for a while.

"He would have died anyway," the colonel said finally. "He killed his wife and her lover."

"He would have had a trial," Stewart said softly. "He would have had a chance to live."

"I thought so. You regret killing him."

"Yes, sir, even if I had to do it."

"If you feel that way, why did you think you had to do it?"

"Another half second and he'd have put a bullet in you, Colonel."

"Exactly. Either Wagner or I had to die, and you chose to kill him instead of letting him kill me. Why?"

Mike stared puzzledly. "I didn't have any choice, sir."

"Yes, you did. You killed him to save my life, put it that way. Why?"

Mike smiled briefly. "I think I see where this conversation is taking us, sir. We've been there before."

"That's right, Mike. And we'll keep going back to the same thing. I'll tell you why you killed that man to save my life. Because you know that my ability as commanding officer of this regiment is worth more than the lives of a hundred men like Wagner. You didn't hesitate at all. It was your duty to kill him. Now I'm telling you that it's your duty to accept a commission in this regiment. You can't avoid it any longer."

"Why can't I, sir?" Mike asked levelly. "I don't want to be an officer."

"I'll tell you why you can't. Because you've learned to trust my judgment, my ability, my training. You've learned that although I can make as many mistakes as any man, I make few of them in command of this regiment. Therefore, when I tell you in strict truth that it's your duty to become an officer, you believe me. Don't you?"

Mike didn't answer.

"We'll be going out against Bragg as soon as we get enough supplies into Chattanooga, as soon as Sherman gets here. We'll lose men when we go, Mike. We'll lose officers. You're my first choice as a replacement. Hanford is my second. What do you say?"

"Let me think about it, sir."

"Decide now. We haven't got time for you to think about it."

"That doesn't follow, sir. If you'd asked me before I was forced to kill Wagner, I'd have refused."

Barnes grinned boyishly. "All right. You have me there. You'd have been stubborn about it. Now you've had this experience. You know as well as I do that you'll kill rebels after this. Why not accept the responsibility you're capable of handling?"

"You're going to give Hanford a commission, too?"

Barnes nodded.

"Well, sir, I told him that I would if he would," Stewart smiled. "I'll say yes."

"Thanks, Mike. I'm very pleased. I'll put it through right away."

Barnes put out his hand and Mike shook it. "I don't know where you're going to get extra uniforms."

Stewart looked down at his worn blue blouse and lighter trousers. He shrugged. "If Grant can put his stars on these clothes, I can put bars on 'em."

28

The wounded round they strewed the ground,
The dead lay heaped in piles. . . .

MISSIONARY RIDGE and Lookout Mountain meant many different things to many people. In Washington a tall, lean man with troubled eyes studied a military map and wondered when his new western commander would move against Braxton Bragg. In Chattanooga the commander looked across the Chattanooga Valley, where the heights ran south from the Tennessee River about four miles apart, thinking about his triple thrust: Sherman on the left with the Army of the Tennessee, Hooker on the right with his dudes from the Army of the Potomac, and Thomas down the middle with the Army of the Cumberland. Sherman fretted for action, knowing that here in battle against these heights his friend Grant and himself would prove themselves once more to be the leaders the country needed; Hooker fretted for action, thinking that now he could start the long road back from Chancellorsville when he had failed to prove that he was the leader the country needed; Thomas waited patiently, confident that once again the country would sound the praises of "the Rock of Chickamauga."

Bragg looked down upon the city of Chattanooga, secure on his heights, knowing the power of his artillery and the strength of his intrenched infantry, but just a shade uneasy when he glanced at a map and saw the broad expanse of Georgia behind him. He couldn't fail, he thought. Not after Chickamauga, certainly. Not on these heights. But supposing he did? What then?

Across the broad nation, North and South, the names Missionary Ridge and Lookout Mountain meant nothing yet to hundreds of thousands of people who wrote letters, wrapped packages, and prayed for their men in Tennessee and Georgia.

To the men of the 195th New York Volunteer Infantry, the names meant little more. That regiment, on the misty morning of November 24, was rewarded for its long, weary days of bridge-building and road-repairing with another job of the same nature. When the right wing began to move before dawn, detachments of the 195th were already at work repairing culverts, corduroying potholes in the muddy roads for the passage of artillery, and bridging Lookout Creek for the crossing of Geary's division, to which the 195th was temporarily attached. They thought they'd been given a dirty job, and they resented it, after more than a month of dirty jobs. They suffered from the gibes and mockery of their companion regiments, who marched swiftly toward the line of battle past the muddy, perspiring New Yorkers.

All through the dawn and early-morning hours they slaved with picks, spades, and axes. Behind them Hooker's batteries on the heights west of the creek thumped the west side of Lookout Mountain while other batteries enfiladed the rebel works on the northern point of the mountain. There was firing on the left, and in the center the dull throbbing of artillery and the fainter, incessant chatter of musketry.

So the battle had started, but the Highland County soldiers could only hear it. A heavy mist hung over the mountain, obscuring the rebel positions and occasionally drifting down so that most of the mountain itself retreated behind the haze. Geary's division was already over the bridge and out of sight among the trees. Somewhere ahead of the 195th the skirmishers were out and the regiments who had been told to fight instead of flounder in the mud were beginning to push forward.

Then the order came from General Geary. Hastily the 195th, company by company, abandoned tools and grabbed their Enfields. They rushed forward toward the low-handing haze, concerned lest the order had come too late and they would be left behind.

As Company A stepped out, First Sergeant Hanford made a decision that he had been deferring for the past three weeks. He looked over his shoulder and called out sharply, "Private Fuller!"

A tall boy, his face flushed with excitement, trotted forward. His uniform, mud-spattered and sweat-stained, was nonetheless obviously new and his rifle was fresh from the factory. Three weeks ago he had arrived with thirty other recruits from Highland County, brought back by Major Sam Bailey, who had gone home on recruiting duty. He had brought a note from his mother: *Dear Jack, I tried to stop him, but I couldn't. Take care of him for me. Carrie.*

"Yes, Sarge?" the boy said, falling into step beside Hanford.

"Stick by me, Pat." The words didn't come easily to Hanford; he wanted to treat the boy as if he were just another soldier, and he had fully intended to do so until the last possible moment. Now he had changed his mind. "Stick by me all the way," he said.

"We're going in, ain't we, Sarge?" Pat said quickly, almost gaily, as if this were the start of a rabbit hunt back home in Highland County.

"Looks that way," Hanford said gruffly. "Remember, when you start shootin', take the ramrod out of the barrel."

"Sure, Sarge. I shot guns before. You know that."

"This is different," Hanford said. "You'll find out."

Lieutenant Michael Stewart, waiting with Captain Colden's Company B to fall into the line of march, saw Hanford and the boy go by. He had time for a moment's brief compassion when he saw the sergeant's big hand touch his stepson's shoulder, and then his voice picked up where it had left off, chanting instructions. His voice joined Colden's clear undertones, both of them talking to all the men, but fixing their eyes on the recruits: "Don't crowd the skirmishers. Remove your ramrods before you shoot. Listen for orders. And keep looking to your corporals and sergeants. That mist is heavy, so be sure you're not firing into the skirmishers. Keep going until you're told to stop. They're just as nervous as you are in that mist. They can't see you coming. Don't run ahead. Stay in formation. The next company on either side may hit rough ground, or we may ourselves. They'll wait for us; we'll wait for them."

It was time. "Let's go," Mike Stewart said. "Let's go, men. Move out! Hump it, now!"

Ahead of the regiment, Colonel Barnes accepted his orders from a courier sent by General Geary, directed his companies into line of battle as they came up, and waved the skirmishers forward. The mist was shifting over the rough terrain; above the 195th it shrouded the tops of the trees, protecting the advance from the rebel guns. The regiment stepped out after the darting skirmishers, slowly at first and stumbling in the underbrush and rocks. A hundred yards went by. The land began to slope upward. The mist billowed and swung ahead of them, as if the pumping breath of seven hundred pairs of lungs was moving it up the mountain. They were out of the mist suddenly, and a rebel battery on the heights swiftly came to bear. Shells burst viciously overhead and in the trees before them. Canister whined and screamed. Rifles in the rebel trenches cracked. Gunfire, yells, screams, and the crashing of underbrush sounded ominously under the blanketing mist.

Jeff Barnes, who had left his horse back at Lookout Creek because of the rough terrain, trotted forward with Major Bailey. Sergeant Comfort, with the colors streaming over his head, held the smooth staff tightly in his right hand, the butt digging into his belly under his belt, and in his left hand he waved a Colt's .44 revolver exactly like the colonel's. It had cost him almost two months' pay to buy it from a soldier in one of Thomas's Ohio regiments. Comfort had to dig in to keep up with the colonel and Major Bailey. His balance was precarious on the rough ground. Comfort's face was red from exertion, but he managed to keep his mouth fixed in a tight grin. He'd follow Barnes to hell or to the top of Lookout Mountain.

Jeff Barnes shared none of Comfort's certainty. The rebels had lines of trenches on the slope filled with veterans. The mist could be just as helpful to them if it continued to climb the mountain as it was doing now. This would be worse than Culp's Hill. It could be very bad.

The skirmishers were darting back through the underbrush under heavy fire from the first line of rebel defenses. Now the trenches came suddenly into sight as the mist lifted. A withering fire struck the double line of attackers.

The charge faltered all along the slope. Regiment after regiment took cover among the ravines and the rock outcroppings. The 195th went down quickly and hugged the ground. Rifles cracked defiance from both sides and powder smoke rolled up to thicken the mist. The rebel artillery was overreaching the Union line.

"We can't stay here, Jeff!" Sam Bailey shouted.

Barnes shook his head. His hand touched his blouse where Kate's portrait, removed from his field desk, rested against his chest. He wondered if he had smashed it when he fell to the ground. Then, just as suddenly, he had another incongruous thought. He'd had no breakfast. A man shouldn't fight on an empty stomach.

"Let's go, Sam," he said. "Get 'em up and running. Tell 'em to yell!"

Within ten seconds officers and non-commissioned officers were on their feet again. They shouted the commands that could scarcely be heard, and then the men were up and running once more.

Private Adam Youngblood ran with Company A. Other men were cursing the rough ground as they stumbled, but Adam had a farmer's respect for natural dangers. He watched where he was putting his feet. A man could break his leg in this jumble of rocks and gnarled brush. He held his Enfield high before him to have it ready to use as well as to balance his plunging body.

Adam looked up every few seconds at the rebel trenches, but he couldn't see a single Johnny. A thick cloud of smoke and mist rolled over the trenches. The flashing orange flames of rebel rifles dotted the face of the cloud. A Minié ball plucked at Adam's hat and sent it flying. Instinctively he crouched lower as he ran. Then he stumbled and went down on one knee, gashing his flesh on the sharp rocks. He looked at the trenches again before he pushed himself back to his feet. Clearly, in a gap in the mist, he saw a rebel crouched at the top of the breastworks, loading his rifle. The rebel raised the weapon. His brown-bearded face turned directly toward Adam Youngblood, or so it seemed.

"Gol, he means to shoot me," Adam whispered to himself. He brought his Enfield to his shoulder at the same time the rebel leveled his weapon.

Adam aimed carefully and squeezed the trigger. The heavy rifle bucked against his shoulder. He saw the rebel's weapon flash, and then the man rolled out of sight into the trench below him.

"It was him or me," Adam whispered. "And I can't let it be me. Not now."

He got up and ran again, limping on the gashed leg. He wondered if that rebel had somebody waiting at home. "It was him or me," Adam said doggedly. "Poor feller."

Other regiments on the lower slope of Lookout Mountain, regiments which had also slowed and stopped at the first smashing im-

pact of rebel fire, were moving forward again. The great line of blue
bodies swept toward the rebel trenches, and here and there along
the line the rebels began to run.

The men from Highland County couldn't see other units. They
couldn't even see full companies on either side of them. The mist
and the brush and the uneven ground kept the arc of vision restricted
to what lay before them. Hooker and his staff, with field glasses
fastened on the wild terrain, cursed the mist that hid the battle. They
had to rely on couriers from Geary, Cruft, and Osterhaus to tell them
how the fight was going.

The fight went well for the Union. The rebels started to abandon
positions as the fierce attack pressed forward in the haze. Dogged
retreat became flight along the west side of Lookout. The Confederates left their rifle pits and pulled in their lines on the mountainside. Geary's division, told to halt at the palisades, would not be
stopped. Over the ledges and boulder-strewn slopes they pushed the
Confederate brigades back up the mountain.

There were pockets of savage resistance. The 195th New York,
after driving the rebels before them from two lines of trenches, ran
into reinforcements for the rebel brigade ahead of them. The Confederates were hastily dug into a brushy ledge footed by a slope of
tumbled rock.

The officers led the charge at the slope and they took the full force
of the first enemy volley. Billy Hasbrouck, leading the right flank,
went down with two Minié balls in his left leg. A rebel ball tore away
Major Hornbeck's jaw. He died slowly. Lieutenant Spector of Company A fell on the slope with several bullets in his chest and belly.
Officers all along the line were wounded, some slightly, some
more seriously. Captain Colden took Company B up the slope on the
left flank and fought his way with revolver and sword into the rebel
position before he was killed by a rifle pushed into his ribs and fired.

Colonel Barnes and Sergeant Comfort went directly up the center
of the rough hill. Comfort yelled savagely as he stumbled ahead
with the colors streaming. Minié balls hit the staff and tore the flag
to tatters, but Comfort was untouched. He fired his revolver at
bearded faces with his left hand. He passed Barnes and reached the
summit. Blue uniforms streamed past him into the breastworks. Comfort thrust the flagstaff into a jumble of rocks and fired his revolver
methodically.

He didn't look back down the slope or he would have left the colors for the first time since he had seized them on Culp's Hill at Gettysburg. Colonel Barnes was on the ground. His right arm had been shattered by a Minié ball just below the shoulder. He tried to get up, but pain and waves of weakness knocked him down again. A soldier helped him to his feet just as the rebels, fleeing, fired another volley. The soldier at Barnes's side crumpled and fell. Another ball struck Barnes's wounded arm. He fell backward and rolled down the slope.

That last rebel volley was succeeded by a few scattering shots from single rebels who reloaded on the run and turned to fire at the Yankees who held the ridge.

One of these shots reached Private Patrick Fuller's heart. He fell dead at Hanford's feet. The first sergeant cried out, then stood staring down at the calm young face of the dead boy. He was a target for every rebel rifle on the mountainside, but he didn't move. His men yelled at him to get his head down, then they stopped yelling. They stared for a second or two at the naked anguish on the sergeant's face and turned their heads away. Tim Tuggle, who had taken young Pat Fuller as a messmate, crawled over to the boy's body. He looked at the boy's bloody blouse, touched the smooth skin of Pat's face, and shook his head sorrowfully.

"I'm sorry, Sarge," he whispered. "I'm awful sorry."

"Back in line," the sergeant cried brokenly. "Leave him to me."

Hanford was crying now, the great racking sobs of a man who has never before in a hard life had reason enough to cry, and so didn't know how to control himself when tears came. His shoulders shook as if he had the ague, and tears flowed like rain down his cheeks. For the first time in his long army career Jack Hanford forgot his duty and deserted his post. He picked up Pat's body in his long arms and made his way down the rocky slope, leaving Company A behind him.

"Where's he going?" a man asked. "What's he going to do with that boy?"

"Never mind," Captain Boudrye said softly. "Load your rifles and get ready. We'll be moving up again."

The order came. Sam Bailey led them out of the rebel breastworks and they headed up the mountain once more, driving the Confederates before them.

On the plateau below, Dr. Renwick had set up his hospital. He worked like a madman, but the stretcher-bearers brought him and his assistant, a young man named Chambers, more casualties than they could handle. Walking wounded were sent back to the division field hospital beyond Lookout Creek. Those who were obviously dying were given morphine and left alone.

"Come here, sir," Chambers called suddenly. He was inspecting the wounds of a row of men who lay on blankets alongside the regimental ambulance. Dr. Renwick was dressing wounds on the other side of the vehicle.

"Take care of it yourself," Renwick snapped. "You know what to do, Chambers. Jesus, man, get busy!"

"This is Colonel Barnes, sir. You'd better come here."

Cursing in a low monotone, Renwick hurried around the wagon. Chambers had already cut away Barnes's blouse and shirt. The two wounds in the colonel's right arm were bleeding steadily. Barnes was unconscious. Renwick sighed heavily and examined the arm with bloodstained fingers. His head shook gently from side to side, as if he were trembling with weariness.

"Get him ready," he said. "I'll go on with these others. Call me when you're all set."

"You're taking it off, sir?" Chambers asked.

"Goddammit, what else?" Renwick turned his back and stumped away, his voice, in helpless anger, trailing curses behind him. Before he could return to the wounded, an excited orderly dragged him off to persuade Jack Hanford to give up the body he had carried down from the mountainside.

"Sergeant, behave yourself," Renwick said sharply, as if scolding an unruly child. "Give that boy to these men here and get back where you belong. They need you."

"Will you take good care of him, Doc?" Hanford said dully. "You do it yourself, Doc?"

"Sure I will," the doctor lied. "Get back to your company, Sergeant. I'm afraid the damn fools aren't done killing each other."

"All right, Doc. You take care of him."

The killing finished, however, at two o'clock in the afternoon, when the rebels had abandoned most of their strong positions, fleeing in disorder toward the Chattanooga Valley. Hooker's men would have swarmed all over them, but the mist settled heavily once more, and orders came to dig in where they were.

During the day Sherman's army had been pounding at the rebel positions on Missionary Ridge, miles across the valley, while the Army of the Cumberland waited in the center for the success of Hooker and Sherman.

When night fell, the campfires of Hooker's troops could be seen everywhere on the sides of Lookout Mountain. The haze lifted and a heavy moon hung over the valley and bathed the sides of the mountain. Telegraph keys were chattering already, bearing fragmentary reports of the first day's action to the waiting governments. "Fighting Joe" Hooker was jubilant in victory; Grant was thinking about what Bragg might be forced to do tomorrow; Sherman paced restively, chewing cigars; Thomas trained his glasses on Missionary Ridge in patient reflection; Bragg was worried.

There was no mist on the twenty-fifth of November. Hooker's army stormed over Lookout Mountain and attacked the rebels on their left flank at Rossville while Sherman pounded all day at the right flank, and Thomas, finally launching his Army of the Cumberland in the center, saw his men refuse to stop when they'd driven the rebels from the first line of rifle pits. Through a day's fighting the men of the Cumberland had watched their rivals, the Army of the Tennessee and Joe Hooker's eastern dudes, pound away at Bragg's forces. Now it was their turn. They paid no heed to officers who told them to dig in at the first line of rebel rifle pits. They eyed the summit of Missionary Ridge, where the great mass of Bragg's army lay waiting in trenches, and they began to yell. Out of the captured rifle pits they stormed, on their way to glory. The rebels retreated slowly, then more swiftly, and soon turned their backs to run all out for the top of the ridge. The men of Thomas's army raced after them. Confederates, astounded by the madness, began to leave strong positions undefended. They turned from the crest of the ridge by the hundreds, then by the thousands, and the Cumberland men had full possession of the height, where they fell exhausted into the rebel trenches.

Braxton Bragg, pressed by Union troops everywhere he looked, retreated sullenly into the state of Georgia, where his gray veterans could lick their wounds.

Back at Chattanooga, Grant was asking Generals Thomas and Granger who had ordered the Cumberland men to keep going up the slope of Missionary Ridge. Thomas said he didn't know; Granger said he didn't order the charge: "When those fellows get started all hell can't stop them."

Jubilation ruled the Union camps that night, excepting here and there around the field hospitals, where men who ministered to the wounded and buried the dead walked softly along lines of blanket-covered forms. The ambulance of the 195th New York had gone along to Rossville with the regiment, with Dr. Chambers in charge. Dr. Renwick had stayed behind at the temporary hospital. Finally he finished all the amputations, probed for all the Minié balls that could be reached, bound and rebound all the wounds, doled out morphine where it was needed, and cursed the war futilely but continuously. Many times during the night of the twenty-fourth of November, and all during the twenty-fifth, he had paused by the cot on which Colonel Barnes lay still and pale, wondering whether the young man would live another hour. He had no fear for the job he had done on Barnes's arm, but he thought the colonel had lost too much blood before and during the amputation. About midnight of November 25, however, he decided that Barnes would live. That was the doctor's victory; he stopped his rounds after looking at the colonel. He wanted to go to bed with victory fresh in his mind; if he continued along the line of wounded, he was sure to find defeat.

Let someone else find it tonight, he told himself. I'm a tired old man and I need some sleep.

29

The sun's low down the sky, Lorena,
The frost gleams where the flowers have been.

FROM THE MIDDLE OF TENNESSEE someone—either Dr. Renwick or Captain Stewart—had reserved a berth for Kate in a sleeping car as far as Cincinnati. She didn't know how it had been done, but she was grateful. When she boarded the passenger train in

Baltimore, the conductor greeted her with cordial respect, telling her with considerable exaggeration that as far as Cincinnati all the services of the railroad were at her command.

It was a long, dreary journey, although the train was comfortable enough and the services offered by the conductor and porters took care of all her needs. She sat by the window gazing out at the wild mountain views of the Alleghanies or the fertile farmlands of Ohio; she read books and magazines, she slept in privacy and comfort in her berth. There were almost interminable waiting periods, however, when the train was sidetracked to allow the passage of military freight and troop trains. Invariably these halts were made at whistle stops or water towers, where there were no accommodations for delayed passengers—no restaurants or tea shops or bookstores or even, in most cases, streets to walk upon and stretch one's legs.

She was alone and lonely; she dreaded the moment that would find her at her husband's bedside in Tennessee, much as she desired to be there; she was weary and worried and sad.

She had no knowledge of Jeff's condition; at times during the long trip she suddenly found herself thinking that he might be dead, that she was on her way to bring his body home. There had been a series of telegraph messages from Tennessee, first from Chattanooga and then from a place called Tullahoma. It seemed to her that this war as it affected her life had been a series of telegraph messages and bulletins. For the rest of her days she would be unable to see a yellow telegraph form without a moment of sudden fear.

Dr. Renwick's messages had been brief and matter-of-fact. From them she knew only that Jeff had been wounded—she surmised that it had been at Lookout Mountain—and that his condition was "satisfactory." That could mean he was recovering, and it could mean that he was dying. Dr. Renwick had had the foresight to know that she would want to go to Tennessee; he had told her with the exasperating economy of the telegraph: YOUR PRESENCE WOULD BE BENEFICIAL.

Michael Stewart—bless the man!—had telegraphed at length three times. The messages had said in turn that Jeff was improved, that accommodations were provided for her if she could come, and that the Baltimore & Ohio was holding the reservation for her from December 1 until she claimed it. More than that, Stewart's words had given her as much sympathy and reassurance as could be conveyed by a mechanical contrivance. The printed signature to his messages, CAPTAIN MICHAEL STEWART, had given her the only pleasure she had known since the casualty lists from Chattanooga had started to come through. She had always believed he would make a good officer, and she was happy that he had been promoted to company command.

The cost of that promotion, however, appalled her. Thank God, Kate told herself again and again, that Ned came through it.

Constantly her thoughts returned to Jeff. Neither Stewart nor Renwick had told her about his wound. It was serious, certainly. "Condition satisfactory," in Renwick's words. They had ominous meaning.

At Louisville, after four days, she changed trains once again, for Nashville and beyond. Tullahoma. What kind of name was that? She remembered that the town had been the headquarters of the XII Corps in the days when the 195th had been shuttling back and forth before the battle. Maybe the regiment was going into winter quarters there.

The journey that had been tiresome and interminable now became an ordeal. The train was made up of an old locomotive pulling a string of decrepit coaches. There were no sanitary arrangements. The heat that was furnished in each car came from a potbelly stove at one end—if you sat near it, you were broiled; if you moved away, you shivered. The coaches stank with the rankness of unwashed bodies and clothing, the odor of stale or decaying food, the sour smell of tobacco juice; they were permeated by the sickening sweetness of raw, cheap whiskey. The plush seats furnished safe transportation for vermin, which, like the rebel cavalry, were ever ready to sally forth to forage.

The train was packed with soldiers. Many of them were bearded, hard-eyed, foul-tongued veterans of the Army of the Tennessee on their way back from convalescent furloughs or duty with funeral parties for casualties of Missionary Ridge. "Uncle Billy's Boys," they called themselves. Hour after hour they cursed Sherman with drunken affection, calling him all the foul names they could think of, but ready to smash in the teeth of any Cumberland or Potomac soldier who ventured to agree with them that he was a crazy son of a bitch.

She tried to close her ears to their talk; apparently they kept forgetting that there was a lady somewhere in the car. After a while she got used to it, realizing that obscenity was second nature to them.

Before the train had rattled very far from Louisville, the officers in the car had congregated in the seats around Kate, as much to be as near as possible to a lovely woman as to protect her sensibilities from the common touch of the enlisted men. There were six or seven of them, young men with the bars of captains and lieutenants. They were all westerners, as far as she could tell, and she was quite surprised at the casual manner in which they wore their military dignity. Their uniforms were a hodgepodge of whatever had suited them in civilian life transferred to Union blue. They were for the most part young men from the midwestern farm states and had none of the spit and polish of the officers in the Army of the Potomac.

She was grateful for their company, although she remained quiet and aloof throughout their many attempts to engage her in conversation. Polite silence and an occasional smile seemed to please them, however. They quieted the more boisterous of the soldiers in the car with an exercise of command that belied their unmilitary appearance. She was particularly glad they were present when the day drew to a close and the train was halted for long periods at one switch or another. She didn't think that she would have been safe otherwise—the single woman in a car with thirty drunken soldiers.

The train stopped at Nashville in the early darkness of the December night. Soldiers and civilians transferred to another train more battle-worn than the first. A half hour later they were rolling south once more. Kate found a companion on the new train, a quiet Tennessee woman on her way to a place called Shelbyville—quite near Tullahoma, she said. She told Kate to close her eyes and get some sleep. There was plenty of time, she said. They wouldn't get to Tullahoma until midnight.

Kate couldn't sleep, however. She was too close now, too near the end of the journey. Soon she would see him. It seemed to her—she tried to brush the thought away and failed—that she was going to meet a stranger, not her husband. In the weeks that had preceded Lookout Mountain, she had sought vainly in his letters for the words of love that would have eased the ache in her heart. Instead, he seemed to draw farther away, as if the miles that separated them had given birth to some kind of geometrical progression in the distance between their spirits. The war, the regiment, the coming

campaigns, the officers with whom he served—she knew too much
about them and not enough about his love.

Now that she had come to nurse him, perhaps she could turn his
mind back to her, back to the tender days of long ago. Long ago?
One year and five months, that's all it was.

The conductor thrust his head through the door of the car and
bawled, "Tullahoma! Station stop, Tullahoma!"

"Here we are, my dear," said the Tennessee woman.

They descended from the train into a mob of unruly soldiers, some
trying to get off, as many more trying to get on. The men on the
train were leaning out the windows, jeering at the men of the XII
Corps who stood on the platform. Kate heard an insistent chant from
the train: "Bull Run! Did you run at Bull Run?"

A soldier on the platform reached out a heavy fist and caught a
jeering westerner flush in the mouth. A tooth bounced on the rough
boards at Kate's feet. With a roar of rage, the XV Corps man came
plunging through the window at the XII Corps soldier who had hit
him. Within ten seconds a free-for-all was going full blast on the
platform. Kate pressed herself against the side of the train. The Tennessee woman had been swept away by the crowd. Kate tried to
shrink, but brawling men fell against her. Above the sounds of combat she heard the shrilling of provost guard's whistles.

Suddenly the melee parted before her. Mike Stewart was pushing his way through. She cried out in relief. He put his arm around
her shoulders and led her through the brawlers. She lost her hat and
took a numbing kick in the shin from an army brogan, but otherwise
she was all right. She shivered with relief when he got her away from
the crowd.

"Are you all right, Kate?" he asked gently.

She turned her face to his. "I'm all right," she said.

"I'm sorry," he said abruptly. "I meant to say 'Mrs. Barnes.' I've
heard your first name so many times I used it without thinking."

She nodded. "I don't know what I would have done without you,
Captain."

"It's over now," he said, glancing back at the milling soldiers on
the lighted station platform. "The provost guard is always ready for
trouble. We don't get on so well with the Army of the Tennessee."

"That's fairly obvious. Where do we go, Captain? Where is Jeff?"

"I'll take you right to him. We're camped outside town, and the colonel has a room in a fine house near by. There's a room for you waiting."

"I can't thank you for all you've done, Captain Stewart."

"No need to thank me." He led her to a waiting buggy. "I'll go back for your bags," he said after he'd helped her into the vehicle.

"Wait," she said swiftly. "How is he? How is my husband?"

"Better," he said. "He's well out of danger, the doctor says."

He left her with a reassuring smile. He was back with her luggage in less than a minute. He climbed to the seat of the buggy beside her and picked up the reins. "It isn't far," he said. "The colonel is with some people named Rush. He's very comfortable."

She remembered the landlady in Baltimore who had taken Yankee money but had made no attempt to hide her rebel sympathies. "They aren't rebels, are they?"

He shook his head. "Lots of Union people here in Tennessee," he said. "These folks have a son in the XV Corps. They're glad to do all they can for the colonel, and they'll be pleased to have you."

"No one has told me," she said hesitantly, "anything about Jeff's wound. How bad was it, Captain? Are you sure he'll be all right?"

He turned his head, surprised. "I thought Dr. Renwick told you. I was sure he would."

"Nothing about the wound," she said. She touched his arm with her fingers. "What is it, Captain?"

"Two Minié balls in his right arm," Stewart answered slowly. "They shattered the bone."

A soft cry escaped her. She bowed her head for a few seconds. When she spoke, he had to lean toward her to hear the words. "Did the doctor—did he operate?"

Stewart nodded. "He had to, Mrs. Barnes. There was nothing else to do."

She was silent for a while. "I see," she said finally. "Yes. Have you talked to Jeff?"

"Every day," he said. "He says he doesn't want company, but I force myself on him. He won't admit it, but it does him good to hear about the regiment."

"Does he know I'm coming?"

"I told him," Stewart answered simply.

"And what did he say?"

"He doesn't say much about anything, Mrs. Barnes. You'll do him a world of good just being here."

"I hope I will."

They continued for a time in silence, until she asked him how long he'd been a captain.

"Six days now," he said, grinning. "I was a lieutenant less than a month. I figure to be a general by Christmas. There have been a lot of promotions since Lookout Mountain. You know our officers were hit harder than the ranks. Your brother is a major now, and I have his company. Sam Bailey is a lieutenant colonel, in temporary command. Jack Hanford is my first lieutenant. The colonel's brother is captain of Company B, succeeding Captain Colden."

She turned in surprise. Ned a major, and Walter Barnes a captain! "Who recommended the promotions, Captain Stewart?"

"Colonel Bailey," he answered. "He didn't waste any time reorganizing."

"Does my husband approve?"

"He hasn't said anything to me about them," Stewart said. "As a matter of fact, Mrs. Barnes, he didn't show much interest when I told him. He just remarked that Hanford was a good soldier and should have been an officer long ago."

They arrived at the Rush house shortly before one o'clock in the morning. Mrs. Rush was waiting for them. She was a tall, lean woman with a broad face and an engaging toothy smile. "I'm sure glad to see you, Mrs. Barnes. A man's wife is his best nurse when he's flat on his back. You come on in right away and we'll get you settled."

"Thank you," Kate said. "I'd like to see my husband first."

"He's asleep," Mrs. Rush sighed. "He sleeps a lot. The operation and all has left him weak. We can look in on him if you want."

She led the way up a flight of carpeted stairs, holding a lamp high to show the way. "Down at the end of the hall," she whispered.

She opened a door and led the way in. The lamp cast its glow over a big room where a massive bed was set between the two eastern windows.

Kate's eyes were on the figure in the huge bed. He was covered to his shoulders by blankets. He lay flat on his back. She crossed and looked down at him. He was breathing heavily, but his face was not relaxed in slumber. There were lines in his forehead as if he were frowning; the corners of his eyes were traced with crow's feet, and his mouth was set grimly. He seemed to sense the disturbance in the room; he rolled restlessly and she had a glimpse of bulky white bandages encasing his right shoulder.

30

Yes, these were words of thine, Lorena—
They are within my memory yet.

HE WAS AWAKE when she entered his room in the morning. He lay on his back with his head turned toward the open window where Mrs. Rush was airing his bedding. She had covered him with a thick comforter to protect him from the raw winter air that whistled through the window.

He turned his head slowly when he heard Kate at the door. She smiled at him, blinking away the tears that came so swiftly when she saw him. She crossed the room quickly and bent to kiss him tenderly.

"Kate," he said softly before her lips touched his. "Hello, Kate."

There was neither warmth nor spirit in the pressure of his thin lips. While she kissed him, his hand went to her shoulder, touched it, then fell away.

"I came as fast as I could, darling," she said, kneeling now and holding her face against his. His arm rested beside her body. Her fingers sought his hand and gripped it.

"It's a long trip," he said simply.

Mrs. Rush, who had been dusting the furniture, started for the door, talking as she went. "I'll leave you two. Mrs. Barnes, you let them bedclothes air for a couple minutes more, then take 'em in and close the window. The fire will warm up the room again right away. Don't let him pull that comforter away from his neck. He mustn't get a chill. I'll bring up a breakfast tray soon as I can."

She left, closing the door firmly.

Kate sat up, putting out her hand to smooth Jeff's sandy hair away from his brow. "I haven't talked to the doctor," she said, "but Captain Stewart said you'd be all right now. I'm so happy, Jeff."

His thin lips drew away from his teeth in a humorless smile. His eyes were cold and hard when they turned from her face to look down at his right shoulder, hidden by the comforter.

"What does a soldier do with one arm, Kate?" he said in a level voice.

"There are a thousand things you can do," she said quickly. "The first thing to do is get your strength back, and then you go home with me for a long rest."

"No, Kate, I'm not going home," he said. "When I'm up and around, I'll go back to duty. I'll spend the winter teaching Sam Bailey all I know about handling the regiment. Then, in the spring, when the campaign starts, I'll step down."

"And what then, Jeff? You'll resign?"

He shook his head wearily. "I can't command in the field, but there must be a job for me in Washington. Some kind of job until the war's over."

She spoke brightly, determined to cheer him. "I'll keep trying to take you back to Highland Landing for a rest. I want you to come."

He smiled briefly. "It won't work, Kate. I must go through to the end, like all the rest." He paused, as if listening to the sound of a drill sergeant's voice that came faintly from the neighboring pasture. "I wanted to take the regiment all the way," he said slowly. "Now they'll have to go on without me."

31

Hark! Was it the night wind that rustles the leaves?
Was it the moonlight so wondrously flashing?

CAPTAIN MICHAEL STEWART and Lieutenant Jack Hanford sat bundled in greatcoats, on upended nail kegs, watching Company B whale the daylights out of Company A in a baseball game. The new sport, which had been slowly growing in the urban centers of the North before the war, had swept like a crown fire through the Union army. There were ten to fifteen men on a side; the players wore no gloves; the pitcher was required to throw with an underhand motion; the bats were often whittled wagon tongues.

Company B of the 195th New York, composed mainly of young men who had played the game in Highland Landing, promised to become the champions of the XII Corps.

Mike was delivered from watching his men absorb the rest of their beating by the arrival of Sergeant Comfort at the frozen pasture that served as a ball field. Comfort eyed the ball game with the disdain of a man who has no time for child's play. He saluted casually, then told Stewart that the colonel wanted to see him.

At the Rush house Comfort vanished into the kitchen, where he was always certain of pie and coffee or cake, served by Winnie Rush, who had never before in her eighteen years been privileged to meet a certified, A No. 1 hero. Winnie was a plain girl, not nearly so pretty or agreeable as some of the girls back in Cedar Bush, but Comfort had learned the prime rule of foraging: take what you can get, better days are coming. As long as the pies, cakes, and puddings continued, he wouldn't complain.

Kate Barnes met Captain Stewart in the vestibule. She took his slouch hat (almost all the officers and most of the men had switched to black felt since coming West, just as the different corps of the Army of the Tennessee and the Army of the Cumberland were sewing corps badges to their uniforms) and she helped him with his greatcoat.

"It's about his brother," she said. "He's worried about Walter. He'll question you."

"I don't see much of Walter," Stewart said easily.

"That's just it. He and Ned go gambling with the sutlers, and now there's a girl. Jeff wants to find out about her."

Stewart nodded. "Yes. I've heard of her. I know nothing about her, though." That was a half-truth at best. He couldn't tell Kate Barnes what he'd heard, but certainly he knew nothing of the woman through personal experience.

"Jeff shouldn't get excited," Kate said worriedly. "I hope you can calm him down. Whatever he knows about this woman, it's troubling him."

She took him upstairs to Jeff's room. The colonel waved him to a chair beside the bed. It had been several days since Stewart had paid him a visit. He noticed that Jeff's color was better, that his face and neck seemed to be filling out, that he was propped up in bed by pillows behind his back. The bandaged stump of his right arm was hidden under a quilted dressing gown.

"Hello, Mike," Barnes said. "Has Hanford stopped brooding about that boy?"

"It's hard to say. I think so, but it goes pretty deep. We had a talk about it just before I came over here. He seems to be feeling better about it."

Barnes nodded, then picked up a letter that lay on the comforter at his side. "This is from my mother, Mike. Walter has been writing her about a girl he's met here. Now he says he's going to marry her. You know about it?"

Stewart hesitated, then nodded. Jeff looked toward the door, where Kate stood silently. "You'd better leave us alone, Kate."

"All right, Jeff." She went out and closed the door.

Barnes looked directly at Stewart. "This girl is a whore, isn't she, Mike?"

"I don't know that much about her, sir."

Barnes nodded impatiently. "Her name is Christine Smithson. She's a widow. Her husband was with Alabama troops, killed at Shiloh. They had money once; she doesn't have any left, but she lives in luxury. She's pretty, she's smart, and she hasn't any morals. She has a mulatto servant named Susie, who entertains enlisted men while the Smithson woman has the officers. Is that about right?"

"Why are you telling me this, sir?"

"If I were able to get out of this bed, I'd take care of the matter myself. As it is, I want you to do it."

"Why me, sir?"

"There's a simple answer to that. You're intelligent, you're Walter's friend, and you can handle it without a hullabaloo. This is what I want you to do: make up a detail from your own company and Walter's company, then you and Walter go to the woman's house. Arrest any soldiers from our regiment or the Pennsylvania outfit you find there, including officers. Give the woman and her servant an hour to pack, padlock the house, mark it 'Off Limits,' and put the women on the train for either Chattanooga or Nashville. Make it Nashville. Get 'em away from the troops."

"This is a job for the provost guard, sir. Division ought to handle it."

Jeff shook his head swiftly. "Orders came down for us to do it. The women have been specializing in our men and the Pennsylvania Dutch boys. General Williams told Bailey to get rid of 'em. Bailey told me, and I'm telling you."

"Yes, sir. Can I speak further, Jeff?"

"Go ahead, Mike. I know it's rough on you to take Walter with you. But he's got to learn."

"That's exactly it, sir. Nobody has had the heart to tell him about this Smithson woman. He's wild about her—he acts like a schoolboy. In the beginning the rest of us thought he knew what he was doing and nobody said anything. But one night at mess Bookstaver made a remark about her—something to the effect that he knew a local widow who slept only with her friends, and as far as he knew, she hadn't an enemy in the world. Walter jumped him and probably would have killed him if we hadn't pulled him away. I could do it quietly, without Walter, sir. She'd be gone; he'd never hear of her again. He's young, sir. He'd get over it quickly."

Barnes spoke impatiently. "You miss my point, Mike. He's been in the army for a year and a half and he still acts like a child. He's got to grow up. He's got to mature. He's leading a company now. To do his job, he has to be as hard as flint. The only way he'll learn is to face up to duty and discipline. What you propose would only shield him from the facts. He'd moon about her, drink more than he does already, get deeper into the sutlers' debt in those card games that Boudrye takes him to."

"If I may say so, Jeff, I don't like it. I'd like to leave Walter out of it."

"You have your orders, Mike. Let me say this. When the spring campaign starts, I'll hand this regiment over to Sam Bailey. He'll take you wherever you're going. I think I can tell you where that will be. Before I do, however, I'll tell you this: when you leave these winter quarters and leave me behind, every man of you must be ready for the hardest, toughest most brutal campaign you've dreamed of. The whole war hinges on what you men are going to do in 1864. There will be no moon-struck boys leading companies of this regiment on that campaign. Walter must learn to be an officer, and he has only three or four months to do it in."

"I don't want to offend you, but you ought to pay more attention to him yourself. That's his main trouble. He takes to Ned because you ignore him."

"While he's an officer in this regiment, he'll get no favoritism from me. You have your orders, Captain."

"Yes, sir. I'll take care of it tonight."

Jeff seemed to indicate dismissal, and Mike saluted and turned away. Barnes called him back.

"Mike, I appreciate what you say even if I don't agree with you. When I get up out of here, I'll treat him less like a plebe at the Academy and more like an officer. He's done well enough, I suppose, except for the drinking and gambling."

"He has, sir. He's a much better officer than he was a year ago."

"I told you before that I think I know where you're going in the spring. Would you care to guess?"

Mike nodded soberly.

"If Grant is the general I think he is, he'll take you to Atlanta. He'll cut the South in half. That will be the beginning of the end."

"Yes, sir. It seems logical. But you'll be coming with us, Jeff."

Barnes shook his head. "I'll be going to Washington to sit at a desk and sort papers. Bailey will take the regiment."

"I hope you're wrong, sir. We've come this far with you. We'd like to go all the way."

"Thanks, Mike. I'm afraid not. Will you tell my wife to come up when you leave?"

"Yes, sir," Stewart saluted once more and left the room.

Stewart informed Walter Barnes that, pursuant to the colonel's orders, he and eight men from his company were to be ready for a provost's detail at nine o'clock that night. Stewart picked that hour because a northbound train was scheduled to stop at Tullahoma at eleven. There would be no delay in getting the women out of town.

"What is this, Mike?" Walter asked when he arrived at regimental headquarters with his men. "It's taking me out of a card game. You're O.D. Can't you handle it yourself?"

"Your brother's orders," Stewart said.

"What's the job? Have the boys been tearing up the town again?"

"No. Nothing like that. It's our problem and General Williams said we had to handle it. Jeff picked me and you to do it."

"Do what?"

"There's a woman to be sent to Nashville with her servant. We're to close up her house, arrest any soldiers we find there—our regiment or any other—and put the woman and her servant girl on the eleven o'clock train for Nashville."

"What are they, spies?"

"No, Walter. They're prostitutes. The woman entertains officers; the servant girl sells herself to the men."

"And we have to run 'em out? All right, let's go. If we get done with it early enough, I can get back to the poker game."

Christine Smithson lived in a rambling, two-storied frame house on the outskirts of Tullahoma, about two miles from the camp of the 195th New York. Stewart had seen the house many times, but he had seen Christine Smithson only once. That had been at a dinner party she had given for the regimental officers shortly after the 195th's arrival at Tullahoma. Mrs. Smithson had been alone, and she had presided at a table lined with officers. Before a half hour had gone by, Stewart had understood her purpose.

He'd been prepared to tell Walter where they were going, but Walter hadn't asked. Now Mike delayed, knowing that he would have to tell the truth before they reached her house but putting off the unpleasant task as long as possible.

They walked side by side on the rough road that led out from town toward her house. The men marched in formation behind them.

"I'd have been out here myself tonight," Walter said suddenly, "if I'd had word from Christine. I'd like to see her every night, but she has a busy life. She always has guests, you know."

Mike looked sharply at him. Was the boy finally suspicious?

"Ladies from town," Walter explained. "Church work and things like that."

The young man's voice fairly sang when he spoke of Mrs. Smithson. There was no doubt that he was completely caught by love.

"We can look at the house when we go by," Walter continued. "If she doesn't have guests, we can stop in. Her girl Susie can give the men coffee. Susie is fond of soldiers."

I should think she is, Mike thought wryly. Give them coffee indeed! Well, it's time. I've got to tell him.

"Walter," he began, "you're very fond of Mrs. Smithson, aren't you?"

Barnes laughed. "As if you didn't know, Mike. Tell you a secret. I've asked her to marry me. She hasn't said yes or no, but I think she will."

"You love her, then."

"I do, Mike." With youthful pride of conquest, he continued haltingly, "And I know she loves me. A woman like her wouldn't——" He stopped. Had it not been so dark, Stewart could have seen his red face. "Well, I just know she does. She's proved it. I've been sort of helping her out, you know. I've been winning lately in the poker games, and that makes it easier. It's funny, but she's too proud to ask for help. I always leave some money where she'll be sure to find it."

"Others have been helping her, too," Mike said.

Walter turned in surprise. "I'm glad of that. I guess she charms everybody."

"Walter, I don't know how to tell you this. The only way to do it, I guess, is to say it right out. Her house is right up the road, isn't it?"

"There where you see the lights. What are you talking about, Mike?"

"That's where we're going, Walter."

"To Christine's? I thought you said . . ." Walter's voice trailed off. "What is this, Mike?" he said suddenly.

"You heard me," Mike said, anger gripping him. He shouldn't be the one to do this! "That's where we're going."

Walter nodded. "I think I see. You mean Susie. All those soldiers who visit her in the kitchen. And I thought she was just a friendly colored girl. Who's the other woman, Mike?"

"The other woman is Christine Smithson."

"What the hell are you talking about?" Walter cried. "You better shut your mouth, Mike, or by God, I'll shut it for you! You're a goddamn liar!"

"No. I've known it right along. So has everyone else, excepting you. She has two dozen officers visiting her at various times. They all pay for the privilege."

Barnes grabbed Mike by the shoulder. "Take it back or I'll kill you. So help me God, I will!"

Stewart shook his head unhappily. "I'm telling the truth, Walter."

A sudden hammering blow from Barnes's right hand caught Stewart on the cheek. He went down into the mud of the road. Soldiers crowded around the two officers, several of them restraining Barnes, who was trying to draw his revolver.

Mike Stewart pushed himself to his feet. "I'm sorry, Walter. I didn't want to tell you. Nobody did. But Colonel Barnes said you had to see for yourself. Now will you calm down and leave that gun alone, or do I have to have the men hold you?"

"Shut your stinking mouth!" Barnes shouted. "Let's go. Let's prove you wrong, Stewart, and then you and Jeff will answer to me. By God, you will!"

A lane led from the house to the main road. Halfway down the lane Stewart posted his men, telling them to surround the house and arrest any man who tried to run. Then he, with Barnes at his side, silent and shaking, went to the front door of the house. He didn't bother to knock, finding the door unlatched. He pushed it open and walked in.

They went up the carpeted stairs to a dimly lit hallway.

"Where's her room, Walter?"

"Find it yourself, goddamn you!"

Mike didn't answer, but looked at the several doors in the corridor. Light was shining at the sill of one of them. Mike walked across to it. "Let me," Walter said suddenly. "I suppose you'd open it without knocking."

He tapped at the door. Instantly a woman's voice answered, "Susie? What is it?"

"It's Walter, Chris. Can you come out a minute?"

This time a man's voice answered, a drunken voice raised in shrill amusement, "Go 'way, Barnes. It ain't your night."

Bookstaver, Stewart thought.

With a swift thrust of his arm, Barnes threw the door open. Bookstaver was in the bed, peering owlishly at his two fellow officers in the doorway. He grinned at them drunkenly. "One at a time, fellers. One at a time."

"Shut up, you lout!" Mrs. Smithson said. She was hastily trying to clothe herself with a dressing gown. Walter Barnes stared at her in sick horror. His lips trembled. He seemed about to cry.

Mike Stewart, looking at Mrs. Smithson, could understand why men would spend a month's pay to visit her. She was undoubtedly beautiful, although the beauty was already beginning to coarsen. She had a firm, full body and an intelligent face, with bright eyes and wide lips. Her hair, dark red, hung gracefully at her shoulders. She had been startled when Barnes opened the door, but she recovered easily.

"What's the meaning of this, Captain?" she asked Stewart.

"You're under arrest, ma'am. You'll place yourself under arrest, Bookstaver, and report to Colonel Barnes in the morning."

"And what am I arrested for?" she asked evenly.

"You know the charges, ma'am. They'll be withdrawn when you get on the eleven o'clock train to Nashville."

"If I don't choose to go?"

"You'll go, ma'am, I'm sure. We'll leave you now to dress. Pack anything you want to take with you. My men will carry it to the station for you."

Walter Barnes spoke then in a low, choked voice. "Christine, tell me it's not true. Tell me, Christine!"

"For Christ's sake, Walter, don't blubber," she said. "Of course, it's true. Why did you think I took your money?"

"I thought——" he whispered. "I thought I was the only man."

She smiled. "Poor Walter. I'm sorry you had to find me out."

He turned and ran from the room. They could hear his boots pounding heavily on the carpeted stairs.

"The end of a good thing," the woman said. "All right, Captain. Send Susie up to me, will you?"

"I will," Stewart said. He went out and closed the door. He hurried for the stairs. He intended to find Walter Barnes right away. What comfort could he give the young man, so deeply in love and now so terribly disillusioned?

He had gone down three steps when he heard the crack of a Colt's .44 revolver. He stopped where he was, listening. He heard the soldiers shouting.

The door of Mrs. Smithson's bedroom opened and Bookstaver stepped into the hall, clad only in his woolen drawers. "What was that, Mike?" he cried.

"I think," Stewart answered heavily, "that it was Walter."
He started down the stairs.

32

Save up yer pennies and put away yer rocks,
And you'll always have tobacco in yer old tobaccy box!

MAJOR EDWARD BOUDRYE never bothered to total the debt
he owed from his poker losses. He knew that Hosea Breed, sutler of
the 195th New York, and Milt Woodward, of the neighboring Pennsylvania regiment, were keeping accounts for him.

Therefore he was disagreeably surprised one night, after two
hours' play in Breed's hut, to be told that he owed almost a thousand
dollars. He realized that he must have lost more heavily than he'd
thought, especially on nights when he was drunk.

"I haven't any chance of getting that kind of money," he said
helplessly. "I didn't think it was that much."

"You got to pay it, Ned," Breed said amiably. He was a big, florid-
faced man with an aldermanic smile. Before he'd obtained the sutler's concession for the 195th, he'd been a court bailiff in Highland
Landing. "We wouldn't press you now, only we need the money for
supplies. We got some business deals on down the line a ways. You
wouldn't want to know the details. They got to do with folks who
ain't what you'd call Union sympathizers."

"Matter of fact, they don't sympathize much with anybody,"
Woodward added, "unless he's got a full pocketbook."

"Let me tell it, Milt," Breed said sharply. "Now, Ned, these folks
has sold us some merchandise, delivery subject to Union patrols.
We're to pick it up south of Fayetteville."

"That's near the Alabama line," Ned said.

"You're right, my boy. They can bring it that far without trouble.
From there on, it's our slice of pie. To handle it, we need two things."

"I'm listening," Ned said.

"First off, we need a pass to show any patrols we might meet on the back roads between the Alabama line and here. A pass signed by somebody like Colonel Bailey, say."

Ned nodded.

"Second off, we need somebody—a major of the 195th, say—in the railroad yards in Tullahoma on the night we bring the merchandise in. Somebody who'd see that the stuff could be loaded into three freight cars, or maybe four, and sent on to Nashville. If it gets to Nashville without no trouble, we don't have to worry. There's folks in Nashville waitin' on it."

"What is it?" Ned asked.

"Cotton."

"And you want me to be the man here in Tullahoma?"

"That's right, Ned. You owe us a thousand dollars. Every time we bring in a shipment, we'll clip two hundred and fifty greenbacks off your account. Four shipments and you're clear. It's easy as pie, Ned. All done at night and nobody the wiser."

"And if I get caught?"

"How you goin' to get caught, boy? That Sam Bailey is slow as molasses and twice as thick. And Barnes still sticks to his room. Who's goin' to catch you? Just let us know a week ahead when you're goin' to be in charge at the railroad."

"Sounds all right," Ned admitted. "I'll think about it and let you know."

He thought over the scheme for twelve hours, then agreed to do it. It was a simple matter to get Colonel Bailey, who signed papers without taking the trouble to read them, to sign the travel and transport papers for the sutlers.

Everything seemed to go well on the night picked for the shipment. Boudrye set his men to unloading ammunition from freight cars at one end of the yards while he hurried to the other end, where a locomotive was making up a string of empties for Nashville. Breed appeared from the darkness to tell Ned that the train crew had been paid to keep their mouths shut, and that the wagonloads of cotton were coming through Tullahoma disguised as bales of straw and driven by Negroes.

"It's goin' smooth as silk," Breed said.

It wasn't quite that smooth, however. Sergeant Sam Comfort, who had spent the early evening loafing in the Rush kitchen with Winnie Rush, and, incidentally, eating large quantities of tapioca pudding, arrived on the scene. He carried a bucket of lunch for Major Boudrye, cold chicken and cornbread sent down by the major's sister. Kate had made a custom of sending her brother good food on nights when he was on duty. Comfort had found the men of the 195th; they'd told him the major was at the other end of the yards.

Comfort paused in the darkness, wondering, as he had all the way from the Rush house, whether he should swipe just one piece of golden fried chicken. Boudrye would never miss it; the bucket was heavy with chicken.

Comfort agreed with himself that he was hungrier than the major was; he sat down on a pile of railroad ties and opened the bucket. He chewed at a chicken breast and watched the string of wagons roll across the freight yard and pull alongside the train. Then he watched the Negroes begin to load the bales.

What were they sending straw to Nashville for? There was never enough straw around here for the officers' horses. By God, Comfort told himself, that was a damn foolish business.

"But that ain't straw," he said to himself in a half whisper. "One man could lift a bale of straw that size with his little finger. Them boys are workin' like mules."

The sutler Breed wouldn't be fooling with straw anyway. Neither would the Pennsylvanian, Woodward, who suddenly appeared in the dim light of the lanterns at the train. And, Comfort added, what's Boudrye doing there?

Comfort stowed the bucket away among the railroad ties. He'd pick it up later and finish the chicken. He made his way carefully out of the railroad area and then began to run. It wasn't more than a half mile to the Rush house. Those colored boys were working slow. There'd be time if he ran all the way. He hoped he wouldn't come up against a provost guard in the streets; they'd want to know why he was running.

Comfort was not an informer or a sneak. He considered himself Colonel Barnes's eyes and ears in the regiment as long as the colonel was unable to move freely in the camp. Everything that Comfort saw or heard was not relayed to Barnes. In his own way, Comfort was as proud of the 195th New York as Barnes was. Now, as he hurried to tell Barnes what he had seen, the sergeant was not thinking at all of Major Boudrye. If he had been, he might have stopped running, shrugged his shoulders, and gone back to finish the chicken. Comfort liked Boudrye for his generosity and friendliness, but he had no respect for him as an officer. Therefore he gave Boudrye's place in the cotton deal no consideration at all.

Hosea Breed, the sutler, was the man upon whom Comfort wanted the ax to fall. "Greenback" Breed, he was called by the men. There were many men in the 195th who weren't experts in the science of arithmetical progression; Breed was known for his speed in fuddling their minds. "Sugar is twenty cents a pound, four pounds for a dollar. Take four—one greenback."

Sergeant Comfort knew he had Breed over a barrel. The prohibition against smuggling contraband cotton had no loopholes.

Comfort was out of breath when he reached the Rush house, where everyone but Colonel Barnes had already gone to bed. The colonel was outside on the wide wooden porch smoking a final cigar before going up to his room. For the better part of a minute he couldn't get the sense of Comfort's story.

"Get your breath, Sergeant. Then tell me slowly."

"We got him cold, sir. Breed, I mean. Loadin' cotton on a freight train. Bales and bales of it."

Finally Barnes understood. He threw his cigar from the porch in a flashing arc. "Saddle my horse, Sergeant! Take Mr. Rush's mare for yourself. Hurry up now!"

Barnes went into the house for his greatcoat and his hat. Kate came downstairs wrapped in a dressing gown.

"What are you up to, Jeff?"

"Trouble at the railroad," he said. "I've got to go down there."

"Let Sam Bailey take care of it."

"We haven't time. You go back to bed, Kate. I'll be all right."

She made no further protests, but helped him with his greatcoat. By the time he returned to the porch, Comfort had the horses ready. He helped Barnes climb into the saddle.

Several times during the fast ride into Tullahoma, Jeff was in danger of pitching from his mount. The loss of his right arm had affected his sense of balance. He gripped the horse firmly with his knees and held tightly to the saddle with his left hand.

They picked up a provost's guard of four men on the way to the railroad depot. Barnes told them to follow to the freight yards.

The cotton was already loaded when Barnes and Comfort slowed their horses at the entrance to the yards. The animals had to pick their way carefully across the tracks. Before Barnes reached the freight train, it was already moving. Even though they couldn't hear him above the noise of the locomotive, the train crew saw his gestures commanding them to halt, but they ignored them. The train gathered speed and rolled north out of the yards.

The two sutlers and Ned Boudrye stood where they were when Barnes rode up to them. The Negroes who had hauled the cotton faded away into the darkness.

"What's the trouble, Colonel?" Breed said pleasantly.

"Have you placed these men under arrest, Major?" Barnes asked Boudrye.

Boudrye didn't answer. He looked from Breed to Woodward and then back at Barnes.

Comfort leaned across to Barnes. "I forgot to tell you, sir," he whispered hesitantly. "Major Boudrye was here all the time."

"Arrest?" Breed asked, laughing. "What for, Colonel?"

"Shipping contraband cotton, as you well know, Mr. Breed. Were you in this, Ned?"

Boudrye belatedly took his cue from Breed. "In what, Jeff? I don't know what you're talking about."

Barnes turned in his saddle to speak to the sergeant in charge of the provost's guard, who had just arrived with his men. "Sergeant, place these two men under arrest." He pointed to Breed and Woodward. "I'll make a report on the charges in the morning. You can tell your commanding officer that they were caught shipping contraband cotton." Then he looked at Ned Boudrye. "Major Boudrye, place yourself under arrest. You'll confine yourself to your quarters until you have orders to the contrary."

"Look here, Colonel!" Breed said quickly, motioning to Woodward to be silent. "Mr. Woodward and I did that train crew a favor. We had a few bales of straw that we picked up out in the country. We came down here and loaded 'em on the train. That crew is bringing sheep down from Nashville on their next trip. Ask Major Boudrye."

"I'd advise you to keep your mouth shut, Breed," Barnes said abruptly. "You can tell that story to the court that tries you."

"He's right, Jeff," Boudrye said. "Where did you get the idea about cotton?"

"It don't take three niggers to lift a bale of straw," Comfort said laconically.

"That's enough, Comfort," Barnes ordered. He turned again to the sergeant of the provost's guard. "Impound those wagons as evidence, Sergeant. I'll explain to your officers."

"Tell you what, Colonel," Breed said with a wide grin, "you're bitin' more off this plug than you can chew. Maybe you'd like to forget the whole thing."

Barnes ignored him. "Major, you can go to your quarters now. Who is in command of the work party here in the yards?"

"Lieutenant Hanford," Boudrye answered sullenly. "You're going to regret this, Jeff."

"Somebody sure is," Comfort said happily. "I seen them niggers breakin' their backs on what you call straw."

Breed and Woodward were marched off to the guardhouse, Boudrye went back to camp alone, and Barnes went with Sergeant Comfort to the telegraph office. Word went through immediately to Nashville to search the train when it arrived. Then Jeff went to corps headquarters to explain the matter to the puzzled captain of the provost's guard.

Comfort made an excuse enabling him to go back for the bucket of chicken and cornbread, while Jeff returned alone to the Rush house. He left the horse at the hitching post for Comfort to take care of and went into the house. Fatigued and troubled by the necessity of telling Kate that her brother faced court-martial, he shrugged his greatcoat from his shoulders and headed slowly for the stairs.

Kate, coming from the kitchen, stopped him. "I've made coffee, Jeff. Come have a cup with me."

"No," he said. "No thanks, Kate. I wouldn't sleep."

"Did you settle the trouble at the railroad?"

"Yes. I settled it. Kate, your brother was there with the sutlers."

She came swiftly to him. "Ned was? What do you mean, Jeff? He was shipping cotton?"

Jeff nodded. "That's right. He's under arrest. He'll be tried."

"Oh my God!" she whispered. "What will happen to him?"

He patted her shoulder gently. "I don't know, Kate. It depends upon the charges. Don't worry about it now."

"You must be wrong, Jeff! Why would he do a thing like that?"

"He owes Breed and that other fellow a lot of money. That's as good a reason as any."

"Where is he, Jeff? I'll go see him. He'll talk to me."

"Not tonight, Kate. He's in his quarters. Comfort can take you to him tomorrow. I don't want you to go through camp at night."

"I must see him now! I must, Jeff."

He sighed. "If you insist, Kate. Wait until Comfort gets back. He'll go with you."

She left with Sergeant Comfort five minutes later. Jeff went to his room. He lay on the bed fully clothed, but he didn't sleep. After a while he got up again and drank a tumblerful of brandy. He stood at the window looking out at the dancing fires of the camp. He wondered if Ned would be fool enough to stick to Breed's story of furnishing straw for the train crew.

He was lying on the bed when Kate returned an hour later.

"Jeff! You didn't listen to him, dear. It's all right. He told me the whole story."

Jeff nodded soberly. "What did he tell you, Kate?"

"There wasn't any cotton at all. It was straw for bedding sheep on the train. If you'd listened to Ned, he would have explained. I'll tell you exactly what he told me, Jeff."

"Don't bother," he said quietly. "I heard it. It's a lie."

"Jeff! He wouldn't lie to me. He wouldn't!"

"I'm afraid he did, Kate. I'm sorry."

"My God, will you listen! Will you, Jeff?"

"No, I won't, Kate. Go to bed now. We'll talk again in the morning."

"Why do you hate him so?" she cried bitterly. "Answer me, Jeff. Why do you hate him?"

He turned to her in surprise. "I don't hate him, Kate. I'm only doing my duty."

Kate tried to calm herself, breathing heavily while she looked steadily at him. She spoke finally in a low and shaking voice. "Jeff, I've done my very best since we've been married to understand that word you use so often. Duty. With you, everything must give way to duty. Family, love, friendship—everything. I don't know if I can go any farther. I'll try. I love you, Jeff, but I'm not sure you love me. If duty as you understand it always comes before love, then you don't need me. All I'm asking you to do, Jeff, is talk to Ned and listen to his side of the story."

"If I'm wrong, Kate, I'll apologize to him and to you. But I'm not wrong."

She left the room.

Jeff turned to the window again, another glass of brandy in his hand. He couldn't sleep now if he tried. He'd take another drink or two. That would do it. He looked out across the camp once more, controlling the desire to go next door to her bedroom to comfort her.

Faintly, carrying through the wall that separated the rooms, he heard her sobbing. At the same time, floating through the cold winter air from the camp, he heard a sentry's call: "Twelve o'clock, and all's well!"

33

A duty stern and piercing broke
The tie which linked my soul with thee—

THE OFFICE of the provost marshal in Nashville telegraphed the following morning. The cotton had not been found on the train. All the cars had been empty.

General A. S. Williams, division commander, took an interest in the case as soon as he heard about it. Two hours after the news came from Nashville, he was in the provost marshal's office at XII Corps headquarters with Jeff and a major on General Slocum's staff, a former prosecutor from Brooklyn. General Williams, called "Pop" by the men of his division, was an alert, lively man with heavy black beard and lively eyes. He was a habitual cigar smoker, although his cigars were more often chewed to a stub rather than smoked.

He heard the news from Nashville and considered it soberly. "That doesn't leave anything to go on, Barnes," Williams said soberly. "What do you think, Werner?"

The major from Brooklyn shook his head. "There's no evidence against Major Boudrye. You can run the sutlers out, of course."

"How about the wagons?" Williams asked the provost marshal, a lieutenant colonel named Stokes. "Was there any cotton in them?"

"A few wisps of cotton clinging to the boards," Stokes admitted. "Lots of straw."

"And the Negroes who did the loading?" Jeff asked.

"Couldn't find hide nor hair of 'em," Stokes said.

"No evidence," Major Werner said. He looked at Comfort, who was standing at attention near the door. "The sergeant's story isn't enough alone. There must be evidence, or corroboration of his testimony."

"How about the train crew?" General Williams said. "Did you try to get them, Stokes?"

The provost marshal threw up his hands. "I sent word to Nashville to send them down with the next train south, but they had already left for Louisville, on their way to Indianapolis. It'll be difficult to get them back here if they don't want to come."

"That's right," Williams said. "We have no jurisdiction over them if they stay in Indiana. And we'd be fought all down the line if we tried to arrest experienced railroaders at a time like this. The best we can do is get depositions from them. See that it's done, Stokes."

"Yes, sir."

"That's your case, Barnes," the general said. "Blown sky-high. Return the major to duty for the present and fire your sutler. I'll see that the other sutler goes. What's his name, Stokes?"

"Woodward, sir."

In spite of his conviction that Ned was guilty, Jeff was relieved that the affair had stopped at this point. Ned could resign his commission without prejudice.

Werner spoke to the general. "The train crew got rid of the cotton somewhere along the line, sir. They must have realized that we would telegraph Nashville. Can't we have a search made for it?"

"We can," Williams said. "They probably stopped the train and dumped the bales alongside the tracks."

"If you find the cotton, baled to resemble straw, then we can proceed against Boudrye. I think that would be enough evidence, with the sergeant's clear testimony. A court might disagree, of course."

"All right, Stokes. Send word to the stations along the line to look for that cotton." The general turned to Jeff. "How are you feeling these days, Barnes? Ready for duty?"

"Desk duty in Washington, sir. I've been writing letters to people I know up there. They'll find me something to do."

"We can use you here come spring. I'd hate to see you go, Jeff."

"Thank you, sir, but I think Washington's best for me."

The general shrugged. "Maybe you'll change your mind. One thing more, Barnes. This Boudrye fellow—what kind of officer is he?"

"Superior in the field, sir. Poor otherwise."

"Then he'll be no great loss to your regiment. You and Bailey will get rid of him, of course. Do it one way or another. Do you think he'll resign?"

"I think so, sir."

"Good. If he refuses, speak to me, and we'll put some pressure on him."

"Yes, sir."

Kate was waiting on the porch when Jeff and Sergeant Comfort returned to the Rush house. "What's happened?" she asked quietly.

"There's no evidence against Ned," Jeff told her. "He won't have to stand trial."

A happy smile came over her face. She clasped her hands gaily. "Go tell him, Jeff! I'll come with you. Oh, I knew it wasn't true."

Jeff didn't answer. He turned to Comfort. "Sergeant, go to Major Boudrye's quarters and tell him he's released from arrest. Tell him I'd like to see him here immediately."

"You ought to go to him, Jeff," Kate said quickly.

Sergeant Comfort turned his mare and trotted away.

"You don't understand, Kate," Jeff said soberly, crossing to a chair on the porch. He sat down wearily, closing his eyes against the pale winter sun. "He isn't cleared, but there isn't any evidence for a court-martial. I can't go to him and shake his hand, saying forgive and forget. He still faces the consequences."

"In other words," she said slowly, "you believe a man is guilty unless he can prove that he's innocent?"

"He's guilty, Kate."

"With no evidence against him? With no testimony but Comfort's? Ned's word means nothing to you?"

"He's lying, Kate."

"And what will army justice be for him? What does duty tell you has to be done to him?"

Jeff kept his eyes closed, trying to ignore the bitterness in her voice. "He has no choice, Kate. He has to resign and go home. The story is probably all over the division by now."

"Oh, Jeff," she whispered brokenly, "what kind of man have you become? He's innocent, yet you will persist in destroying his career."

"He's done that himself, Kate."

"Oh, my God, Jeff. Don't do it. If you love me, don't do it. He's my brother!"

"I have my orders from General Williams, Kate. I couldn't disobey them even if I wanted to."

"You've convinced the general that Ned is guilty?"

Jeff got up from his chair and went to her. He took her hand in his. She pulled it away and averted her face.

"Listen to me, Kate. I want you to go home with him when he resigns. You shouldn't have come here at all. Go home to Highland Landing, dear, and wait for the end of the war."

She looked up at him suddenly. Her face was white and her eyes flashed. "I'll go, Jeff, if you force him to resign. I'll go home. And that will be the end of everything between you and me. When I married you, I was sure that together we could add one more word to the three that West Point had given you. I thought that love could become equal to duty and honor and country. I was wrong. You've changed so terribly, Jeff. You're hard, cold, brutal. I can't stand it any longer, Jeff!"

She ran into the house, leaving him with her words biting coldly into his mind. He wanted to run after her, ask her gently to forgive him, to try to pick up the threads that had broken, but he knew he could not. His duty was clear. Ned Boudrye must resign.

His conversation with Ned a few minutes later was brief and cold.

"They didn't find the cotton in Nashville, Ned."

Boudrye shrugged. "There was no cotton to find."

"You know there was. I know there was. By this time the entire regiment knows there was. You'll have to resign and go home, Ned."

"Whatever you say."

"All right. The sooner the better. There are two trains to Nashville today. Take one of them. If you'll write out your resignation, I'll put it through the proper channels. Kate will be going with you."

"I see. She's leaving you? She said she would."

"Yes, she's leaving me. Perhaps she wouldn't if you told the truth."

Boudrye laughed. "Once I called you a son of a bitch, Barnes. I'm saying it again."

"Say it all you please, Ned, if it gives you satisfaction. It's eleven o'clock. I want your resignation by noon."

"You'll have it."

Boudrye turned on his heel and walked away.

Captain Stewart went to the depot with Kate at the colonel's request. He had been the only witness to their parting. She turned to Jeff at the steps of the Rush house, standing calmly before him. Her voice was quiet. "Good-by, Jeff. Take care of yourself. Let us know if you ever need anything."

"Thank you, Kate. There'll be nothing I'll need. Good-by."

She walked gracefully to the buggy without looking back. Stewart helped her into the seat, crossed to the other side, climbed in, and picked up the reins.

"Hurry," she whispered. "Please hurry."

When the buggy was out of sight of the Rush house, she began to cry softly. Stewart spoke to her comfortingly, but she continued to cry all the way to the depot. Finally she wiped away her tears with a handkerchief and managed an unhappy smile.

"I'm sorry," she said.

"It's all right. I understand."

"Mike," she said quickly as the buggy pulled up before the depot, "will you write to me and tell me how he is and what he's doing? Will you write often?"

"Of course I will."

"Thank you. And watch out for him, will you, Mike?"

"He can take care of himself."

"Not any longer. He's driven himself too far now. He thinks his career is over. It's broken his heart, Mike. He doesn't want me or need me. All he has left is whatever the army sees fit to give him. I hope they don't throw him aside."

"Don't worry. They need him and everyone like him."

"You've been wonderful, Mike. I thank you for everything."

She leaned over and kissed him on the lips, lightly but tenderly. "It would be wrong to go away without kissing somebody."

He smiled. "I'm glad you kissed me, Kate."

Ned Boudrye, accompanied by a Negro who took Kate's bags, came to the buggy. He helped Kate to descend, then reached up and offered his hand to Mike.

"Good-by, Stewart," he said gravely. "Give 'em hell in the spring."

"Good-by, Ned. Good-by, Kate."

They went into the depot. Stewart sat in the buggy for several minutes until the train that was taking them north had pulled away from the station. He was rewarded for his wait by a last view of Kate waving to him from a train window. He picked up the reins.

"Wait a minute, Capt'in!"

The telegrapher ambled from his shack alongside the depot. "Can you take a message to the provost marshal fer me, Capt'in?"

"Sure," Mike said.

The man handed over the envelope. "Can't find no orderlies around here when you need 'em. Other times they're all over the place. That there is an important message."

"Is it?" Mike said.

"Must be. It's all about cotton. Seems to me them two provost marshals, here and in Nashville, got little to do, sendin' one message after another about cotton. This one says they found some bales of cotton in a ravine about thirty miles up the line. Why in hell do they keep talkin' about a few bales of cotton when they got deserters and criminals and such runnin' around loose?"

"I wouldn't know," Mike answered.

"Guess you wouldn't. You ain't but a capt'in. Talk like that is for majors and such. Thanks a lot for bein' my orderly, Capt'in."

"You're welcome," Mike said.

He drove away from the depot.

They won't bring him back, he told himself. They'll forget the whole business now that he's gone.

Part Three

"It was, in my judgement, the most magnificent army in existence. . . ."

(W. T. SHERMAN, *Memoirs*)

34

When a rider came out from the darkness
That hung over mountain and tree,
And shouted: "Boys, up and be ready!
For Sherman will march to the sea."

IN APRIL 1864, the mountains of eastern Tennessee echoed the sounds made by a great army massing for a campaign. Locomotives chugged along the railroads, hauling the long strings of rattling freight cars filled with food, clothing, and ammunition. Men marched the muddy roads converging on Chattanooga. They were veterans of the Army of the Cumberland, the Army of the Tennessee, the Army of Ohio. They were weather-beaten, bearded, and lean. They came in from winter quarters all over eastern Tennessee, carry-

ing everything they needed on their backs, for the order from Uncle
Billy was exact: one wagon and one ambulance per regiment. They
stepped out with the long stride of the western armies, cursing
amiably at the mud, gnats, cavalrymen, generals, staff officers, politicians, and rebels. They were ready to go against Johnston in
Georgia, one hundred thousand of them.

One evening in the middle of April their leader sat in his quarters
in a comfortable house in Chattanooga trying to catch up with his
correspondence. There seemed to be five times as many letters to be
answered now that he was commander of the Department of the
Mississippi.

Grant had gone to Washington to command the armies of the
United States, and was now in the field in Virginia. Sherman was
alone.

He sat at the desk tired and hungry after a long day. His red hair
was tousled as usual; he gnawed at a cigar; his fingers pawed at his
wiry beard. He was ready to call it a day, but there was one more
letter marked for his personal attention by one of his aides, Captain
Audenreid. Rolling the cigar over his stained teeth, he picked up the
letter and began to read. It was from a place named Highland Landing, New York—he remembered it as a small city upriver from West
Point—and it was dated April 11, 1864. It was addressed to Major
General W. T. Sherman, Commander, Department of the Mississippi,
Nashville, Tennessee. It had followed him to Chattanooga.

Dear Sir: [the letter began]
I regret this intrusion upon your valuable time. . . .

Sherman skipped the first paragraph. They always regretted in-
truding, but they always did it just the same.

You may remember my husband, Colonel Jefferson Barnes, whom
you met early in the war while he was on duty at the War Department in Washington. At that time you urged him to serve in
the western theatre of operations.

Barnes? Jefferson Barnes? The general's mind turned back the
months, remembering his visits to Washington. Would this young
man be the young Academy graduate who had been serving on
General Scott's staff? He thought so. That had been during the period
when his brother John had been looking for suitable officers for Ohio

regiments. Sherman had checked this Barnes's record in case he was willing to take an Ohio commission.

Just out of the Academy, as well as the general remembered, with a brilliant record. That was the boy. Now what did his wife have to say?

> He is presently in command of the 195th New York Volunteer Infantry, stationed in Tullahoma, Tennessee. He was grievously wounded at Lookout Mountain and lost his right arm as a result. Since that time he has been exceedingly despondent, believing that his military career as an active officer has ended.

> He has, I am told, sought and received from friends in Washington a post with the War Department, the only kind of position he thinks he is now qualified to hold. I am not certain of this, because my husband and I have been estranged for several months. The circumstances of our separation have nothing to do with this letter.

The general chewed his cigar savagely and stopped reading, viewing the entire letter as if it were some kind of serpent that he'd handled inadvertently. He'd be damned if he'd get involved in somebody's domestic difficulties. She'd probably go on to say that she wished that General Sherman would ask her husband to write home and apologize for whatever it was they'd fought about. No, that wasn't likely. Audenreid would never have given him a letter making such a silly request. He read on.

> The men of the 195th, I am told by one of their officers, have circulated a petition requesting my husband to remain with the regiment. Every man in the regiment has signed the petition, as have all the officers, including the lieutenant colonel who normally would succeed to the command.

> My husband has steadfastly refused to consider this course. He is devoted to his duty, and insists that it is his duty to relinquish his command because of his disability. No amount of argument will persuade him otherwise. You need him, sir, in whatever campaign you undertake this spring. He is personally responsible for the transformation of the 195th New York from green recruits to soldiers as fine as any in your army. His training at West Point, where he graduated with the Class of 1861, is too valuable to be lost to the Union at this critical point.

> I realize that you are a better judge of your needs than anyone else, and I of course understand that you may not agree with me.

> It is reasonable to ask why, when so many wives are praying that

their husbands retire from active service, I should make an appeal to you to change my husband's mind on that very subject.

There are two reasons. I have known the men of the 195th New York since the regiment was activated, and their record is a source of pride to me and to all of the people here in Highland County. My husband is the man most suited to command them, no matter what his disability may be. The second reason is personal. If my husband and I are ever to repair our shattered marriage, we must do it with pride and confidence and faith in the future. These are now lost to him entirely, because he considers himself useless. If he were to march on to victory with your great army, I am sure that he would have a long and brilliant career in the service of the United States.

Therefore I ask you to refuse his request to be relieved of his command, if it is within your power. He would be persuaded by you, I am sure, because he admires you above all the general officers of the Army.

If you communicate directly with him, sir, please do not mention me or this letter. I would not have him think that I interfered in his military career.

With respect and admiration and my best wishes for victory in the coming campaign, I am

Sincerely yours,
Kathleen Barnes
(Mrs. Jefferson Barnes)

"Audenreid!" the general called harshly. His voice rang sharply against the walls of the room. While he waited, he ground the coals of his cigar in an ash tray.

A youthful-looking officer wearing captain's bars appeared in the doorway, a faint smile on his face as he looked at the letter in the general's hand.

"Sir?" he said.

"Does our train to Nashville make any stops?" Sherman asked abruptly.

"Wood and water only, sir. You and General Howard must be back here as soon as possible, sir."

"Instruct the engineer to stop at Tullahoma."

"Yes, sir!" Audenreid grinned. "I've checked, sir. He's still at Tullahoma. His regiment hasn't left winter quarters yet."

"Are you reading my mind, Captain?" the general asked sharply.

"Yes, sir. She writes an appealing letter."

Sherman grunted and reached for another cigar.

"Your dinner is ready, sir, and the train leaves in an hour. General Howard is waiting at table."

"All right, Audenreid. We'd better not serve any whiskey with General Howard dining with us."

"No, sir. And another thing. You'd better not start eating until General Howard says grace."

Sherman nodded. A faint smile trimmed the corners of his stern mouth.

35

Then cheer upon cheer for bold Sherman
Went up from each valley and glen—

SERGEANT COMFORT, so noted for his excellence at housekeeping, was performing his present task most inefficiently. He was packing Colonel Barnes's personal effects for the trip to Washington. It was a job he hated, and he did it with a long face and a steady flow of grumbling. The colonel paid no attention to Comfort's comments; he was busy settling last-minute details with Lieutenant Colonel Bailey.

"Goddammit, Jeff, I wish you'd change your mind."

Barnes shook his head, then, attracted by an unusual hubbub coming from camp, walked to the window. "What's that racket?"

He saw soldiers streaming from every direction to line the road from town. In solid ranks at the roadside, they waved their caps and shouted. He saw that their attention was centered on a small group of mounted officers trotting toward the Rush house.

"Hell!" he said. "It's some general paying a visit. The way the men are yelling, they must know him."

Bailey looked over his shoulder at the road. "Maybe it's Hooker. They'd yell for Hooker."

Barnes shook his head. "Hooker's in Chattanooga."

"Well, here he comes, whoever he is," Bailey said. He pulled his blouse straight and looked unhappily at his scuffed and dusty boots. "I hope he's a westerner. He'll look worse than I do."

"Let's go downstairs. Mrs. Rush must have some coffee on the stove," Barnes said. "Leave that, Comfort. We may need you to serve coffee to the general."

Mrs. Rush met them on the stairs, her skirts in her hand and her legs pumping frantically to push her upstairs in a hurry. "Oh, my God, Colonel! It's General Sherman. Oh, my God, I've got to change my dress. Don't let him go until I've changed my dress."

She brushed past them and ran for her room.

A captain appeared in the vestibule as Barnes and Bailey reached the foot of the stairs. "Colonel Barnes?" he asked sharply, looking at Jeff's empty sleeve.

"That's right," Jeff answered.

"General Sherman's compliments, sir. He'd like to talk to you. Can you step out on the porch?"

"We can serve the general coffee if he'd like to come in," Barnes said quickly, gesturing toward the parlor.

"We haven't time, sir. If you please, Colonel." The captain stepped back toward the door.

Sherman was alone on the porch, slouch hat over his eyes, black cigar gripped by his tight mouth, his restless gaze darting over the countryside as if he were drawing a mental map for some future military operation in this area. He turned when Barnes and Bailey came out. The rest of his party had remained with the horses, and his aide now left the porch and joined them.

He raised his hand casually when Barnes and Bailey saluted and then put his hand out to Jeff. "How are you, Barnes? I see you took my advice to come West."

"Yes, sir. Pardon my left hand. I'm glad to see you again. General Sherman, this is Lieutenant Colonel Bailey, 195th New York."

"How're you, Colonel?" Sherman shook hands with Bailey, nodding impatiently, as if he were dispensing with everything but the business at hand. "What's this about you going to Washington, Barnes?"

"That's right, sir. Colonel Bailey will relieve me."

"He will like hell! You're going South, not North."

"I'm sorry, sir. I've given it a lot of thought. I can't do it. I'd be too much of a liability in a hard campaign."

"Is that right? That's your opinion, eh? You didn't ask anybody's advice. You just made up your mind that you were useless. You might be at that, Barnes, if you keep up the kind of talk you put in this letter." Sherman pulled a sheaf of papers from the inside pocket of his blouse. He leafed quickly through them. "Here we are. 'Liability.' That's what it says here. '. . . unfit for active field service . . .' Are you, Barnes? Another one: '. . . crippling disability . . .' Is that what you have, Barnes? Bah!"

The general flipped his cigar over the railing. Then, deliberately, he gripped the papers in both hands and tore them in half.

"You'll take this regiment to Chattanooga, Barnes. That is an order."

Bailey pounded one fist into the other and grinned delightedly.

Sherman's face wrinkled with impatience. "I can't stay here forever, Barnes. Acknowledge that order."

Jeff's face was deep red. His lips tightened before he answered. "I request that you approve my relief, sir."

Sherman dropped the torn papers to the porch. "You listen to me, Barnes. What do you think this country sent you to West Point for? To sit in a chair in Washington and give a lot of sweet talk to Congressmen? My God, man! We didn't educate your right arm. We put the military science into your head. Now you have to use it. To hell with your right arm! A liability, are you? I'd like you to meet another liability." He turned swiftly and called the group of officers some distance from the porch. "Howard! Come here a minute, will you?"

A tall, full-bearded man wearing the twin stars of a major general left the group and walked to the porch. The empty right sleeve of his blouse was tucked neatly into his belt. He nodded gravely as he mounted the steps.

"General Howard, Colonel Barnes and Colonel Bailey," Sherman said briskly. "Howard, shake left hands with this liability here. He says he can't go after Johnston with us because he left his right arm on Lookout."

"I know Colonel Barnes," Howard said quietly. "I taught him mathematics at the Academy. How are you, Barnes?"

"Good to see you again, sir," Jeff said awkwardly, embarrassed at the grace with which Howard shook hands.

Howard looked quickly at Barnes. "Why do you think you can't come with us? I've been on active duty since the rebs emptied this sleeve for me at Fair Oaks."

"We're losing time," Sherman said abruptly. "You haven't acknowledged that order, Barnes."

Jeff's throat constricted and the muscles in his jaw worked for a second or two before he answered. "You're sure you want me, sir?"

"Damnation, man! What do you think I came here for?"

"Yes, sir!" Jeff managed to say. "I'll be proud to serve under you, sir."

"Good. Let's go, Howard. They're waiting for us in Nashville."

Mrs. Rush came to the door too late to have any more than a glimpse of General Sherman's face as he mounted his horse. She stamped her foot in disappointment; she'd changed her dress and put on face rouge and powder. It wasn't fair. She went back into the house shedding tears of vexation which streaked the powder and rouge.

36

Bring the good old bugle, boys,
We'll sing another song,
Sing it with the spirit that starts the world along—

A COMMANDING GENERAL trying to defend a railroad with less than seventy thousand troops against a commanding general with one hundred thousand veterans must possess the qualities of genius. Joseph E. Johnston undoubtedly had them, and had the railroad itself been the only prize in sight for Sherman, the spring campaign of 1864 might have taken another course. Johnston, however, had not only to consider the fragile line of steel that snaked its way across

Georgia. He had one of the two great armies left to the Confederacy, and he was dedicated to its preservation as a fighting force. Behind the army lay the great city of Atlanta, the "gateway of the Confederacy." In every direction from Atlanta stretched the rich state of Georgia. Above Georgia lay South Carolina, and above South Carolina lay disaster.

Disaster might be averted if the rebel army in Georgia was kept intact. Sherman could never threaten to form the second jaw of a pincers designed to squeeze Lee's Army of Northern Virginia if Johnston's army could be preserved. Grant from the north and Sherman from the south—Johnston saw the danger.

He had hoped to fight at Dalton, where he had all the natural and artificial advantage. Sherman had refused to fight, but had swung around the right flank. Johnston hoped to fight at Resaca, and he used all his wiles to bring on a general engagement. This time Sherman fought, but on his own terms, not Johnston's. He was content with standing off the rebel attacks that were launched from the tight ring of defenses at Resaca, and countering them with the massive pressure of his numbers. The XX Corps hit Hood in the flank when Hood came out to test the Army of the Tennessee. Osterhaus gained the heights of Bishop Polk's lines outside Resaca, and General John "Black Jack" Logan of the XV Corps of McPherson's army pushed his artillery to the ridges and blew the railroad bridge to pieces—the bridge that promised safety to the rebel army. General Howard with his corps punched at Hardee's rebels in the center. All day long the rebels braced for the great assault, but it didn't come. What came instead was pressure on the ring, pushing and probing and poking and pounding. Added to the pressure were the reports from excited red-grimed couriers, who came into Resaca from the rear, telling of Union cavalry striking toward the railroad far down the Oostanaula, and warning that Yankee divisions were on their way around the right flank again, now threatening Calhoun, seven miles below Resaca.

Fight it out at Resaca? Protect the railroad? Preserve the army? Fall back toward Kingston, extending Sherman's line? Which was Johnston to choose?

As if he could read Sherman's mind, Johnston withdrew his army during the night of May 15. As at Dalton a few days before, he got away, with scant hours separating him from disaster.

In the darkness near the center of the Union line, where the bivouac fires were already gleaming, the 195th New York Infantry made ready for sleep. The flashing and booming of Logan's artillery on the right, pounding Resaca, furnished lightning and thunder for the warm spring night.

Colonel Barnes stood wearily in the shadows, with his back against a tree, waiting for Comfort to bring him something to eat. He didn't care so much what it was, so long as it filled his belly. Bookstaver and Bailey were near by, writing reports by the light of candles, using bayonets as candlesticks. Other officers lounged and smoked, talking quietly of the day's action, in which the 195th had skirmished with Hood's advance through most of the day. Mike Stewart stood alone about ten yards from Barnes, staring steadily at the distant flashing of Logan's guns.

Barnes hoped he could get some sleep. The stump of his arm throbbed steadily, causing him to wonder if he were going to be a weather prophet, as all old soldiers who had been wounded claimed to be. He wished that he had allowed Comfort to pack some brandy for him before they left Tullahoma. He could use it tonight. He hadn't had a drink since Sherman had ordered him to take the 195th into the campaign. He didn't need it any longer, but he had been wrong to ignore its power to bring sleep. He wondered if Stewart had any whiskey or brandy.

"Mike," he called softly.

Stewart turned and came to him. "Yes, sir?"

"You wouldn't have any whiskey, Mike?"

"I'm sorry, Jeff. Maybe I can get you some."

"Don't bother," Jeff smiled, "I'll put Comfort to work. He could forage a flask of Napoleon brandy in a Methodist revival."

"It was a rough day," Stewart said.

Barnes nodded, dropping his hand to the holstered Colt's .44 at his belt. He no longer wore a sword; he'd had Comfort send it home to Kate. During the day's skirmishing the revolver had been awkward in his hand; he'd never before fired a shot left-handed. He'd also have to devise a method of reloading with one arm.

"Your boys did well," he said to Stewart. "You had three wounded?"

"Dr. Renwick says they'll be back to duty in a few days. All three were hit by spent balls."

"Hood's a fool," Barnes said suddenly. "He came boiling out to test us and got slammed back. I wish he were in command over there instead of old Johnston."

"What will they do now, Jeff?"

"Retreat. What else can they do?"

They were interrupted by the approach of a young officer mounted on a long-barreled roan horse. The officer spoke to Sam Bailey, who pointed with his pen toward Barnes and Stewart. As he came closer, Jeff recognized him as Captain Audenreid, Sherman's aide-de-camp.

"Evening, sir," Audenreid said, swinging down from the saddle and saluting. "General Sherman's compliments, sir, and will you have dinner with him?"

"Hello, Audenreid," Jeff said. "Where is General Sherman?"

"A mile or so." Audenreid gestured into the darkness. "At General Hooker's headquarters. Come anyway, even if you've eaten. I think he wants to see you."

Jeff laughed. "I haven't eaten yet, Captain. Shall I go along with you?"

"By all means. The general said you were to bring any of your officers you'd care to ask, sir." Audenreid glanced at Mike Stewart.

"Captain Stewart, Captain Audenreid," Jeff said. "What do you say, Mike? Want to meet Uncle Billy?"

"Yes, sir! I'll borrow a horse and be right with you."

"Ask Comfort to saddle mine, will you, Mike?"

In a few minutes they were on their way, moving carefully through the bivouac areas, where the exhausted soldiers already slept heavily, wrapped in their blankets in the darkness.

Hooker's headquarters showed that the general had followed Sherman's orders against unnecessary equipage. There was a tent fly stretched among tree branches like an awning, a roll of blankets underneath the fly, and a folding desk near the blankets.

Two Negroes whom Hooker had brought from Chattanooga were setting places for the dinner on a long, uneven table made of a row of quartermaster's clothing boxes. The seats were the wooden boxes in which hardtack was packed. Standing around the table, waiting to be seated, were perhaps a dozen officers of various ranks, most of them generals. Sherman himself, dressed in a gray flannel shirt, open blouse, baggy breeches, and the black slouch hat that he wore in the field, was striding up and down among the officers. He chewed viciously on a long black cigar, stopped to dictate notes to an aide who sat on a cracker box with notebook on his knee, and kept up an intense, rapid-fire discourse with several officers as he passed them. It was difficult to tell where conversation, dictation, order, or greeting began or ended.

Barnes and Stewart stood in the background waiting to be directed to a place at the table by one of Sherman's aides. Stewart recognized a few of the generals: Hooker and Williams, of course, and Howard, whom he had seen at Tullahoma and on the march from Chattanooga, and McPherson. The others were strangers to him, although several of them nodded or spoke to Barnes.

Then suddenly Sherman was standing before him, looking alternately from him to Barnes and back again, lined face screwed into a fierce frown. "Good to see you, Barnes," he said harshly. "This one of your men?"

"Yes, sir. Captain Stewart, sir."

Sherman thrust out his hand. Stewart was surprised at the steeltrap strength of the wiry fist.

"You were hit by Hood today, weren't you, Barnes?"

"Yes, sir. We had some sharp skirmishing."

Howard and McPherson came closer when they heard Sherman mention the rebel general. They stared at Barnes speculatively.

"What did you think of that attack? Pretty snappy piece of work, wasn't it? Hah?" Sherman chewed the cigar, his hard blue eyes fixed on Barnes's face.

"No, sir," Barnes said abruptly. "There was no reason for it. General Howard's corps was strongly placed, and we were ready to counter from the left. It was a waste of men."

McPherson grinned and nudged Howard with his elbow. Howard shrugged, still watching Barnes and Sherman.

"You think Hood's one of these rash fellows, do you?" Sherman asked. "The kind who wants to win all the battles with charges?"

"I know nothing about him, sir, except that today's attack was ill advised and badly executed."

Sherman turned swiftly. "What do you think of that, Howard? Isn't that what McPherson and I were saying?"

He didn't wait for an answer. He looked toward General Hooker, who was talking animatedly with General Williams. A kind of polite formality came into his voice when he spoke, as if he had great respect for the former commander of the Army of the Potomac. "General Hooker, can we eat now? I have to be on my way."

"It's ready, General," Hooker nodded. "Just give the word."

"Let's go, then," Sherman said. "You two sit by me," he added to Barnes and Stewart.

The food was simple and not too plentiful: hardtack, bacon, sweet potatoes, and black coffee. Sherman immediately picked up knife and fork and attacked the bacon. A word from Audenreid at his shoulder stopped him. The general glanced toward the other end of the table, nodding.

"Oliver," he called to General Howard, "would you like to say grace?"

Howard nodded gravely and bowed his head. His short prayer carried clearly, but it did not drown out Sherman's comment to Jeff Barnes.

"How is your wife, Barnes?"

"I haven't heard from her lately, sir."

"A fine woman," Sherman said. "She recognized the difference between an asset and a liability. Do you know Mrs. Barnes, Stewart?"

"Yes, sir," Mike answered quickly.

"Fine woman," Sherman said again. "It's not an easy life, being married to an officer in the regular army. It takes courage in a woman to stick it out. I often wonder how Mrs. Sherman lasted so long at it."

"You've never met my wife, sir," Jeff said puzzledly.

"Don't have to meet her to know about her. I never met Lieutenant General John Bell Hood either, but I know what kind of a man he is from that attack he made today. McPherson was with him at the Academy. He says Hood is apt to yell 'Charge!' as soon as he sees a bugler standing around with nothing to do. A good man, for our side. Why haven't you heard from your wife?" Sherman held up his hand swiftly. "Don't tell me about it. I've got enough on my mind already."

"Yes, sir," Jeff said evenly. His face was darker than usual.

"I know," Sherman said. "It wasn't anybody's fault. Just one of those differences of opinion. All right, Barnes. You're a young man just out of the Academy a couple of years. You've still got the books in your head. Here we are at Resaca. Johnston will move out tonight, and we'll go in first thing in the morning. What do we do then?"

"Chase him as fast as we can, sir. Don't give him a chance to fortify another place like Dalton or Resaca."

"It's not enough to chase a fox, Barnes. Sooner or later you've got to try to catch him. How would you do that?"

Jeff didn't notice that everyone at the table was listening to the conversation between him and Sherman. He had his eyes fixed on Sherman's seamed face, and his voice became animated. "He'll stick close to the railroad, sir, as far as Atlanta. It's all he can do. He wants us to attack him in intrenchments and he wants to pick the place. It's probable that we could overpower him if we had to make a general assault, but I don't think it's necessary."

"You don't, eh? What do the books say to do instead?"

Jeff grinned. "The books don't say it, General. You've been doing it. You flanked him at Dalton; you threatened to flank him here at Resaca. When we get into the flat country below, you can flank him at will. The men in my regiment gave it a name at Dalton. 'Ring around Rosie,' they call it."

"And what should I do when we've flanked him as far as Atlanta, Barnes?"

Jeff nodded. "Flank him again, sir. Flank the whole city. Cut off the railroads, and Atlanta will die."

Sherman laughed harshly. "Put a ring around Rosie, eh? Well, if we're going to do it, we'd better get at it." He picked up his tin cup of black coffee and drained it quickly, piping-hot though it was. "Audenreid, let's go!" he called. He nodded down the table, with the quick change to formality when he spoke to Hooker. "Thanks for your hospitality, General. I'll do my best to repay it somewhere along the line."

Before they left for the 195th's bivouac, Barnes and Stewart were approached by General McPherson. He smiled genially at them.

"Were you warned, Colonel, that he would ask you those questions?"

"No, sir, I wasn't."

"You gave the right answers, then. That was his way of telling us how we're going to fight Joe Johnston. 'Ring around Rosie,' indeed! This army will be swinging like a gate all the way to Atlanta. Good night, Colonel. Good night, Captain."

On the way back Jeff was silent. He nodded but did not reply when Mike thanked him for the invitation to accompany him.

"I'll never forget it, Jeff."

"Yes," Barnes said absently. "I wonder how he knew about Kate?"

Stewart could have told him, but he didn't. In her letters Kate had asked him to keep her secret.

37

Yet praying
When this cruel war is over,
Praying that we meet again.

184 Liberty Street
Highland Landing, N.Y.
May 10, 1864

Dear Captain Stewart:

The word of the spring campaigns has finally come, and everyone talks of nothing but the prospects for victory this year. I am not so sanguine as some, but the skies are bright, are they not?

We know now that the 195th is part of the XX Corps in the great army that General Sherman is leading into Georgia, and our hearts are with you every step of the way. You cannot know yet that General Grant has already begun to hammer at the rebels in Virginia, and while we are appalled at the severe losses our troops have sustained in the opening days, we say this to each other: He fights, and then he fights again! Maybe this is the man, after so many failures.

There is no word from your army yet, but I hope and pray that you will meet success in all you try. My brother Ned, who left yesterday for Virginia to take a company in a New York regiment commanded by an old friend of my father, told us that Johnston is a great general, as clever as a fox. Ned also said, however, that Sherman finally with his own command cannot be beaten by a dozen Johnstons. It is to Ned's credit, considering his bitterness toward my husband, that he likened Sherman to Jeff so that we might see Sherman more clearly. They are the same kind of man, Ned told us—dedicated, determined, and indomitable. It seems to me that this must be true in many ways, even in their weaknesses. For instance, it is common knowledge that Sherman was prepared to throw up his command when things went wrong earlier in the war, but Grant made him stay, just as Sherman made Jeff stay when Jeff was ready to quit.

You must write me, Michael, as soon as you can, telling me how it is with Jeff. Do all you can to ease his burden.

I am afraid that I can never help him again, although I understand him well. The others here do not. My parents are silent when he is mentioned: his mother and father grieve for Walter and try to hide their pain in realizing that their other son is a stranger to them.

Please relay to me any needs that Jeff has, and I will see that Comfort is supplied with whatever they may be, so long as packages may be sent to your army. With my fond wishes, as ever,

Kate.

38

We've been tenting tonight on the old
camp ground,
Thinking of days gone by. . . .

MICHAEL STEWART would have written to Kate every day if he had had the chance, but as it was, twice a week was about the best he could do. He wrote his letters at night in his bivouac wherever the 195th New York threw down its gear to sleep on the ground.

Sometimes he wrote by firelight; often he shared a precious candle with Jack Hanford, who appreciated help with his spelling in his letters to Carrie. Usually before he started to write his letter, Mike read through several that Kate had sent to him. He carried her letters with him, wrapped and tied in oilcloth.

One night near Cassville, Georgia, they were fortunate. The officers of the 195th had taken as quarters an abandoned house at the edge of the town. Stewart and Hanford had a table to write on and cane-bottomed chairs to sit on. A coal oil lamp flickered on the table before them. Their letters that night were far longer than usual. In the dark night a thunderstorm raged; the camp was quiet, with most of the men forced to huddle miserably in damp blankets under their pup tents. Johnston's army was somewhere near Allatoona, waiting for the Yankees to move again, but Sherman had declared a three-day rest.

Mike let his pen fairly fly across the pages that night; there was so much to tell her about the campaign three weeks old, and if he could not give her much news about her husband—for there was no change in Colonel Barnes, other than a leaner, sterner look about him—there was much to say about the progress of the army across the state of Georgia.

> In the field before Cassville, Ga.
> May 22, 1864

Dear Kate:

Your letter of May 10 arrived here today from Chattanooga, proving that the rebels have not made good their boast that they would cut the railroad behind us. Rest assured that they will not.

By this time the newspapers are probably filled with accounts of our campaign, but perhaps I can add details that they have not carried.

The XX Corps has fairly earned the flanking championship of the world. This is the way it goes: we're on the right wing, facing the rebs in their strong positions. Then the word comes from Thomas to Hooker, and away we go! All the way around the army to the left and keep on going. Next thing we hear, the rebels have skedaddled, Thomas in the center is chasing them, and back we go to the right again to wait for the next order to swing around the end.

After Dalton and Resaca, we got down into the open ground, and Joe Johnston laid a beautiful trap for us at a place called Adairsville. I don't know what the papers said about it, but this is how it went. He made a semicircle with his flanks on opposite hills and his center strongly entrenched across the valley. He thought we'd come boiling down the middle and be caught. But by the time our center approached his trap, we had a corps far beyond the rebel right wing, McPherson and most of the Army of the Tennessee were below him on the road to Kingston, and we even had an infantry division in sight of Rome, far to his left. What could he do? Retreat again.

He tried once more here at Cassville. This time we understand he'd told his troops they'd retreat no farther, but fight the great battle we have been expecting. We pressed in; the next morning Johnston was gone across the Etowah River to Allatoona. Flanked again!

We have discouraged the rebels in several ways. First, our flanking tactics. Jeff and I interrogated a prisoner that some of my lads captured yesterday. He said nothing of military value that we did not already know, but one of his remarks amused us. "Ole Joe is the post, and Sherman is the gate. He just swings around." Our railroaders also are too much for the Johnnies. This same prisoner, while we were talking to him, suddenly cocked his head and listened. "What's that?" he asked. "A locomotive whistle," I told him. He shook his head sadly. "I dunno how you fellers do it," he said. "We ripped up them tracks day before yestiddy."

I tell you, Sherman is a marvel. After our progress during these first weeks, he has the men wild about him. They have sense enough to know that sooner or later Johnston will stand and give us the battle of our lives, but they have gained so much confidence in themselves by our speed and success that when the day of battle comes they'll not be beaten by Johnston and Lee put together.

All is not perfect, however. This army, which has had but little opportunity for bathing and laundering since we left Chattanooga, is suffering from the usual plagues of vermin that beset soldiers in the field, and in addition, we fight a losing battle daily against a universal southern blight known as the "chigger." This insect's bite is worse than that of flea or louse, it seems to me, and is far more likely to fester. Those men who are particularly susceptible to the chigger's poison require treatment from Dr. Renwick.

Then, too, the weather has played us false. It rains almost every day, turning the roads to gumbo. If it doesn't rain, the sun beats down unmercifully. After this short experience with Georgia, I'm tempted to advocate letting her secede and stay seceded if she so wishes.

We have had a good many casualties in the fighting so far, and I suppose these have been reported back home or will be shortly. Jeff continues well, although this hard campaigning is a strain upon us all. I think he needs nothing any more than the rest of us do. It is surprising how little a soldier can do with when he must.

Your letters, Kate, fill me with longing to be back home. I re-

member well the day you left Tullahoma, and I will never forget
your farewell to me. With every day that goes by, I desire more to
be with you. Remember that you have my love and devotion always.

He signed his name, read the paragraph, smiled, and then ripped
the page into small pieces. It had become a ritual with him. The
last page of every letter he wrote to her was written twice. He would
write of love, as if she knew how he loved her, and then he would
tear up the page and write another, wishing her good health and
assuring her of his respect.

A childish trick, he told himself as he signed his name to the
second attempt. Yet it does no harm. She'll probably never know
how I feel about her.

39

We've been fighting today on the old camp ground,
Many are lying near. . . .

THE JUNE RAINS came and put an end to the wide flanking
sweeps. The rebel lines stiffened. Johnston had stopped retreating.
His men dug in on the rough hills behind Dallas and Allatoona.
Pine Mountain, Lost Mountain, Kenesaw Mountain—there they
would fight it out with Sherman.

For twenty-seven days there was steady fighting along a ten-mile
front. Day after day the Federal army poked and probed at the
rebel lines, looking for the weak spot. Casualties were never severe
on any one day, but in the aggregate they showed that Johnston
was doing effectively what Jefferson Davis demanded—he had
ended the series of brilliant withdrawals. That wasn't enough, however, for the desperate leaders of the Confederacy. They needed a
victory to restore their sagging hopes.

There was great pressure put on General Johnston to take the
offensive. He did not, believing that his role was to preserve his
army. A disaster could end the war in Georgia. Day after day he

strengthened his trenches in the hills, knowing that Sherman could not flank him now without so weakening his lines that any Confederate attack would succeed. The old gray fox waited for Sherman to act.

Bishop Polk was killed by artillery fire on Pine Mountain, June 14. The next day Johnston withdrew his troops from Pine, and two days later, from Lost Mountain. He was secure on Kenesaw. He waited, watching Sherman.

All the way down from Chattanooga, Sherman had pivoted his forces around "Pap" Thomas and the Army of the Cumberland in the center. Sweep to the left, sweep to the right; the men likened the flanking marches to a square dance they often performed in bivouac, in which the caller would cry, "Forward six and back, side gents docey-do!" Thomas in the center would sidle forward to Johnston politely enough, bow and retire; meanwhile McPherson and Schofield were swinging around each other.

Now, for the first time, with Atlanta twenty miles away behind the rough green slopes of Kenesaw, Sherman stopped the dancing tune. He ordered a frontal assault.

On June 27, early in the morning, the Union guns began to roar. Crouched in their breastworks on the mountainside, the rebels listened to the whining of the shells. They waited. As soon as the guns stopped, the blue-bellies would be coming.

At nine o'clock the Federal guns went silent. Confederate gunners, with their pieces trained on the Yankee trenches in the flatland at the foot of Kenesaw, waited for the tidal wave of blue. Logan's XV Corps jumped up and ran for the mountain. Several divisions of Thomas's Army of the Cumberland stepped out in formation. The rebel cannon poured destruction upon them.

Within two hours it was over. The attack reached the rebel trenches and spent itself. The XV Corps and the Cumberland divisions stumbled back to their trenches, dazed, battered, bleeding. They left behind them twenty-five hundred men among the rocks and pines of Kenesaw.

The square dance music started again. The attackers had gone "forward six and back"; before the fight was over, Schofield and McPherson were swinging around the ends again. The rains stopped; Schofield on the right pushed beyond Johnston's flank and held his ground tenaciously.

On July 2, Johnston answered to the tune. He abandoned Kenesaw and fell back toward Atlanta. He intrenched at Peach Tree Creek.

The telegraph wires hummed between Richmond and Atlanta. Jefferson Davis asked Joe Johnston when he intended to fight. Johnston said that his operations must depend upon Sherman.

Davis to Johnston: ". . . you . . . express no confidence that you can defeat or repel him, you are hereby relieved . . ."

Johnston to Davis: ". . . Confident language by a military commander is not usually regarded as evidence of competency."

The handsome, gallant John Bell Hood succeeded to the command. He had lost an arm and a leg in the service of the Confederacy. He was the idol of the ladies, and a favorite of the troops. There were those among the gray veterans, however, who shook their heads and muttered, "I dunno. He seems like a man who'd draw to an inside straight."

Along the great blue ring that stretched around him Hood's acquaintances of former years cheered the news. McPherson grinned at Sherman. "Just a horse and a bugler, and here he comes!"

40

The same canteen, my soldier friend,
The same canteen,
There's never a bond, old friend, like this!
We have drunk from the same canteen.

THERE WERE many horses and many buglers available, and on the twentieth of July the opportunity to draw to the inside straight was presented.

Thomas's Cumberlanders were moving in, pushing at the rebel defenses on the Peach Tree line. Schofield was on the left, with McPherson beyond. There was a gap between the halves of the Union army; Thomas had moved too far too quickly. On the left side of the gap Hooker's XX Corps was moving to join the left wing.

John Bell Hood saw the gap, listened to couriers who told him of its size, looked at his men in the trenches, and told them to smash through the hole in the Union line.

The XX Corps had stopped in the brushy fields of the gap, thrown up breastworks, and its men were eating a late dinner in midafternoon. The 195th New York held the left wing of Williams's 1st Division, next to Geary's division. Some of the skirmishers, not content with bacon and hardtack for lunch, were picking blackberries in a briar patch beyond the skirmish line.

They had plenty of time to get back to the regiment when the rebels stormed into the gap, but they had a better view of the impact upon Ward's and Geary's divisions than did their comrades behind the breastworks of Williams's division. They saw Ward's men take the blow and stumble back; they saw Geary's regiments fighting hand to hand, and then the rebels were upon them. Wave upon wave of screaming men in butternut poured out of the pine trees on the slope before them.

For the first time since Gettysburg, Sergeant Comfort did not hold the colors high with one hand and fire a revolver with the other. Instead he planted the staff in the soft earth of the breastworks and began to pump the lever of the Henry repeating rifle that he had acquired after Kenesaw. He'd given thirty-five dollars for it to a wounded soldier of a Wisconsin regiment in Howard's corps. This was the weapon of which the rebels said, "Them Yanks got a gun they load on Sunday and shoot all week." It held sixteen cartridges.

Comfort pumped the lever, fired, pumped again, fired, and yelled with delight. He'd stop the rebels all by himself! At least, he would if he kept his butt down.

It would be hand to hand in a few seconds. The rebels were thirty yards away. The deadly waves were crumbling, but they closed the gaps and kept coming.

There were no orders to be given, no companies to be moved; Colonel Barnes and Colonel Bailey stood shoulder to shoulder in the center of the 195th's line, firing methodically at the screaming rebels.

The gray line howled as it slammed into the blue. Bayonets clashed and rang. Disarmed men grabbed their enemies and wrestled them to the ground. Comfort swiveled the Henry this way and that, dropping rebels who sought to seize the colors. Dead and wounded sprawled all over the parapets and were trampled into the earth by the wild men who fought above them.

The desperate rebel attack was slowed but not stopped by Hooker's men, who fought valiantly in open ground. Regiment by regiment the blue lines fell back in the hand-to-hand combat, and still the rebels came pouring through the gap. The 195th New York, protected somewhat more than the other Union forces by breastworks, managed to hold its position, beating off successive waves of screaming rebels.

Jeff Barnes, his revolver empty, stood in the center watching the rebels pour past both flanks of the Highland County regiment. The 195th stood alone now, facing an entire rebel division. Jeff began to count slowly to himself, unmindful of the withering fire from Confederate muskets. His hat went spinning; Minié balls tugged at his clothing; a ball carried away the heel of his left boot. He continued to count; he would hold the breastworks for thirty seconds. If he waited longer, the entire regiment would be captured.

Sam Bailey yelled in Barnes's ear that they must retreat. Barnes shook his head and counted: "Twelve . . . fifteen . . . twenty . . ." The rebel fire grew in volume as the third assault wave fell back. Casualties piled one upon another behind the breastworks or fell across them to lie on the bodies of the men in brown.

Jeff stopped counting the seconds and raised his arm. A few men had already turned to run. Then, on the left, a brigade of Geary's division rushed back into the fight, cutting like a knife through butter the rebels who had advanced beyond the 195th's left flank. The 3rd Brigade of Williams roared into the rebels on the right.

Jeff grinned savagely at Bailey. "There they come!" he yelled. "Let's go, Sam!" He jumped to the top of the breastworks and slid down into the twisted bodies of the Confederate dead. Every man of the 195th who was still on his feet followed Barnes over the breastworks. Yelling wildly, they struck the rebel line, which was already falling back in confusion from the impact of the counterattacks on the left and right. Again the fighting was hand to hand; this time the rebels retreated slowly to the edge of the woods from which they'd come. Once more the 195th New York, having been in a salient of the Union line, was caught up in a pocket of fighting far in advance of the rest of Williams's regiments. They stood their ground again for a minute or two, but the weight of the rebel fire was too terrible to bear. Like skirmishers scattering before an enemy advance, men of the 195th came back to their breastworks.

Jeff Barnes, watching the withdrawal, saw Mike Stewart trying to take his company out of a gully into which the rebel retreat had drawn them. The men came scattering in a storm of Minié balls, but Stewart went down. He lay still. Two or three of his men looked at him, but they ran on. Jeff rapped Comfort's arm with his revolver. "Come on," he shouted, pointing at Stewart's body.

Comfort lumbered beside him as they crossed the open ground, where the rebel bullets whistled viciously. There was momentary protection on the incline of the gully into which Stewart's body had rolled. Jeff saw blood pumping across Stewart's blouse from a body wound.

"Help me with him!" Jeff shouted to Comfort. The colonel dropped his revolver and bent over Stewart.

Comfort looked unhappily at his prize Henry, then at the colors in his left hand. Groaning, the sergeant placed the rifle gently on the ground and used his right arm to help Barnes lift Stewart.

Together they hauled the unconscious captain across the open ground that was carpeted with the bodies of dead and dying men. They had fifty yards to cover. It seemed impossible that they would make it. Comfort was certain that a rebel bullet would slam into his backside, exposed to the enemy for the first time in the battle.

A dozen men from Stewart's Company A poured over the breastworks to take the burden from Barnes and Comfort. Stewart was carried on a stretcher to the rear, where the surgeons of several regiments had improvised a field hospital.

The XX Corps had held the gap. Three times more the rebels tried to smash through, but now there were Union reinforcements to throw them back. Hood suffered heavy losses at no profit to the defense of Atlanta. The fighting was ended at dark with the gap in the line repaired and Sherman advised that his information on Hood was correct: the new rebel commander was brave, determined, and rash.

Hooker's troops had suffered fifteen hundred casualties in repulsing the Confederate onslaught. The 195th New York counted 104 dead and wounded.

Jeff Barnes went to the field hospital.

"I think he'll live," Dr. Renwick told him as they stood above the still form of Mike Stewart. "The ball broke three ribs on the right side, far as I can tell, but it went right through. Nice neat hole. There's lots of others that weren't so lucky."

"Is there anything else we can do for him?" Barnes asked.

"Sit there and hold his hand if you want," the doctor answered grumpily. "I can't do anything else. There's too many others. My God, Jefferson, you must have been right in the middle of it. More than a hundred of our boys!"

"It was hot," Jeff agreed. "So there's nothing I can do?"

"You can take his personal things with you. They'll get lost or stolen here." The doctor pointed to Stewart's hat, on the ground beside the wounded man. "Watch, money, ring, letters, and such."

Jeff picked up the hat and folded it under his arm. "Do all you can for him, will you, Doctor?"

"I do all I can for all of 'em, son. I just can't do enough, that's all. Be ready in the morning to read burial services. A lot of 'em will die tonight."

"All right. Let me know when you want me."

Late that night Jeff decided to make a neat bundle of Stewart's possessions. He'd give the bundle to Bookstaver to keep with the regimental records. Then he remembered that he couldn't give the bundle to Bookstaver. The adjutant had been killed that afternoon. Jeff sighed; Bookstaver had been an insipid, colorless fellow, but he'd done his job well. Jeff would miss him.

Who will take his place? Jeff thought wearily. Maybe young Tuggle. No, he's too efficient as Company A's top sergeant. Well, I'll find somebody. There'll be a lot of promotions tomorrow, but I'm not going to think about them tonight.

There were several letters among Stewart's effects bearing the return address of Summit House. There was also a packet of letters bound in oilcloth. To conserve space, Jeff decided to put all the letters together in the oilcloth. He untied the cords that bound it and picked up the Summit House letters to put them inside. His glance fell on the handwriting of the letters in the packet. He recognized it at once.

Kate writing to Mike Stewart? There were at least a dozen letters folded into their envelopes.

He stared at the packet for a long time, then slowly and carefully tied it together again. He put all of Stewart's things into one of

Bookstaver's file envelopes and put the envelope away in one of the wooden boxes containing regimental records and correspondence.

Sam Bailey was already asleep in the pup tent that he and Barnes shared. He was snoring heavily, but the snoring could not be heard five yards from the tent because of the constant rumbling of McPherson's guns far to the left on the hills at Decatur. Barnes sat down near the pup tent, with his back against a tree, to have a final cigar before he turned in for the night. The bivouac was quiet enough; all the men not on picket duty were sleeping. In the distance, sometimes sharp and clear above the sound of the artillery, the cries of the wounded carried on the still air.

The sky above Atlanta glowed dull red where buildings burned. Occasionally a rebel battery replied to McPherson's bombardment, and here and there a rifle cracked whenever a picket thought the enemy was creeping in from the opposing lines.

Jeff smoked his cigar slowly, thinking about the letters. He did not regret putting them away unread. He would not have read them in any case, even had he had reason to believe that there was anything more than friendship between his wife and Mike Stewart.

Kate was lonely back in Highland Landing. She wrote to Stewart, but not to her husband, and Jeff was sure that Stewart replied with the news of the campaign and the regiment—all the things that he, Jeff, should be writing to her.

Was it up to him to repair the break between them? Of course it was; there was no question of pride or face-saving involved. He should write her a long letter, telling her how much he longed to see her, how much he wanted to come home to her when the war was over.

He shook his head. He would be lying if he said those things. He knew that he cared now about only one thing—victory. To be truthful, he had scarcely thought of Kate since the army had marched out of Chattanooga. There were too many responsibilities crowding his mind. Sometimes at night, busy with paper work, he would look at her picture in his field desk, and then he would regret all the barriers that had been thrown up between them. Such moments were infrequent, however. There was too much to do and too little time to do it in. Whatever future he and Kate might have could not be decided until the war was over.

He touched the stump of his right arm with his left hand, doubting that there was any future. All his ambition, all his dreams, had been left on Lookout Mountain. Twenty-five years old, and he looked to be forty. All the young man's fire was gone, leaving only the hard core of duty—the determination to drive on to the end.

He thought grimly of the day when victory would be announced to the nation. He supposed people would go mad with joy: whistles would scream, guns would blast, men and women would dance in the streets. What would that day mean to him? The end of his life, because the army had no place for a one-armed lieutenant in the permanent establishment.

Kate had been right to leave him, and he would never ask her to come back. She was too young, too bright and gay to share the bleak gray days that peace would bring him.

He wondered idly if Stewart loved her. The care with which the letters were wrapped showed that they meant a great deal to Stewart.

Maybe I'm wrong, Jeff thought. Maybe those letters tell him that she loves him, too. They were together often in Tullahoma. It could have happened. She knew by then that our marriage had gone up. Why not?

Jeff got to his feet, checked briefly at the headquarters tent with Hanford, the O.D., and then made his way again to the field hospital.

"How is Captain Stewart?" he asked Renwick.

"Not bad," the doctor said wearily. "We got some that won't last till morning. I'm not worried about Stewart. You going to fight again tomorrow?"

"Depends on what Hood does," Jeff said.

"I'll need more morphine, bandages, surgical thread——" Renwick threw up his hands. "I need everything, Jefferson."

"I'll see what I can do for you," Jeff said. "Mind if I walk around among the men?"

"Go ahead." Renwick smiled briefly. "Give them a good word or two."

Jeff walked quietly along the rows of blanketed forms on the ground. There were a few lanterns to throw light on the wounded men and several campfires to take the chill from the night air.

He could call them all by name; he stopped for a few seconds with each man who was conscious. They wanted to know how the regiment had come out of the battle, if this friend or that had survived, if the rebels promised to fight again tomorrow. Some wanted word to go to their families or sweethearts; Jeff promised them he'd do his best.

A young man from Company A named Jimmy Wilson was obviously dying. He lay with open eyes, staring at the stars. His left leg was gone and his shoulder was shattered. Dr. Renwick had given him all the morphine he could spare, but the boy was still awake. He smiled weakly at Jeff and tried to speak.

"Easy, Wilson," Jeff said, bending low. "You don't have to talk."

"Licked 'em, Colonel?" the boy whispered.

"We licked 'em, Wilson."

Wilson's tongue moved over his dry lips. "Come a long way with you, Colonel."

"You did, Jimmy."

"Got a long way to go." The boy's eyes closed. He opened them briefly once more. "I'm dyin', sir. You say a word when they put me under?"

Jeff's throat constricted; he couldn't speak. He nodded to the boy. Wilson closed his eyes again.

41

Just before the battle, the Gen'ral hears a row,
He says, "The Yanks are comin', I hear their
rifles now."

AT PEACH TREE CREEK the first assault was shattered and was succeeded by several others that ground themselves to bloody bits against the XX Corps and the supporting troops of Thomas. A few days later Hood tried again. He saw the Army of the Tennessee alone at Decatur on the ring around Atlanta. He threw four divisions against it. This was Sherman's own army; it had never been whipped.

The XV Corps alone beat off seven frontal assaults in one afternoon of fighting.

Hood withdrew once more, having accomplished nothing but the slaughter of several thousand veterans who could not be spared.

The ring tightened; the guns boomed night and day; the city was a shell. The men in butternut crouched in their trenches, wondering when the President in Richmond would bring old Joe back to the command.

Sherman fretted and fumed, wheeled and marched. He offered dare after dare, knowing his opponent, but the gallant Hood tended his wounds and refused the dares. Sherman wanted Atlanta, and now wanted it badly. All his future action depended upon the taking of the city.

When McPherson was killed in the fighting of July 22, Howard was appointed to the command of the Army of the Tennessee. Howard was a compromise with "Pap" Thomas; Sherman wanted to name "Black Jack" Logan, but Thomas objected. Hooker thought he deserved the post by virtue of experience, reputation, and seniority. He resigned his command of the XX Corps and went home to sulk. Slocum was brought in from his command on the Mississippi to take over the XX.

Hood held fast to his trenches through August. Skirmishing was constant, but the great battle that would force a decision was avoided. Sherman wondered if somehow Johnston had not again taken a hand in the game. Great siege guns were brought down the railroad from Chattanooga. They pounded the city into rubble. "There goes the Atlanta Express," said the Yankees in the trenches when the shells screamed overhead at exact five-minute intervals. The gunners chalked the shells: "Love and kisses to Jeff Davis!"

Sherman's cavalry raided the railroads that fed Atlanta, making a lot of noise with small result.

Then Hood made one of the inevitable mistakes of so restive a spirit. He detached his cavalry under young Joseph Wheeler to rip up the railroad between Sherman and Chattanooga. Wheeler did little ripping and finally wandered off into eastern Tennessee. Hood had cut off the eyes and ears of his army.

On August 25, Sherman offered another dare. Leaving the XX Corps to look upon Atlanta from the north, he marched off with the rest of the army, swinging around the end again to menace Atlanta by the south, and to capture and destroy the fragile rail lines that kept the city alive.

The rebels investigated the empty Yankee trenches. The city went wild. "Sherman has retreated." Hood telegraphed to Richmond, telling of his victory.

The time was drawing near. It was August 30 before Hood knew he had been duped. There was heavy fighting at Jonesboro to the south of the city on September 1. Hardee's corps was thrown back by the Yankees, barely escaping destruction.

That was the night that Hood blew up the ammunition stores and told his ragged men that they were leaving the city. They were departing at one end of town while the XX Corps came marching in the other.

The word went by telegraph to Washington. The President lifted his bowed head from his desk. He had been contemplating the image of defeat in the November elections. The capture of Atlanta would now destroy the "peace platform" of the Democratic Party and its candidate, General McClellan.

Slocum's men tramped into Atlanta to the music of the band of the 33rd Massachusetts; the fires left by Hood coated the blue ranks with red shadows; General "Pap" Thomas, when he heard the news, tossed aside his studied dignity and essayed a jig; Sherman flashed the message: "So Atlanta is ours and fairly won. . . ."

42

And I warm to you, friend, when I think of this:
We have drunk from the same canteen.

THE DAY after Atlanta fell Dr. Renwick appeared at regimental headquarters in a field on the outskirts of the city.

"Well, Doc, what can I do for you?" Barnes asked. The doctor stepped into the weather-beaten Sibley tent that Comfort had foraged among the abandoned equipment of the rebels.

"Stewart is ready to travel, Jeff," the doctor said wearily. "So am I."

"You are, Doc? What are you talking about?"

"I'm going home, son. I've seen enough. I can't bear any more of it."

Jeff looked at him silently for a few seconds. Then he nodded. "I see, Doc. Whatever you say. Will Chambers stay with us?"

"He'll see you to the end. He says he will. He can do the job. I'm tired and I'm sick, Jeff. I've got to go home. Stewart and I might as well make the trip together."

"Does Stewart want to go?" Jeff asked. "When I saw him three days ago, he was talking about getting on his feet and returning to duty."

Renwick shook his white head. "He'll be flat on his back for another month or so. When he does start to move around, he's going to have trouble. That Minié ball smashed a couple of his ribs to smithereens. He won't be much good for soldiering. I told him this morning. He's willing to go home."

"How will you move him from train to train?"

"Stretcher or wheel chair. He's able to sit up all right."

"When do you want to go, Doc?"

"Today, if we can. Will there be trains going to Nashville?"

"Not from Atlanta. They're fixing the tracks between here and Marietta. We'll take you to Marietta."

"Good, Jeff. I'll go get our things ready."

"And I'll get your travel orders, Doc. You just can't pick up and leave, you know. I have Stewart's personal property here," Barnes said, turning to the boxes of regimental records. He took out the bulky folder and handed it to the doctor. "I'll come around to see you both before you leave."

"You don't think I'm quitting, do you, son?"

Jeff shook his head soberly. "The quitters are gone long ago, Doc. None of us quits any more. When a man gets worn out, he's got to stop. You reached that point long ago. Remember that we'll be grateful forever for what you've done. Some of us would be dead and buried but for your work."

"I couldn't face another battle, Jeff. Not another one, with them screaming and crying and praying all around me and nothing for me to do but cut off their arms and legs and wonder if they'll die while

I'm cutting. Before I'd do it again, I'd put a gun in my mouth and pull the trigger."

"I understand, Doc. Of all of us, you've had the worst of it ever since we left home."

"No, Jeff. Not the worst. You had that. You had to tell 'em to go out and get mangled; all I had to do was try to patch 'em up. But you're a strong man, Jeff. You've had to be to last so long in this business."

"I'm wearing thin, Doc," Jeff said with a smile, "and we've still got a long way to go."

"Not so far now," Renwick said. "They can't stand up to Uncle Billy and Grant together. By the way, Jeff, can I take any messages home for you?"

Jeff shook his head. "No, Doc. Not a one." Renwick hesitated, then shrugged. "All right. See you later."

At noon the 195th's ambulance wagon brought Mike Stewart and the doctor through the regiment's bivouac area on the road to Marietta. Hundreds of soldiers lined the way to say good-by to Dr. Renwick. The old man had tears in his eyes as he shook hands with all the men who could press close enough to him.

"God bless you, boys," he said again and again as the ambulance moved slowly away. "Good-by, and God bless you!"

The ambulance stopped at Barnes's Sibley tent. He came out and climbed into it. He called to Comfort to bring his horse along; he'd ride a short way with Captain Stewart.

"Well, Mike," he said to Stewart, who lay on a mattress in the bed of the wagon, "so you're off to God's country."

"I wanted to stay, Jeff, but Doc Renwick convinced me I'll be an invalid for a long time."

"Don't resign your commission," Jeff said. "It may be years yet before they give up."

"No, Jeff. The Confederacy has gone up. A few more months, that's all they have left. I'll try to get back before it's over, but I doubt if there'll be time."

"I envy you," Jeff said, smiling. "You'll have some fishing this fall and some hunting on the mountain."

Stewart nodded. "Maybe. I ought to be off my back in a couple of weeks." He looked soberly at Barnes. "Doc Renwick brought the stuff you kept for me. Did you see the letters, Jeff?"

"From Kate, you mean? I saw them. Of course I didn't read them."

"You could have, Jeff. All she ever wrote about was you. Is there anything you want me to tell her?"

"No, nothing. Thanks, Mike."

"When it's over, Jeff—can I tell her you're coming home?"

Barnes shook his head. "I don't know what I'm going to do. It'll have to wait, Mike."

"Before I go, I'd like you to know how I feel about her."

"I think I know without your telling me. Does she feel the same way?"

"You know she doesn't."

Barnes nodded. He put his hand down and grasped Stewart's hand warmly. "Have a good trip, Mike. Come back if you can. Good-by."

Barnes climbed out of the wagon, accepting Comfort's help on the retractable steps. He watched the ambulance roll away in a cloud of dust on the Marietta road.

43

The bee shall honey taste no more,
The dove become a ranger,
The dashing wave shall cease to roar,
Ere she's to me a stranger.

"WE'LL NEED this house, ma'am," Sergeant Comfort said to the woman who answered the door at his knock. It was a two-story brick building with a wide, pillared veranda across its front. It was on Marietta Street, several hundred yards from General Thomas's headquarters.

The woman looked at Comfort briefly and then down the brick walk to the gate, where a tall officer with one arm was dismounting from his horse. He was accompanied by three other officers.

"Yes," she said simply, letting the door swing wide. "I understand. Tell your officers to come in, Sergeant."

She stood aside as Bailey, Hanford, and the new adjutant, a former sergeant of Company C named Secord, came across the broad porch of the door. Barnes stood on the brick walk, shading his eyes with his hand and looking down the broad expanse of Marietta Street.

She was young, probably less than twenty-five, Hanford thought. She was dressed in plain black; most of the women in Atlanta wore black, or so it seemed. Her hair was straw-colored, brushed back from her forehead. She was a good-looking woman, Hanford told himself. Her face was more angular than round, her features sober without seeming severe.

Bailey and Secord swept their slouch hats from their heads when they saw her. They stared admiringly. They'd seen no young, pretty women since leaving Chattanooga in May. Hanford touched his fingers to the brim of his hat, then turned to look at Barnes, who was still on the walk.

Bailey bowed politely. "I'm Lieutenant Colonel Bailey, ma'am. 195th New York Infantry. These officers are Major Hanford and Adjutant Secord. Colonel Barnes there on the walk, ma'am."

"Did you say Barnes, sir?" She came out of the shadowed hallway and moved through the door. She stood looking at the colonel, who now turned to face her. "Jeff?" she asked tentatively. Then she smiled. "Jeff Barnes!"

His weathered face broke into a warm smile. "Ruth Meyer!" He came forward with his hand outstretched. "How are you, Ruth?"

"You've changed so," she said. "I wasn't sure it was you until you turned around. Hello, Jeff." She had a level voice, low and rich.

"Gentlemen," he said to the others, "this is Mrs. Corwin, daughter of Brigadier General Meyer of the Army of the Potomac."

"There's news!" she said quickly. "I didn't know my father was a general."

"Glad to meet you, ma'am," Bailey said politely but puzzledly. He looked at Hanford for enlightenment, but Hanford was obviously as much at sea as he was.

Barnes laughed. "It's no mystery, Sam. I knew Mrs. Corwin when her father was instructor in military drawing at the Academy."

"Come inside, Jeff," she said. "Come in, gentlemen. You're very welcome here."

Sergeant Comfort, intent on duty and not at all astonished that his colonel should have found a pretty young woman to call by her first name, even in the heart of the Confederacy, broke in politely. "Excuse me, ma'am. You got a stable round back? I ought to put up the horses."

"Of course, Sergeant. Go ahead. I'm afraid you'll have to furnish your own forage. General Hood's men cleaned out the grain, hay, and straw."

In the vestibule she took their hats, then led them into the parlor. It was a light, airy room with many windows and two pairs of french doors leading to the veranda. Most of the glass in windows and doors had been broken by the concussions of artillery fire during the siege of the city. The empty panes were covered with netting. The room was comfortably furnished. A portrait of a young Confederate officer in dress uniform hung on the wall facing the door through which they entered.

Barnes walked across and looked at the portrait.

"That's George to a T," he smiled. "Where is he serving, Ruth?"

"He was killed at Chancellorsville."

"I'm sorry, Ruth."

"That was a long time ago," she said quietly. "I'm used to being a widow now. There are many of us in Atlanta."

Barnes looked again at the portrait, then explained to Bailey and Hanford: "Major Corwin was my classmate at the Academy," he said.

"When did you see my father, Jeff?" she asked, then answered her own question. "Of course you couldn't have. He's in Virginia and you've been down here."

"I saw him less than two years ago, Ruth, in Baltimore. He was well. You haven't heard from him?"

"Not since I left West Point," she said. "It's amazing to hear that he's a general. But then, you're a colonel already."

Barnes laughed. "I'm still a lieutenant in the regular establishment." He turned suddenly to Hanford. "I'd better put you to work, Jack. Go find us another house. We can't use this one."

"Why not?" she asked quickly. "There's plenty of room, Jeff. Only George's aunt and myself live here."

"No, Ruth. We need a house for regimental headquarters. Part of our duty will be as provost guards in this section of the city, and that means noise, drunken soldiers in the middle of the night, constant traffic through the house. It would be an imposition."

"Please, Jeff. Don't refuse. I want you to stay. There are twelve rooms. We'll take the three upstairs in the back and leave the rest to you."

He hesitated.

"During the siege," she added, "we had part of General Hardee's staff quartered here. I'd much rather have Federal troops after all these years of gray uniforms."

"We'll make noise, we'll track mud, we'll break things, we'll get in your way."

"So did Hardee's officers. I didn't mind."

"All right. Remember that I warned you, Ruth."

Sam Bailey got to his feet. "Come on, Jack. Let's get the gear and start moving in. Which room can we use for an office, Mrs. Corwin?"

"This one. The rebels used it."

When the others were gone, Ruth brought a decanter of brandy and poured Jeff a drink. "Can you talk awhile, Jeff, or must you be as busy as the rest of your army seems to be?"

"I can't help them to move us in here," he said, nodding down at his empty sleeve. "Let's talk. You must have known that some of us who knew you at the Academy would be with Sherman. Why didn't you come looking for us? You knew Jud Kilpatrick, didn't you? And Archie Smith is with the XX Corps artillery."

"I planned to see General Howard. He's one of Father's friends. But your men were boisterous in the streets, and I was waiting for them to calm down a little. Instead, you found me. I'm glad, Jeff." She laughed brightly and, moving closer to him, lightly touched the fabric of his blouse. "It's been so long since I've seen that blue uniform." Her voice softened. "Where were you wounded, Jeff?"

"Lookout Mountain. From the way you've been talking, I gather that George never made a rebel of you?"

"He tried. God knows he tried. I was in love with him, and I listened to him in the beginning. But it was all a mistake, Jeff. I should have known it wouldn't work. By the time he went off with the troops to Virginia, we were quarreling bitterly. Then I was an alien here. George's aunt—she's the only family he had, you know—

used to talk nothing but states' rights, secession, the glorious cause. Since his death she's scarcely talked to me at all. At least we get along without open warfare. These people, Jeff, thought they'd whip the North in six months. I don't think they've realized yet that they've lost, but at least, now that you're here, they see what they've brought on themselves."

"It'll be worse before it's over," he said, "unless they quit now. Haven't they had enough, Ruth?"

"They'll never have enough. You'll beat them to the ground, and while they lie there, they'll talk about the cause. They'll insist on destroying all they have to keep fighting, not that they have much left now. You should have seen the home guard going out to man the trenches during the siege so Hood could make his foolish charges with the veterans. Little boys and old men, marching through the streets singing 'The Bonnie Blue Flag.' I think you'll have to kill them all, because they'll never admit they're whipped."

"Wasn't there some way you could come North? You shouldn't have stayed here, Ruth."

"I wanted to. I could have arranged it, I suppose. George had many friends who would have helped his widow, even to go to Yankeeland. Then the fighting started here in Georgia and it was too late."

"So your marriage didn't work. Neither did mine, Ruth."

"You're married? Someone I knew at the Academy?"

"No. A girl from Highland Landing. It's been difficult for her. I guess she didn't realize how much the army would demand of me."

"I can see what it's done to you, Jeff. At least now you'll have a rest, won't you? You'll stay here in Atlanta?"

"Who knows what Uncle Billy will do next? We won't go far until Hood is disposed of. That won't be a job for the XX Corps. We're the occupation troops for the city."

44

What Captain leads your armies
Along the rebel coasts?

DURING THE AFTERNOON that followed, Comfort took the lead in transforming the Corwin house into regimental headquarters. Informed that the Corwin servants had long since run away from the incessant cannonading of the siege, Comfort turned up with a homeless Negro couple. They were far from being expert house servants, but they were eager to learn under Comfort's benevolent tyranny.

He established himself in the kitchen, where he lounged with coffeepot and pipe, directing the activities of the Negroes and the enlisted men whom he had dragooned into headquarters service.

Comfort smiled complacently and sipped his coffee. Goddamn, this was the life! He didn't know what Sherman had in mind, but he'd be content if the XX Corps occupied Atlanta for the rest of the war.

General Sherman's mind was revealed in part to Jeff Barnes that evening. Jeff, Bailey, and Hanford had finished dinner and were lingering over coffee with Ruth Corwin, who was giving them a graphic description of the city of Atlanta under siege.

She was interrupted by Comfort, who appeared at the doorway of the dining room. "Beg pardon, Colonel," he said abruptly. "General Ruger is outside. He says get your hat and come on. I told him come in and have a cup of coffee, but he says he ain't got time."

"All right, Sergeant," Jeff said. "Excuse me," he said to the others.

Comfort brought the colonel's horse from the stable. Jeff joined Brigadier General Ruger in the street. Ruger was a capable, earnest officer. He was heavy-set, with a flaring mustache and a square, stern face. "Good evening, Barnes," he said brusquely. "They want to talk to us. Williams said I was to bring you with me."

"What do you think it's about, sir?"

"You'll find that out, Barnes. I'm not the one to tell you."

Sherman was already launched into the subject when they arrived. He paced the long wooden veranda of the house that General Thomas had chosen for temporary quarters. He talked at his usual rapid-fire pace while his aides scribbled notes of his conversation. Sherman nodded to Ruger and Barnes when they climbed the steps, but kept talking. General Thomas rocked his portly body in a comfortable porch chair, General Slocum eyed Sherman impassively from a similar chair, and General Williams chewed nervously on a black cigar. Every division and brigade commander in the XX Corps was on the porch. Jeff Barnes was the only regimental commander among them. He and Ruger perched on the wide steps and listened to Sherman.

"They'll scream, all right," Sherman said. "Oh, they'll howl! They'll call me a brute and a barbarian, but they've got to go. I don't care what they call me. War is war, and not popularity-seeking. Let them stop the war and then I'll listen to 'em."

"Nobody here is arguing with you, General," said Thomas mildly.

"That's because you all know I'm right. We garrisoned Memphis and Vicksburg and Natchez, and I saw what happened. We'd need a division or two to control Atlanta with the people still here. We can't spare the men. They've got to go, every man, woman, and child except those that work for us or are necessary to keep utilities going.

"Slocum, your corps will do the job. I don't care which way they go, north or south. Let 'em choose. We'll give the ones who want to go north food and transport. The ones who want to hang on to the last ditch can go to Hood. He's at Lovejoy's Station. I'll write and tell him they're coming. We'll move them to Rough and Ready Station, let Hood take 'em from there. I'll set up a two-day truce with him. Now listen to me, gentlemen. They all must go, every noncombatant in Atlanta, and that includes the blacks. But don't force the slaves to go south to Hood. If they want to go north, let them. You'll have plenty of time to set up a schedule for moving the people out. Hood isn't going to agree to this without howling, and the mayor is already yelling his head off. I told him today what I was going to do."

"The ill and the aged, General?" Slocum asked. "What shall we do with them?"

"There will be few who can't travel the few miles to Rough and

Ready, Slocum. Use your judgment. Humanity, but not sentimentality, will do the trick. Any questions, gentlemen?"

General Geary spoke. "Do we use force if they don't want to go, sir?"

"If it's necessary, Geary. They must go."

"When will we start moving them, sir?" Geary asked.

"Perhaps next Monday. That should be time enough. I'll publish an order with the details. Anything else?"

"Maybe, General, you'd better tell us where we're going next," Thomas said lazily. "We're not going to sit here in Atlanta for the rest of the war, are we?"

"You know where I want to go, Tom," Sherman answered, "but you also know that until I get approval from Mr. Lincoln and General Grant, I'll keep it to myself." He looked at General Thomas, a wry grin breaking his wrinkled face. "That question, Tom, was designed to make my tongue slip. You know me better than that. In due time, gentlemen, you'll all find out where we're going. Your first job is to plan your transport for the evacuation of the civilians." He turned once again to General Thomas. "Tom, did you bring Thomasville into Atlanta with you? If you did, I suggest that it's been a hot, dry day and these gentlemen are probably thirsty."

All the others smiled at the reference to "Thomasville." It was a dig that had given rare glee to Sherman on the way from Chattanooga. General Thomas, a lover of comfort in the field, had been the only general officer to ignore pointedly Sherman's order that field equipment be kept to a bare minimum. He had traveled with a carnival-type wagon, loaded with a massive tent, tables, chairs, desks, filing cases, and enough supplies to last through three campaigns. Sherman had dubbed the spectacle "Thomasville" or "Thomastown" early in the march.

"I imagine something can be done for their thirst," Thomas said equably. He had never risen to Sherman's gibes. He lifted himself ponderously from his chair. "I'll see to it."

Several conversations immediately started among the officers on the porch. Jeff Barnes stood on the steps with Ruger wondering why he had been included in this council.

He didn't have much time to wonder about it because he heard his name called by General Williams. "Barnes, come over here!" Williams was standing in a group that included Sherman and Slocum.

"I was wondering when they'd get around to it," Ruger said with a slight smile on his broad, stern face. He nodded toward Williams. "Go on over, my boy."

"How are you, Barnes?" Sherman said abruptly. "I see you managed to get here with the rest of us."

"There were times when I thought I wasn't going to make it, sir."

Sherman smiled. His harsh voice was softened when he answered: "One of those times was at Peach Tree Creek. How many assaults did your regiment hold against?"

"Three, sir."

Sherman nodded. "I read the reports. You didn't think a one-armed man could be a hero, did you, Barnes?"

"There weren't any heroes, sir. Just several hundred veterans who stood their ground."

"You're right, quite right," Sherman agreed, nodding. "All the heroes went home long ago, I guess. How many men are left in your regiment fit for duty?"

"Four hundred and twenty this morning, sir."

"That's not so bad. I understand some regiments are down to two hundred. Well, Barnes, I'll tell you why you're here. You're getting a brigade. Confirmation came through from Washington today. Didn't you hear it through the grapevine?"

"No, sir. Not a word." Jeff's throat tightened; he could scarcely make the words audible.

"That's remarkable!" Sherman said. "Usually my staff has all messages decoded and spread through the army in less than an hour. That's it, Barnes. We're adding a brigade to Williams's division. And you can keep your New Yorkers, can't he, Williams?"

"Yes, sir!" Williams said, chewing his cigar vigorously and winking at Jeff. "Congratulations, General Barnes!"

Sherman shook Jeff's hand firmly, and the others did the same. General Ruger pressed forward when the hand-shaking ended. "I demanded the privilege of giving you your stars, Barnes," he said. "Here you are, General, and may they bring you good fortune." He handed Jeff a pair of shoulder tabs of fine blue cloth. The borders and single stars were done in untarnished gold embroidery.

"Thank you very much, sir." Jeff said softly, unwilling to trust his voice.

"And a pair from me," General Williams interposed, putting a pair of shoulder tabs into Jeff's hand. "Ruger insisted on the honor, and I gave it to him, so put this second pair on another uniform and wear them with my best wishes."

"Thank you, sir."

"Come and see me tomorrow," Williams said. "We'll work out the brigade together. You'll keep your boys, and I'll give you the New York bunch in the 2nd Brigade, the Wisconsin regiment from the 3rd, and probably another. With every unit at such low strength, some brigades are going to have six regiments."

It was almost dark when Jeff left Thomas's headquarters and rode back toward the Corwin house. His spirit was higher than it had been since the 195th had left Highland Landing. That seemed ages ago, yet he remembered that it had been only two years.

He was a brigadier general at an age when Academy graduates in the old days were looking for their first promotions. He was twenty-six; his birthday had been last week, he remembered. He had his stars, although he hadn't been the first in the class to get them.

Now the years that stretched ahead of him would be years of service in the army; they wouldn't retire a general officer when the war was over. A brevet brigadier general ought to rate a captaincy in the regulars. How thankful he was that Sherman had taken the time from a heavy schedule last April to stop in Tullahoma! He would be, like thousands of other men in this army, ever grateful to Uncle Billy. A life that had once seemed broken and empty was now filled with confidence.

A sudden blast of music made the bony old gray horse dance all over the street. Jeff had a moment's hard work to keep his seat before he could look for the cause of the disturbance.

Ahead of him, before the Corwin house, a band was blaring away at the apple-knockers' song. In the dusk the six companies of the 195th New York Infantry were standing in formation as if for review.

The old horse continued to fret at the blaring band music, arching his neck at the pull of the reins. He lifted his hoofs coltishly. As the horse danced before each company in turn, Jeff inclined his head in salute. He was unable to slacken his firm grip on the reins.

Comfort was waiting at the hitching post to take the horse. His tanned face was split by a boyish grin, although he stood stiffly at attention when Jeff was dismounting.

"All right, Comfort," Jeff told him. "At ease. Put him away."

"By Jesus, General!" Comfort said brokenly. "I think it's prime! I just think, by God, that it's prime."

"Can you sew on a pair of stars, Comfort?"

"By God, I sewed the eagles on, didn't I, General? By God, I did!"

Jeff turned to meet Sam Bailey, who snapped a salute and smiled happily.

"Let 'em go, Sam," Jeff said. "Put them at ease and let 'em go. They don't have to parade for me."

"They wanted to, Jeff. They've known about it all afternoon, but they kept the secret. Say a few words to them, General. Go ahead."

Jeff nodded. "If I can. I wouldn't be surprised if I started to cry." He stepped a few paces into the street, where all six companies could see and hear him. "Thank you, men," he called. "Thank you very much. General Williams tells me that we're to stay together. You'll be transferred to the 4th Brigade with me. We'll go on to-gether."

Discipline was cast aside by a shout from Company A. "Three times three for the Ramrod!"

The cheers thundered behind him as he walked up to the house. His eyes misted, although he brushed his hand across them to clear them.

45

Yet praying
When this cruel war is over,
Praying that we meet again.

"I'M SORRY, RUTH," Jeff said, "but there can be no exceptions. You'll have to go."

They were sitting on the veranda in the darkness long after night-fall. The house was quiet; Sam Bailey was working alone in the parlor. Hanford was on provost duty and Comfort was eating pie in the kitchen.

"I know," she said. "I'd like to stay and run the house for you, but I suppose it wouldn't be proper. George's aunt will go south to Hood. She has a brother near Millen, Georgia, I believe. And I'll go north. You're sure I can?"

"The general said so. Where will you go, Ruth?"

"To Cincinnati. I can wait for my father there. It's where his family lives."

"What will you do in Cincinnati, Ruth?"

"Who knows? Wait for the war to end. Teach school perhaps. You remember that I taught for a while in the grade school at Highland Falls when my father was at the Point."

"Maybe you'll get married again, Ruth."

"I hope so," she said simply. "It would have to be someone in the army. It's the only life I know."

"I guess army officers should pick army wives," he said. "It's a hard life for anyone who wasn't raised to it."

"You'll go home to your wife, won't you, Jeff?"

"I don't know."

"Do you want to tell me about it?"

"Not now, Ruth. Sometime, maybe."

They sat in silence for a time, then she said reluctantly that it was time to go inside. He got up and stood aside to let her pass. She brushed against him in the darkness, and his senses responded to the touch of her body and the fragrance of her perfume. He caught her hand and turned her to him. He kissed her.

She answered the kiss, then pulled away.

"Good night, Jeff."

"Good night."

The days went swiftly by—warm, sultry days during which the XX Corps marshaled the horses, mules, and the wagons that would carry the civilian populace of Atlanta to Rough and Ready Station, south of the city and halfway to Hood's lines. The people wouldn't believe that they were to be shipped away from their homes; sullenly they eyed the preparations and waited for word from their civic leaders that Sherman had been prevailed upon to change his mind. Even their worst estimates of Sherman's ruthlessness had not prepared them for this extreme measure.

Hood agreed to the truce that Sherman proposed for the transfer of civilians, but he protested the order "in the name of God and humanity."

That started an exchange of bristling letters between Sherman and Hood, in which Sherman's sharp words cracked like pistol shots and his sentences rattled like musketry. Hood relied upon frequent references to gallantry and justice. The rebel general accused Sherman of "studied and ingenious cruelty," to which Sherman replied with a list of rebel crimes against the nation, telling Hood to "talk thus to the marines, but not to me, who have seen these things."

At length Hood stopped writing letters, and the preparation for the evacuation of Atlanta went ahead. General Barnes took command of the new brigade in the 1st Division, XX Corps, and put all five of his regiments into the task of clearing the city. He and his staff—he took Secord from the 195th to be one of his aides; a second lieutenant from the Wisconsin regiment was another—worked long hours through the rest of the week, knowing that when Uncle Billy said the town was to be empty of civilians at dawn on the following Wednesday morning, the job had better be done.

There was sometimes enough leeway in his day for Jeff to have dinner with Ruth Corwin, or at least coffee and brandy before midnight. Neither of them mentioned again the kiss on the veranda. It had put a barrier of uneasiness between them. For the first time in many months, Jeff was conscious of emotions not connected with duty.

She was alone much of the time now; her husband's aunt had not spoken a single word to Ruth or to any of the officers, soldiers, or Negro servants since Sherman's edict had been told her.

"Her first reaction," Ruth told Jeff, "was to call Sherman a barbarian and you a coldhearted ruffian. Then she said we'd go to her brother's plantation. I told her I was going north to Cincinnati. She hasn't spoken to me since. She leaves the room whenever I come in."

As the week went by, Ruth tried to spend as much time as she could with Jeff. She ordered Comfort and the Negroes out of the kitchen every morning at dawn, and she prepared breakfast for herself, Jeff, and sometimes the brigade staff. She delayed dinner for him if he was late, and sometimes until ten or eleven o'clock. Twice she asked him if he couldn't secure a delay in her departure from Atlanta. Each time he refused, although reluctantly.

Monday came, and with the dawn the streets began to fill with wagons, carriages, and buggies, most of them moving slowly through the city to the south, and a few moving to the huge railroad terminal, where trains waited for those who had elected to go to Tennessee and points north.

The crowds moved slowly and sullenly, quiet for the most part but for the barking of dogs and the wailing of frightened children. All of these people had hoped until the last possible minute that Sherman would change his mind, but now their hopes were ended; they told themselves they were helpless in the hands of a modern Attila. They were participating in the writing of a new page in the history of warfare; their journey into Hood's unwilling arms would be studied by military leaders yet unborn as a prime example of the art of forcing an enemy to encumber himself during retreat.

"If you wait until tomorrow," Jeff told Ruth, "the trains won't be so crowded, and they'll move faster without delays along the line. You'll go straight through to Chattanooga without stopping."

"I'll wait," she said. "Will you be here for dinner? I'll try to make something special."

They had dinner that night alone. Mrs. Corwin had gone to Rough and Ready; the Negroes had piled into a boxcar headed for the mysterious land of freedom in this Year of Jubilo; Comfort was on the town, seeking with other men of the Highland County regiment to give solace to some of the fancy ladies who would leave in the morning to ply their trade with their former customers of Hood's army; the other officers quartered in the house were on provost duty to prevent looting in the largely deserted city.

Jeff and Ruth went to the shaded veranda after dinner to catch the cool evening breeze, each of them remembering the kiss of a few nights before. It could easily have been repeated; they could have shared a few hours of love. The war had long denied them any tenderness. The time passed, however, without incident; neither of them found by accident or design the words that would have aroused passion. They might have been subdued by the somber silence that held the city, or perhaps by the passage of occasional groups of roistering soldiers. At any rate, when Jeff arose at eleven o'clock to make the brigade grand rounds—a duty he usually delegated to a junior officer, but preferred to do himself on a night like this when looting was likely—there had been no suggestion that this night was different from any other.

"Will I see you in the morning, Jeff?" she asked.

"Of course you will."

"Jeff, do you think—after the war, do you think we'll see each other again?"

"There are only a few army posts, Ruth. I think we will."

"I hope we do, Jeff. If you're free——" She stopped talking and turned away. "Good night, Jeff."

"Good night, Ruth. I'll post a sentry at the gate until I get back. Sleep well."

He stepped off the veranda and his long stride carried him quickly into the darkness. She stood there until she could no longer hear his steps on the sidewalk, then she entered the deserted house, crying softly.

46

When Johnny comes marching home again,
  Hurrah, hurrah!
We'll give him a hearty welcome then . . .

IT HAD BEEN a long, leisurely journey from Atlanta, with Dr. Renwick insisting on stopping here for a day and there for another, while Mike Stewart fretted and fumed at the delays. Because of the doctor's insistence on taking the trip in easy stages, Mike was strong enough to sit in a wheel chair on the forward deck of the *Oregon* when it steamed into the bay at Highland Landing.

"You'd have been flat on your backside moaning and groaning," the doctor said mildly, "if I'd listened to your damned yelling about speed." He peered nearsightedly at the steamboat landing, trying to recognize the people who waited in the shade of the pavilion roof. "Can you make out my wife in there, Mike? Likely she's got that purple parasol of hers over her head."

"I see her," Mike said. "How'd she know we would be on this boat?"

"I used the telegraph, my boy. When you were pounding your ear in bed in that high-priced hotel in New York yesterday. Sent one for you, too."

"You shouldn't have done that, Doc," Mike said with a show of irritation. "I could have made it out to Summit House without my father. It's the end of the season; he can't spare the time for trips to Highland Landing."

"Didn't send it to him," the doctor said equably, at the same time waving with surprising vigor to the woman with the purple parasol.

"Who, then?"

"Figured you'd have to stay here in town for a night to rest up after the trip and all. I said to myself, young Mike don't want to stay with me and Mame, nor in the hotel, either. So I sent word to Mrs. Barnes to be down here to get you."

"Dammit, Doc, what'd you do that for?"

Mike's face flushed, his mouth set in a thin line of anger, but his gaze went again to the dock. He saw Kate then, standing just behind Mrs. Renwick. Her father was with her, and between them was a wheel chair. Mike lifted his arm and waved tentatively to her. She smiled and returned the wave.

"What'd I do it for?" the doctor asked in a tone of mild surprise. "Why, boy, do you think I'm blind altogether? I could see how you looked at her down there in Tennessee. And maybe sometimes she looked back at you the same way. Anybody but a complete ninny could have seen what was in your mind. Maybe not in hers, not then, nor maybe not even now. Sometime, though. I'd bet on it, unless Jeff gets around to understanding that he ain't married to the United States Army. I don't blame you, boy, not at all—a pretty girl like that one!"

"You're all wet, Doc," Mike said abruptly. "They'll patch up their troubles when Jeff comes home."

"I dunno about that," Renwick said musingly. "He doesn't make it easy to patch anything up. I won't fault him for what he's done these two years and more, but he could have used a softer touch."

"They're married, Doc. You shouldn't have interfered. You shouldn't have sent her a telegram."

"An old man like me makes a career out of interfering. Now let's get over to the gangplank so you can get ashore and let her take care of you for a day or two. It'll do you both a power of good."

When the gangplank went ashore, Sheriff Boudrye came aboard with the second wheel chair, transferred Mike to it with the help of a deck hand, and then wheeled the chair slowly to the landing. The crowd parted to let the wheel chair through. As Kate came swiftly to greet him, Mike heard a bystander say to another, "That the poor feller's wife? Ain't she pretty?"

She took his hands in hers and bent to kiss him. "Welcome home, Mike!"

His throat was constricted; his words came with difficulty. "Thanks, Kate. It's good of you to be here."

"We'll get you home and then you can start talking about Sherman," the sheriff said.

"The hotel would suit me," Mike said. "Dr. Renwick sent you that telegram without my permission."

"You'll stay with us," Kate answered him. "The hotel indeed!"

"This is an imposition," Mike said.

"Not at all, Captain," the sheriff said. "We've got your room ready, and I'm all set to hear firsthand about the Atlanta campaign." He looked at Kate. "And the regiment, of course. Jeff and the rest."

Dr. Renwick removed himself from his wife's tearful embrace. "Mike, you're my first patient back in civil life. I'll be over to see you every day. I told you that I wasn't going to let you go back to that mountain of yours without watching that wound for a few days."

Mike surrendered, smiling. "All right. A day or so."

Kate walked beside him while the sheriff pushed the wheel chair along the landing to the street.

Suddenly she asked, "How is he, Mike?"

"The same," Stewart said. "Maybe a little thinner, more tired, but just about the same."

"How does he manage with just one arm?"

"Comfort does everything for him that a man needs two arms for. It's no handicap to Jeff."

"Has he spoken of me, Mike?"

"Just before I left, Kate. I asked him if he would come home when it was over."

"And what did he say?"

"No answer, Kate. Neither yes nor no."

"He won't come home."

"Now, Kate," the sheriff interrupted in a worried tone, "we've told you and told you to stop thinking about it. Married folks are always getting themselves into fixes the first few years. He'll come back when it's over and then everything will be fine again. You'll see."

She smiled but didn't answer.

47

Still onward we pressed till our banners
Swept out from Atlanta's grim walls. . . .

THE SICK AND THE WOUNDED boarded the trains that rolled away to Chattanooga and Nashville. The great exodus of civilians had ended long since, but there were many who had been permitted to stay for one reason or another; they too were boarding the trains and leaving the city day after day.

Hood feinted one way, then another, and Sherman's corps wheeled and countermarched to meet the threats. In Atlanta the XX Corps soldiers grew fat and lazy in the shortened defenses. Provost duty was a lark. Rarely did any one regiment have to work more than two days in a row in the railroad yards, and the only other disturbances to the urban holiday were drills and parades. The band of the 33rd Massachusetts gave concerts in the Athenaeum, and other regiments responded with plays, musicales, lectures, and dances—in which most of the "ladies" were distinguished from the gentlemen by bands of cloth tied to the arms of their blue blouses.

The men of the XX Corps relaxed and sorrowed mockingly for their brothers of the Armies of the Tennessee and the Ohio, who were being marched day after day through the rough hills along the railway, ready to meet Hood at any point.

Hood hit the small garrison at Allatoona, and General Corse threw him back in a day's fierce fighting. Then Hood swung north again, toward Resaca and Dalton, and Sherman went after him. A stern chase on land is often as difficult as one at sea; Hood easily escaped into Alabama.

The men wondered what came next—what would Uncle Billy do? They had no idea. When he sent Thomas with the Army of the Cumberland all the way to Nashville, and Schofield with the Army of the Ohio to Knoxville, they couldn't understand the general's mind. With reinforcements since the Atlanta campaign, they'd had more than a hundred thousand men in Georgia. Now they had just about sixty thousand, counting the cavalry. Would Sherman follow Hood into Alabama? Would he swing north, abandoning Atlanta, and wait for Hood to come to him? Would he garrison the railroad line between Chattanooga and Atlanta and sit out the winter?

The men in the ranks, and, indeed, the men on Sherman's staff, had no way of knowing the contents of the correspondence that had been passing to and from Washington since early September. On one end of the line was Sherman, who confided in few men except Thomas and Howard. On the other end were the two men who held the power to make the decision.

Sherman insisted that his plan for a new campaign would put Georgia and the Carolinas out of the war; Grant was dubious; Lincoln, who had seen so many generals fail, was fearful.

The messages hummed over the wires, with Sherman refusing to be denied. "I can make this march," he told Grant, "and make Georgia howl!"

He held to his guns, and finally the day came when permission was given, grudgingly and cautiously. Grant wired, "I say, then, go on as you propose."

Sherman grinned in delight, shouted for his staff, and the orders began to fly.

"Call in the detached commands," he said.

The legions groaned, groused, and put on their marching boots.

"Rip up the railroad," Sherman said.

The legions set their shoulders to the crowbars; the rails tore loose from the ties; the ties were piled and set afire; the rails were heated on the fires and then twisted into pretzels.

"Abandon all unnecessary equipment," he said.

The legions grinned to a man and stripped down to rifles, cartridge boxes, blankets, and mess kits.

Then they listened to the general's words in Special Field Orders, No. 119, Military Department of the Mississippi.

"The general commanding deems it proper at this time to inform the officers and men of the XIV, XV, XVII, and XX Corps that he has organized them into an army for a special purpose, well known to the War Department and to General Grant. It is sufficient for you to know that it involves a departure from our present base, and a long and difficult march to a new one . . ."

48

Bring the good old bugle, boys,
We'll sing another song. . . .

THE XX CORPS was to be the last to leave the city, as it had been the first to enter. All day long on the fifteenth of November, 1864, the men made ready. The throwing away of luxuries began at daybreak. The old campaigners knew what they could carry on their backs.

The few tents that had been carried stubbornly from Chattanooga to Atlanta now went into the fires; veterans had come to regard the pup tents with contempt because they were no protection at all in a driving rain. These went into the flames with the other tents. The average soldier selected only a blanket wrapped around an extra shirt and a pair or two of socks; these in turn were rolled inside his poncho, if he had one. Forty rounds of ammunition in his cartridge box and twenty in his pockets, plus his food and mess gear—these things and his rifle were all a veteran carried. Haversacks—for those who did not wrap rations up in their blankets—contained plenty of coffee, sugar, and salt, along with a scrap of salt pork and three days' supply of hardtack. A man could renew the staples on the march once every ten days.

Everything else was thrown away. One man in each group of messmates carried a hatchet and an extra stewpan; another lugged the coffeepot if the group was fortunate enough to own one. If not, each man carried his own tin can with his mess gear. Usually one man was entrusted with the group's playing cards, which had been thumbed and flipped daily all the way from Chattanooga and now were ragged and almost illegible.

The other three corps were outside the city while the XX waited for Sherman to give the word to go. The men of the XX watched the destruction of Atlanta with hard eyes. In the wake of dozens of battles and skirmishes along the Potomac and in the West, they had picked up rebel equipment marked: "Made in Atlanta, Ga." This city, with Richmond and a couple of others, furnished the major part of the equipment that kept the Confederate armies in the field.

Captain Poe, Sherman's chief engineer, was in charge of the demolition. First went the railroad bridge over the Chattahoochee, and then the mammoth railroad depot in Atlanta. Both were rammed, without explosives, to piles of rubble. Sherman's orders to Poe provided for the destruction of depots, warehouses, machine shops, factories, and all other buildings which, in the chief engineer's opinion, might later be of industrial and military use to the enemy. With Sherman's arrival from Marietta at noon, the engineers began to apply torches and explosives to buildings not already rammed.

The bursting of the demolition charges started early in the afternoon. Then clouds of heavy black smoke began to rise and roll in the clear sky above the doomed city. As the afternoon wore on, the fires began to spread in the heart of the city. The dull explosions of munitions abandoned by Hood thundered constantly, punctuated by the incessant crackling of small arms ammunition in the sheds and warehouses.

The few people remaining in Atlanta streamed for the outskirts, frightened by the fires, the blasts, and the dread of violence from the scattered regiments remaining in Atlanta.

Toward evening the entire area around the railroad depot was a mass of flame that was visible for a score of miles on every side.

High above the soaring flames the black clouds of smoke billowed. Through the fiery haze, midway between flame and smoke, the sun glowed like a blood-red ball of fire. Blazing cinders started more fires, tossed as they were by the shell explosions. For miles around the city the men of the waiting army felt the oppressive heat beating against their bodies.

There were thousands of Union soldiers that night who watched the conflagration for a while as they waited in bivouac, then rolled in their blankets for a few hours' sound sleep before the long march began. They were old campaigners—the kind of soldiers who were little impressed by anything after three years of war. Sherman wanted to burn the city? Let him burn it! Whatever Uncle Billy wanted to do was all right with them.

Other men, recruits since Chattanooga or since the siege of the city, stayed awake far into the night to watch the awful spectacle.

There were a few regiments, in addition to the men under Poe's direct command, who were in Atlanta on duty, protecting dwellings and stores against looting. The regiments of the 4th Brigade of the 1st Division were among them. Through most of the night their companies patrolled the streets in the glare of the fires.

Brigadier General Barnes, mounted on his bony gray, directed the flow of frightened civilians and detached commands of Union soldiers who poured out of the flaming heart of the city. Toward midnight the streets were almost deserted of all but the soldiers of his own brigade and those of the regular provost guard, the 111th Pennsylvania and the 2nd and 33rd Massachusetts. He passed the order to his regiments to bivouac on the Decatur road, by which the XX Corps would take up the march in the morning.

Jeff Barnes didn't sleep that night. He and Sam Bailey sat on a stone bench on the vast lawn of a deserted mansion, talking desultorily and watching the wild fires consume Atlanta. Near by, Jeff's gray horse, painted by the glow of the fires to a strawberry color, cropped contentedly the grass that once had been so carefully tended. Around the house, out of the light, the four hundred or so men of the 195th New York were rolled in their blankets.

Neither Barnes nor Bailey showed any emotion as they watched the destruction of the city. They speculated on Sherman's destination, agreeing that the seacoast was most likely; they talked of Hood moving against Thomas in Tennessee, agreeing that "Pap"

Thomas would have an easy time handling Hood's forty thousand weary veterans. They planned briefly the system of foraging that would be instituted on the march, letting details go by to be adjusted as experience demanded. They spoke of necessary promotions in the 195th. Finally Bailey said he was going to roll in his blanket and try to get some sleep. Before leaving Jeff, Bailey looked at the fire as if it were a brush-burning in the fields around his home outside Highland Landing. He remarked that the absence of a steady wind had given Poe an easy job.

"Wonder why he was so careful today," Bailey said. "Burn the place to the ground, that's what I say."

"The public buildings are enough. It's ruined as a base of operations for them. Good night, Sam."

"Good night, Jeff."

Alone for the two hours or more that remained before reveille, Barnes went over in his mind the condition of the brigade and the prospects for the campaign ahead.

He had five regiments totaling less than two thousand men. The 195th New York was the only one of the five with a complete complement of staff and line officers. Other brigades were in far worse shape as far as returns of men fit for duty, but the army itself was the perfect machine for the job Sherman had undertaken.

Sixty thousand men were ready to swing eastward across Georgia with the coming of the dawn. They were an army of veterans. The world had not seen their like since Caesar's legions. The old men and the heavy men and the weak men had been weeded out long since—they had either fallen by the wayside in the Atlanta campaign or had gone back to Nashville with General Thomas. The men whom three years of grim war had broken in spirit were also gone; they had not re-enlisted as "veteran volunteers."

Thousands of the young men who slept under the rolling smoke of Atlanta's ruins had been in the field for three full years and yet had not been old enough to vote for Mr. Lincoln in the regimental elections not quite two weeks before. Young as they were, they were hard and tough and battle-tempered. They worshiped Sherman. They didn't give a damn where they were going as long as Uncle Billy took them there.

They had ripped up the railroad with enthusiasm, knowing that once it was gone, they'd be on their own. They'd torn down the wires and the poles of the telegraph line with as much glee as Wheeler's rebel cavalry showed in the same task. With the telegraph dead, there could be no link with the north.

As soon as Sherman gave the word, they'd march straight into the heart of Georgia without a thought for Hood's ragged soldiers ranging behind them. If Uncle Billy thought that Thomas could take care of Hood, then they had nothing to worry about.

The regiments were, many of them, down to a third of the number that had so gaily enlisted long years ago; Sherman wanted no recruits—let Thomas have them at Nashville. There were colonels in this army who had come to war with eight hundred men and now could muster two hundred. A brigade parade during the occupation of Atlanta sometimes took as little time to pass in review as had one of its regiments upon enlistment.

Sixty thousand, Jeff Barnes told himself. They think they can march straight to Richmond if Sherman leads them. And, by God, I guess they can!

It's the beginning of the end, he thought. We can't be stopped now. Johnny Reb is finished. He's gone up the flue.

How long? Six months? Eight months? With a winter campaign, it will be no longer.

His eyes closed in weariness as he considered the future. He tried to picture Kate at home in Highland Landing, but the image would not clarify. That was a world far away. It had existed long ago. Could he return to it? He wondered if he could even try. He had left it sometime before Gettysburg. That was a long way to retrace one's steps to find something that had been lost.

He dozed on the bench for a while, warmed by the air that billowed outward from the glowing embers of the city. The old gray horse cropped the lawn serenely, undisturbed by the explosions that shook the ground, heedless of the strange red glow that cast away the darkness.

When the bugles blared just before dawn, the 4th Brigade tumbled out of blankets and got ready to go. Bacon, hardtack, and coffee were downed quickly, and the five regiments fell in on the Decatur road. Behind them the black smoke billowed everywhere in the sky, red-tinged by the glowing embers of Atlanta's ruins. An occasional shell or cache of power exploded sharply amidst the distant dull thunder of crashing walls. Behind the 4th Brigade came the three regiments of the final provost guard: the 111th Pennsylvania, the 2nd Massachusetts, the 33rd Massachusetts with its noted regimental band.

General Barnes gave the order to march. The ranks stepped out with the long stride of the western armies. The band in the distance began to play "Old John Brown," as the soldiers called it. Jeff Barnes reined in the gray at the side of the road until Company A of the 195th New York came swinging by. Jeff called First Sergeant Tim Tuggle.

"Go ahead, Sergeant," Jeff said, "sing the song for 'em."

"Yes, sir," Tuggle said, smiling.

He stepped back into place as the band blared into the chorus. His voice lifted the ringing words and rolled them back over the long column:

> *"Glory, glory, Hallelujah!*
> *Glory, glory, Hallelujah!*
> *Glory, glory, Hallelujah!*
> *His soul is marchin' on!"*

Company by company, regiment by regiment, the men picked up the words and roared them forth as they marched into the dawn. They exhausted the verses of the older song, and Tuggle led them into the new ones:

> *"Mine eyes have seen the glory of the coming*
> *of the Lord,*
> *He is trampling out the vintage where the*
> *grapes of wrath are stored,*
> *He has loosed the fateful lightning of His*
> *terrible, swift sword,*
> *His truth is marching on!"*

In Atlanta the fires were burning out and the embers were turning black. In Tennessee, Hood prepared to batter his ragged army to pieces against Thomas, the Rock of Chickamauga. In Virginia, Lee braced his weary regiments to meet the endless waves of blue. In Washington, Lincoln confessed that he was anxious, fearful when he considered the danger of Sherman's march.

On the Decatur road, Uncle Billy rode forward along his swinging columns on his way to make all Georgia howl.

49

I asked my mother for fifty cents,
To see the elephant jump the fence.
He jumped so high, he touched the sky,
And never came down till the Fourth of July.

THE TALL FRAME of Sergeant Tuggle was a formless blur of motion in the moonless darkness before dawn. He walked swiftly along the row of sleeping men, carrying a long stick, which he used to rap the sleepers' feet. His voice carried sharply as he repeated, "Come on! On your feet!"

James Handy heard the sergeant coming. He was lying on his back with his arms raised and his fingers laced beneath his head. He had been awake a long time, staring upward at the dark sky and listening to Adam Youngblood's snoring.

The sergeant's stick tapped Handy smartly on the legs. "Off your butt and on your feet. Come on!"

"I'm awake, Sarge," Handy answered softly. "I'll get Youngblood up."

The sergeant went to the next row of sleeping men. As Handy lifted himself on one elbow to shake Youngblood awake, men near by began to stir. They muttered sleepily, cursed out of habit, cleared their throats, and growled at one another.

Youngblood said he was awake, so Handy stopped shaking him. They pulled on boots and breeches, then bent to roll their blankets. By nightfall this bivouac would be only a date line in the adjutant's records.

Two dozen other soldiers were also rolling blankets and clothing. They did it quickly with a few deft motions. Private Handy struggled with his; if he didn't get it right it would chafe his shoulders, bang his butt, and otherwise annoy him all day long. Handy was still trying to smooth the wrinkles from his blankets when Youngblood finished his own roll.

"Ain't you ever goin' to get the knack?" Youngblood said mildly. "Let me do it, Jimmy."

In a few seconds Youngblood had the pack rolled and roped.

The men sat down to eat. Cold salt pork and hardtack made their breakfast after two days of poor foraging. If they were lucky this day, they'd have plenty to eat within a few hours. They were sure they'd be lucky; the 1st Division had yesterday moved to the head of the line of march of the XX Corps, after two days of bringing up the rear. The first foragers out would get the best pickings.

Private Handy was one of the few men who ate only pork for breakfast. He wasn't going to eat hardtack in the darkness when he couldn't see the weevils. Actually, he didn't even relish the pork because he could hear other men's teeth crunching the hardtack and then hear the occasional laconic remark, "Fresh meat!" as a man spat out a weevil.

A mounted officer reined in before them. He slumped heavily in the saddle, his slouch hat pulled low on his forehead. Peering at him, Private Handy recognized Major Hanford.

"It's Old Jack," he said to Youngblood. "He's takin' us out hisself."

Youngblood grunted. He was munching the hardtack that Handy had set aside; it was a sin and a shame to waste good food—besides, if he had a dollar for every weevil he'd bitten into in this war, he could buy another farm.

"All ready, Sergeant?" Hanford asked gruffly.

"Ready, sir," Tuggle answered.

"Let's go," the major said. "You men hump it this morning. We've got a regiment to feed."

They moved out of the bivouac of the 4th Brigade of the 1st Division. They heard other foraging parties moving in the darkness. Tousled heads poked from blankets as the foragers passed. In the still morning air rose the usual valedictory chorus for the "bummers" upon whose efforts the regiment's stomachs depended. Roosters crowed, turkeys gobbled, geese honked, cows bawled, and mules brayed. As usual, a wag here or there called out: "Paragraph No. 4: The army will forage liberally on the country. Go, you bummers!"

A misty rain began to fall before the foraging party was long away from the bivouac. The road was already muddy; the rain would make it worse. The party's route was east, away from the Milledgeville road along which the XX Corps was marching. A winding side road,

Major Hanford had been told, led to a spur of the Macon & North Central Railroad. There were plenty of farms and plantations along that spur, and if his party reached the rail line first, there'd be good eating in the 195th for a day or two.

The trick was to beat other regiments to the booty. The army hadn't been on the march a full week, and already a code for bummers was in force. First come, first served—that was the cardinal rule. If a bunch of bummers ran into Georgia militia or a troop of Joe Wheeler's cavalry, every other foraging party within hearing of the guns would come running. After the rebs were driven off, then it was every party for itself as far as foraging went. A man kept his eye on his own regiment's plunder, or it would vanish in an instant.

As the party marched, a soldier near James Handy asked if anybody wanted a drink. He had a bottle of whiskey left from the previous day's foraging. When the bottle came to Handy, he didn't hesitate, but took a short pull, gasping as he swallowed. It was raw stuff; he felt it burn its way down to his stomach.

"You like that rotgut?" Youngblood asked mildly.

Handy didn't, but he felt obliged to say he did. It was the first drink he'd ever had; he didn't think he'd take another very soon.

"Sure," he answered Youngblood. "Sets a feller up."

Private Handy felt fine when the burning of the whiskey stopped. He was ready for anything. He grinned in the darkness, flexing his shoulder to feel the heavy rigid length of his Enfield. He spoke to Youngblood, trying to keep his voice casual.

"S'pose we'll run into any secesh cavalry, Adam?"

"I sure to God hope not," Youngblood said.

Private Handy laughed. "You afraid of a few rebs on horses?"

"I sure to God am." Youngblood paused reflectively. "I'm afraid of 'em off horses, too."

"I ain't," Handy said. "Not with forty rounds in my cartridge box, I ain't."

Youngblood didn't answer for a few seconds. When he did, his voice was characteristically gentle. "That's right, Jimmy. I keep forgettin'. You ain't seen the elephant yet."

Handy's boyish anger flared. It wasn't his fault he hadn't seen any fighting. They wouldn't let him.

"Never mind," he told Youngblood. "It ain't my doing that I ain't been in a battle. Old Jack keeps sendin' me back to help the doctor or bring up the ammunition or some foolish thing. It ain't my fault, so quit throwin' it up to me."

"Don't get mad, Jimmy," Youngblood said. "It's goin' to be a long day."

They all said the same thing to Handy. All the old soldiers, the veterans of Gettysburg and Lookout and Resaca and Kenesaw and Peach Tree Creek: "You ain't seen the elephant yet, Jimmy." How could he when the major kept singling him out for jobs that took him out of danger?

As dawn was coloring the eastern sky, Major Hanford's voice rose above the sloshing of feet through the soft red mud. "All right, you men! Keep your eyes peeled for rebs. Sergeant, I want flankers in the fields."

Sergeant Tuggle called out a string of names. Cursing men began to climb the rail fences that lined both sides of the road. Even if the road was ankle-deep in mud, it provided easier walking than brushy fields and wood lots.

"I want scouts up ahead," Tuggle said. He looked at Youngblood. "Take somebody up front with you, Adam. Come a-runnin' if you see any rebs."

The men around Youngblood bent their heads and trudged along. Scouting duty meant getting shot at by bushwhackers, and no man was fool enough to volunteer to get shot at. Youngblood eyed the men speculatively.

Private Handy's eager voice broke the silence. "Take me, Adam."

Instantly every head rose from contemplation of the red Georgia mud. Two or three men clucked their tongues, shaking their heads in disapproval. They'd learned long ago that only damn fools and recruits volunteered. Also, they didn't like the idea of young Handy going into danger. It had been apparent to all of them from the moment that the boy had joined Company A during the siege of Atlanta that Old Jack had taken a liking to him. They remembered how Hanford's stepson had died at Lookout. They didn't want anything to happen to this boy.

Youngblood and Handy trotted past the head of the column under the casual eyes of Sergeant Tuggle. Major Hanford's gruff voice halted them.

"You want to take him, Adam?"

"Why not, Jack? I mean—sir."

"I know what to do, sir," Handy told the major.

Old Jack stared at him. Then he shrugged. "I guess there's got to be a first time. Adam, don't do nothing foolish out there."

"That ain't likely," Youngblood said.

By double-timing, the two scouts soon put more than a quarter of a mile between themselves and the rest of the bummers. The road was bordered alternately by open fields and pine wood lots. Every few minutes they passed abandoned houses, most of them shanties, and all showing signs of their owners' hasty departures.

While they trotted along, Private Handy reflected morosely on the conspiracy that seemed to be operating against him. He was a man now and could take care of himself. He'd have to, after all. He'd been an orphan since infancy, and had enlisted direct from the Highland Landing city orphanage. He'd joined the army to fight, and he didn't intend to be done out of fighting when it came.

Private Youngblood did nothing to lift his companion's spirits. He seemed deathly afraid of rebels. At every roadside shanty he insisted on taking cover until they were certain it was deserted. He walked crabwise past wood lots that bordered the road, jumping for the ditch every time a rabbit or a squirrel rustled in the underbrush. Before the sun was midway across the morning sky, Handy was thoroughly disgusted with Youngblood's timidity. No wonder Adam had come through so many battles and skirmishes without a scratch!

They had the first sign of human life about ten o'clock. Youngblood suddenly stopped Handy and cupped his hand behind his ear to listen. Handy thought Youngblood had the frightened look of a mongrel dog caught raiding the garbage bucket.

"What's that noise?" Youngblood whispered.

Handy could hear it now, the distant chuffing of an idling locomotive. "Engine on the railroad," he said.

"Let's go back and tell the major," Youngblood said.

"Tell him what?"

"We found the railroad. What else?"

"We knew it was there all the time. Ain't we even goin' to take a look at it?"

"Where there's a train, there's Johnnies. Let's get on back."

"We got to look, anyways."

Handy trotted ahead, with Youngblood following reluctantly. "Stick close to the fences and brush," Adam called.

They went a quarter of a mile, then they could see the railroad clearly. The bed was raised a few feet above the neighboring swampy fields. Directly ahead of the two soldiers was a cluster of buildings, all seemingly deserted. Standing alone to the right was a station house. A faded sign hung awry, facing the road. Handy could make out the letters. The first one or two letters were missing. The rest of the sign read: "—owville." He tried to fit the missing letter or letters. "Lowville. Towville. Crowville."

"I don't give a durn," Youngblood said nervously. "Let's beat it out of here."

Now they could see the locomotive. It stood on a siding several hundred yards to the right of the station. A dozen Negroes were loading grain sacks and wooden boxes into three freight cars attached to the engine. The sacks and boxes were being taken from a string of mule-drawn wagons at the siding. As the two soldiers watched, the Negroes climbed into the empty wagons and began to drive away, heading to the right, away from the station.

"There ain't no rebs here, Adam," Private Handy said.

Youngblood shook his head. "Somebody's bossin' them slaves. They won't work without somebody around to tell 'em what to do. Come on."

"I want to take a look at them buildings," Handy said. "Might as well get first pickin's on whatever's good to eat."

"You listen to me," Youngblood said. "I been at this game a long time. I'm tellin' you you'll get your durn head blowed off. Let's go back."

Jimmy couldn't understand Youngblood's uneasiness. Most of the time Adam was calm and untroubled.

"You go ahead and tell the major," Handy said. "I'll lay here and watch things."

Youngblood hesitated, then nodded. "Don't show yourself. We'll be here in four–five minutes."

Private Handy watched his messmate trot back along the road. Then he started for the hamlet ahead. He was in full sight of anyone watching, but he was sure that no one saw him. The Negroes were quite a way along the tracks now, and no white man had joined them.

He'd gone about ten yards when the first shot was fired. It came from the buildings to the left of the station. The report was the flat crack of a musket. Handy didn't hear the bullet whine. He had thought that bullets always whined. He noted with surprise that he felt exactly as he had before. He had expected some emotion—elation, perhaps, because he could now qualify as a veteran.

He took three quick steps to the shelter of the rail fence on the left side of the road. Two more shots were fired. He was pleased to hear a sound as if a very swift hornet had zipped by his ear. A half minute went by, he moved his head, and two Minié balls picked splinters from the rail above him.

Handy settled himself in the brush and cautiously poked the muzzle of his Enfield through the rails. A fast look behind him showed the Negroes in wild flight across the fields. He parted the bushes and looked toward the buildings where the pair of rebels were hidden. His heart was pumping rapidly now and his body tingled as the blood rushed through his veins. So this was what it was like!

What should happen next? Handy wasn't sure. He thought he could try to cross the field at the next intersecting rail fence. He could sneak around the buildings and capture two prisoners to present to Old Jack when he arrived with the foraging party.

He decided to try this flanking movement. He'd heard all about flanking—how Sherman had shoved Johnston all the way from Ringgold to Atlanta by flanking runs. Private Handy decided to play his own game of "Ring around Rosie."

He looked toward the nearest line of fence that crossed the field behind him. He started in surprise when he saw a line of figures in brown clothing moving along the fence at a rapid trot. Three—five—seven—ten of 'em! They were cutting him off from the foraging party. The flanker was being flanked.

His heart raced. He was in a fix, but he vowed to remain calm. He glanced toward the station. If he could reach it, he'd hole up in there until the rest of the foragers rescued him. There were only a dozen rebels, after all.

He was worried, and now he was angry at himself for not realizing that Adam Youngblood had known what he was talking about.

He jumped to his feet and ran as fast as he could, slipping and sliding in the mud of the road. The rebels in the hamlet fired at him. He looked back. The ten men at the fence had come into the open. They were about three hundred yards away. His strained face relaxed. He'd get to the station easily. Then the rest of the foragers would come to rescue him.

His courage lasted through ten strides. It was dashed away by a glance along the railroad track to the left beyond the buildings. In the distance, where the shining rails tapered to a meeting point, he saw a group of horsemen riding hard and approaching with what seemed to be incredible speed. He knew they were rebel cavalrymen. There were maybe a dozen, maybe fifteen of them.

Handy's confidence fled instantly. They'd shoot him down! He was suddenly terrified because he knew he'd be caught in the open. He was going to die. He saw himself sprawled in the red mud with his life's blood flowing from a dozen wounds. He hadn't imagined that war was going to be like this.

He knew he had to run for his life. He swerved to the right, vaulting the rail fence on that side of the road. He stumbled through the swamp grass of the field, panting the prayers he'd learned at the orphanage.

He headed for the puffing locomotive, not because it offered a refuge, but because that was the only place in sight where there were no rebels.

The wild, piercing rebel yell rose behind him. He turned his strained face to look back. The running rebels had picked up some of the distance. The riders were much closer. Handy tried vainly to make more speed. He stumbled and fell into the bog. Scrambling to his feet and running on, he began to sob frenziedly.

He heard two or three scattered rifle shots, and then a volley. The rebel yell tore the air once more. Handy looked back. The rebels who had been chasing him on foot were jumping across the rail fence again and running for the buildings. Handy heard more scattered rifle shots. Then he saw a line of blue figures dodging along the rail fence in pursuit of the rebels. The foraging party had arrived. He was saved.

His wild fear receded, leaving him trembling. Then it returned when he looked at the cavalrymen. They had almost reached the station. They had cut him off from his comrades. He expected the foragers to fall back immediately when they saw the troopers, but they didn't. They kept moving forward along the rail fence. Now they were exchanging long-range shots with the cavalrymen as well as with the dismounted rebels in the hamlet.

Handy crouched in the grass, watching the blue-clad soldiers advance. He thought they'd all gone mad. Did they want to get killed?

Swiftly the Yankees moved toward the station. The rebel horsemen fired a scattered volley, wheeled their mounts, and retreated down the track, turning to vanish among the houses and shed of the hamlet.

The Union soldiers in the road stopped their dodging advance and joined in a run for the station. Handy saw the major trotting his horse behind them, reining in now and then to fire calmly at the hamlet with his revolver. While the soldiers were crowding through the doors and windows of the station, the major carefully tied his horse to the hitching post outside.

Private Handy, still crouching in the grass, shook and shivered as if he had swamp fever! How could the major act so methodically when all the men in the station were going to die! And when the rebels finished them, they'd come after Jimmy Handy.

He wouldn't let it happen. He'd get away. He crawled through the bog toward the tracks. He could run faster on the railroad ties.

The Enfields cracked steadily against the sharp popping of the rebel cavalry's carbines.

Handy clawed his way out of the marsh grass to the stone bed of the railroad. He got to his feet a few yards from the locomotive. He ran to the right, away from the station.

He didn't pass the end of the train before terror caught him again. Coming toward him this way was another bunch of rebel horsemen! He threw himself away from the tracks into the swamp once more.

It didn't occur to Handy in his fright that he could probably crawl well into the swamp and be safe. His only thought was that he was sure to be killed.

He was lying in the evil-smelling bog beside the train. He had to do something to save himself. The Johnnies would shoot him down if he tried to run in any direction.

The answer came to him as he stared wildly up at the train. During the occupation of Atlanta he'd worked just as often as the other men of the 195th New York in the freight yards. He'd ridden in the cabs of locomotives many times. He knew what to do. He leaped to his feet and raced for the cab. The approaching cavalrymen were perhaps two hundred yards away. Scrambling up the high steps of the cab, Handy sprawled forward and grabbed the drive lever. The

driving wheels moved, slipped, and then began to turn steadily. The
train rolled slowly toward the station. Its speed increased gradually,
but a wild look back showed Handy that the rebels were getting
closer. He gave the locomotive full throttle for a few seconds. Then
he had to shut it off. He knew nothing about allowing the engine to
brake itself, and he didn't want to roll past the station.

The train was still moving when it reached the building. Handy
leaped from the cab and fell on the wooden platform as soldiers in
blue rushed past him to reach the freight cars. Vaguely he heard
the squealing of brakes as they turned the brake wheels on the cars.

Handy crawled for the open door of the building. His mud-plas-
tered Enfield was still slung on his shoulder.

Major Hanford hauled him into the station. All the other men were
firing through the windows and doors, covering the soldiers who had
braked the train. Handy lay gasping on the floor, looking up at the
major. He couldn't understand why Old Jack was grinning at him.

"That was a neat trick, son," the major told him. "You stole that
train from under their noses."

Handy tried to deny it; after all, he'd been saving his skin. His
words wouldn't come out straight. He could only mumble.

"Take it easy," Hanford said. "We're all right here. There's another
bunch of bummers coming up the road and the brigade is right on
their heels, fixing to rip up this railroad."

Handy pushed himself to his feet and crossed to a window that
faced the road. At his shoulder Youngblood fired, pulled in his rifle
to reload, and tunelessly hummed the apple-knocker song.

Handy saw blue-clad soldiers coming on the run. The firing at the
other windows died away to a few scattered shots.

"There go the rebs, sir!" Youngblood called. "It's all over. The
general is coming up the road, sir!"

Hanford pushed James Handy down to a bench beside the door.
"Sit there and get your wind back, son. You did a good job. They
didn't want to fight us, but they wanted that train. You took it away
from 'em. From here they could of run it right into Macon."

Most of the soldiers went outside to secure the train and its load of
supplies for the 195th New York against the other foraging parties
of the 4th Brigade, who were now crowding the tracks outside the
station, looking enviously at the boxcars.

Handy realized, as his fear ebbed swiftly, that nobody knew he'd been a coward. Not a man among them seemed to suspect that James Handy had tried to run away in his first meeting with rebel soldiers.

Handy thought about it while he tried to scrape the mud from his clothes and rifle. If he kept his mouth shut, he'd be a hero. No one would ever know the truth. He would be a veteran now, accepted as one of them, instead of being treated as a child. It didn't sit well with him, however. He'd always hated a liar.

The men still in the station suddenly snapped to attention as General Barnes came through the door, followed by Colonel Bailey.

"At ease," Barnes said quietly. He looked around for Major Hanford.

This was the first time that Private Handy had ever been close to the general. He'd seen him dozens of times, of course, in Atlanta and on the march. Handy was surprised to see a man so young. At a distance the general looked old enough to be Handy's father. The face was lined, the eyes were hard, the sandy mustache covered a stern mouth.

He looks awful hard, Jimmy Handy thought. I'm glad he don't know I was scared. I bet he's never been scared of anything. "We heard the shooting, Jack," the general said to Hanford. "We were coming here anyway to rip up this line, so we did some running to get here faster."

"Nobody hurt, sir," Hanford said with a grin. "The whole shindig didn't amount to a damn thing. You take a look at the grub on that train?"

The general nodded. "Share and share with the other regiments, Jack."

Hanford frowned. "We captured it, sir! This boy here——"

"That's an order, Jack," the general said abruptly. "What about this soldier?"

"He nabbed the train all by himself, sir. It was down the line from the station and he brought it in under fire. Private Handy, Company A."

Handy flushed under the scrutiny of the cold blue eyes. Old Jack should have kept his mouth shut!

"Good work, soldier," the general said. "Make a record of it, Jack."

"Yes, sir!" The major beamed.

Handy was astonished to see the touch of a smile twist the general's stern mouth. He'd been told that the general never smiled.

"Is this the fellow you told me about, Jack?"

"That's right," Hanford said. "Don't you think he'd make a pretty good farmer, General?"

Private Handy looked puzzledly at Hanford. There was that farm talk again, and what was more, the general seemed to understand it.

"I think he would, Jack," said the general in a voice that was very soft, almost gentle. Then it changed instantly, becoming incisive.

"All right, let's get to work outside. We meet the division at sunset at the end of the spur. By that time this entire line must be ripped up. Jack, your boys can ride the train down to the main line."

"Thanks," Hanford said. "We'll split the grub when we get there."

The general astonished Handy again with a boyish grin. "Remember what I said, Jack. Share and share."

"Absolutely, sir." Hanford grinned back. "I'll see that the other regiments get exactly what they've got coming."

The general cocked an eyebrow. "I'm sure you will."

General Barnes and Colonel Bailey left the building.

Hanford paused to light his pipe, winking at Handy. "The Ramrod won't check those shares," he said. "We'll take the best for ourselves, Jimmy."

"Sir," Handy said awkwardly, "I was awful scared out there. You talked like I was a hero or something. I was just scared I was goin' to get killed."

Hanford nodded. "Everybody's scared, boy. I been soldierin' all my life, and I still get scared."

Handy shook his head doggedly. "I don't want no credit for it. I ain't brave, sir."

"Glad you ain't. The brave ones usually gets killed. The rest of us will be around when the war has gone up."

50

*How the darkies shouted when they heard the joyful
    sound,
How the turkeys gobbled that our commissary found. . . .*

FIRST SERGEANT TIMOTHY TUGGLE, who had been reared in
a law-abiding and God-fearing family in Highland Landing, had
never in his twenty-two years broken the Seventh Commandment.
Therefore, the practices of his foragers in the days following the
army's departure from Atlanta rested heavily upon his mind. He had
never before been called upon to draw a line between plain stealing
and the appropriation of material useful to the enemy.

He recalled time and again Paragraphs 4 and 6 of Special Field
Orders No. 120, as well as General Slocum's general order to the
Army of Georgia, as the left wing of the Union forces was now called.
Slocum had made clear the limits of foraging and had announced
severe penalties for pillaging by the soldiers in his command. It
seemed to Tuggle that the orders were direct and specific, but that
it was going to be impossible to enforce them, because not even the
officers took them very seriously.

First Lieutenant Justin Miller, who had taken command of Company A when Mike Stewart was wounded at Peach Tree Creek,
shared none of Tuggle's concern. Miller was a debonair young man,
who had before the war sold tickets on the Highland Landing ferry.
His only ambition was to marry a beautiful girl with plenty of money.
He would even marry an ugly girl with plenty of money. When he
did, he would never do another day's work in his life. He had a
cherubic face and an easy grin, and had never been known to lose
his temper with the men.

Company A had come a long way from the slapdash days of Ned
Boudrye. The men still acted, dressed, and marched like an assort-
ment of file-closers, but their discipline was excellent. As reckless and
carefree as the frontier men in the Army of the Tennessee, Company

A was earning the reputation of being the most enterprising group of bummers in the XX Corps. This was principally because Lieutenant Miller interpreted Sherman's and Slocum's orders to mean that his men were free to take anything that wasn't red-hot or nailed down.

In the early days of the march Tuggle tried to argue with the lieutenant. "The men entered those two plantation houses today," Tuggle would say as the foraging party was returning to the line of march at the end of the day. "They stole a lot of valuable things, Lieutenant."

"Damned rascals!" Miller would grin. "If you watch the front door, Sarge, they go in the back. If you watch both doors, they go in the windows. These Georgians brought it all on themselves, anyway. They put too many temptations on the men, with all those doors and windows."

"General Slocum said that looters were to be shot, sir," Tuggle said doggedly. "Our men have been looting every house we come to."

"Have they now?" the lieutenant said. "I'll speak to 'em about it. I thought they were just foraging."

"I try to keep 'em out of the houses, sir, but I can't do it alone. Maybe we ought to grab one of 'em and send him to division court-martial for an example."

"Division would send him right back, Tuggle. Look—the way I read it, the order said pick up forage of any kind, pick up meat of any kind, and so forth. Just because the boys have to go through a door or two to get at the meat and flour and such is no reason to accuse 'em of looting."

"Nobody keeps meat in the clothes closets and in chests of drawers, sir. They've been stealing left and right."

"I'll keep my eye open, Sarge. Don't you get all steamed up about it. I haven't seen 'em take a thing yet they didn't need, one way or another."

"It'll go bad for us, sir, if the Ramrod comes along someday when the boys are loaded down with silk shirts and linen underdrawers and table silver and stuff like that."

"Hell, Sarge, you ever take a look at what Sergeant Comfort forages for the general? We get milk—Comfort takes the cream. We get turkeys—Comfort takes the breast meat. We get beef—Comfort takes the tenderloin. Don't you worry about the general, Sarge. He isn't going to get rough with the boys for being a little light-fingered."

Major Hanford, who had been appointed to the new job of chief foraging officer for the brigade, therefore accompanying the daily foraging parties to supervise the selection of food and forage, usually kept an amused silence during the arguments about the ethics of bumming. One day, however, when Tuggle protested vehemently about the appropriation of a leather-seated spring buggy of handsome design, Hanford spoke his mind.

"You're right, Tim. We don't need that buggy. It'll be burned or abandoned tonight when we bivouac. We don't need a lot of things the boys haul away with 'em. But I'll tell you this. That buggy they're skylarking in—I'll bet a month's pay it carried some rich rebel around the countryside a few years ago talking treason and secession to his neighbors. I'll bet lots of times it carried him to Milledgeville, where he could sit in the legislature and vote for rebellion. I wouldn't be surprised if Jeff Davis rode in that same buggy a few weeks ago when he came through this part of Georgia hollerin' about us being vandals and brutes and scum. That there buggy, to me, is just as much war equipment as a commissary wagon."

Hanford paused and looked steadily at Tuggle.

"The men can burn it up for firewood or leave it in a ditch or ride in it from here to Savannah. I don't give a damn, and you shouldn't either. Don't worry about the rights and property of these rebels. That's just what they want you to do. They want Sherman to put a guard around every house, to leave a division here and a brigade there to protect them while their menfolks are off in Virginia with Lee or in Tennessee with Hood killing our soldiers. To hell with 'em, Sergeant! Our job is to whip 'em, to beat 'em into the ground, to make 'em wish that they'd never started this war. If Sherman thinks that the best way to do that is to take or destroy everything they own, I'm all for it."

Hanford paused. "That boy of mine at Lookout, Tim. He wouldn't have died if these folks hadn't started this war. So I'm not going to fault the men if they pick up a few gimcracks here and there. It's all right with me."

Tuggle's stubborn conscience wasn't pacified by Hanford's words, but it was forced into submission as the days went by and the men became expert in the ruthless art of devastating a countryside. The two wings of the army cut a path sixty miles wide across the state of Georgia, averaging ten to twelve miles in a day's march. Behind the army lay a wasteland—all food, hay, grain, and farm supplies either gobbled up by the grinding jaws of sixty thousand men and countless thousands of horses and mules, or smoldering in black embers while Lee in Virginia and Hood in Tennessee cried for supplies for their hungry and ragged veterans.

After the first week houses began to burn. In the right wing Sherman's old soldiers of the Army of the Tennessee considered that they had a special license from Uncle Billy to do their damnedest to the state of Georgia. Some of the fires were accidental, others were set by deserters and stragglers, still others by foragers whose officers enforced no discipline. Many of them, however, were the result of the bushwhacking campaign urged upon the citizens of Georgia by their leaders and by their newspapers. When a party of bummers was fired upon and the bushwhackers turned out to be local civilians, then every house in the neighborhood might be in flames before nightfall.

Company A of the 195th New York, however, burned no houses or barns from Atlanta to Milledgeville. Sergeant Tuggle saw to that even though he had given ground in his fight against pillaging.

More and more often, as the XX Corps swept toward Milledgeville, the capital of Georgia at the time, Company A was sent out as the foraging party for the 4th Brigade of the 1st Division. Lieutenant Miller's men became famed throughout the corps for the quantity and quality of the food they brought back to camp.

Daily they rode off on captured horses and mules, or in farm wagons that they had appropriated. Before the army behind them had stirred itself for the day's march, the foragers were scattered over the countryside, miles ahead of the column or wide on its wings.

Lieutenant Miller seemed to have developed a nose for the richest, most rewarding plantations. As he pounded down a back road early in the morning, his eye would sweep across a farmer's fields and gardens, view the house and outbuildings, and then come back to Sergeant Tuggle. "Not this one, Tim. There's a bigger one down the road. We'll leave this for the 3rd Brigade."

He was usually right. The men would cheer him handsomely when they rounded the next bend of the road and came upon a view of rich fields, bulging barns, and a stately mansion. Whooping like madmen, they'd stream down the lane and fly into action to clean out the place before other bummers arrived. Lieutenant Miller and Major Hanford followed more leisurely, with Miller pointing out that he'd known this rich plantation was sure to be here because of the excellent condition of the road, or because he'd seen well-kept fences bordering the poorer farmer's land, or because he'd seen the chimneys of the house through the treetops.

Swiftly the wagons ranged in a train and the supplies would begin to flow into them. Chickens, turkeys, geese, ducks, pigs, hogs, sheep, calves, hams, buckets of honey and molasses, pots of lard, baskets of sweet potatoes, a hundred other items—all would be piled into the beds of the wagons. Then the plantation's vehicles would be brought into the train loaded with hay and grain for the brigade's animals. If a plantation that seemed conspicuously rich yielded at first efforts only a small supply of food and forage, then the bummers went to work with a will to find the hidden wealth.

It was comparatively easy to find if the owners had not taken all their slaves with them when they fled before Sherman's approach. Early in their foraging days the men of Company A had learned the secret: just ask the slaves where their masters had hidden the food and valuables. Then the garden would be turned up or an outbuilding pulled off its foundations, and the wagons would be loaded high with the provisions so easily found.

If there were no slaves, the job was harder. Bayonets and sabers were brought into play, and the gardens were poked and pierced until a man shouted that he had "found a vein." Then the digging would begin. It was a rare planter who managed to hide his goods and provisions from the zealous explorers of Company A.

Once the wagons were loaded and on the way to the appointed rendezvous with the army column, Sergeant Tuggle's task of preventing pillaging became difficult. Men would hide from Tuggle's sharp eyes to remain behind to loot the house. An hour later several of them would rejoin the party laden with shirts, trousers, boots, linen, wine, whiskey, odds and ends of every description. When Tuggle braced them for entering dwellings, they would grin roguishly at him and say that they'd found the booty buried in the garden.

Lieutenant Miller would wink at Major Hanford, the men would wink at each other, and Sergeant Tuggle would ride down the road fuming at the conspiracy that would get them all shot when the Ramrod found out they were looting.

The campaign all through central Georgia was a gigantic, prolonged picnic. There was little or no fighting, and the best living most of the men had ever had.

In all the regular foraging parties, even more so than in Company A, there were pillagers, since the men believed that Sherman wished it so. Most of the outrages against the people of Georgia, however, were committed by the independent bummers, stragglers, and camp followers who skirted the fringes of the army columns, looting and burning.

Officers' orderlies, Negro mess attendants, and the idlers of every brigade took advantage of the license to forage. They scattered everywhere over the land, sometimes remaining away from their commands for days at a time. They descended in groups on the outlying plantations, stripping them of all provisions, jewelry, silver, and other valuables. Many times an organized foraging party under a responsible officer would take from a plantation the food and forage that its brigade needed for the next day, leaving the inhabitants a sufficient supply for themselves and disturbing neither the house nor the people's possessions. As soon as the foraging party left, however, a mob of independent bummers might swarm from the woods to overrun the place. Trunks and clothes boxes would be smashed; the finest clothing would be taken for the adornment of the Negro prostitutes who could not be kept away from the bummers' bivouacs; pictures, books, and furniture would be ripped and smashed. As likely as not, the bummers would burn the house before they left.

In both wings of the army general court-martials sat in judgment on bummers accused of serious crimes, and while punishment was swift and severe in a few cases, most generals and field officers were inclined to agree with the men in the ranks that Sherman "wished it so."

As far as Milledgeville, the organized foragers seldom violated the spirit of Special Field Order No. 120. Then, in bivouac in Milledgeville on Thanksgiving Day, while the entire army was feasting on turkey, goose, or chicken, there were three events that changed the temper of the men in the ranks and cost Georgia's citizens dearly.

A few ragged, emaciated prisoners who had escaped from Andersonville Prison stumbled into the camps of Sherman's well-fed veterans, weeping at the sight of the blue uniforms and the waving flags. Thousands of soldiers left their feasts to stand watching in silence.

as the fugitives gorged themselves on the rich food that the bummers had assembled. At the same time newspapers from Richmond, Savannah, and Augusta were being passed through the regiments, all proclaiming the call to duty for the citizens of Georgia—bushwhack Sherman's invading legions!

The Savannah *Daily Morning News* demanded that the people seize their weapons and attack the Yankee columns, which were "sprawling all over the country . . . those who are not willing to surrender can be beautifully bushwhacked."

The third event that caught the soldiers' minds was the swift passage of news that units of Confederate General Wheeler's cavalry, harassing the Yankee advance, had taken to executing bummers who had been unwary enough to be caught far from their commands.

Flushed with pride in the victory of the Atlanta campaign and contemptuous of the opposition they had so far encountered on the march to the sea, Sherman's men brought themselves up short at these evidences that they still had to fight a harsh, bitter war. Perhaps the joyful outing that Uncle Billy had embarked upon was over now. There'd be rough times ahead. They vowed to make them just as rough for the citizens of Georgia who ventured to follow their leaders' suggestions about burning bridges, blocking roads, and bushwhacking foragers.

First Sergeant Timothy Tuggle saw the escapees from Andersonville when they first arrived in Sherman's camps. He joined the crowd of curious, silent officers and men who ringed the area where the fugitives were being fed and doctored. At his side was Private Adam Youngblood, who whispered again and again, "The poor fellers! Why didn't they feed 'em, Tim? Why did they let 'em starve? The poor fellers!"

Tim Tuggle had no answer. He stared with hard eyes at the toothless mouths that sucked in the food and then spewed it forth again from stomachs unable to hold it. He saw the festered feet with open, running sores and the gaunt bodies gray with dirt and disease.

Why, Tuggle asked himself, why indeed? This was a land of plenty. Sixty thousand men were moving through this rich country, each man gorging himself on fresh food. The XX Corps alone had left tons of supplies to rot by the roadsides in the past few days. The XIV Corps also had been unable to consume the provisions brought in by its foragers. The left wing of the army was reportedly living even more riotously. Why had not the men in Andersonville been fed?

Tuggle had already heard the story that was spreading through the watching crowd of soldiers: hundreds of Union soldiers died every day in Andersonville of malnutrition and disease. Why?

Tuggle became aware that a tall, silent man had come to stand beside him. The sergeant glanced aside and saw General Barnes.

"Not a pleasant sight, Sergeant," Barnes said.

"My God, sir, I've never seen human beings look so bad and still live. Why were they starved, sir?"

"It wasn't done deliberately, Tuggle. The Johnnies don't have enough to feed their armies, let alone tens of thousands of prisoners."

"With all this, sir?" Tuggle cried, waving his arm as if to include the state of Georgia. "There's enough food for the whole Confederacy right here in Georgia."

"It isn't quite so simple as that. They can't transport it. The rolling stock on their railroads can't even carry food to their armies."

"Then they should have exchanged the prisoners!"

Barnes shook his head. "That would be an exchange of able-bodied veterans for these poor skeletons. No, Tuggle, it wouldn't work."

Tuggle clenched his fists. "I don't care what the reasons are! They didn't have to starve those men."

"Sergeant, the food is no good to the rebels if they can't move it when and where it's needed."

Tuggle refused to backtrack. "No, sir! They could quit the war and keep people from dying. No, sir! They could give up today just by using the telegraph wire and saying so. Tell Sherman and Grant they're quitting! Goddamn them! I never cursed before in my life, General Barnes, but I say it again. Goddamn them! Every rebel son of a bitch!"

"Easy, Sergeant," the general said. "Don't blame the people. Their leaders run the war, not the people."

"Who chose the leaders, sir? Who did the hooting and hollering in the beginning? Who waved that bonnie blue flag and screamed with joy when our boys ran at Bull Run? No, sir! Don't tell me that Jeff Davis starved those men all by himself."

A ripple of approval came from the grim-faced soldiers gathered around Tuggle and the general.

"I'm not arguing with you, Tuggle"—the general smiled thinly— "but remember that they haven't long to go now before we finish them. Every step we take on this march brings us closer to the end."

"Yes, sir. And every step I take from now on, I'll be remembering those men there. And I'll be remembering who did it to them."

Out from Milledgeville the great army rolled, with the organized foragers and the hobo soldiers sweeping ahead and to both sides, a tide of tatterdemalion riders on captured horses. Wheeler's cavalry worked closer and more daringly to break the wave, but the bummers soon became the most proficient skirmishers in the history of modern warfare.

Often they might be attacked by rebel horsemen while they were sacking a village or plantation. Fearlessly, riotously, they would form a ragged line of battle and fight like demons until the cavalry was driven off or another wild mob of bummers came gallivanting down the pike. If attacked by vastly superior forces, the bummers fought in dogged retreat until they backed into one of the army's marching columns. Then they sallied out again to put the rebels to flight. It was said in the army that one of the chief reasons that Sherman showed so little inclination to curb the bummers' lawless activities was the value he placed on their skirmishing. They furnished a widespread screen of mobile mounted infantry that kept Wheeler away from both wings of the army.

The rights and property of Georgia's citizens were certainly not assured of safety when the Macon *Telegraph* printed this charge:

". . . the cesspools of Northern infamy and corruption have been dredged to their vilest dregs in order to collect the infamous spawn of perdition sent out to despoil our country. . . ."

The men of Company A, 195th New York, found that copy of the Macon paper on the veranda of a plantation house in central Georgia. In five minutes the flames and smoke were rising high into the pale December sky while the bummers watched with sober satisfaction.

"Who set that fire?" Major Hanford asked brusquely when he came up from the barns, where he had been supervising the loading of fodder.

ant soenfrrir soenfrrir

"I did, sir," Sergeant Tuggle answered. He looked levelly at Old Jack.

"What the hell for, Tuggle? You had no reason to burn it."

"Bushwhackers, sir."

"Bushwhackers, my butt! There weren't any shots."

"Yes, sir. Four shots. All the men heard them."

"Damn it, Tuggle, that was my men at the barns shooting pigs."

"Was it, sir? My mistake, then. Too bad. It was a nice house."

"If you pull another trick like that, Sergeant, I'll take it up with General Barnes."

"Yes, sir. Maybe you can give him that newspaper at the same time. He'd probably like to read about the dregs of cesspools, too."

Hanford turned away. He had also read the Macon *Telegraph*.

At another plantation house Sergeant Tuggle, who had not obeyed the order against entering dwellings since Milledgeville, called to Private Youngblood from an upstairs window, "Adam, come up here!"

Youngblood went up the stairs. In a spacious bedroom Tuggle was at an open clothes closet while two women stood on the other side of the room. One of them, a gray-haired woman with bitter eyes, sheltered the other, a weeping girl of twenty or so. The older woman was harshly demanding that Tuggle leave the house.

"Shut up, lady!" the sergeant said. He pointed into the closet. "Take that white dress, Adam. It's a wedding dress."

"What for?" Youngblood asked.

"You're going to marry that girl you sent home, aren't you? Take the dress for her."

"These folks here——" Adam said, gesturing toward the women. "Maybe I better not, Tim. It don't seem right."

"Take it!" Tuggle said in a savage voice.

Youngblood moved forward and bundled the silk dress under his arm.

Tuggle turned again to the women. "Where's your menfolks, lady?"

The woman set her lips and refused to answer. The girl was sobbing fearfully.

"Where are they?" Tuggle demanded. "Bushwhackers shot at us this morning. A mile down the road. You better have a good answer for me."

"My husband is in Virginia with his regiment," the woman said.

"Prove it," Tuggle said. "You got letters from him?"

She opened a drawer in a chest beside the bed, showing the sergeant a bundle of letters tied with ribbon. Tuggle walked over and examined them.

"You're lucky," he said coldly. "I was going to burn you out. Pass the word, lady, when you see your friends. Any shooting at us and we'll burn you all out. Come on, Adam."

Youngblood followed Tuggle down the stairs and out of the house, uncomfortable with the silk dress under his arm, wondering how he could dispose of it without angering Sergeant Tuggle. He couldn't ask Susan Connor to get married in a stolen dress. It was white, anyway; one of his messmates had told him that a widow never wore white when she got married. The wedding was a subject that was often in Youngblood's mind. Susan would have just the kind of wedding she wanted. A stolen dress wouldn't do at all.

Youngblood couldn't get used to the change in Tim Tuggle. He was sorry for the young sergeant. The sight of those Andersonville prisoners had made a terrible transformation in Tuggle. He seldom sang, told no jokes, and never entered comradely conversations around a bivouac fire. He concentrated all his time on doing what Sherman had said they would do when they left Atlanta: make Georgia howl.

Youngblood wondered sadly if there ever would be an end to this savage war. He wanted only to get home to the farm—to Susan and the boy, to his father.

He dropped the dress beside a hedge in the driveway when they were leaving the plantation. Maybe the women would find it there. Then he poked through one of the burlap sacks tied to the saddle of his mule. Finally he pulled out a child's toy—an artistically fashioned miniature of a coach and four horses, cast in iron. The coach was lacquered bright red with yellow wheels. The horses were black.

Youngblood quickly replaced the toy in the bag after assuring himself once again that it wasn't broken.

He didn't want anybody to think he was stealing. He'd found the toy in a playroom of the house, a room that was filled with a boy's playthings and books. The room had evidently been unused for many years. Youngblood wondered what had happened to the boy who owned the toys. His guilt ebbed from him as he remembered the dusty look of the room. It wasn't stealing to take something that nobody ever used. His own boy would treasure the toy.

How long would it be before he could give it to him?

Color Sergeant Samuel Comfort rapidly established himself as one of the most proficient bummers among all the sixty thousand men who marched from Atlanta to the sea. There was a gentlemen's agreement between him and Lieutenant Secord, who was in charge of mess facilities for brigade headquarters. Secord left all the details to Comfort, assured that the 4th Brigade's mess would be equal to any in the army. In return, Secord never questioned the sergeant's comings and goings, nor did he ever investigate the contents of the pair of light freight wagons that Comfort had commandeered. Secord knew that much more was transported in those wagons than ever was unloaded at brigade headquarters.

The wagons, painted bright blue with gold trim, were seen everywhere on the periphery of the XX Corps' route. Neatly lettered in gold on the sides of the wagon beds was the inscription:

HEADQUARTERS MESS
4th BRIG., 1st DIV.
XX CORPS

Comfort had his personal foraging party to do the hard work of bumming while he supervised. Near Covington, Georgia, on the second day's march, he had enlisted in his service two strong and amiable Negroes whom he had found begging food at the mess fires of the 195th New York.

The fourth member of Comfort's command was a shy, slim boy of twenty from the Wisconsin regiment of the 4th Brigade. His name was Buddy Adams. He'd been a bugler until the battle of Peach Tree Creek, when a rebel Minié ball had smashed his bugle. He was polite, soft-spoken on the rare occasions when he said anything, and an expert poker player. He'd been detailed to brigade headquarters as an orderly during the occupation of Atlanta. He'd canceled Comfort's sizable poker debt to him in return for permanent foraging duty as Comfort's assistant.

Every morning at dawn Comfort set out with his caravan, usually leaving camp with the regular foragers of Company A. While the Negroes handled the mules that pulled the wagons, Comfort took his ease on the sheepskin-padded seat of the first wagon, feet propped on the dashboard and pipe or cigar in his mouth. Before him, bracketed to the dashboard, were a shotgun and a rifle. A Colt's .44 was slung in a holster at his hip. Private Adams was similarly armed in the second wagon.

The handsome wagons would pull into a plantation drive and the two Negroes, after Adams had reconnoitered the place, would spring to the ground and go to work. They were adept in the art of nabbing guinea fowl, turkeys, geese, and chickens. They skimmed the rows of vegetable gardens for the choicest vegetables and fruits. They wandered, eyes to the ground, across flower beds and lawns, looking for the telltale spot of disturbed earth that indicated buried valuables. They could stick a pig, bleed it, and have it butchered and wrapped in sacking before Comfort and Adams had finished their inspection of the plantation house. If there were slaves on the place, the Negroes immediately assumed the authority relegated through Sergeant Comfort by "Mistah Linkum," and then they became the taskmasters and the slaves did the work. If the owners of the plantation had not already abandoned it, Comfort engaged them in pleasant conversation, as if it were natural circumstance that he should be talking to them about the weather, the condition of the roads, or the harvest while his Negro assistants were trussing the poultry and sticking hogs. Sometimes these people—most of them women or old men—would protest the quantity of provisions that piled into the spick-and-span blue wagons, believing that the heavy-set sergeant with the cheerful smile and the handsome young soldier with him would surely prove to be gentlemen, not brigands like the rest of Sherman's invading horde.

Comfort would smile easily at the protests and say politely, almost regretfully, "You should of thought of your chickens when you started the war, ma'am. You started it, and we aim to finish it if it takes every last chicken and pig you got."

If the lady of the house pointed out angrily that Comfort's bummers were trampling her garden, he would issue the warning, "Walk between the rows, boys."

Even though Comfort and his bummers ranged farther than most, they seldom ran into trouble. Once, a few days after leaving Milledgeville, they stood off a party of Wheeler's cavalry for two hours before the shooting attracted another party of bummers to the rescue. Another day they had to abandon the wagons and take to the woods when an entire troop of cavalry caught them rifling an abandoned house. Company A arrived in time to recover the wagons from the rebels, but under cover of the rescue Lieutenant Miller's men stripped Comfort of all the provisions he had collected.

General Barnes and his staff usually lived well: baked ham, roast pork, fried chicken, broiled quail, all served with fine wines and good brandy. Bumming, however, was not always one pleasant outing after another. Sometimes the weather was bad; sometimes a stretch of country was thinly populated by poor farmers rather than rich planters. And sometimes the inhabitants did their best to answer the call to bushwhack the Yankees.

Comfort and Adams ran into a couple of them one chill December morning. The place was a few miles from Sandersville, Georgia.

One of the men was the old planter who had refused to abandon his plantation; the other was his overseer. They knew the Yankees were near. The day before, the XX Corps had started ripping up the rails of the Georgia Central Railroad beyond Sandersville.

The two men crouched as comfortably as they could below the wall of a stone pavilion in the garden of the plantation house. A lane wound up from the main road between twin rows of live oaks. The old planter had made up his mind to get some Yankees before he fled his home. He knew, however, that he couldn't hold off a strong foraging party. For the necessary escape, he had tethered a small brown mare for himself and a mule for his overseer out of sight behind the house.

The two men had been waiting since dawn. The cold stone had chilled the old man's feet. He moved his toes in his fine calfskin boots to keep the blood circulating. The overseer was motionless, watching the lane.

Suddenly the overseer spat tobacco juice on the pavilion floor. "Yankees comin' up the lane," he said mildly.

The old planter drew his revolver and peered across the wall. Two bright blue wagons were rolling up the drive. A Yankee soldier and a Negro sat in the first one. There was a Negro on the seat of the second wagon.

"Get ready, Jim," the old man whispered.

"I been ready a long time," Jim answered.

The planter leveled his revolver, a Colt's navy model that his son had taken from a dead Yankee at Chickamauga. "I'll count three," he said, "then we'll shoot. I wonder where the others are. There can't be only one of 'em. Here goes. One, two——"

A revolver cracked behind them. The old man slumped against the wall. Jim tried to bring his musket around, but a second shot caught him in the head. A brown line of tobacco juice streamed down his chin.

Private Buddy Adams walked into the summerhouse, holding his revolver ready. He looked at the dead men briefly, then called, "Come on, Sarge. Two of 'em, both gone up."

A few seconds later Comfort vaulted the wall. He looked down at the bodies. "You have to shoot 'em, Buddy?"

"They was fixin' to shoot you."

Comfort nodded. "All right."

"You want his boots or his revolver, Sarge?"

"I'll take the gun. The boots wouldn't fit me, anyways."

Comfort picked up the revolver and held it, looking down at the stern gray face of the dead planter.

"Old man," he said softly, "how come you didn't know enough to watch behind you? Even that wouldn't of done you no good. We been a long time at this game."

51

So we made a thoroughfare for Freedom and her
*   train,*
Sixty miles in latitude, three hundred to
*   the main,*
While we were marching through Georgia!

MILLIONS OF PEOPLE across the northern states waited for news of Sherman. He had disappeared into the heart of Georgia with sixty thousand men, cutting all communications, leaving no base of supply, marching into the face of what might be the greatest disaster ever to overtake a modern army.

The people up North had no way of knowing that the march for Uncle Billy's boys was a picnic, an outing, a traveling carnival. They had no reason to be amused at the sparse reports culled from rebel newspapers by northern editors, all of which, summed up, predicted that Sherman's army would be annihilated next week or the week after.

Highland County, with some hundreds of its sons plunged into the unknown with the "lost army" in Georgia, waited in fearful suspense.

In the post offices, general stores, taverns, and courthouses of the county men gathered to talk in low worried voices about the audacity of Sherman's campaign. The literate among them, the men with more schooling than most, were usually pessimistic. They talked of Napoleon's Moscow march, of Hannibal's passage of the Alps. Always they spoke with troubled authority of supplies and communications essential to any army in the field. They had no way of knowing that Sherman's men were faring as richly as any invading army in history, or that the rebel resistance consisted of a few troops of Wheeler's cavalry harrying the bummers. They could not realize the temper of Uncle Billy's boys, who saw no need for communications as long as Sherman led them, who didn't care a damn where they were going or what they would do when they got there.

Kate Barnes, in addition to her own concern for Jeff's safety, was pressed to share the worries of many other women who had sons or husbands with Sherman. Daily there were women who visited the Boudrye house on Liberty Street to ask if she'd had any word from Jeff. She was the general's wife; they expected that she surely would have news before anyone else did.

Some women knocked at the door and asked diffidently if she had heard anything, then went on with their marketing or other errands. Others accepted her invitation to come in to talk for a few minutes. A few came frequently to tea in the weeks after Sherman left Atlanta. These, most of them, were wives and mothers of officers in the 195th New York. Sometimes Kate had meager bits of news to pass on to them, some disquieting rumor relayed by the *Statesman's* editor, Adam Colden, which he had received through the Associated Press or from metropolitan newspapers. These rumors, invariably southern in origin, prophesied disaster to Sherman's army.

Mike Stewart, recovered from his wound except for stiffness in the damaged muscles of his side and shoulder, furnished brightness to an otherwise dark world. He was a frequent visitor to Highland Landing, ostensibly on business for the hotel. He had dinner four times with the Boudryes during November and December.

Mike had no fear for Sherman's sixty thousand. Again and again he told Kate to tell the women who worried to calm their fears.

"Sherman will march wherever he pleases, and the rebs can't stop him. If he's going to the sea, he'll get there. If he's going to Florida or straight through the Carolinas, he'll come out all right. Then Grant will drive against Lee, Sherman will be on the other side, and it will be all over."

"But where is Sherman now?" the sheriff asked dubiously. "Folks all agree that you can't march into the heart of the enemy's country and let them close in around you. He left Atlanta three weeks ago. We should have had some word by this time."

Mike smiled, shaking his head. "I can't tell you where he is. On the way to Savannah or Charleston, likely. Your question reminds me of a story I heard the other day when I was in New York. I had lunch with a man who is close to some of the people around Lincoln. It seems the President is as worried about Uncle Billy as anyone else. But he can still make jokes. Senator Sherman went to the White House and asked the President point-blank if anyone knew where his brother was heading.

"The President said even he couldn't tell that. 'I know what hole he went in at,' Lincoln said, 'but I can't tell you what hole he will come out of.'"

Stewart was always welcome at the Boudrye house. Kate and her parents, all three, found pleasure in his company and each had a particular reason for greeting him warmly. Kate, of course, found in him the only link with her husband; Mike seemed to have an inexhaustible supply of stories about Jeff and the 195th.

The sheriff was always glad to see Mike, not only for his good company, but because Boudrye was already embarked on plans for a political career for Mike. It would be difficult, the sheriff reasoned, to find a man more suited for public office in Highland County—young, personable, well educated, a war hero who had risen from the ranks to company command. What more could the voters want? The sheriff was determined that Mike should run for supervisor of the township of Cedar Bush in the following year's election. After that who could say what success would lie ahead? Mike smilingly turned him down time and again, but the sheriff was a hard man to dissuade.

Mrs. Boudrye kept to herself her reason for offering her best hospitality to Mike. Kate, she believed, had suffered too much from Jeff to return to him as his wife. A divorce was possible, and could be managed quietly. When Kate was free of Jeff, what better man could she find than Michael Stewart? He was young, handsome, wealthy, and he was obviously in love with Kate. Mrs. Boudrye was determined that when the time came, she would speak her mind.

One night early in December, Mrs. Boudrye told Kate what she had been thinking. "What will you do, Kate," she asked, "when the war is over and Jeff is able to come home?"

"I don't know," Kate said slowly. "What can I do?"

"It seems to me that the only answer is a divorce. It can be arranged quietly. Your father hasn't been in politics all these years without storing up a few favors here and there."

"I've thought of it," Kate admitted. "If Jeff wants a divorce, he can have it."

"You can't leave it to him, dear. He wouldn't consider you; he never has."

"The end of the war may change things, Mother. I'll wait."

"Don't wait too long. Mike is in love with you."

"I know, Mother. But I'll wait until Jeff comes home. If it's what he wants, I'll do it."

"Think of yourself, dear. Promise me you'll write and ask him what he intends to do."

"All right, Mother. I'll write to him."

In mid-December the news flashed across the thousands of miles of telegraph wires in the Union.

SHERMAN HAS REACHED THE SEA!

There were parades and bonfires and civic celebrations in every northern city. In the western farmlands the families of the men in the Army of the Tennessee passed the word down country roads choked with snow, plowing the drifts to tell the back-country people that their men were sitting on the beaches beside the salt water of the Atlantic, filling their bellies with the fresh oysters they'd talked about so often but had never tasted.

From Tennessee a few days later came the second message of jubilation—old "Pap" Thomas and the Army of the Cumberland, at Nashville, had smashed Hood's army to pieces, destroying its effectiveness as a fighting force.

General Hardee, with ten thousand rebel veterans, waited in Savannah for Sherman's frolicking bummers to calm down for the expected assault on the city's fortifications. Instead, Sherman gave the orders to besiege, knowing that he could starve Hardee out. On the twentieth of December, Hardee evacuated the city, and the long columns of bummers, now trailed by thousands of slaves who insisted on joining "Mistuh Linkum's army," marched into Savannah.

On Christmas morning President Lincoln released to the Union the message he had received from Uncle Billy the night before:

"I beg to present you as a Christmas gift, the city of Savannah, with one hundred and fifty heavy guns and plenty of ammunition, also about twenty-five thousand bales of cotton."

52

*Mine eyes have seen the glory of the
coming of the Lord;
He is trampling out the vintage where
the grapes of wrath are stored. . . .*

THERE HAD BEEN many recruits, many men who had not seen the elephant, among the hundred thousand who had marched out of Chattanooga on the way to Atlanta. The sixty thousand who had made the march to the sea were veterans, old soldiers on a rollicking campaign. They punished Georgia severely, but not many of them had Tim Tuggle's grim intensity.

When they left Savannah, however, in the first days of February 1865, another change had come upon them, among the many changes wrought by war.

They struck into South Carolina with the ruthlessness of a champion fighter in prime condition who sees his opponent reeling with weariness.

They were determined to end the war quickly, with savage blows. In South Carolina secession had been born; in South Carolina it would die.

This was the state that had plunged a nation into civil war. Sherman's army was determined to teach its people a lesson they would never forget.

There were other changes in them, both physical and mental. The diseases and sicknesses that had plagued them as recruits were gone. They were lean, fit, and healthy. Earlier in the war they had generally been clean-shaven; now they were bearded. Their skin had been tanned by the sun, roughened by wind, and smoke-cured over campfires. They wore their ragged uniforms with a devil-may-care air; they would walk for the rest of their lives with the long slouching stride of Sherman's army.

They'd discarded the sentimentality and emotion that had softened their days as recruits, but they'd retained the raucous, bawdy humor of the frontier army. They were profane and far less religious than they'd been at enlistment. In most regiments the discipline was more casual than ever, but this condition was offset by the fact that almost all the inefficient officers had been weeded out of the army long since. It would have been difficult, in the South Carolina campaign, to find an officer who didn't have the respect, if not the affection, of his entire command.

The long months of war had made remarkable changes in one man among the many thousands. Brigadier General Jefferson Barnes had left on each battlefield, each skirmish line, a fragment of the strength and purpose of his life. His youth had been replaced by weary maturity, won, as Jack Hanford had said long ago that it would be, at a heavier cost than most men had to pay.

Infantry command had taken too great a toll. In the cavalry, for instance, he might have fared differently. The leader of mounted troops could be a "hell of a damned fool," as Sherman called Kilpatrick, and yet make himself a brilliant record. "Did you ever see a dead cavalryman?" It was a common jest in Sherman's army.

There had been no elasticity in Jeff Barnes's spirit since Gettysburg. He had watched his men die in battles and skirmishes; he had seen them waste away in field hospitals; he had seen them go home maimed and broken. Each casualty had been another drop of corrosive acid eating away his strength.

Now, as the army headed into South Carolina to finish the war, General Barnes was leaner than ever, almost gaunt, in spite of Comfort's splendid foraging. The lines in his face and around his eyes were deeper and longer; they gave him the same expression of stern, unrelenting austerity that marked Sherman, who was almost twice his age. Also, like Sherman, he·grew more nervous and intense, smoking cigars one after another (he never questioned Comfort about where they came from). He took his sleep in cat naps wherever the army halted. He worked far into the night while the soldiers slept. When the army was on the march, he slouched in the saddle on the old gray horse, his eyes and his mind keenly attuned to the innumerable details and decisions required of a brigade commander.

He gave himself so little time not devoted to duty that he had not yet written an answer to Kate's letter, which had arrived at Savannah in January, forwarded by the sea line that the Union Navy had furnished Sherman. He had considered his answer, however, many times.

Each time he read her letter he sought from her words his own answer. Should he interpret her letter literally, or should he act upon the urges of his lonely spirit and assume that she wanted him to come home?

Dear Jeff: [she had written]
The months have gone by more swiftly than I thought possible, and I realize that my congratulations on your promotion are belated. Nonetheless, they are warmly offered.

I suppose you do not know how tensely the entire country waited for news of Sherman while you were making the grand march to the sea. Among us here, only Michael Stewart had no fear that Sherman would make the coast without disaster. In December, when the news arrived that you had reached the Atlantic, Highland Landing went mad with joy. The celebration far surpassed in tumult any that I have ever seen, including firemen's carnivals. We all assume that final victory and peace are now in prospect.

I regret that I have not written before this. I had hoped that you would write to me. The bitterness of our parting in Tennessee has been eased by time, but I understand how deeply it has scarred us both.

I suppose there is no blame to be taken. What happened to us is simply one of the myriad evils of this war. I pray that they come swiftly to an end.

If we must find a reason for what happened, I would say that the terrible strain of war changed you so rapidly and so deeply that I could neither understand nor adapt myself to what was happening to you.

In the year that has passed, I've thought constantly about our marriage. Your silence for so long seems to indicate that you agree with me that it would be fruitless to try to repair the damage.

You have entered a world that lies beyond all I know, Jeff, and I cannot bring myself to believe that you will find a way back, or that I can follow you.

Would it not be wise to end our marriage? My father tells me that it can be done without disagreeable publicity. If you wish it, I will tell him to arrange it. Probably Judge Crist will help.

On the other hand, if you refuse, or if you want the decision to wait until the war is over, I will understand. Please consider it carefully, as I know you will, then write and tell me what you think about it.

Many people who do not know why I came home from Tennessee so suddenly tell me often to send their best wishes to you. There are so many I cannot name them in one letter. Michael, of course, speaks of you often with affection and respect. He stops to visit when he is in Highland Landing. He talks of the day when he can rejoin the regiment, but I am sure he cannot. He has recovered from his wound, but its effects are still quite evident.

My fond wishes for your health and safety, Jeff, and I will await your answer to this. Please pass my regards to all the officers and men whom I knew so well.

Your wife,
Kathleen Barnes

In the quiet stretches of the night, when tension kept him from sleeping, he knew what he wanted to tell her. He wanted to ask her to wait until he came home. They could try to heal the wounds.

At other times he considered the life that lay ahead of him—it might be dreary duty for years at some frontier post, or occupation service in the defeated and bitter Confederacy. These would never do for Kate.

There was no one to confide in, no one to talk to in the night hours, no friend among the officers who might counsel him. In a sense, he was alone among the multitude that stormed out of Savannah to strike savagely at South Carolina. He carried the unanswered letter with him.

He did not ride alone, however. Sometimes Secord was with him, sometimes Bailey or one of the other regimental commanders, and often Hanford, whenever the bummers were not out. Color Sergeant Comfort sometimes sent out his blue wagons in command of Buddy Adams, spending the day himself riding at his general's side. Comfort rode the small brown mare that he had picked up at the Georgia plantation where Buddy Adams had killed the planter and the overseer; as an official bummer, Comfort was entitled to maintain a horse.

Comfort, too, showed the multiplicity of changes brought by war. To some degree his transformation was even more startling than that of the general. The fat, bumbling, eager-to-please boy of Camp Chapman in '62 was now a big man, hard-muscled, brown-bearded, with a go-to-hell air about him. His eyes were narrowed in his weathered, pouched face; they were hard eyes that would have made his mother cry if she had looked into them.

More or less unconsciously Comfort aped the general's habits—he wore his battered slouch hat low over his eyes; his hands were gauntleted; his navy Colt's revolver was worn on his right hip with the butt forward, to be easily drawn with his left hand. Comfort chewed his cigars exactly as did the general. He lounged in the saddle as Barnes did.

By this time Sergeant Comfort knew that he had found his life. He would never return to the sleepy village of Cedar Bush. He would be a soldier for the rest of his days. The general had promised that wherever the army assigned him after the war, Comfort would go, too.

It quickly developed that the campaign in the Carolinas was as different from the march to the sea as that outing had been from the hard fighting of the Atlanta campaign.

The men called it the "Smoke March." In the wake of four corps black smoke rolled in clouds across the sky. Everything burned. The destroying flames leaped from factories, public buildings, railroad depots and piles of ties, warehouses, barns, and deserted dwellings. Vast stretches of pine forest flamed in the night, with here and there a holocaust as stored turpentine caught fire.

Sherman's army, almost to a man, was determined that South
Carolina should suffer. "They started it, now let's give it to 'em!"

The bummers, as usual, ranged far ahead, skirmishing with Wheeler's cavalry, sometimes outdistancing the Federal cavalry under the wild man, Kilpatrick. General Howard, bringing up his
troops in battle formation to capture a fortified railway, was startled
to see a bummer, dressed in top hat and frock coat, riding hell-bent
on a mule from the direction of the rebel lines, screaming at the
top of his lungs, "Hurry up, General! We've got the railroad!"

It was easy for conscientious officers to keep the troops from pil-
lage, vandalism, and rapine. The record of the various corps was
good in that respect. It was inpossible, however, to put a checkrein
on the bummers. Robbery and violence increased tremendously; the
bummers put into harsh practice the army's attitude toward South
Carolina.

They knew as well as anyone else that Sherman was determined
to make South Carolina pay. Wheeler had informed Sherman that
he would stop burning cotton if Sherman stopped burning houses.
Sherman answered sharply:

"I hope you will burn all cotton and save us the trouble . . . All
you don't burn, I will . . . Vacant houses, being of no use to anybody,
I care little about, as the owners have thought them of no use to
themselves. I don't want them destroyed but do not take much care
to preserve them."

The bummers believed their spree was justified and condoned.
After all, hadn't they heard the rumor that Kilpatrick had filled the
saddlebags of his troopers with matches?

The army couldn't be stopped, because such an army had never
existed before. When it plunged into the Salkehatchie swamps, rebel
leaders who knew the country allowed themselves rare grins and
made plans for overwhelming the Yankees as soon as they mired
themselves deep in the flooded swamps.

While the rebels waited, Sherman's army made ten to twelve miles
a day, corduroying roads in muck up to their knees, wading all day
long in waist-deep water, bridging streams that rebel engineers said
were impassable. Soldiers "camped" in trees above the rolling flood-
waters, and after a night's roost in the branches they greeted the
dawn by crowing like cocks.

Out of the swamps they came storming, and rolled on through

South Carolina. The city of Columbia burned to the ground in mid-February while the XV Corps—Sherman's own—surrounded and occupied the town. Who did it? It might have been slaves, escaped prisoners from the rebel military prison, rebel deserters, or it might have been the Federal soldiers in the city. The controversy raged, but the men in Sherman's ranks didn't care. The city was the birthplace of secession. What the hell did it matter who burned it? If Uncle Billy had ordered it done, the soldiers said, it was all right with them.

The old gray fox of the Confederacy, idle since he had been relieved of command before Atlanta, was called back to make the last desperate attempt to stop Sherman. Lee, in supreme military command, told Johnston to do his best. Johnston knew that the effort could not succeed. He had heard how the Yankee army had crossed the Salkehatchie swamps, and had made up his mind that there had been no such army in existence since the days of Julius Caesar.

He answered the call, however, and the weary and ragged veterans in gray began to assemble in Sherman's path. Sherman was headed for Goldsboro, North Carolina, where the campaign of the Carolinas would end and the final phase of crushing Lee would begin.

Johnston marched and countermarched, feinted and withdrew. Sherman grinned at the old game, and returned to the tactics of the Atlanta campaign. He flanked, and Johnston had to fall back. This time Johnston had not even the chance to make a sudden march and a surprise attack on any of Sherman's four corps. The bummers made a screen miles wide ahead of the main columns. At Fayetteville, North Carolina, they'd rushed into the city and tried to capture it from General Wade Hampton's cavalry. They'd been driven back, but they held tenaciously to the outskirts of the town until the troops behind them moved into line.

Sherman was confident. He knew that Johnston had to fight, but the swift-moving blue columns weren't going to let Johnston pick his spot this time.

The rebel veterans, knowing they were making their last retreat, loaded their rifles, fixed their bayonets, and cleared their throats to scream their last rebel yell.

53

*He has gone to be a soldier in the army
of the Lord. . . .*

RAGGED and almost barefooted, the blue columns swept out of
South Carolina, leaving a path of devastation that would scar the
land for generations.

The shattered Confederacy had one move left. If there was time,
Lee could join Johnston in North Carolina. If he did so, there was
an outside chance that the merged armies could smash Sherman,
then turn to fight Grant, who would be in close pursuit.

The XX Corps marched in review before General Slocum at Fayetteville on March 13, then crossed the Cape Fear River on a pon-
toon bridge. Somewhere ahead Johnston waited.

On March 14, Ward's division skirmished with rebel cavalry. On
the same day Kilpatrick's hard-riding troopers fought with rebel infantry near Averysboro. On the sixteenth of March, in a pouring rain,
most of the XX Corps engaged the rebels in day-long skirmishing
before Johnston pulled his troops back toward a town named
Bentonville.

On the morning of March 19, Jeff Barnes was invited to breakfast
on a hillside twenty-five miles east of Fayetteville, where General
Slocum had his headquarters. Sherman was Slocum's guest.

The early-spring morning was soft and balmy, fruit trees near by
were in full bloom, and birds sang beautifully with the dawn. It
was Sunday, and in the distance the band that the 33rd Massachusetts had tenaciously maintained through three years of campaigning
softly played the familiar strains of "Old Hundred."

The officers on the hillside were infected by Sherman's buoyancy
of spirit as well as by the beauty of the peaceful morning.

"The way it looks to me, Slocum," Sherman said to the commander
of the left wing, "we're not going to give Joe Johnston the fight he
wants until we get to Goldsboro. He wanted to fight at Averysboro,

but your boys pushed him back. And if we can put him on the run again at Goldsboro, he'll retreat all the way to Raleigh. If Grant can push 'em from his side, we've got 'em at last."

"Sounds fine," Slocum said, "but Williams and the others in the XX Corps all think he's going to try to fight as soon as he can. Williams thinks he's picked his spot. I'm inclined to agree."

"Slocum," Sherman answered with a grin, "you and Pop Williams ought to know better. You're like the old maid who looks under the bed every night before she dares get in it. I'll bet a box of my best cigars that Johnston won't risk a fight. When you flanked him at Averysboro, he pulled out fast enough. It's the Atlanta campaign all over again. He won't risk a fight until he knows what Lee is going to do."

"I think it's closer to the mark, General, if you don't mind my saying so, that it's you who doesn't want to fight. You've said time and again you wanted a base at Goldsboro before you tangle with Johnston."

"I admit it," Sherman said agreeably. "What would we do with the wounded? What's more, your wagons are empty, same as the right wing's wagons. And Schofield will be in Goldsboro with the Army of the Ohio when we get there. Then we'll fight Johnston."

"What will we do if he insists on a fight?"

"You engage him, and then we'll flank him. He'll have to retreat."

Slocum then went into detail on the caliber of the rebel troops the XX Corps had met on March 16.

"Did you see them in line, Slocum?" Sherman asked.

"No, sir. I saw prisoners. All veteran regiments, or what's left of them. Most of 'em were at Chickamauga, some as far back as Shiloh."

"Let's hear from a man who saw Johnston's army in line of battle," Sherman broke in. "You, Barnes. Your brigade was in the action at Averysboro. What did you think of their behavior?"

"They were good, sir," Jeff said, stepping forward. "They're ready to fight. They know it's their last chance. I talked to prisoners, General. They'll fight."

"You, too, Barnes?" Sherman smiled. "I can't get anybody to agree with me this morning."

"I hope I'm wrong, sir, but I think it's the same as Kenesaw. He can't let us come any farther without engaging us."

"We'll see about that," Sherman said. "I think we can get to Goldsboro without meeting him. You think we can't. You want to bet a box of cigars, Barnes?"

"Yes, sir. I think I do."

Sherman laughed delightedly. "All right. You're on. Pay me in Goldsboro."

He turned swiftly away, calling to Slocum, "Let's go see if Joe Johnston wants to fight."

Joe Johnston did.

On that day, along the road from Averysboro to Goldsboro, two divisions of the XIV Corps discovered, as usual, rebel cavalry harassing the advance.

"Drive 'em!" said headquarters.

The skirmish lines answered laconically, "They won't drive worth a damn."

Almost immediately the XIV Corps found itself engaged with a major part of Johnston's army, which had taken its stand at Bentonville. The objective seemed to be to catch first the left wing of Sherman's forces, smash it to pieces, then swing around to face the right. Except for the road and some farmland bordering it, the ground where Johnston was picking the fight was covered by wood lots and dense thickets of scrub oak. The low land was swampy.

The XIV Corps, fighting savagely, had to fall back before repeated rebel attacks.

The 1st Division of the XX Corps, moving into the line, took position southwest of the battle line on elevated ground. The veterans listened to the cannonading and the musketry from the XIV Corps' position with casual interest. If a battle was coming, they'd be ready for it when it reached them, but they'd long since quit worrying beforehand. The inevitable card games blossomed along the line of breastworks thrown up by the 1st Division.

General Barnes, taking advantage of the halt, asked Comfort to brew him a cup of coffee. While he drank it, he read Kate's letter again. He would answer it when they reached Goldsboro. He'd tell her to wait until he came home.

They needed each other, he and Kate. There could be other children, there could be a quiet family life for them to share.

His thoughts were interrupted by Comfort and Lieutenant Secord.

"Beg pardon, General," Comfort said. "You'd best come up. Johnnies formin' in the woods yonder."

"That's right, sir," Secord said. "Looks like at least a division movin' into line. Maybe more."

Jeff put Kate's letter away in his blouse pocket, mounted his bony gray, and rode down the brigade lines. The card games had ended swiftly, the cards were put away, and the men were watching keenly the scrub oak in the middle distance and the pines beyond.

Sergeant Comfort trotted after the general until he reached that portion of the breastworks held by the 195th New York. Comfort was handed the regimental colors by Sergeant Tuggle. "Don't want anybody else to carry 'em," Tuggle said with a smile. "Keep your butt down, Sam."

Comfort eyed the distant pines. "They ain't comin' yet. Time for a cigar."

"I thought Sherman said the Johnnies had enough," Tuggle remarked, keeping his eyes also on the pines.

"Them bastards ain't never got enough," Comfort answered. "You want a cigar, Tim?"

"No, Sam." Tuggle looked at General Barnes, who was talking earnestly with Colonel Bailey. "Is the Ramrod going to stay with the 195th, Sam?"

"I dunno. He just jumped on that old nag and come over here. This is as good a place as any. Wonder what's holdin' up the fireworks, Tim. They ain't even started yellin' yet."

"This may be their last one. They want to make it a good one."

"I don't give a goddamn about their last one," Comfort said. "I just hope it's our last." He held his cigar half raised to his lips for a second, then put it into the corner of his mouth. He reached for the revolver on his hip. "Here they come, Tim."

The rebel yell, shrill and defiant, rolled across the open ground. The scrub oak thickets shuddered and rocked, then into view came rank upon rank of gray-brown men running low and hard.

The Yankee veterans crouched behind the breastworks and waited. Evidently this was a general assault along the entire line of the XX Corps. To the right the cannonading was thunderous.

The rebels came swiftly, firing as they ran. In a matter of seconds, the fighting was hand to hand. It was brief and bitter, then the rebels' attack spent its force and they started to run back to the protection of the pines.

Before they had disappeared, a mounted courier from General Nat Jackson, now in command of the 1st Division, rode down the brigade position crying, "General Jackson's orders, sir. Drive them out of the pines. Attack immediately."

Barnes nodded, handed the reins of his horse to Bailey's orderly, and said to Bailey, "All right, Sam. Let's take 'em out."

A boiling line of blue poured out of the breastworks into the open field. Somewhere in the woods a Confederate battery was wheeled into place and opened fire. The shells burst in the breastworks and beyond them. Three brigades of the 1st Division were crossing the open ground. The rebel fire was heavy against all three, but particularly so against the brigades on the wings. The 4th Brigade, in the center, went forward swiftly when the others faltered.

The wing brigades had failed before they managed to do more than penetrate the scrub oak. Jeff Barnes saw the blue troops in the distance falling back.

His decision had to be quick. Could his brigade hold on in the scrub oak until another attack was formed? A salient might be the margin of victory in a second attack. He pressed forward swiftly through the brush to get a good look at the rebel lines. Comfort, with the colors, was right behind him. Most of the men were down in the scrub oak expecting the order to fall back.

Jeff mounted a slight elevation in the brushy terrain and looked at the pine trees. A division, Secord had said. There were at least three divisions massing in the pines! This was Johnston's major effort, and Sherman had been wrong.

He had to pull the brigade back immediately.

"Get 'em out of here, Sam!" he yelled to Bailey. "Take 'em back."

Two or three hundred men of the 195th heard his call above the crackle of musketry. They turned and raced for the breastworks. The other regiments of the brigade also wheeled and ran.

Jeff Barnes waited too long, trying to gauge the strength of the rebel troops. He and Comfort were in plain sight. The rebels had plenty of time. They aimed carefully. Three Minié balls struck Barnes, tearing through his chest. He fell forward on his face and died.

Sergeant Comfort, holding the colors high, was one of the few who saw the general go down. With a bitter cry he started forward again, but other rebel rifles were ready. Sam Comfort stumbled and fell with a ball in his belly. He got to his hands and knees and began to crawl toward the general, dragging the colors with him.

"I'm comin', sir," he whispered brokenly. "I'll get there. I ain't leavin' you."

He crawled five yards before he collapsed. He lay there with his hand reaching toward the dead body of his general, then he died.

The XX Corps moved forward in the next attack, and the rebels gave ground. Before the day was done, Johnston's desperate army was retreating again. It was all over but the shouting.

54

> *Sing it as we used to sing it, sixty*
> *thousand strong,*
> *While we were marching through Georgia!*

THROUGH THE WORKINGS of the close fraternity of hotel owners, Mike Stewart had reserved rooms for himself and for Kate Barnes and her mother in a small pleasant hotel not far from the White House. They arrived on May 22, 1865, the day before the Grand Review of the Army of the Potomac. Sherman's army would march on the following day. Weeks before, when Mike had read of plans for the parades, he had asked Kate and her mother to accompany him on the excursion to Washington.

The accommodations that were waiting for them were comfortable, even luxurious, on a day when generals' wives were crowding without protest four to a room at the Willard and other big hotels in Washington.

The city had never been so crowded in all its years as the center of the republic. From all over the nation people had come to watch the Union's two great armies march in review.

Every wheeled vehicle in Washington was in constant use that night, but Mike had only to tell the hotel owner that he wanted to visit Alexandria—within five minutes a buggy and driver were waiting at the door of the hotel.

The city was in a turmoil. Sherman's bummers, four corps of them, were determined not to be awed by the nation's capital. They were under orders to remain in their camps on the other side of the Potomac, but thousands of them managed to get into the city. They would not take a back seat to the bandbox soldiers of the Army of the Potomac, who were inclined to stroll the streets as if they owned them. Lean, brown, and bearded, the men of the western army drank cheap whiskey, caroused in bawdyhouses, roistered through the streets, and fought Potomac soldiers wherever they found them. The legions of provost's guards broke up the brawls and managed to keep the wild men from the West herded into areas of the city where broken windows and street fights had been common during the war. Washington's saloonkeepers and prostitutes did a record-breaking business.

For his trip to the camps in Alexandria, Mike had put on his uniform. The red star of the 1st Division, XX Corps, showed prominently on his slouch hat. The uniform helped ease the passage of the buggy through the jammed streets. As he neared the Long Bridge, the provost's guards were predominantly units from Sherman's army, who looked at the red star and waved Mike's driver on with friendly grins. If reeling soldiers blocked the way, one of them was sure to cry, "Make way for the Star Corps! The captain's a bummer, boys. Let 'im through. Let the Star Corps through!"

Many of them, far gone with drink, were simply standing in the streets, passing bottles around and singing the new song with the rollicking Irish air:

> "Bring the good old bugle, boys, we'll sing
>   another song. . . ."

Mike noticed that the men from the Army of the Potomac were hanging together and quietly giving the westerners street room.

His driver, a dignified Negro with a pleasant manner, remarked while they were passing a free-swinging brawl: "Them are the wildest men I ever seen, sir."

"They're pretty rough," Mike agreed.

"You was an officer to 'em? I reckon you had a terrible job, sir."

"No, it was a wonderful job, because they're the greatest soldiers the world has ever seen."

The buggy threaded its way through the streets of the old camps in Alexandria among thousands upon thousands of tents. Campfires burned brightly, coffeepots boiled over the flames, and the men who had marched with Sherman relaxed at the end of their long journey. They played poker, sat around the fires singing the old songs, or listened to the brigade bands rehearsing for the Grand Review. It seemed to Mike as he traveled through the endless rows of tents that every band was bent upon playing "Old John Brown" all through the review.

Soon enough the buggy passed through the bivouacs of the XV Corps, where the tents were all stenciled with that corps' badge, a cartridge box with the figure "40" superimposed, then Mike saw rows of tents sporting the star of the XX. Provost guards directed him to the 1st Division, and he was soon pumping Sam Bailey's hand. Then Hanford was there, pounding Mike's back and booming, "Mike, my boy! How are you?"

Other officers crowded into Bailey's tent to greet Mike. He had a drink with them, then Bailey and Hanford took him to Company A's camp area. It was heart-warming to have the men throng around him—twenty-six of them were left on the company rolls. They had dozens of questions to ask about Highland County; they told him tale after tale of Company A's achievements as the best bumming party in Sherman's army.

"You come to march with us, Captain?" one of the men yelled to Mike. Instantly the rest of them changed the question to a demand. Justin Miller, now wearing captain's bars, grinned at Stewart. "You're elected, Mike. You'll parade 'em down Pennsylvania Avenue."

"That wouldn't be right," Mike said quickly. "I haven't been with you since Atlanta."

"You'll do it, Mike," Bailey said, grinning. "Remember how the Ramrod used to get that stern look and say, 'That's an order, Captain!' Well, I'm saying it for him."

Mike tried to stand fast on his refusal, but they wouldn't listen. Finally he promised to be with them at dawn of the twenty-fourth.

They left Company A and returned to Bailey's tent. As they walked, Mike observed the changes in the two men with whom he had campaigned so long. Bailey, not yet thirty-five, now had a lined face, weary eyes, and a tic in the muscles on the left side of his face. He spoke in a harsh, tired voice. He had become a chain-smoker of cigars, lighting one from another. When they were back in the tent, he dashed off two tumblers of bourbon whiskey in rapid succession, but they didn't seem to relieve his tension.

Hanford, on the other hand, looked not a day older than he had when he enlisted with Stewart in Cedar Bush. He was harder and leaner, however, and his voice had sharpened with the responsibility of command. He had shaved the beard he'd worn through three campaigns. There seemed to be more strength and youth in his craggy features.

"I brought Mrs. Barnes and her mother with me, Sam," Mike told Bailey after sipping at his bourbon.

"She's pretty as ever, I'll bet," Hanford said. "How did she take the news about the general?"

"I don't know," Stewart said. "I was at the hotel when it came through. I didn't hear he was dead until a week or so later. When I saw her, she was all right, and she's been fine ever since."

"You got a place in the stands for her and her mother?" Bailey asked.

"No. That's one reason I came over tonight. Can you do something about tickets, Sam?"

"Damn right I can! If we have to go to Uncle Billy himself, we'll get 'em for her."

"Mike, do you think she'd like to know about it?" Hanford asked. "I was looking back and saw how it happened. I could tell her about it."

"She'd like to see you, Jack. She's had letters from all of you, of course, and from Williams, Slocum, and Sherman, but I'm sure she'd like to hear you tell it."

"We'll go on back with you," Bailey said. "First, I'll ride up to headquarters and get the passes for the reviewing stand."

Bailey's errand took a half hour; the passes came directly from Colonel Audenreid of Sherman's staff. With them, Bailey brought a rectangular package addressed to Mrs. T. J. Barnes, Highland Landing, New York.

"Sherman sent it himself," Bailey explained. "Said he was going to mail it, but told me to deliver it instead. I don't know what's in it."

Kate greeted them warmly when they reached the hotel. Her mother was already sleeping in the next room. Kate served coffee while Bailey told her about the regiment. Then she opened the package from Sherman.

"A box of cigars!" she said wonderingly. "Now why in the world——" She took an envelope out of the box and opened it.

The officers looked at one another puzzledly. Had Uncle Billy gone out of his head?

She read the letter enclosed in the envelope to herself. She closed her eyes and sat without speaking for a minute or so. Then she lifted the letter again and read it aloud.

"Dear Mrs. Barnes:

On March 19, near the town of Averysboro in North Carolina, General Barnes and I made a wager. The stakes were small—a box of cigars. Your husband said that General Johnston would stand and fight; I said he would not.

"I have made many mistakes in my lifetime. The one I made that day hurts me deeply. If I had listened to General Barnes and to other officers of the XX Corps, the action at Bentonville would have taken a different course. We drove the rebels finally by the weight of our superior numbers, but we might have avoided the casualties that the action cost. Perhaps the fates that govern the destinies of soldiers would have turned the blow that cost the nation a gallant soldier and you a beloved husband.

"As I wrote you in my formal letter some weeks ago, you have my deep sympathy. My words, I know, cannot go far to ease your pain. Perhaps you will remember, however, over the years that lie ahead of us, while the cigars in this box are crumbling into dust, that Uncle Billy sent it to you as a token of the debt he owes to one of the finest soldiers of 'Sherman's army.' With deep respect, I am

Sincerely yours,
W. T. Sherman, Major General, U. S. Army."

Kate was crying when she looked up at the three men. Sam Bailey rubbed his hand swiftly across his face, blinking his eyes. Hanford cleared his throat and looked at the floor.

"Tell me about it, Major Hanford," Kate said softly. "Tell me just how it happened."

She listened with bowed head while Jack Hanford told the story of Bentonville. When he had finished, she smiled at them.

"Thank you for coming," she said. "You'll hear my voice cheering you when the 195th marches past the stands. I only wish——" Her voice faltered. "If he could have led you to the end . . ."

"He'll be there, Mrs. Barnes," Sam Bailey whispered. "I promise you that."

They left her, and Mike went downstairs to arrange for the buggy to take them back to camp.

Kate stood alone looking at the letter in her hand.

"Jeff," she whispered, "if you had only come home to me."

55

Hurrah! Hurrah! We bring the jubilee!

AT DAWN of May 24, Sherman's army began to move into Washington. It wound through the streets beyond the Capitol, moving corps by corps closer to Pennsylvania Avenue. The XV Corps had the honor of marching first, right behind its own Uncle Billy.

Nervously Sherman sat his black horse and stared at his old command while he waited for the nine o'clock starting signal. This was to be the greatest day of his life. He hoped his boys would behave themselves.

At his side General Howard was unperturbed. With his keen insight, he had sensed the temper of the thousands of men in the restless ranks. He knew that they would march to glory as they had never marched before.

Sherman, however, was fearful lest his beloved bummers arouse the ridicule and scorn of the scores of thousands who lined Pennsylvania Avenue. The men had been ordered to get haircuts. Scarcely one in a hundred had complied. They'd been told to draw necessary items of uniforms from the quartermasters; now as they waited, the broken and dusty boots were painfully obvious, the old uniforms were faded and tattered. Their rifles and bayonets, however, gleamed in the brilliant morning sun.

The day before, Sherman had held an honored place in the presidential stand, where he had watched the Army of the Potomac march proudly past. The eastern soldiers had been spick-and-span in clean uniforms. They had stepped precisely in drill field manner, although Sherman had noticed that some of them gawked at the notables in the stands. It had been a grand parade the day before. Sherman feared that the vast audience would not look kindly upon his tatterdemalion columns.

Mike Stewart had reflected Sherman's anxiety about the western soldiers. Sitting with Kate and Mrs. Boudrye in one of the reviewing stands near the White House, he'd watched the Army of the Potomac.

"They'll laugh at us tomorrow," Mike said glumly as he watched the trim, precise ranks of the IX Corps sweep past the stand. "Our boys won't march like that. They'll be all over the street. They'll wink and yell at all the pretty girls. They'll sing every song the bands play. I'll bet that every time the column halts, every fourth man will bring out a deck of cards for a poker game."

"Nobody will laugh at them," Kate told him. "Not at Sherman's army."

The Army of the Potomac had had a beautiful day for its parade. The skies were bright. A breeze stirred the colors on their staffs, making them dance brilliantly over the marching columns. The review itself had been almost perfect in its execution. The only incident to mar it had been caused by General Custer's horse, which had shied at a garland thrown from the crowd, thus giving the dashing cavalryman a chance to ride madly past the stand, saluting with his saber, before he reined in his mount and gracefully returned to his division. The crowd cheered the debonair young general, and all the newspaper correspondents made full accounts of the incident.

The eastern army had given the nation a splendid show. Now it was Sherman's turn.

At nine o'clock precisely a gun boomed. Sherman touched single spur to his horse. He and Howard moved into Pennsylvania Avenue. Behind them came Sherman's staff.

A tremendous roar lifted from the packed ranks of spectators. Sherman frowned, shook his head slightly, glanced briefly at Howard. Was that great shout to be replaced by laughter?

Suddenly the red-bearded general smiled, lifted his shoulders, and stared straight ahead down the broad avenue. Come what may, he would ride with pride!

Before he had ridden a hundred yards, he and his horse were garlanded with flowers. He didn't dare look back, once he was started, to see if his ragtag army was behaving itself.

He could have dismissed all his fears. Rank upon rank, the regiments of the XV Corps moved into the avenue. Their shoulders were straight under the loose blouses, so different from the tight jackets of the easterners. Their black slouch hats were pulled forward over their eyes. Here and there bare feet slapped the pavement. Their lean brown faces looked straight ahead; their hard, slim bodies swung into the stride.

They marched in the old way of Sherman's army. The long stride, in perfect cadence, caught the hearts of the multitude as if people saw instantly that this was the step that had carried these men through the center of the Confederacy, from the Mississippi to the Atlantic.

Had Sherman looked back, he would have exulted. The far-reaching swinging stride carried them after him in perfect step. The gleaming rifles and bayonets were in alignment, rank upon rank, regiment after regiment. The crowd went wild as the westerners swept by. Cheer upon cheer thundered from the massed spectators. The soldiers hid their grins with tight lips. They stared straight ahead. Sherman's army would show the world what marching was!

Seated in the reviewing stand near the White House, Kate and her mother could hear the bands blaring long before the head of the parade made the turn at the Treasury Building. The crowd before the White House was silent, tense with expectancy at the approach of the strangers from the West. They'd been hearing tales for years about the undisciplined mob that Sherman commanded.

Suddenly Sherman and Howard were there, riding in front.

Kate Barnes fixed her eyes on General Sherman. So this was the man! She stared at the wrinkled face, the stern mouth, the wiry red beard. Her eyes blurred with tears.

The general went by, to leave his horse and take his place of honor with Grant and the President on the reviewing stand.

Then the legions came. Division after division rolled by the stands, carried swiftly by the proud, swinging pace. Above them danced the thin battle-torn colors and regimental flags. Behind each division came its ambulances and wagon train. The bummers made their mark on the day: the wagons were loaded with pigs, chickens, turkeys, geese—livestock of every description. With the wagons marched the slaves who had attached themselves to the bummer brigades, hundreds of Negroes dressed in rags. They bounced merrily along in the wake of their horses.

The XVII Corps followed the XV, marching with the same perfection. Then, with its bands blaring the new song with the jaunty air, telling how they'd marched through Georgia, the XX Corps came down the avenue.

"Here they come, Mother," Kate whispered as the 1st Division with its red-starred flag rounded the turn at the Treasury Building.

"Our boys?" her mother asked.

"Yes, our boys."

The brigades were scarcely more than regiments in size. The first three went quickly by, stepping to the music of the 33rd Massachusetts band. Each brigade commander, followed by his staff, preceded his unit.

Then the 4th Brigade appeared. Kate stared for a few seconds, then drew in her breath with a low cry.

Alone in front of the brigade, First Sergeant Timothy Tuggle marched, holding in his hand the reins of General Barnes's bony gray horse. Fastened to the empty saddle was a dusty gauntlet and a holstered revolver.

Ten yards behind the gray horse, Private Adam Youngblood led Sergeant Comfort's dancing brown mare. A flagstaff was fastened in a saddle boot, and above the empty saddle the thin, faded, ragged flag of the 195th New York Volunteer Infantry streamed in the breeze.

The crowd, which had been wildly cheering a moment before, fell silent as the 195th marched on.

The legends on the flag could easily be read: Gettysburg, Lookout Mountain, Kenesaw Mountain, Peach Tree Creek, Atlanta, Bentonville.

Kate Barnes cried quietly.

TENNESSEE
Tennessee R.
Ashville
Chattanooga
Dalton
Greenville
Resaca
Oostanaula R.
Chattahoochee R.
Saluda R.
Etowah R.
Rome
KENESAW MT.
Savannah River
Marietta
Atlanta
Madison
Augusta
McDonough
Monticello
Milledgeville
Waynesboro
Clinton
Millen
Macon
Irwinton
GEORGIA
15 th Army Corps
17 th Army Corps
14 th Army Corps
20 th Army Corps
Cavalry
Sherman's Army from Chattanooga to Atlanta
Alabama R.
Arno